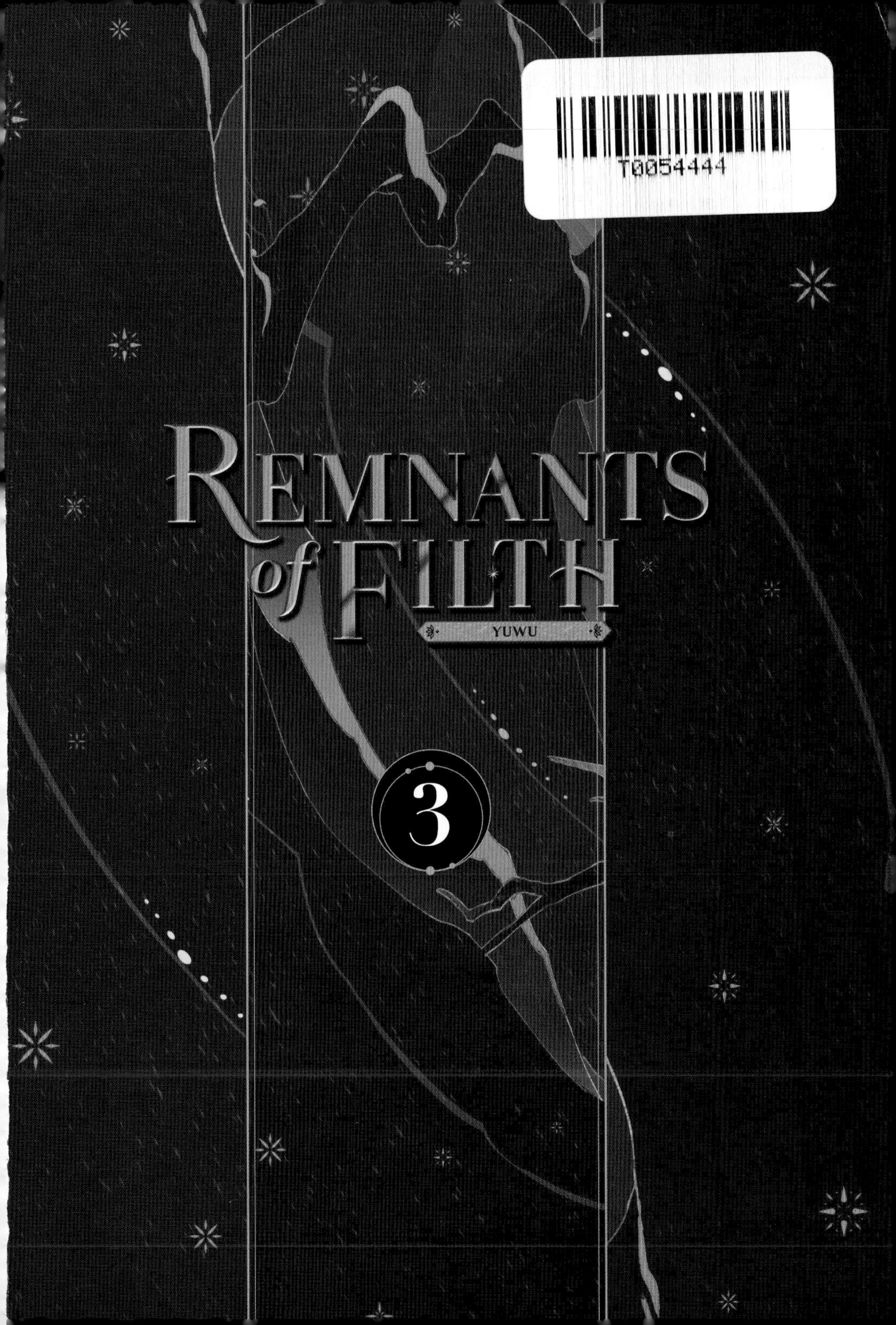
REMNANTS of FILTH
YUWU
3

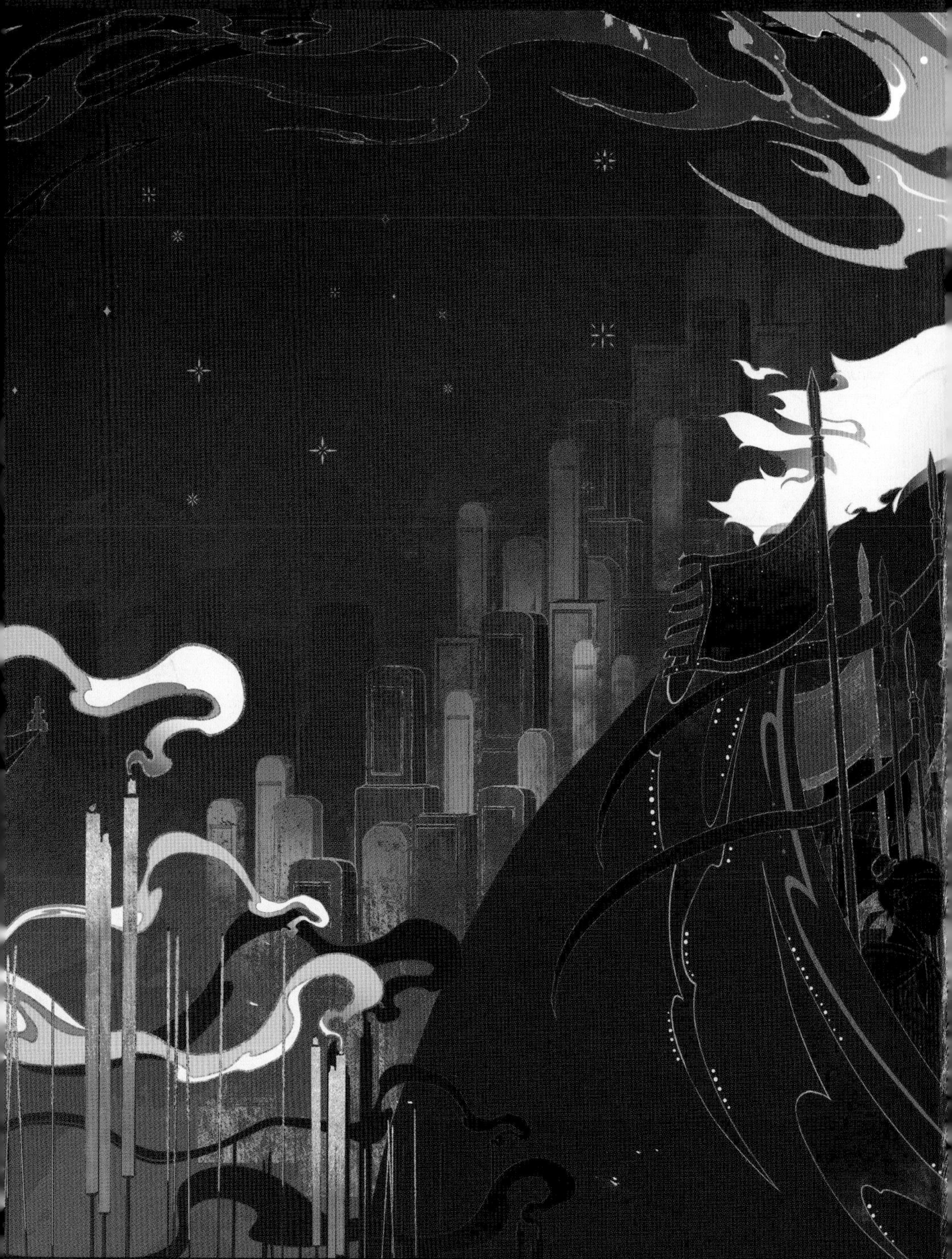

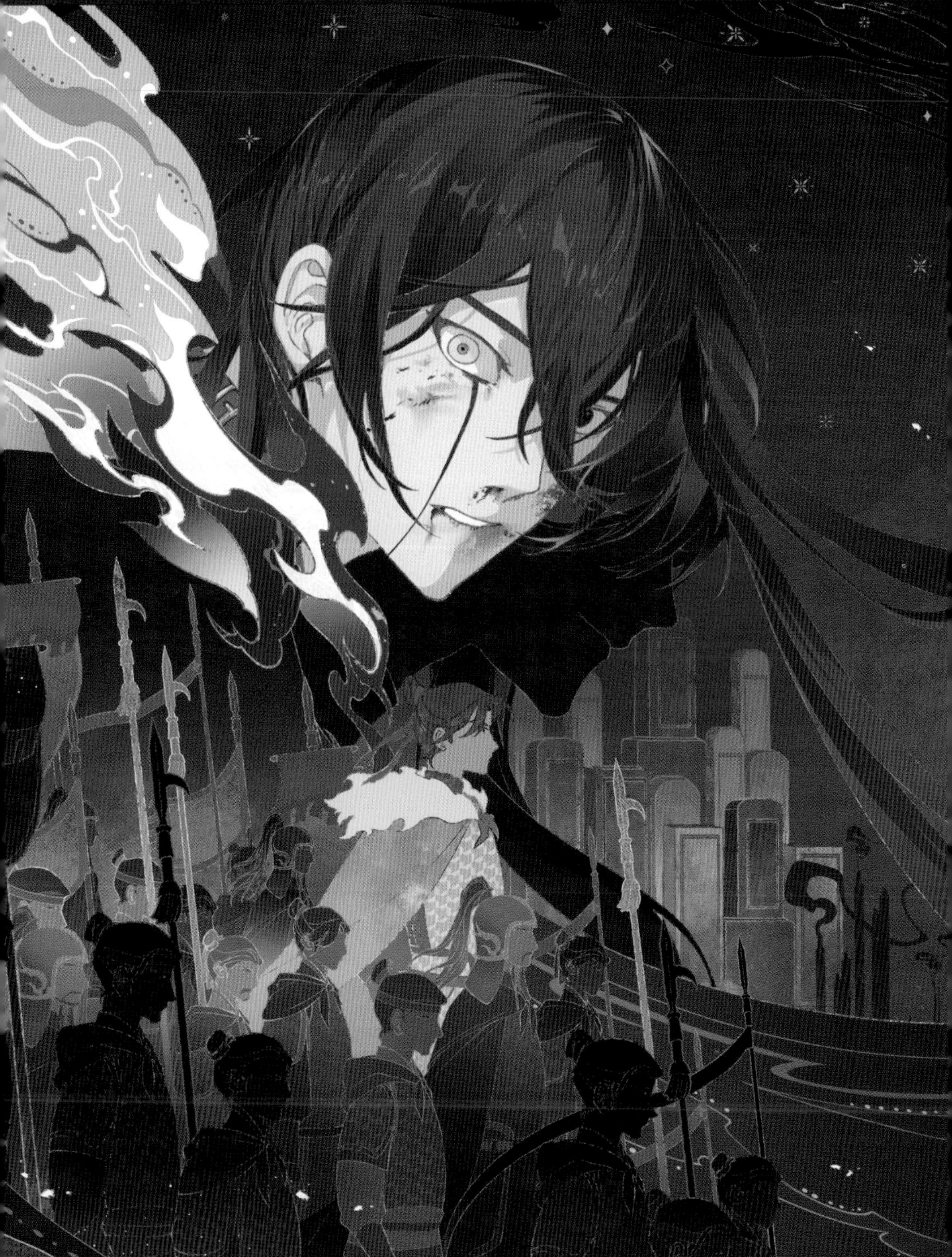

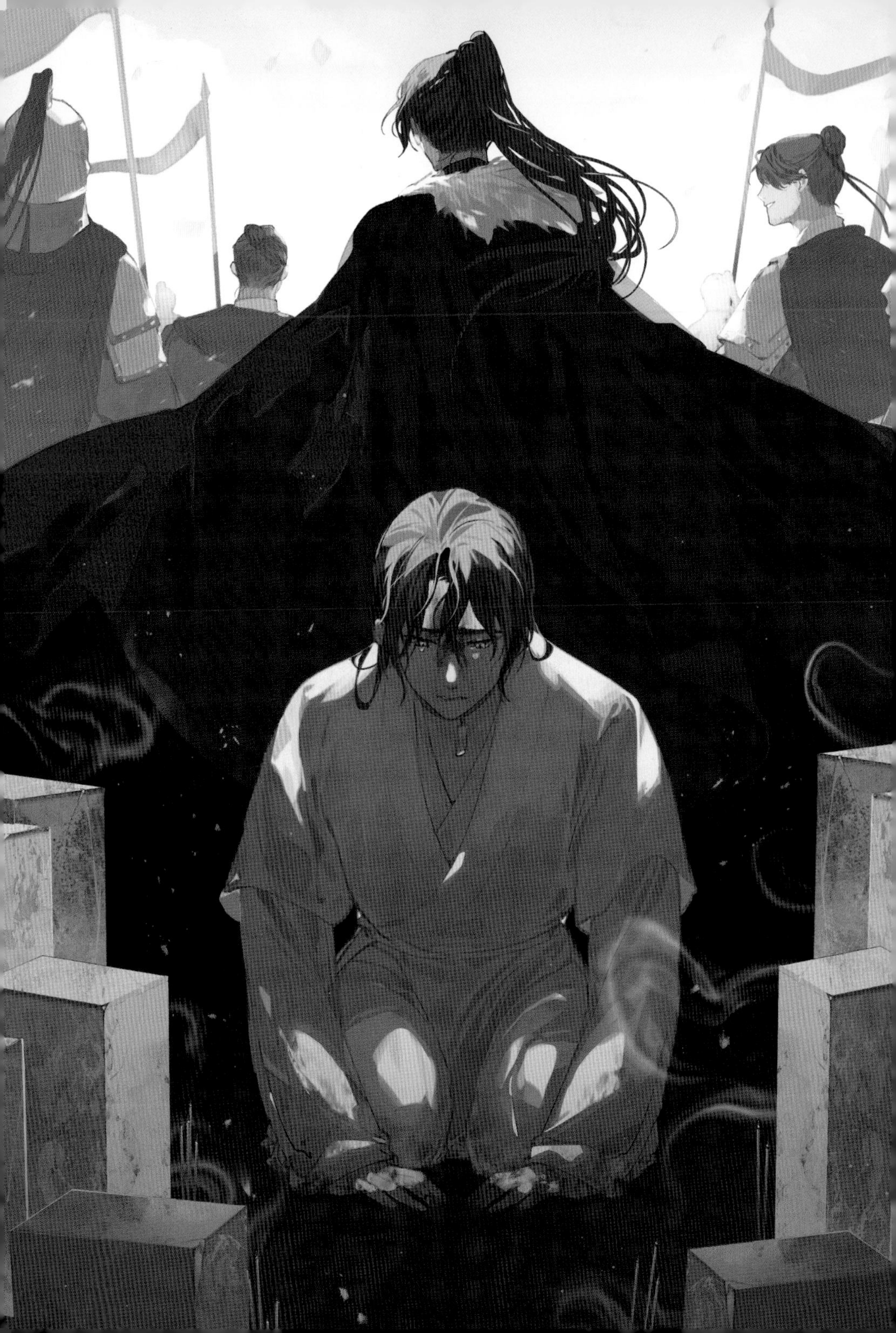

REMNANTS of FILTH

YUWU

3

WRITTEN BY
Rou Bao Bu Chi Rou

ILLUSTRATED BY
St

TRANSLATED BY
Yu & Rui

Seven Seas

Seven Seas Entertainment

REMNANTS OF FILTH:
YUWU VOL. 3

Published originally under the title of 《余污》 (Yu Wu)
Author © 肉包不吃肉 (Rou Bao Bu Chi Rou)
U.S. English edition rights under license granted by 北京晋江原创网络科技有限公司
(Beijing Jinjiang Original Network Technology Co., Ltd.)
U.S. English edition copyright © 2023 Seven Seas Entertainment, Inc.
Arranged through JS Agency Co., Ltd
All rights reserved.

Cover and Interior Illustrations by St

Seven Seas press and purchase enquiries can be sent to press@gomanga.com.
Information regarding the distribution and purchase of digital editions is available
from Digital Manager CK Russell at digital@gomanga.com.

Seven Seas and the Seven Seas logo are trademarks of
Seven Seas Entertainment. All rights reserved.

Follow Seven Seas Entertainment online at
sevenseasentertainment.com.

TRANSLATION: Yu, Rui
ADAPTATION: Neon Yang
COVER DESIGN: M. A. Lewife
INTERIOR DESIGN & LAYOUT: Clay Gardner
PROOFREADER: Stephanie Cohen, Hnä
COPY EDITOR: Jehanne Bell
EDITOR: Kelly Quinn Chiu
PREPRESS TECHNICIAN: Melanie Ujimori, Jules Valera
MANAGING EDITOR: Alyssa Scavetta
EDITOR-IN-CHIEF: Julie Davis
PUBLISHER: Lianne Sentar
VICE PRESIDENT: Adam Arnold
PRESIDENT: Jason DeAngelis

ISBN: 978-1-68579-760-7
Printed in Canada
First Printing: March 2024
10 9 8 7 6 5 4 3 2 1

TABLE OF CONTENTS

67

Trust Me Once More

GU MANG'S BLUE EYES looked into Mo Xi's as the smoke of the incense drifted past them in silence. He didn't speak. He seemed to hear Jiang Yexue sighing right by his ear. *Mo Xi was only seven years old when Fuling-jun died. He was betrayed by his second-in-command, his corpse mutilated, his spiritual core dug out. In the letter he didn't live to send, he wrote, "Who says we have no clothes, for we share the same robes of battle." You did the exact same thing his killer did. And you expect Mo Xi to forgive you?*

The ash dispersed on the wind and incense smoke clouded the air. "Mo Xi, I don't think...I like war either."

For some reason, his heart and throat both ached as he spoke; he choked with it. Although he had no memory of the past, he felt that his words were sincere. Mo Xi didn't understand him. Mo Xi was mistaken. How could he like going to war...? So many dead, bathing wretchedly in blood; a singular achievement paid for with ten thousand withered bones. How could he like that? He hadn't fought for himself, or for honor, or for an opportunity to advance. If he had, he wouldn't now see so many ghosts. Wouldn't see them questioning him, blaming him.

He'd been living with guilt all along.

"I know...how you feel."

I know how it felt to lose your father. I do, I swear...

Mo Xi was silent. He didn't want to argue in front of his father's grave. It was true that he had once believed without reservation that Gu Mang valued human life and camaraderie above all else, but now, he found Gu Mang's words entirely ridiculous.

Gu Mang who had once said, "You can't be too attached to past affections," and stabbed his former brothers in the name of revenge. How could *he* understand how Mo Xi felt? He was nothing like Gu Mang. There was no way he could excise past attachments and feelings from his heart, just as he still couldn't stand the sweet scent of osmanthus in full bloom. Just as he could never forget all that happened while his father had been alive, despite how young he'd been. He could close his eyes whenever he wanted and be met with scenes from the past—Mo Qingchi standing under the osmanthus tree, his silhouette tall and upright. Mo Xi couldn't even bear to handle his own weapon. Despite the passage of years, he could never forget the question he had once asked his father: *Papa, what's your weapon made of?* It was like a curse.

As Mo Xi looked at the golden strings of characters that read *Fuling-jun, Mo Qingchi. May his valiant soul rest in eternal peace,* he could picture every single plant in the Mo Manor's back garden without effort. He remembered the promise his father had made to him.

Mo Xi closed his eyes. "You can't understand me."

At the age of seven, he had learned what the fires of war meant. That understanding came at the cruelest price—his father's life. The child Mo Xi had been was tender and immature; he hadn't understood what battle entailed. He only thought it ferocious and found the thrill and vengeance of fighting terribly attractive. He badgered his father constantly with questions about weapons. He liked how his father looked in military uniform: stately and commanding, imposing and impressive. He liked when his father rushed to the battlefield. In his heart, his papa couldn't lose. All that the fires of war bestowed on the Mo Clan was supreme glory.

He had been too naive. He'd had no idea what war would take from him.

As for Mo Qingchi, he'd probably thought Mo Xi too young to bear such heavy talk of life and death. "Papa has two spiritual weapons," he had said with a smile. "One is cast with Shuairan's soul, passed down through generations of the Mo Clan. It'll be yours eventually. The other, Papa received when he first entered the academy."

Mo Xi looked up at his father with shining eyes and tugged his sleeve. "I wanna see, I wanna see!"

Mo Qingchi reached down and plucked off an osmanthus blossom that had fallen in Mo Xi's hair. Smiling, he raised his hand, palm up. "Xiaoyue, come."

A beam of golden light rose in the center of his palm. Flecks of brilliance coalesced into the shape of a sperm whale that swam with leisurely strokes around the tree. It flicked its tail, and osmanthus flowers rained down across the courtyard.

The little boy stood at his father's side, his dark eyes wide in wonder as he watched.

"Weapon transformation." At Mo Qingchi's command, the spiritual form of the sperm whale transformed at once into a golden shield. Mo Qingchi grasped the shield and smiled down at his son. "Xiaoyue is cast from the spiritual core of a whale that had become a spirit. Once transformed into a weapon, it becomes a shield. This is Papa's second weapon."

Back then, Mo Xi had burned with admiration and curiosity. He very carefully reached out to touch the shield. "Are all cultivators' weapons made from spiritual forms?"

"Just about." Mo Qingchi chuckled. "Bronze and iron weapons often can't handle the flow of spiritual energy, nor can they be summoned at will, so they have to be carried around with you. That's why most people don't choose weapons made from common metals."

This explanation was a little over Mo Xi's head. Blinking in confusion, he looked at the shield again. "Papa, will I have one too?"

"You're the only son of the Mo Clan. You'll enter the cultivation academy soon, so of course you'll get one too."

Mo Xi's spirits instantly soared. He was filled with the naive fearlessness of youth; he yet felt no reverence for arms or mortality. He only thought that having a weapon was something amazing. In the future, he wanted to be just like his papa, fighting on the frontiers astride a splendid warhorse. Having never experienced eternal separation, he ignorantly and impetuously believed that he would adore such a blood-soaked career. To let loose an arrow that pierced the storm, to surrender his life on the fields of slaughter— what a heroic daydream that had been. Mo Xi couldn't help but touch his father's shield, his eyes sparkling. "Then what will mine be? Will I have a big fish just like Papa?"

Mo Qingchi bent until he and his son were nearly eye-to-eye. He smiled as he patted Mo Xi's soft, black hair. "The elders at the academy will set you a trial. During it, you'll summon the holy weapon that fits your soul best. You might get a big fish just like Papa, or it could be something else—it could be anything, from magical flora to spiritual fauna."

"I'll get it as soon as I enter the academy?"

"Pretty much." Mo Qingchi smiled.

"Then let's go to the cultivation academy!" Mo Xi tugged on his father's sleeve, eyes huge. "Can we go tomorrow?"

"Not tomorrow," Mo Qingchi laughed and explained patiently. "You'll have to wait till you're seven at least. The academy doesn't take students any younger. Once you turn seven, Papa will ask His Imperial Majesty to admit you into the academy, and then you can undergo the trial. Then our Fireball will be a real little cultivator."

Mo Xi, all unknowing, had grinned. Then something seemed to occur to him. He asked hesitantly, "Papa..."

"Hm?"

"Is the trial hard? What if I can't pass and they send me home?" After all, it was only natural for such a small child to be nervous.

"Don't worry," Mo Qingchi smiled. "Even a fool would be able to pass the trial; you'd have no trouble even if you took it with your eyes closed. You have nothing to fear at all." He smacked his own forehead. "Right—a shixiong or shijie will accompany you. If you encounter any challenges, they'll help."

Hearing that, Mo Xi relaxed. He'd absorbed his father's words raptly, as though he wanted to grow up as fast as possible and receive his own weapon. Papa had promised to take him there once he was seven; so from that day on, Mo Xi counted the days until his seventh birthday in eager anticipation. He diligently marked off each passing day in a Chonghua calendar before he went to sleep at night. With every stroke of the brush, it seemed he was nearing his dream of becoming a powerful war god. He liked battle, and he couldn't wait to get his weapon, to dedicate himself to learning cultivation, to grow up and fight shoulder to shoulder with his father. How thrilling that would be!

Then the Liao Kingdom attacked. Mo Qingchi was appointed to his usual post of commander and rushed off to the battlefield.

That year, Mo Xi finally had his longed-for seventh birthday. But what he received was neither weapon nor admittance to the academy. Instead, it was a military report from a very long way away. Before he could begin to wrap his young mind around the idea of mortality, Mo Manor was draped in white silk, and mourning bells tolled from the imperial palace.

"Fuling-jun has passed!"

Cries of grief rang across the city, and paper money covered the ground like unmelting snow. People came in droves to Mo Manor to shed their tears and pay their respects. Regardless of whether Mo Xi knew them or not, regardless of whether they were familiar faces or practically strangers, each one wailed as they knelt on the ground. His mother sobbed herself into a stupor more than once, and his perfidious uncle feigned heartbreak as he arranged his foster brother's funeral.

All were in mourning garb—even the emperor himself came in white. "To lose Fuling is to lose a part of me..." Forehead pressed to the coffin, the late emperor wept, his voice cracking. "Heavens, why must you be so cruel!"

The court officials were on their knees; their sobs filled the air. Outside the main hall was piled a mountain of sacrificial treasures. The high priest blew into the horn of a spirit yak and a beam of golden light rose from the casket, motes of brilliant warmth melding into a whale that swam circles in the hall before gliding out into the courtyard.

The osmanthus tree there had long shed its flowers. There would be no rain of petals as that great creature swam by for the last time. It soared into the lofty skies and returned to its sea of drifting clouds.

"The holy weapon has been released," the high priest cried, kowtowing as he knelt. "May his spirit rest in peace."

The crowd wept as they pressed their foreheads to the ground.

"Fuling-jun was a hero."

"May his valiant soul return home—"

Among this crowd of otherworldly apparitions clad in white, Mo Xi was the only one who didn't cry. He silently knelt, watching in dazed confusion. Who had left?

Who had passed...

Who was the hero?

Who had become a valiant soul?

What did *hero* mean, exactly? Growing up, he had often heard that word, but with his father's death, it was suddenly horribly foreign. This word, which had once seemed so dazzling, the battlefield he had endlessly yearned for—what were they, really?

"May his valiant soul return home—may his spirit rest in peace—"

No, no—Mo Xi's body shook. He didn't want any valiant deeds; he didn't want his father to be a hallowed hero; he just wanted his papa to be standing in the courtyard, to take him to pick osmanthus blossoms in the autumn and brew a pot of sweet flower wine.

He just wanted his papa to return, to come back and take his hand, to lean down and say cheerfully, "Little Fireball, you're seven years old, so Papa will take you to the academy. Be good and learn diligently from the elders."

At that thought, he almost seemed to see his papa standing in the doorway, turning his head to smile at him. "Little Fireball," he said, "good boy—come here, let Papa take a look at you."

Dazzled, Mo Xi walked toward the silhouette in that beam of sunlight. It was just then that the funeral firecrackers went off. Their crackling seemed to wake him from some dream deep in his soul. "Dad?" he asked blankly. "Dad, where are you?"

Wh-where are you? There was no one at the door, only a bolt of white silk hanging low. His fingertips were ice-cold. In that cruel moment, he finally, dimly, understood the meaning of death.

With a great wail, he shouted for his papa, pelting out of the hall. The crowd of court officials were shocked and grieved by the sight as they wiped their endless tears. His uncle rushed after him and scooped him up as he struggled. "Xi-er, be good," he said, eyes red. "Come to Uncle, come to Uncle..."

"I saw Papa! I saw him!" Mo Xi cried, his voice cracking as he threw himself into his uncle's arms and bawled. "I saw him... Why did he leave? Why did he leave? Why doesn't he want me anymore?!" The child shouted himself hoarse. Each cry was more mournful than the last, his entire face blotchy with tears.

In the end, his trembling lips formed one last question. "Why doesn't he want me anymore...?"

That was the year he turned seven, the year he had yearned for with his papa. When it came, it wasn't what he had expected at all. So this was war. This was the price of glory.

Months later, his birthday arrived. He was still dressed in mourning clothes, sewn with the most exquisite thread and finest workmanship. The Mo Clan's stature had only risen after his father's death, but what did that matter?

He walked to the window, where the osmanthus tree outside was once again in bloom. Golden stars were scattered between slim leaves of jade, each like a tiny reflection of the past year. Awash in their fragrant scent, he sat down with the Chonghua calendar he'd marked for two years. A thick layer of dust had accumulated on it.

His own voice from years past seemed to echo in his ears. "How many days are left until my seventh birthday?"

Back then, Mo Qingchi had patted Mo Xi's head with a large palm. "There's no rush."

"But I'm in a big rush, Papa," Mo Xi grumbled. "I really want to skip these two years and wake up when I'm seven."

Mo Qingchi burst into laughter, the sound at first vivid, then muffled, then gradually subsumed in the soft rustle of the leaves outside.

Back then, Mo Xi hadn't known what the future would hold. He only felt that those two years would be so very long and boring. He wanted to get through them as quickly as possible so he could turn seven and take one step closer to the battlefield he yearned for. He had no way of knowing that those two years he rushed through were the last with his papa. And afterward, no matter how deep his regret, no matter how thoughtful or sensible he became, he couldn't go back. He could never relive those last seven hundred days, the days he had resented and wished to discard.

He hugged that big calendar, its reckoning forever paused at the sixteenth Lunar New Year's Eve of the era. The day they'd received the battle report.

"Papa..." he whispered. "Today's the day. I can go to the academy now." He waited a while, but there was no response. There never would be.

Mo Xi buried his head in his arms, curling up on the table. Shoulders shaking, he sobbed himself breathless.

"Papa...what if we stopped going to war... Don't go... Come back..."

Come back...

Hero is such a cruel word. I just want you to stand in the great hall and watch the osmanthus flowers bloom in autumn with me.

Come back...

When I grow up, I'll take your place on the battlefield, okay? I won't do it for rank or fame. I don't like battle anymore—I just want to protect you; I just want to be at your side.

I wish you'd come home. Papa...

"You'll never understand me." On the cloud-draped peak of Warrior Soul Mountain, Mo Xi had risen to his feet. Now, he slowly opened his eyes. His gaze paused on Fuling-jun's jade gravestone before shifting to Gu Mang. "If you weren't reveling in battle for the sake of your own ambition, then I don't understand why you would defect to the Liao Kingdom."

Gu Mang was silent.

"It's true that Chonghua wronged you—we owed a debt to you. But there was more than one path before you, and more than one country you could have fled to. Yet you went to the Liao Kingdom." Mo Xi's eyes were clear and cold. "You wanted revenge. For your dashed prospects, for your dead comrades-in-arms, for your own advancement. You didn't care whose blood you spilled."

"Mo Xi..."

"Sorry, I'm the useless one here," Mo Xi said, self-mocking. "Not even the price of my life was enough for you to turn back."

Gu Mang watched Mo Xi's eyes; they were too dark, too cold, too deep. In the sunlight at the summit of Warrior Soul Mountain, the near decade of disappointment they carried was so clearly visible.

His heart was suddenly seized by an overpowering impulse. He didn't know what kind of emotion it was—all he knew was he didn't want to see Mo Xi like that.

He didn't want Mo Xi to look at *him* like that.

Heart pounding, the words slipped from his mouth. "Can you trust me again?"

They were like an assassin's arrow: these words caught both of them off guard. Mo Xi's eyes widened. Astonishment was clear on that handsome face, paired with an extremely rare blankness. He seemed almost dazed. "What?"

Gu Mang bit his lip and stood, looking at Mo Xi with his back to the sky. "I don't know how bad I used to be. I've forgotten everything from before. But right now, I agree with you. I don't like to fight either, and I don't like to be betrayed either."

The brisk spring breeze ruffled his white robes. As a dense cloud withdrew from the path of the sun, a thousand beams of gold cascaded around Gu Mang like a shower of arrows—as though flying down to kill a man from years ago, or as if to pierce someone's heart.

The former Beast of the Altar stood before Mo Xi. Backlit as he was, Mo Xi couldn't make out Gu Mang's features, but the voice he heard was no less determined than before he lost his memories.

"I want to atone. I don't want to disappoint you," Gu Mang said, his voice overflowing with a deep, soul-stirring conviction. "Can you trust me once more?"

Without waiting for Mo Xi's response, Gu Mang got down on one knee, white sleeves fluttering. For the first time, he lowered his head in true deference and shame. Harboring hope and earnest warmth, burdened by bloody crimes and freezing with cold, he softly said, "I beg my lord to teach me."

Mo Xi was struck speechless.

At that very moment, there came the sound of clapping. A voice diaphanous and chilly as smoke drifted over. "Good heavens, how moving. What a lovely performance—pray tell, what tale of redemption is this? *Tsk*, I might just drown in my own tears."

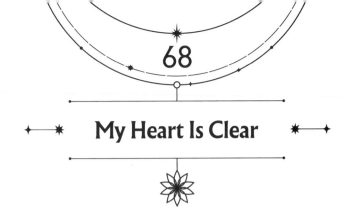

68

My Heart Is Clear

THE TWO OF THEM turned to see Murong Lian saunter out
of the shadows, white clothes aflutter and pipe in hand.

In addition to the gravestones at the mountain's summit,
there were also eight jade statues, each as tall as ten men, carved in
the likeness of the seven sovereigns and one extraordinary guoshi
since Chonghua's founding. Murong Lian had been skulking behind
one of these sculptures without attracting the notice of either Mo Xi
or Gu Mang.

Mo Xi glared at Murong Lian. "Wangshu-jun, do you *really* have
nothing better to do?" he asked flatly.

"This lord came to pay respects to my late father. Afterward,
I found myself wanting to gaze upon this majestic scenery while I
contemplated the ephemeral nature of life. Thus, I paused here to
admire the mountains, the rivers, and the drifting clouds."

Murong Lian narrowed his eyes and took a drag on his pipe.
He slowly exhaled. "Does Xihe-jun think I would listen to such a
ridiculous conversation otherwise? *I want to atone*," he snickered.
"I'm going to laugh myself sick."

He stepped onto the jade-plank path, one spotless white silk shoe
after another, and strode over to Mo Xi and Gu Mang. His gaze
was full of undisguised malice as he looked Gu Mang up and down.
"Sweetheart, don't you know what kind of trash you were?"

Gu Mang's serenity was infuriating. "I know," he said. "I am a traitor."

Murong Lian blew a ring of smoke and scoffed, sneer unchanging. "Oh, so you do know. I thought after living it up at Xihe Manor for so long, you might've forgotten your place and your status."

With a single long stride, Mo Xi stepped between Murong Lian and Gu Mang, his face impassive as ever. "Murong Lian, know your bounds."

Murong Lian let out a rather sinister laugh. "What, I can't even scold the dog I raised anymore?"

"He belongs to me now." Mo Xi made no effort to soften his tone.

Murong Lian's facade of indifference, thin as a cicada's wing, sloughed away in an instant. "You don't have to say it—I can tell you think he belongs here. Only the people of Chonghua may bow at the graves of our heroes buried on Warrior Soul Mountain." Murong Lian swooped in close to Mo Xi, eyes glinting and teeth gritted. "So, Xihe-jun, tell me the truth—you still see him as your brother, don't you? If we are to fraternize with our enemies so, why don't we roll out a red carpet and invite the King of Liao to tour the tombs of our fallen heroes while we toss flowers and light firecrackers?"

Mo Xi had ignored Murong Lian's gibes, but Gu Mang spoke up. "I came to apologize."

Murong Lian looked as if he'd heard a brilliant joke. "Apologize?"

Gu Mang thought he hadn't explained himself clearly enough. "I came to apologize to them—" He turned to look at the lofty gravestones. "To apologize for my crimes."

This time, Murong Lian really did burst out laughing. The tassels on his pipe swayed with his cackling, each guffaw louder than the one before. "Ha ha ha—apologize for your crimes? Your *crimes*?"

He stared at Gu Mang with the sly eyes of a fox. His laughter hadn't yet faded, but viciousness had already risen in his gaze. The overlapping mirth and malice made his pale face seem extraordinarily malevolent. "How will you apologize? How *can* you apologize? Don't make yourself ridiculous, Gu Mang. Do you think stumbling to your knees at the grave of Mo Xi's father, bowing once or twice and burning some paper counts as apologizing? Chonghua's heroes can't bear such an insult!"

"Murong Lian!" Mo Xi snapped.

"What, are others not allowed to speak to him? I can't even berate him a little?" Murong Lian spun around to glare at Mo Xi. "Little Fireball, we both lost our fathers young. How deficient Wangshu Manor must be in your eyes, that you dare order me around like this. Your old man and mine are both lying on this mountain. Maybe you don't mind that he's here, but I do. As is my right!" Murong Lian jabbed a vicious finger in Gu Mang's direction. "Look at him! How can he speak of apology with that carefree expression!"

Without warning, Gu Mang walked right up to Murong Lian, stepping around Mo Xi. "I didn't say that was my apology. I'm not smart, but I know that's far from enough."

"Bullshit!" Murong Lian snapped. "You're not dumb, no—you're far too clever. You pretended to be obedient and resigned at Luomei Pavilion, but now that you're in our General Mo's hands, you start faking remorse and come here to burn a few sheets of paper money for sympathy. Gu Mang, are the spirits of Chonghua's valiant martyrs so cheap? Do you think a couple sheets of paper money can write off your sins? Do you think all the descendants of Chonghua's heroes are as easily appeased as your Xihe-jun?"

Gu Mang looked at him, gaze unfaltering. "I don't."

"Then you never should have come, you bastard!" Murong Lian suddenly hooked his pipe around the back of Gu Mang's neck. Gu Mang shuddered as the scalding metal pressed into his skin, but he didn't struggle free, as though he'd steeled himself against it. His pristine blue eyes fixed wordlessly on Murong Lian's face. Ash fell into his loose lapels, the sparks leaving burns on his exposed skin.

Gu Mang didn't flinch, but Mo Xi couldn't stand to watch any longer. Whether it was because of Gu Mang or the solemnity of the heroes' tombs, he had no desire to see Murong Lian carry on with this farce. He grabbed Murong Lian's arm and lifted the pipe away from Gu Mang's neck.

The skin beneath was blistered and raw, but Murong Lian was yet unsatisfied. "Mo Xi, let fucking go of me!" he snarled.

"Murong Lian, you plan to throw a fit on Warrior Soul Mountain?"

"You're the one who brought a traitor here to offend generations of Chonghua's martyrs! And you have the nerve to tell me off?"

"He came to apologize!"

"Only to your dad! Did he apologize to any other? Did he kneel before any other? What kind of apology is this? He's just sucking up to you so you'll let him off easy; I can see he's already gotten what he wants. And what do you plan next? Will you ask His Imperial Majesty to reward him for his newfound contrition? Have you any idea what he's plotting?!"

It was no rare thing for such fury to lead to physical violence. Murong Lian was certainly trying to get a rise out of Mo Xi, yet to avoid coming to blows atop Warrior Soul Mountain, Mo Xi silently endured his taunts. When Gu Mang saw Murong Lian goad Mo Xi, he stepped forward to try to get between them. Unexpectedly, Murong Lian whipped around and slapped Gu Mang across the face with an audible *crack*.

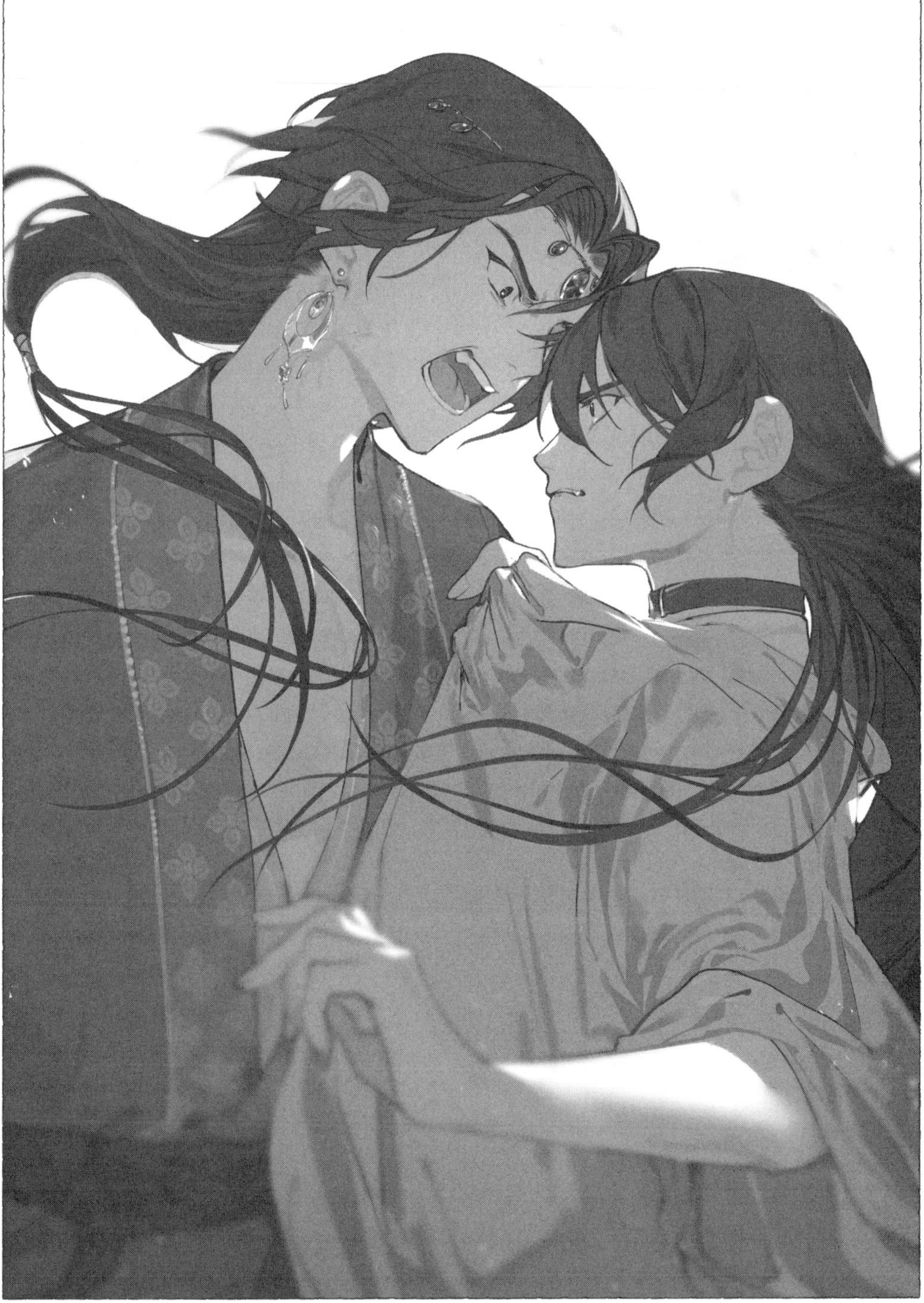

The red lotus sigil on Gu Mang's neck glowed to life, but he suppressed the spell. He had heard the conversation between Mo Xi and Murong Lian; he understood that it would be wrong to brandish weapons or shed blood here.

Murong Lian wasn't satisfied with one slap. The sight of Gu Mang's face filled him with indescribable frustration and disgust; he delivered a vicious kick to Gu Mang's chest.

Caught unawares, Gu Mang crumpled onto the steps and coughed up a mouthful of blood.

"Gu Mang!" Mo Xi cried out sharply.

Gu Mang brusquely swiped at the blood on his mouth and looked up at Murong Lian. A bestial savagery gathered in his eyes, but he determinedly restrained himself. Heaving to catch his breath, he lowered his eyes and pushed away Mo Xi's outstretched hand. He used his sleeve to wipe the blood from the steps.

Murong Lian narrowed his eyes, his fingertips trembling from anger. "What are you doing *now*?"

"This place shouldn't...get dirty." Gu Mang lifted his head. "I said I wanted to apologize for my crimes. It's the truth. I said I wouldn't betray anyone ever again, and that's the truth as well."

Murong Lian said nothing.

"I didn't lie." Gu Mang's bloodstained lips parted. "Everything I said as I knelt here today was true."

Those limpid blue eyes were so clean and so clear that Murong Lian couldn't help taking a step back. Under his sleeve, he fiddled with the sapphire-colored ring on his thumb as his shuddering became more and more uncontrollable. As if determined to ignore some emotion that threatened to overcome him, Murong Lian paused for a moment and suddenly gritted his teeth. "Fine. You want to apologize for your crimes, to kowtow, to start anew—is that right?"

"Yes," Gu Mang replied firmly.

Murong Lian looked up and took a deep breath. When he gazed back at Gu Mang, his eyes shone with an indefinable light. Hidden within his sleeve, his fingers tightened around his thumb until that sapphire-blue ring dug into the flesh of his palm.

"Kneel before every single gravestone in the cemetery, regardless of when they were erected or whether they died because of you. With each kowtow, say 'the traitor Gu Mang deserves to die ten thousand deaths.'"

Murong Lian bent his smoke-scented lips to Gu Mang's ear. He said softly, "Only after you've knelt at every single grave on the mountain will you have the barest of rights to claim sincerity in apologizing to the departed souls."

Murong Lian straightened and glanced at Mo Xi. Then, as if he never expected Mo Xi to agree, he turned back to Gu Mang. "But you belong to Xihe-jun now, so I can't give you orders. It all depends on how regretful you really are."

Gu Mang didn't hesitate for a moment. He got to his feet, the brilliant sunlight illuminating the reddened skin of his cheek and the blood staining the corner of his mouth. "I'll do it."

I said I meant it. Once I've decided on something, I'll never turn back.

It was hard to gauge whether malice or shock was more prominent on Murong Lian's face at Gu Mang's swift reply. Or perhaps it was some secret feeling, unfathomable to anyone but himself, that lurked within his expression. Murong Lian's eyes flashed as he whispered, "You'd better not have second thoughts. There are tens of thousands of graves here. Three full days and nights may not be enough to kneel to them all."

"Whether it's four days and four nights, or ten days and ten nights,

I'll do it," Gu Mang replied. He turned to glance at Mo Xi. "I want to…show you my heart."

Mo Xi's hands had long since clenched into fists, but he held his tongue. He knew Gu Mang too well, and he knew that look in his eyes. Blocking his way would be like barring a wild beast from blood—there was no way Gu Mang would obey.

Furthermore, Murong Lian wasn't wrong. Even minor mistakes had their consequences. And the sins Gu Mang carried amounted to battlefields strewn with corpses and endless trails of blood.

Still, Mo Xi murmured hoarsely, "Gu Mang, think it through carefully. Even if you do this, no one will forgive you. It doesn't matter if you kneel for three days and three nights or ten days and ten nights. Even if you die kowtowing on this mountain, you will be a criminal in Chonghua. Nothing will change."

"I want to show you my heart," Gu Mang repeated.

Mo Xi felt as though a boulder had rammed into his chest. Hearing Gu Mang say these words a second time, he suddenly understood. Gu Mang had never imagined his crimes and betrayals would be written off. He had known long since that nothing of those could be erased. He just wanted to live differently; he just felt that the way he was had been wrong. He just—he just wanted…

"After you see it, if you're willing to trust me, will you teach me what to do? This time, I don't want to walk the wrong path."

Mo Xi couldn't say a word—his heart ached so fiercely he nearly crumpled to his knees. Braced against the cold mountain wind, his face was deathly pale, his blood like ice. He looked at Gu Mang's upturned face, so naive and ignorant.

After a long pause, he heard someone speak in a voice so rough that he only realized belatedly that it was his own. "Don't be fool-ish, Gu Mang," he sighed. "There's no path forward for you."

Gu Mang's eyes widened.

Murong Lian went pale. "Mo Xi—don't tell..."

But Mo Xi didn't listen. He felt as if his heart was being cut open and his throat was raw and bloody, but still he spoke, enunciating each word with such cold cruelty.

"No path remains for you. His Imperial Majesty gave you the death sentence. The sole reason you're still breathing now is to keep you available for use in black magic experiments."

"Mo Xi!" Murong Lian shouted furiously. "Why are you telling him this? Are you crazy?"

"What do you want? For him to atone with his whole heart, just so you can tell him on his dying day that all he did was use-less?"

Murong Lian fell silent.

Mo Xi turned back toward Gu Mang. "Since you want to do it, then I'll tell you the truth. It could be tomorrow or next year, but in the end, you will die. No matter what you do, you'll never earn a chance to start anew."

Gu Mang said nothing. His wide-eyed gaze slowly drifted downward and his long lashes lowered, casting a tracery of delicate shadow over his ocean-blue eyes. Just as Murong Lian and Mo Xi both thought he would drop the matter, he said, "I understand."

The wind whistled past like the wailing of war drums, like the weeping of the dead.

"But it doesn't matter," Gu Mang continued. "Even if I could start over again for just one day, if I could live properly for just one day—I still think that would be the right thing to do." When he looked up, he resembled once more the passionate youth from the past, who charged headlong even into the face of death.

"I'll go as far as I can," said Gu Mang. "If I die tomorrow, then I'll have been a good person for a day. If I die next year, then I'll have been a good person for a year. This is the last thing I can do."

This is the last redemption I can ask for, after years of wandering lost.

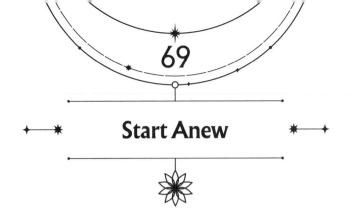

69

Start Anew

A DROP OF DEW rolled off of a cypress leaf. The wind fluttered through Mo Xi's wide sleeves as he stood beneath a copse of trees on Warrior Soul Mountain. He gazed at the small silhouette moving among the vast forest of gravestones in the distance.

It was the night of the first day. Stars blanketed the sky.

After the earlier confrontation with Murong Lian, Gu Mang had indeed started to kowtow at each tomb and gravestone. Murong Lian unmistakably meant to humiliate him, but Gu Mang had taken it as an opportunity. Spurred by a profound stubbornness, he sought to prove his newfound resolve.

"You're really going to do this?"

"I am."

"Even if nothing will change?"

"Something will change," Gu Mang said. "At the very least, I'll feel better."

In the end, Murong Lian knew that he'd gotten his way, while Mo Xi knew that Gu Mang had made his choice and wouldn't turn back.

Eventually, Murong Lian left, and Mo Xi had no choice but to leave as well. Gu Mang kowtowed alone amid the birdsong of the cemetery. In time, the weary birds returned to their forests. The setting sun sank below the horizon, and the silver sickle of the moon glinted like frost. Not a sound could be heard in the silent night but for Gu Mang's movements through the city of the dead, kneeling and bowing again and again.

As time passed, Mo Xi couldn't dispel his uneasiness and made his way back to the peak of Warrior Soul Mountain alone. Revealing his presence would only create trouble, so he stood among the trees, watching that distant, white-robed figure.

Gu Mang knelt the entire night, and Mo Xi watched until daybreak. When other mourners arrived after dawn to pay their respects, Mo Xi left silently. He was expected at morning court and couldn't stay staring at gravestones all day.

Perhaps Murong Lian had fanned the flames of rumor; this matter of Gu Mang kowtowing at Warrior Soul Mountain seemed to have grown wings. By noon, the tale had spread throughout Chonghua's capital.

"What's that guy planning now?"

"I heard he had a sudden epiphany and realized he'd done wrong, so now he wants to apologize."

"Really? It'd better not be a trick."

"Why don't we go take a look?"

Chonghua's high-ranking nobles didn't have so much free time on their hands that they could go pick a fight on Warrior Soul Mountain, but common idlers swarmed toward the heroes' graves like mosquitoes scenting blood. They claimed they wanted to pay their respects, but in reality, they wanted to personally get an eyeful of this exciting new development.

Afraid of offending Xihe-jun, these busybodies didn't make trouble for Gu Mang directly—but this didn't diminish their cutting mockery in the least. As Gu Mang knelt at each grave, the onlookers chattered to one another behind raised sleeves.

"He's actually kneeling all proper. Back when he was taking clients at Wangshu-jun's Luomei Pavilion, he wasn't anywhere close to this docile. Xihe-jun's only trained him for about half a year, so how has he gotten this obedient?"

"Xihe-jun must be good at it, duh."

"If you ask me, everyone knows Xihe-jun may be coaxed but not coerced. That Gu asshole must've figured out Xihe-jun's personality, so he decided to put on this act and deceive everyone."

"Aha—that actually makes a lot of sense! Aiya, if he really felt so guilty, why not just off himself?"

"There's no question, he's a liar!"

Gu Mang turned a deaf ear to it all. As these snatches of criticism buzzed around him, he slowly walked up the steps, kowtowing and kneeling as he went. Over and over, he repeated the words Murong Lian taught him: "The traitor Gu Mang deserves to die ten thousand deaths." He chanted devoutly, as though this was a rebirth mantra that could deliver his guilty soul from the abyss of worldly suffering.

But too many people hated and disdained him. He thrashed in that sea of misery while those on the shore cast stones at him. *Go away, go drown,* they jeered. *This is the only kind of ending your life deserves.*

Against this onslaught, Gu Mang repeated the endless motions of kowtowing, striking his forehead thousands upon thousands of times against the cold, hard stone. His footsteps were leaden, his shoulders stooped, but his eyes shone with a light that pushed him onward. He bent his spine; he lowered his head. From the brightness of day through the vast darkness of night, he piously put his hands together.

"The traitor Gu Mang deserves to die ten thousand deaths..."

On the third day, a dense thicket of clouds covered the sky, blanketing Chonghua City in an interminable drizzle. Gu Mang's robes were thin, and after kneeling for so long in the frigid wind and rain of early spring, his body was on the verge of collapse. He forced himself to crawl up another stone step on his hands and knees and knelt at the first jade gravestone. His lips moved, but he couldn't make a sound. Rain streamed sluggishly down his face.

He looked up at that towering and stately hero's gravestone.

Wangshu-jun the Seventh, Murong Xuan. May his valiant soul rest in eternal peace.

So he had made his way up to Murong Lian's father...

Gu Mang looked at the imposing golden characters on the tablet. The inscription was pristine and solemn; before it, he was like a mound of mud cowering before a god. His lips trembled, and his nearly useless throat strove as he mumbled, "The traitor Gu Mang..."

A crash of spring thunder boomed in the distance. The sound was dull, as if the sky had become a massive drum.

Gu Mang trembled as he raised his numb palms. He brought them together before his forehead, and then closed his eyes to bend down, pressing his head to the ground.

"Deserves...to die...ten thousand deaths..."

Rumbling thunder split the skies.

As if the sound had shattered his soul itself, Gu Mang didn't rise after this last kowtow. Three days and three nights of kneeling, without sleep or cease, had finally rendered him unconscious.

The sight of him crumpled in the rain, curled at the foot of Murong Xuan's grave, was like the rank smell of carrion to those sightseeing vultures. They scurried closer for a better look, glancing sidelong at his weak, rain-soaked body. Many were aware of Gu Mang's mad rampage from months earlier, and they hadn't dared raise their voices above a whisper when Gu Mang was conscious. But now that he had fainted from sheer exhaustion, these people gained courage.

"This damn slave said he wanted to apologize for his crimes, yet he collapsed before he even knelt to all of them. Is he really passed out or is he faking it?"

"Kick him and find out."

At that, someone walked over and kicked Gu Mang's pale face. When he didn't react, they shouted, "He's really knocked out!"

Noisy chatter spilled forth as if unleashed from a dam.

"He's here on Warrior Soul Mountain to kowtow, not to take a nap!"

"Beat him!"

Curiously, most of those gathered weren't sons of heroes or descendants of martyrs. The high-born nobles who had genuine blood debts with Gu Mang had better things to do than to spend a day hauling themselves up a mountainside to gawk at him. They wanted only to see Gu Mang executed; if that wasn't possible, they would rather not see him at all and spare themselves the displeasure. And those who possessed true ability and power—such as Princess Mengze, Jiang Fuli, Yue Juntian, or Murong Chuyi—well, nobles or powerful subjects at that level were even less likely to get mixed up in this mess.

As the saying went, birds of a feather flocked together. Those who hiked all the way to see Gu Mang humiliated were alike in their craven shamelessness, and most were incompetent idlers. None of their dead could be laid at Gu Mang's feet, yet this group was far more outraged than the actual descendants of those deceased heroes in their passionate fight for "justice."

In this world, people who fought for justice could largely be split into two types: those who acted out of righteousness and spoke up to redress wrongs, and those who acted out of boredom and stirred up naught but trouble. The group at Warrior Soul Mountain was no doubt the latter.

But these idlers who had come to pick fights were not the only ones on the mountain; there were also those who came honestly to pay their respects to the deceased and had run into this scene by chance. In the midst of the chaos, a child's soft voice was raised, teary with sobs she could no longer suppress. "Aunties and uncles, can you... Can you stop hitting him—"

A large hand covered her mouth before she could finish her plea.

The crowd turned, slightly panicked at the thought that this girl was some noble maiden who'd called out to stop them. But once they saw the speaker clearly, their panic disappeared faster than ripples in water and transformed into raw malice. "Changfeng-jun? What kind of fit is your daughter having *now*?"

It seemed that the child who had just spoken up was little Lan-er. She had come with her father to pay her respects at the cemetery; they hadn't expected to run into this kind of situation.

Ever since she had fallen sick, Lan-er had been scorned wherever she went. No one dared play with her, nor did they pay any heed to what she said. Other than her papa, no one so much as smiled at her. She and Gu Mang had merely exchanged a few words when they met at the medicine master's manor, but those words and the slight weight of the dragonfly on her head amounted to the first gentleness she had known in many, many years. Now, as she saw Da-gege bullied like this, she couldn't stop the tears that streamed down her face.

"My apologies, my apologies," Changfeng-jun blurted.

But the rabble wouldn't let it go. "They're right to call your daughter a mad dog," someone mocked. "She's even pleading on behalf of a creature like *him*."

"Control your daughter's filthy mouth. The only reason she still attends the academy is out of pity. If you don't watch yourself, sooner or later her blighted core will be torn out!"

Someone else took it a step further: "Changfeng-jun, surely your daughter's too young to be chasing after men? What's wrong, did she take a fancy to this dog?"

Such filthy talk would've infuriated any normal father, but Changfeng-jun could no longer be described as normal. He was a deer cornered at the edge of a cliff. Faced with these bloodthirsty predators, what could he do? It didn't matter if his anguish tore his heart to shreds and set his hands to shaking. He forced it all down. Even if the tendons in his neck protruded with rage, he had no choice but to laugh along and agree.

They were right. Little Lan-er couldn't afford any more missteps. Every day that went by, she risked expulsion and having her core pulled out. Changfeng-jun bowed and apologized as he hurriedly scooped up his daughter and carried her away from this dangerous place.

The moment he let go of Lan-er's mouth outside the graveyard, the child burst into tears. "Papa," she sobbed into his shoulder, "what did that Da-gege do wrong...?"

Changfeng-jun stroked her hair. "He committed a crime punishable by death—the crime of treason. Lan-er, you need to watch what you say."

"There's no way to forgive him?"

"His crime is unpardonable. There's no chance he'll be forgiven."

Lan-er's tears rolled like beads coming off of a string. "But...but..."

Her father carried her down the mountain path. She watched with her head on her father's shoulder as Gu Mang and that crowd of people faded into the distance. Young and naive as she was, she didn't know that Gu Mang had long ago lost his own parents. "But... the way he's being treated..." Her voice hitched with sobs. "If his parents saw...wouldn't they be sad?"

If his mama and papa could see, wouldn't they be sad?

Little Lan-er didn't know that Gu Mang had no mother or father. He had lost his family long ago, then later his brothers, his army, his glory, and his reputation—he had nothing left but his own filth. There was no one left who would feel sorrow on his behalf; only those who would rejoice at his suffering.

No one cared for Gu Mang. The only one who would stay by his side was shackled by destiny and status; a man who had long since lost the freedom to do as he wished.

"Xihe-jun."

In the hall of the Bureau of Military Affairs, Mo Xi had just finished his work and was preparing to once again leave the capital for Warrior Soul Mountain. For each of the past few days when Gu Mang had been in the cemetery, Mo Xi had dealt with his military duties as quickly as possible before heading back to that copse of trees to keep an eye on Gu Mang from afar.

But today, the attending official stopped him.

"What is it?"

"There's been an urgent missive from the eastern frontier. His Imperial Majesty requests your presence in the throne room to discuss it this evening."

Mo Xi paused halfway through pulling open the collar of his military uniform. The clever attending official noticed immediately. "Does Xihe-jun have other important matters to attend to?"

"What's the situation at the eastern frontier?"

"Yun Country fell to the Liao Kingdom's demonic magic and has amassed great numbers of ghost troops. Three villages at the eastern frontier were massacred..."

Mo Xi refastened his collar with slender fingers. "Tell His Imperial Majesty I will be at the throne room as soon as I sort through our records on ghost soldiers."

"We'll await Xihe-jun's arrival."

Thus the one in the throne room stayed awake all night, engaged in candlelit discussion, while the one on Warrior Soul Mountain lay unconscious all night, with no one to care.

On the dawn of the fourth day, Gu Mang awoke from his stupor.

He blearily blinked his eyes open. The sky had cleared, and he was sprawled in a puddle. The azure expanse above him seemed so close, he could reach out and touch it. He stirred and sensed that new wounds had somehow appeared on his body, but he wasn't much alarmed.

"Mngh..." He rubbed at a lump on his head. Did he fall? Or was this from his kowtowing? He couldn't figure it out, so he let it go.

A dozen or so gravestones remained. He crawled upright and scooped a handful of the water pooled in front of Murong Xuan's grave. Unbothered by its cleanliness—or lack thereof—he drank it slowly, then clambered forward on all fours to continue his penance. Like the sky clearing after the rain, like the sun shining through the clouds, he felt that the weight of his crimes might finally be lessened, ever so slightly. He bowed without pause, kneeling before all of those vengeful ghosts in his dreams, kowtowing to the past and present.

Level by level, one jade step at a time. Gravestone by gravestone, one deceased soul after another.

Mo Xi arrived an hour later. He had worked through the night at the Bureau of Military Affairs, and his eyes were red after two nights without sleep. Another might've hurried home to their bed after spending all night at work, but Mo Xi seemed possessed by some waking nightmare as he took breakfast at the Bureau of Military Affairs and walked up Warrior Soul Mountain alone.

Gu Mang had already spent four days on his knees. Four days and four nights without rest might have been nothing to the General Gu of the past: he had a singularly strong spiritual core, which was more than enough to keep him burning hot and bright like a torch. But all that remained for the Gu Mang of the present was a damaged body and a shattered soul.

Still, he forced himself to endure the hardship.

Mo Xi silently watched over Gu Mang from afar. He counted each grave for Gu Mang as he knelt. Here was the nine thousandth one hundredth and sixty-first plaque...the nine thousandth one hundredth and sixty-second plaque...

He was almost there. He was almost done.

By noon, Gu Mang finally reached the gravestone of Mo Xi's father once again. He looked like a beggar who had rolled in mud, soaked in dirty water from head to toe. His face was begrimed, his forehead rubbed raw, and his knees had long become a bloody mess, but his eyes were extraordinarily bright. No one who looked into those eyes could doubt his sincerity or shatter his hope.

Carefully, attentively, Gu Mang kowtowed thrice.

It was over.

He let out a breath and tried to stagger to his feet. Exhausted by his long trial, he collapsed almost instantly, crumpling back toward the ground. But the pain of impact never came.

He felt a cool breeze. Someone was holding him; someone had taken his filthy body into their arms. They had a faint scent about them—one that Gu Mang recognized. Honey and jasmine. And though they tried valiantly to hide it, their hands were shaking.

Gu Mang turned and caught sight of Mo Xi's face.

Mo Xi had stood in the shadows all this time, enduring the torment of waiting with Gu Mang until he had finished his apology. He'd been waiting for so long to help him up at the very end.

Gu Mang looked at Mo Xi, and then looked at the hand bracing his arm. Slowly, a smile that was nearly lighthearted spread across his dirty face. But as his eyes crinkled, hot tears sprang forth. Embarrassed, he wiped wildly at his face. He wanted to speak, but after repeating *the traitor Gu Mang deserves to die ten thousand deaths* so many times, it was all he could do to swallow. He couldn't say anything else. He looked at Mo Xi, smiling and crying at the same time.

He felt so stupid. His broken brain was uselessly stuck, but he still urgently wanted to express himself. He tapped his own chest. "Do you understand...my heart now? I didn't lie to you."

Every word came out clumsy. He tried his hardest to smile, but he couldn't stop the tears that fell freely. "I didn't...lie."

Mo Xi said nothing.

"It was true..." he said haltingly. "This time...all of it is true..."

Caught between the desires of his heart and the vengeance of his nation, Mo Xi's soul was tearing itself asunder. He couldn't find a word to say. In the end, he helped Gu Mang to a stone bench in silence.

Gu Mang looked at the gravestones covering the slope below. "How nice," he mumbled. "I've knelt before all of them..."

The cool breeze blew softly over the mountaintop.

"I can start over again..."

Each word Gu Mang said was a knife digging into Mo Xi's heart. Lowering his head, Mo Xi took out a bamboo box, which he placed on the bench. This box was from the dining hall in the Bureau of Military Affairs and had been imbued with spiritual energy to preserve the temperature and flavor of its contents for hours on end. Mo Xi unpacked it without looking at Gu Mang. "Eat something," he murmured.

Within was straw mushroom and pork congee, rice cakes, meltingly tender braised dongpo pork belly dripping with savory juices, thinly sliced cucumber with sweet tianmian bean sauce, and some fluffy, white steamed buns.

Mo Xi held out a pair of chopsticks for Gu Mang, but Gu Mang didn't take them. He looked at his dusty hands in distress and made a great effort to wipe them on his clothes. No matter how hard he wiped, they were still filthy. Helpless, Gu Mang sat and stared vacantly into the distance.

Mo Xi sighed and produced a spotless silk handkerchief. He wet it with a water-channeling talisman and turned to Gu Mang. "Give me your hands."

"They're dirty..."

Instead of repeating himself, Mo Xi tugged Gu Mang's hands toward himself. When they touched, he could feel Gu Mang's fingers trembling in his own.

Mo Xi looked down. Slowly and carefully, he wiped Gu Mang's hands with his damp handkerchief. When he finished, those hands were clean, and his once-spotless handkerchief was thoroughly dirtied.

"Go ahead," Mo Xi said.

Gu Mang looked at the food, genuinely ravenous. He gulped. "Can I eat the steamed bun and meat without using chopsticks?" He raised his newly pristine hands to show Mo Xi. "Look, they're clean."

Mo Xi swept a silent glance over him. Those thin scars on Gu Mang's hands were only more painful to see on his spotless skin. He looked away. "Just for today."

Gu Mang nodded at once and took a hungry bite of the steamed bun. Mo Xi, who had also toiled all night without stopping for a meal, looked at Gu Mang and tried to affect a careless tone. "No one's going to take it from you."

In response, Gu Mang dug in with even more haste, unintelligible sounds issuing from his steamed-bun-stuffed mouth. After a beat, Mo Xi's voice softened even further. "Slow down a little," he said gently. This was met with more incomprehensible noises, muffled by steamed bun and braised meat.

It had been a long time since the two of them had sat together so amicably. For a moment, Mo Xi had a powerful urge to pat Gu Mang on the head, just as he had in the past. But in the end, he raised a hand only to let it fall back to his side.

The movement was subtle, but Gu Mang noticed. However, he mistook Mo Xi's intentions. After a moment's pause, with his mouth still full of steamed bun, he falteringly tore the remaining bun in two.

Tendrils of steam rose into the air. Gu Mang kept the smaller piece for himself and passed the larger one to Mo Xi. Above his bulging cheeks, his blue eyes were so clear they seemed to have been rinsed by the rain.

"Are you hungry too?"

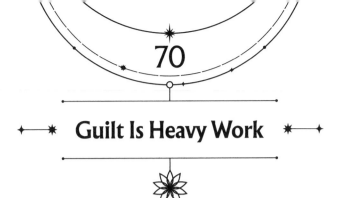

70

✦ Guilt Is Heavy Work ✦

MO XI BLINKED. "I don't need anything," he said slowly.
"If you don't like steamed buns...there's meat too."
Gu Mang replied. "I'll split that with you too."

Mo Xi turned his face to hide his stinging eyes. "I just ate. All of this is for you."

Only then did Gu Mang resume his chewing, appeased.

After he finished, the two descended the mountain together. The path was steep and long; Gu Mang didn't like to rely on others, so he stumbled and limped in front, while Mo Xi followed, wordlessly watching his figure from behind.

This view was so familiar. Many years ago, there had been a young general who doggedly led his brothers over hill and dale, blazing a trail through the thorny wilderness. He wasn't particularly tall or imposing, and he had no time to fuss over his appearance, so he was often grimy, and sometimes hunched and ragged. He was like a mayfly trying to topple a tree, whom anyone could crush with their pinky. But this mayfly would always struggle back up after being struck, tenacious and indefatigable. He would never be defeated.

He had once been the army's invincible god of war. He had given countless people faith that they would be victorious, and hope that they would return safely home.

Mo Xi had thought it was for this reason that he yearned to see Gu Mang repent and apologize for his wrongdoings. But when he saw Gu Mang kneeling before each grave in that forest of tombs, kowtowing to the heavens for his crimes, Mo Xi's pain only deepened. The sight of Gu Mang with his spine bent, his spirit broken— this wasn't pleasing at all. Very few enjoyed seeing the strong made fragile, let alone a person who had been your guiding light.

As Mo Xi's thoughts wandered, Gu Mang stopped and turned to look at him. "What is it?" Mo Xi asked.

Gu Mang pointed at the three-way fork in the road, "I don't remember which way to go. Is it left?"

Mo Xi glanced to the left, where the trees had fallen and left a patch of bare ground. The path was blocked off with military-issue chains, and two elite guards from the imperial palace kept watch. A barrier shone behind them, obscuring everything beyond from view.

"That's the forbidden area of Warrior Soul Mountain—no one is allowed in," said Mo Xi. "Go to the right."

Gu Mang looked thoughtfully toward that mysterious restricted area, his eyes slowly growing unfocused. An expression of sorrow washed over his face, as though he had remembered something.

"What's the matter?" Mo Xi asked.

It was precisely sunset. Before Gu Mang could answer, the bleak peal of bells rose from behind the distant city walls, echoing between the heavens and the earth. The wind picked up in the mountain forest, gusting from the depths of the forbidden area and over the meandering mountain path. Leaves rustled on the trees, and birds flitted to and fro. In the cool breeze, Gu Mang slowly closed his eyes.

"I don't know," he said. "But I think I've dreamed of this place before..."

This strange, offhand comment could not be true. When the emperor sealed this area, Gu Mang had already defected. He couldn't possibly have been there before.

"No one can go in there," Mo Xi said. "There are guards keeping watch at all hours. How could you have come here?"

Gu Mang's lips parted, but he didn't know what to say. He could only hum in agreement and walk away, even as he cast longing looks over his shoulder.

Many days of kneeling had left Gu Mang exhausted and half-starved. When they returned to the manor, Gu Mang ate and bathed, then burrowed into his den to drop off to sleep. He made no more mention of the restricted area.

Gu Mang slept soundly all night and well into the next day. When he woke at last, he saw Mo Xi standing in Osmanthus Hall in black and gold robes, his hands behind his back. Upon hearing movement behind him, Mo Xi turned around and tossed Gu Mang a scroll. "Catch."

"What's this?"

"*Introduction to Magic* and *History of Chonghua* combined," replied Mo Xi. "Yesterday, I spoke to His Imperial Majesty about your desire to turn over a new leaf. He told me to give you these books."

Gu Mang had been noisily flipping through the scroll. At this, he looked up, eyes shining. "He's agreed to let me start over?"

Mo Xi shot him a strange look before responding. "Let me remind you—I've warned you already that there's no chance His Imperial Majesty will retract your execution order, regardless of what you do to make amends. You cannot change the final outcome, no matter what."

The flowers in the courtyard cast gentle shadows within the hall, but these words were cruel. Mo Xi said: "You will still be used for black magic experiments, and once you lose your value, you will die." He paused. "Do you understand?"

"I do."

Mo Xi closed his eyes. "Think it over carefully and make up your mind before you answer."

"I've knelt for four days; my mind is made up." Gu Mang's bearing was serene, so much so that it reminded Mo Xi of the man from days past, the one who could hold the sky aloft on his shoulders if ever it should fall. "I know His Imperial Majesty only wants me to learn what's in these books so he can continue to use me. Instead of getting a free lunch, it's better if I work for my food. I understand."

"Not only that," Mo Xi said. "The reason he wants me to teach you these subjects is because he holds out hope that you will remember something useful."

"What's wrong with that?" Gu Mang asked. "I too want to know what happened to me in the past. I want to know whether what you all say is true."

Mo Xi's hands clenched into fists, nails sinking deep into the flesh of his palm. "I've explained everything. If you choose this path, don't blame Chonghua for its ruthlessness on the day of your execution. You'd better not be bitter about it."

"Of course I'll be bitter; but you'll die someday, and so will I." Gu Mang caressed the bamboo scroll as if laying a hand on his own future. His thought process was almost bestial in its simplicity. "But if I can do better for some little while before then, I might as well."

He looked up, limpid eyes staring squarely at Mo Xi. "Otherwise, why shouldn't I just die tomorrow? It would be better than spending my days in pain."

Mo Xi found himself at a loss for words. It seemed he always arrived here, whether he was talking to the shameless General Gu or this thoughtless Gu Mang. He silently stared at Gu Mang for a while. "From now on, come to my study every day after sunset, at the hour of xu. I will do my best to teach you."

Hugging the scrolls to this chest, Gu Mang nodded.

Thus Mo Xi began to teach Gu Mang a few beginners' spells that didn't require much spiritual energy, as well as pieces of Chonghua's history. Gu Mang had used to know all these things. According to Jiang Fuli, learning them a second time might help Gu Mang recall the memories he was missing. And indeed, it turned out to be quite an effective method.

Day after day passed like this, and the end of spring arrived before they knew it. Gu Mang recalled memory after memory from the past, but perhaps Jiang Fuli's calming medicine was too potent—all he regained were light and unimportant fragments. Most were related to his studies at the cultivation academy.

These memories weren't very useful; perhaps their greatest utility was in letting Gu Mang recover a shadow of his old self, such that he was no longer quite so brainless. Sometimes he swaggered about like General Gu, but other times, he crouched silently in a corner like a wolf. At some times his speech was clever and sparkling with wit, but at others, he stumbled over every word, halting and incoherent.

Much to Mo Xi's vexation, as fragments of Gu Mang's memories returned, he began to inadvertently repeat things he used to say. For example, he would often speak with an absurdly arrogant cant and nearly get his legs broken by Li Wei. Or he'd call Mo Xi "Mo-shidi" and nearly get his legs broken by Mo Xi. Gu Mang had yet to find a balance between his instincts and the rules, and often found himself in situations where he'd have to swallow the latter half of a sentence after starting it.

Once, for example, he thought to help Li Wei sweep the courtyard. With a sudden flash of inspiration, he waved his hands and pushed up his sleeves as he strode up to Li Wei and called out, "C'mere, lemme—"

Before he could finish his statement, he met Housekeeper Li's quizzical look and was quickly startled out of General Gu's shadow. He shook his head and carefully stuttered: "Sweeping...h-help you."

As time went on, Gu Mang found he hardly knew how to speak anymore. He often stood in the courtyard with his mouth open, staring vacantly into space. When others called for him unexpectedly, the expression on his face seemed caught between Gu Mang and General Gu, flickering back and forth. He had no idea how he was supposed to act, or what to say to avoid annoying those around him, so when confronted by others, he was wont to simply purse his lips, reduced to long spells of plaintive silence.

Housekeeper Li was compelled to pronounce candidly, "If you ignore the fact he's a felon, that look of his is pretty cute and pitiful."

Mo Xi's sole response was a cold snort.

Nevertheless, whenever he wasn't at court and didn't have other matters on his plate, Mo Xi stayed in the manor and taught Gu Mang to read. As in his youth, Gu Mang liked to scribble in cursive but disliked writing in formal script; he liked *Introduction to Magic* but disliked *History of Chonghua*.

On one particular day, however, Mo Xi returned to the manor to find Gu Mang sitting by the Taihu stones near the pond's rippling waters. He was eating an apple and engrossed in reading *History of Chonghua*. The sight was so unexpected that Mo Xi couldn't help but walk up behind Gu Mang and lean in to see what he was poring over. "What is it? Is this part particularly interesting?"

His voice was low, slow, and deeply charismatic, and his lips were a hair's breadth from Gu Mang's ear. The heat of his breath made Gu Mang jump and whip around to stare, a piece of apple still held between glossy lips. The two were so close Gu Mang's lips nearly brushed Mo Xi's cheek. Although Gu Mang hardly noticed, Mo Xi's ears instinctively reddened, and he abruptly straightened up.

At length, he said stiffly, "Don't turn around so quickly in the future."

Gu Mang swallowed his bite of apple with an audible gulp and licked his lips. "You're the one who snuck up behind me and spoke in my ear. How is it my fault?"

Mo Xi had no retort. The wolflike and witless Gu Mang from several months ago would have never said anything of the kind. But his expression right now held some of the former Gu-shixiong's unreasonable manner. Still, Mo Xi knew that he was the one being unreasonable in this situation. "Any more backtalk and you'll be coming to the study tonight to copy *Legends of Divine Catastrophe*."

Gu Mang opened his mouth. The haughty spirit of the war god Gu Mang itched to make a snappy comeback, but in the end, the shell of the traitor Gu Mang deflated. Pliant obedience once more filled those blue eyes.

Mo Xi couldn't tell which state displeased him more. And he had no desire to continue this frustrating comparison. He lifted his chin and prodded the bamboo scroll in Gu Mang's hand. "Why are you still on this part?"

"Oh..."

Virtue, Mind, and Wisdom were the titles of the three gentlemen of Chonghua. This particular chapter told of the best of them—Wisdom. In the past century, the titles of Virtue and Mind had been passed down to younger generations; Wisdom alone had found no worthy successor.

Gu Mang pointed at the small painting of the Wise Gentleman. "This person looks familiar."

71

Chen Tang and Hua Po'an

MO XI WAS SILENT for a moment. He crossed his arms and stretched his long legs to lean against the pillar behind Gu Mang. "You think the Wise Gentleman looks familiar?"

"Mn. I think I've seen him before, but I forget who he was."

Mo Xi arched one sharp brow. "The Wise Gentleman died hundreds of years ago. Perhaps you've gotten him mixed up with someone else."

Gu Mang didn't appear to accept that explanation. He stared at the painting for several more seconds, and then proclaimed resolutely, "I've definitely seen someone who looks like him. Do you think he could have ascended and become immortal, so he wouldn't have died?"

"That's impossible."

"Why?"

"The Wise Gentleman died of a shattered core in the battle that consecrated his name in history. Chonghua has never again named anyone Wisdom in honor of his memory."

Having personally experienced the pain of a shattered core, Gu Mang flinched involuntarily. "Why was his core destroyed? Did he do something wrong?"

"The Wise Gentleman was always pure and beyond reproach. But if you were to say he did something wrong...it was probably in making an exception to shelter an academy disciple." Mo Xi paused. "He trusted the wrong person."

The painted subject gazed out from the silk scroll, his expression serene. His eyes seemed to contain compassion as well as gentleness. "Trusted the wrong person," Gu Mang murmured. He hesitated. "But it's not written in the book."

"*History of Chonghua* is an abridged history. It doesn't contain the biographies of every notable person—it only lists the spells they created and their achievements. Of course you won't find every detail here."

"Will you tell me about it, then?" Gu Mang turned around and propped his long legs on the bench, gazing at Mo Xi in anticipation.

Mo Xi paused. "Sit properly, not like a ruffian."

Gu Mang reluctantly set his feet back on the ground.

Happily, Mo Xi had nothing else to attend to. After a moment spent recalling this particular history, he began to tell Gu Mang of the past.

"The Wise Gentleman was named Chen Tang. He was once the headmaster of the cultivation academy as well as state preceptor. Under his leadership, the academy produced countless talented commanders and grandmasters and devised many new spells and techniques. There was a saying back then that, with Preceptor Chen Tang's guidance, even the least talented disciple could transform themselves and achieve success. Thus people named him 'The Wise Gentleman with the Golden Touch.'"

"Then wouldn't everyone be begging him to teach them?" Gu Mang asked.

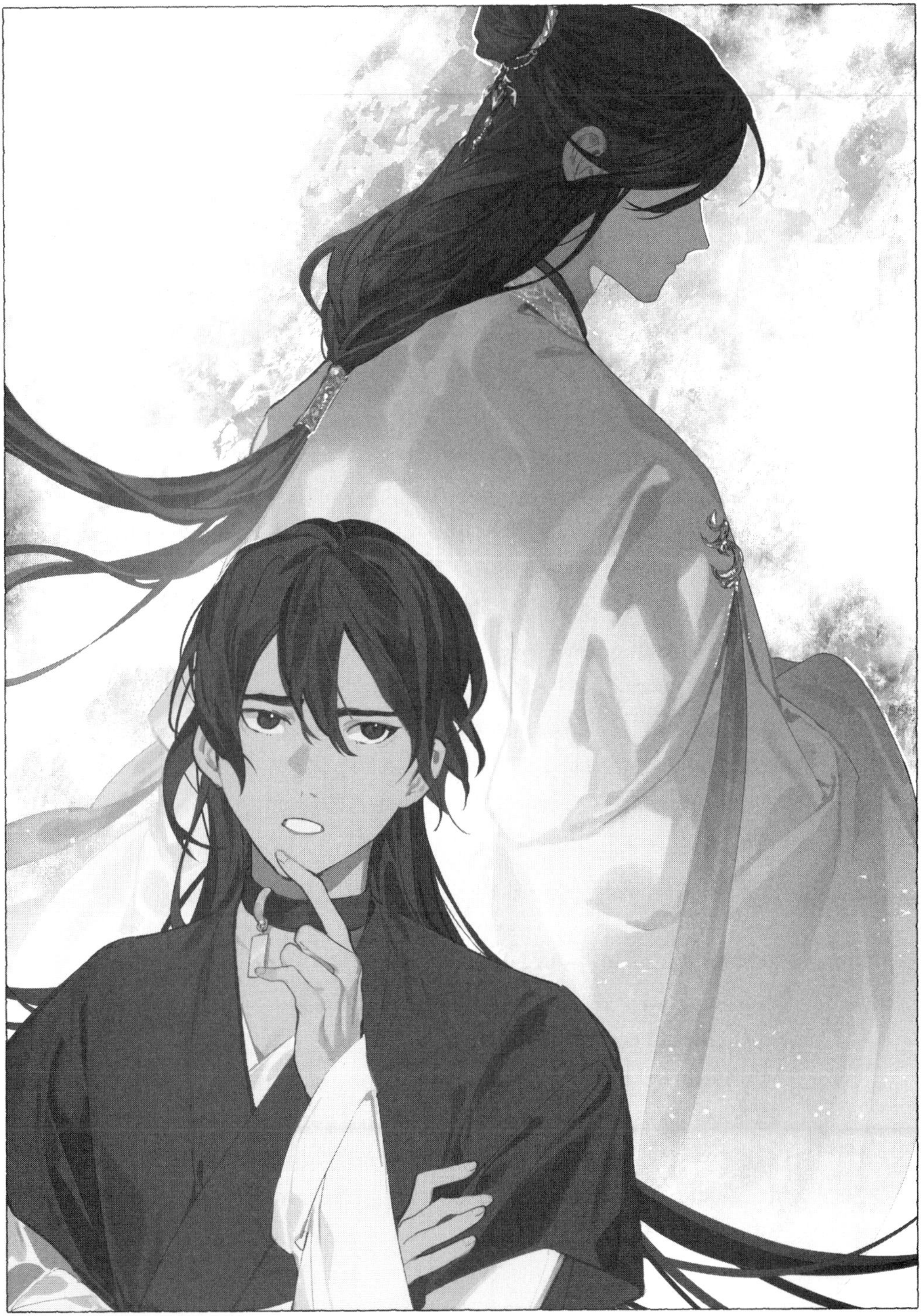

"There was no need to beg—Chen Tang taught everyone regardless of background. As the headmaster of the academy, he paid personal attention to every single disciple." Mo Xi paused. "Even the academy's slaves.

"Back then, there was a young slave at the cultivation academy who refused to resign himself to a lifetime of inferiority. He wished to wield the same power as cultivators, so each time Chen Tang gave a lecture, he would pretend to be cleaning the seats very slowly in order to eavesdrop next to the platform."

"Ah...how daring. Wouldn't he get shooed away?"

"Other elders might have done so, but Chen Tang didn't," said Mo Xi. "That slave knew the headmaster's benevolence and picked his lectures for that very reason. What's more, he was very intelligent; he memorized nearly everything Preceptor Chen Tang imparted to his disciples."

Gu Mang raised his hand: "I got it! And then this little slave secretly cultivated and became terrifically powerful, and then fought Princess Haitang—"

Mo Xi blinked, his habitually grave expression giving way to rare confusion. "Who?"

"That amazing princess, like Mengze. Princess Haitang."

"...It's *Preceptor* Chen Tang, not Haitang. Preceptor as in headmaster of the academy—it's a different thing from Princess Mengze."

"Fine," Gu Mang answered, "but it sounds the same to me. Princess Chen Tang, then."

Mo Xi pursed his lips slightly. Gu-shixiong had always liked to tease Mo Xi by calling him "Princess." It turned out this rascal's habit of calling men *princess* hadn't changed even now. Mo Xi kneaded his temple with slender fingers, as if afflicted with a sudden headache. He didn't want to discuss semantics of preceptor or princess, so after taking a few breaths, he continued, "You guessed the first part right: that slave indeed cultivated in secret, but things weren't so neat. Developing a spiritual core is a dangerous process. The stronger a cultivator's innate ability, the more torment they must endure. That slave had no idea he possessed astonishing potential, to the extent that he lost control and went berserk as soon as he started developing his core. The academy dorms burst into flames, and the secret of his cultivation was exposed. He was brought before Preceptor Chen Tang."

Gu Mang was entranced. As soon as Mo Xi stopped to take a breath, he blurted out: "Then what happened? Did Princess Chen Tang break the slave's spiritual core?"

"No. The slave's core hadn't yet fully formed—it was still in the process of coalescing, and he was in a great deal of pain. Chen Tang knew that if no one reached out to guide him, he would combust and die. So, because of his great compassion, he defied the law that forbade slaves from cultivating and helped the young man through his trial."

The plants in the courtyard swayed. Mo Xi gazed at the glimmering ripples on the water and continued. "After Chen Tang helped him, the slave knelt and thanked him profusely; he would do anything to repay this gift of life. Seeing that the slave had a strong spiritual foundation, Chen Tang's heart softened. He reported the incident to the emperor and took the young man in as an academy disciple."

Gu Mang sighed. "That slave was so lucky. In any case, what was his name?"

"He had no parents to give him one. The academy overseers usually called him Thirteen, his slave registry number. But after Chen Tang took him in, he gave him a new name." Mo Xi hesitated for a moment. "Hua Po'an."

Chen Tang, Hua Po'an. As if spooked by the sound, several birds in the surrounding trees startled into flight, clearing the high walls and soaring into the sky.

Mo Xi shot a glance at Gu Mang. Here was an interesting situation—Hua Po'an's infamy was such that his name was almost an unspeakable taboo and uttering it akin to a curse. Even now, many in Chonghua wouldn't dare mention him in casual conversation.

But Gu Mang didn't react at all to this monster's name, as if it was that of any ordinary person. He merely asked, "Was Hua Po'an the person Princess Chen Tang shouldn't have trusted?"

"Correct. Chen Tang's faith in him was misplaced. He had no idea what kind of evil he'd taken in and was completely oblivious to the fact that he had personally bestowed a name on the monster who would bring disaster to the Nine Provinces for nearly a century. He thought things would carry on as usual, and that he'd only performed a truly insignificant action."

Mo Xi lowered his head and gazed at the painting of Chen Tang, saturated with sunlight. The brushstrokes lent him a gentle and warm appearance, as if the subject were gazing through time to meet the viewer's eye.

"Years went by. Chen Tang's care wasn't wasted on Hua Po'an—he grew stronger and more powerful. He accomplished many remarkable feats for Chonghua and received the emperor's regard and commendation. The emperor even tried to end the ban on slaves cultivating in hopes of finding more incredible talents like him."

Gu Mang was amazed. So Chonghua had thought of putting slaves to use en masse even back then? He couldn't help but ask, "Did he succeed?"

"No. Abolishing the prohibition was no trivial matter. The emperor first specially allowed Hua Po'an to select some clever slaves from among the people and instruct them in cultivation."

Gu Mang seemed somewhat disappointed, but he said, "That's all right too—at least they had an opportunity to prove themselves..."

"Prove themselves?" Mo Xi scoffed as though he'd heard a great joke. "Yes, they proved themselves. But what they proved wasn't impressive spiritual power, but rather ravenous ambition."

As he spoke, he met Gu Mang's blue eyes, clear as river water. "Gu Mang, do you know why Chonghua's nobles are so skittish about allowing slaves to cultivate?"

Gu Mang shook his head.

"Because of Hua Po'an. The emperor gave him the power to raise an army, but in the end, he turned this knife against the heart of Chonghua." Mo Xi's face was grim. "The cultivators Hua Po'an taught didn't seek to repay the country's kindness—rather, they wanted to overturn established order and throw Chonghua into chaos. Hua Po'an defected."

Gu Mang fell silent as a realization slowly dawned. "Then...the army I had was very similar to Hua Po'an's, wasn't it?"

"Yes." Mo Xi also paused for a beat before slowly continuing. "Many people saw Hua Po'an in you. Back when Hua Po'an made his move, Preceptor Chen Tang was there to stop him. But if you were to repeat his crime, a similar disaster would undoubtedly befall Chonghua. And if it did, no one knew who could stop it."

Gu Mang paled slightly, his knuckles whitening as he gripped the scroll. "Are we alike?" he asked quietly. "Hua Po'an and I?"

Noting Gu Mang's unease, Mo Xi softened his tone. "You aren't the same. It's true that you also committed treason, but Hua Po'an was a madman beyond imagination. In order to strengthen his slave cultivators as quickly as possible, he kidnapped many Butterfly-Boned Beauty Feasts for military use."

"What are *Butterfly-Boned Beauty Feasts*?"

"They are people with a special constitution." Mo Xi's tone held disgust; he was unwilling to say much on the subject. "They can be used as dual cultivation vessels, or eaten directly," he simply said. "Even the most ordinary cultivator can improve their cultivation instantaneously by consuming the flesh of such people. Hua Po'an used this cruel method of cannibalism to pull up a group of slaves sworn to him with their lives. He left to establish his own country on Chonghua's northern frontier and proclaimed himself king."

As he spoke, Mo Xi closed the scroll of *History of Chonghua* on Gu Mang's knees. "Now that I've said all this," he said, lowering his head, "let me ask you: Do you know which country Hua Po'an was the founding monarch of?"

Gu Mang looked at him blankly. "L-Liao..." he stuttered.

"Correct." Mo Xi's expression became graver. "The Liao Kingdom's founding monarch, Hua Po'an. He was the ruinous consequence of the first time Chonghua trusted a slave."

Mo Xi had only meant to tell Gu Mang something of the Liao Kingdom and Chonghua's history; he hadn't meant to insinuate anything about Gu Mang. Nevertheless, his words were taken with intent. Gu Mang was overcome with embarrassment and shame. He felt as though a hand had tightened around his throat, rendering him momentarily unable to speak.

As he had regained some sense of his past self in recent days, he'd felt ever more strongly that his actions from before he lost his memories had been incomprehensible. Even if Chonghua had its flaws, at least it was a nation that had once tried to change for the better, only to end up as the victim of other schemes. Chonghua had believed in Hua Po'an, but Hua Po'an turned and dealt a blow to the nobles led by Chen Tang. If Gu Mang were in their shoes, could he ever unreservedly trust a slave-born person again? Who knew if that person might become the next Hua Po'an, or whether they would found the next black magic Liao Kingdom.

Yet, under these conditions, Chonghua had still given its slaves a second chance. Whether to achieve a balance of power, or to exploit them, or for other reasons, Chonghua once again gave power to a slave—to Gu Mang and his army. How much determination and courage must it have taken the former emperor to make such a decision?

But in the end, Gu Mang had become an exemplary Hua Po'an. He might not have led his army in an uprising, but he still defected and fled to the very Liao Kingdom that Hua Po'an founded. He'd walked a path far too similar to that of his predecessor.

After a long, conflicted silence, Gu Mang slowly set down the bamboo scroll. "I'm sorry..." The most worthless phrase in the world. One Gu Mang had already repeated thousands of times in front of those heroes' gravestones.

It took Mo Xi a moment to understand what Gu Mang meant. He didn't know how to respond. He heard Gu Mang speak up again: "What about Princess Chen Tang? In the end, how...how was his core destroyed?"

72

Yesteryear Defeat

"IT WAS BECAUSE of Hua Po'an."

"What did Hua Po'an do?" asked Gu Mang.

"After founding the Liao Kingdom, he delved into the ancient writings of the demon race and used other unorthodox methods to hatch a Demonblood Beast of devastating power."

"A Demonblood Beast..."

"Indeed," Mo Xi said. "This Demonblood Beast possessed terrifying abilities. Once it grew and matured, it threatened to swallow the entire population of Chonghua in a matter of days."

Gu Mang's blue eyes widened. "Then what did they do?"

"It happened too quickly. The nation's forces were helpless in the face of it." Mo Xi paused briefly. "The only person in Chonghua who understood Hua Po'an's spiritual techniques was Chen Tang. He felt every kind of regret and shame at having taught Hua Po'an magic and believed it was his failure of judgment that had led Chonghua to this calamity. Thus, in the final battle with Hua Po'an, he chose to die with the demon, using his own spiritual core and souls to seal and slay the Demonblood Beast."

Gu Mang was caught in his words as if in a trance. In his mind's eye, he could almost see Preceptor Chen colliding with the Demonblood Beast's spiritual power, their spells arcing and exploding across the battlefield.

"Chen Tang met his end with a destroyed core and a consumed corpse," Mo Xi said. "Forget ascending as an immortal: his souls and those of the demon beast's perished together. Reincarnation isn't even a possibility. So there's no way you could have seen the Wise Gentleman." Mo Xi met Gu Mang's azure gaze. "You probably met someone who looked like him."

Gu Mang lowered his head. "But..." He hesitated for a long while, but no words came. After a long beat, he could only concede haltingly, "Probably, then."

In the days after he heard this story, Gu Mang became somewhat absent-minded. His dreams were full of scattered reflections. Sometimes they were things he'd dreamed about before, sometimes the scenes were completely new. Sometimes, he even dreamed of Preceptor Chen Tang from the story. Clad in snow-white robes, the man from the painting stood amid flower petals raining from the sky. Gu Mang couldn't quite make out the man's face, but he was vaguely aware that this was indeed Chen Tang. Yet when he tried to step closer to see his features more clearly, the falling haitang blossoms turned into a great deluge of blood.

Chen Tang's voice was dark, filled with resentment, disappointment, heartbreak, hatred. "Traitor," he said. "How could you be worthy..."

Traitor...

"When did Chonghua ever do you wrong? When did I ever do you wrong?"

Every word seemed to weep blood.

Traitor. Traitor!

Gu Mang stared blankly; he didn't know why he would dream of Chen Tang or why Chen Tang would speak to him thus. Still, he thought...why *had* he committed treason? He writhed in misery, his thoughts a roil. Under Chen Tang's questioning, his dream-self knelt, clutching his head... Why had he committed treason?

The vision shattered; Chen Tang and the bloody rain dispersed. Gu Mang slowly raised his head to find he was kneeling in the throne room, covered in filth and weeping in sorrow.

Up on the throne, the emperor's expression was one of apathy. Within the hall, ridicule was written on the officials' faces. Gu Mang resembled a soul boiling in the bloody pits of asura hell, ceaselessly slamming his forehead against the ground as he kowtowed. "Please... just let us build gravestones... *Please*, I'm begging, there're too many dead... There're really too many dead..."

Your Imperial Majesty... Marquis... I beg of you...

This nightmare plagued him for days. On the evening of the fourth, the situation became dire—even dinner couldn't lift Gu Mang's spirits. He sat on his little stool, chewing on his chopsticks as he stared into space.

Since Princess Mengze's visit, Gu Mang had stopped sitting in the seat across from Mo Xi. Li Wei would bring a small stool for a seat and bench for a table, and Gu Mang would hunch over to eat there. Each day Mo Xi directed the servants to send Gu Mang food from his table, using excuses like "This doesn't taste good, I don't want it" or "It's too much, I can't finish it." Gu Mang would happily take the offending morsel off Mo Xi's hands.

Today was no different; Mo Xi picked at his food before pointing at the roast goose on the table, the sweet-and-sour crispy meats, and steamed perch. "Give these to him," he said to Li Wei, clearly referring to Gu Mang, who was sitting at his little bench.

Gu Mang had been well-behaved recently; he had long ago learned to say "thank you" after receiving each dish. But today,

Gu Mang didn't say anything. He stared with empty eyes at the servants placing the sumptuous dishes before him, not even the ghost of happiness appearing on his face.

Mo Xi dismissed the servants and took a couple mouthfuls of hot soup. "Your eyes used to light up at the mere sight of a pork bun. Now, you have all sorts of meat before you, but you don't speak a word of praise."

Gu Mang turned his head, hands clasped around a meat pie. "I'm thinking."

"What are you thinking about?"

Gu Mang lowered his head. "I've been thinking all day about why I would defect," he said in a muffled voice.

Mo Xi was still for a moment. "I've told you before, Lu Zhanxing was the fuse, and your ambition was the gunpowder. His Imperial Majesty stripped you of authority, but you refused to bend the knee."

"But..." Gu Mang said softly. "But I remember...it seems like many people died."

Startled, Mo Xi looked up, a chill in his expression.

"I only remember a little," said Gu Mang. "I remember kneeling in the great hall—I kept kowtowing, begging you all for leniency... But no one listened to me," he murmured.

Mo Xi was silent for a long while. A question issued from his mouth, deep and low, burdened with accumulated suffering. "When...did you remember this?"

"Just yesterday," Gu Mang answered. "Is something wrong?"

Mo Xi's heart pounded, his eyes flashing with complicated feeling. He hadn't expected that Gu Mang would recover this scrap of memory. Even if Gu Mang didn't understand the context of that scene, this information would be enough to shock all of Chonghua. It was this dispute in the throne room that had led Gu Mang to lose faith, and it was difficult to judge who had been in the right. If Gu Mang recovered this memory alone from among his destroyed recollections, he would be prone to develop hatred and the desire for vengeance against the nobles of Chonghua.

"Mo Xi?"

After a moment's silence, Mo Xi decided to speak frankly. Firstly, he disliked lying; secondly, telling Gu Mang everything from the start might at least prepare him for the truth.

"Listen, Gu Mang, this matter is not as simple as you think. No matter what memories you recover related to this, you must come to me for an explanation first. Don't try to guess anything on your own."

Gu Mang nodded. After a while, he raised his hand. "Then I have something to ask right now."

"Go ahead."

"When I was kneeling in the great hall, was I begging for mercy for Lu Zhanxing?"

"Not entirely," Mo Xi replied.

Mo Xi hadn't personally witnessed this confrontation at court. When Gu Mang returned to the capital to make his report, Mo Xi had still been on the battlefields at the western frontier, unable to extricate himself. He had only learned what happened later from watching the imperial scribe's history mirror. All he knew was that Lu Zhanxing, Gu Mang, and Murong Lian had led the army to Phoenix Cry Mountain, where Gu Mang had split off from the others. Gu Mang had gone directly to the hinterlands of the Liao Kingdom's southernmost city while Lu Zhanxing and Murong Lian kept watch over their troops.

It should've been a flawless plan, if not for Lu Zhanxing's quick temper. An envoy from a neutral country started an argument with him. In the heat of the moment, Lu Zhanxing beheaded the envoy.

This third country immediately sided with the Liao Kingdom as a result and attacked Chonghua's encampment from behind Phoenix Cry Mountain. Disaster befell Chonghua's armies.

At the time, Gu Mang had been personally leading his troops on the front lines; they had planned to infiltrate enemy ranks and splinter the Liao Kingdom's power from within. However, this effort was unsustainable for long; by the third day, Murong Lian's imperial army was meant to rush over to reinforce their numbers. Then, co-ordinating the offensive from within and without the enemy forces, they would be poised to break through in one blow. But thanks to Lu Zhanxing's rash action, Murong Lian's troops were diverted into fighting the third country and couldn't provide assistance. Gu Mang bitterly waited for reinforcements that never came, and their original plan of attack became a fatal dead end.

When the besieged Gu Mang learned that the third nation had allied with the Liao Kingdom because Lu Zhanxing killed their envoy, he burst out cursing in indignation and sorrow. "Lu Zhanxing, are you fucking trying to kill me? Why the fuck are you so stupid? How selfish can you be? *How selfish can you be?!*"

But what use were his complaints? A hundred thousand soldiers had put their lives on the line with Gu Mang. They'd come from nothing to reach the heights of fathomless glory at his side—but overnight, they were annihilated. How many of them would return in one piece?

At that time, Gu Mang could think of nothing else. When he was done cursing, he wiped his tears and clenched his teeth, setting his shattered heart on fire to light the way home for those hundred thousand brothers. He counted each and every one—every man he kept alive, every man he brought back to their homeland. In so many battles, Gu Mang had fought for victory. This time, he fought to go home.

Later, he realized that the one at fault in this campaign hadn't been Lu Zhanxing—it had been him. He was well aware of Lu Zhanxing's fiery temper, but he'd still believed this brother of his could handle such a weighty responsibility. It was Gu Mang who had made an outrageous mistake, who had erred beyond belief.

Gu Mang had no intention of absolving himself of responsibility. He had been prepared to make penance with his own death—but he couldn't let his hundred thousand comrades be tarred with the same brush. The mistake had been his. All who had lost their lives and shed their blood—they were innocent. They deserved respect; they shouldn't be erased. He was willing to sacrifice all he had achieved so those brothers who died in vain could receive a gravestone with their names on it. It was he who led them to their deaths. Whenever he closed his eyes, he recalled those humble names, those dirty smiling faces, their eyes shining with boundless trust. Some of the cultivators were so young—barely fifteen years old—dressed in shabby clothes, their voices full of reverence and hope when they called him "General Gu."

General Gu... General Gu.

Each cry echoed; each word was stained with blood. Was he worthy? He wasn't! The General Gu they admired was a useless good-for-nothing who cared only for the code of brotherhood. He'd led them to die inglorious deaths on the battlefield—he simply couldn't let them go to their graves without even a name.

So he begged. He knelt at the foot of the throne, covered in blood and filth, mud streaking his face, and he begged.

Please, give them a name. I'll take all of the blame myself. Give them a gravestone. An army's defeat is the fault of the commander; the soldiers are blameless. Please...I'm begging you...

But His Imperial Majesty refused, and the hall full of onlookers sneered at his grief. He was like the lowly Hegemon-King who had finally reached the battlefields of Gaixia on the eve of his defeat. What did his enemy, Liu Bang, care if he was alone and doomed?[1] They wanted nothing more than to hand him that fatal sword—their eyes flashed red and they longed to see him bare his neck for the blade. Only when he was dead would they be at ease. Only then could they be sure that there wouldn't be another slave in this century who would upend the heavens and tread upon the heads of the aristocracy. No few of the onlookers brimmed with secret delight, practically on the verge of clapping and cheering at Lu Zhanxing's error—for without this defeat, how else could they have brought Gu Mang and his slave army to heel? The timing couldn't have been more perfect.

"There will be no gravestones, no state funeral. Deputy General Lu Zhanxing will be interrogated and executed at the end of autumn. General Gu will be stripped of his military rank. The remaining soldiers will be provisionally detained to prevent any violence."

This was the emperor's final judgment and punishment.

Battlefields were fickle things; there was no such thing as a god of war who could weather a hundred battles unscathed. Murong Lian, Yue Chenqing, and Mo Xi could afford to lose battles because they stood shoulder to shoulder with imperial power. The same noble blood ran in their veins. It was only Gu Mang who couldn't. He needed to fail but once for these powerful officials to come swarming, trampling over him so he could never rise again, nor lift his head.

So the emperor's refusal was quite correct. The callous voice that floated down from the imperial throne became the final straw that

---

1   Xiang Yu, the Hegemon-King of Western Chu, was a prominent warlord who fought Liu Bang (eventual founding emperor of the Han dynasty) and was defeated at the Battle of Gaixia. He committed suicide in disgrace.

broke Gu Mang. "It is at our mercy that you keep your life. You are standing here today because of the late emperor's divine grace. Do you think your life is worth the cost of a formal burial for these defeated troops? You have no right to discuss it with me."

Thus was Gu Mang's last attempt and only plea mercilessly dismissed by the emperor before the watching court. He couldn't honor his promise in the end. The dead were denied grave inscriptions, the living were taken into custody, and Gu Mang's brother-in-arms had his head lopped off and his corpse displayed at the eastern market for three days and nights.

He lost everything in the blink of an eye.

Mo Xi had been far from the imperial capital during all of this. By the time he held up the history mirror and saw what happened—by the time he saw Gu Mang slamming his head into the ground until it was bloody, sobbing as he knelt and cowered, plummeting from hope to despair, from impassioned pleading to despondent silence—by the time he saw all of this, Gu Mang had already left the capital. Everything was already over.

Perhaps his obsession ran too deep; Mo Xi dreamed of this sight for years. He dreamed of Gu Mang howling in grief, smashing his head against the floor in heartbreak. The palace hall filled with the mocking faces of court officials, and the emperor handing down his verdict without mercy.

In Mo Xi's dreams, he would often be in the hall too—perhaps because he'd always thought that everything might have gone differently had he been there. Or perhaps none of this would have happened if, after Mo Xi returned to the capital, he had noticed Gu Mang's growing desire to defect.

What a fool he had been. He had seen clearly Gu Mang's deterioration and heartbreak when he returned from the front lines.

But Gu Mang then had seemed so listless, like he might spend the rest of his life in a morose stupor. Mo Xi had feared that Gu Mang wouldn't be able to get back on his feet, but he'd never thought that Gu Mang would defect.

He'd never imagined that Gu Mang *could* defect.

Gu Mang had always been like a god to him. Mo Xi had been so young then; how could he know that even gods could crumble and collapse. He had thought Gu Mang invincible. When he considered that righteous, enthusiastic, smiling shixiong—the shixiong whom nothing could break, the General Gu who could endure any misery—Mo Xi simply couldn't believe that Gu Mang's heart had died in that throne room, that it had shattered into fragments and been crushed to dust, never to be put whole again.

"Actually, I couldn't argue when you left and defected," said Mo Xi. "But out of all the Nine Provinces and Twenty-Eight Nations, why did you have to choose the darkest one?"

Gu Mang didn't immediately respond. After a lengthy pause, he said, "I don't know." He was struggling to relate to his former self in the story Mo Xi had told. His mind was in a mess. He could perhaps understand the despair he felt and the motives he had, but it was just as Mo Xi said—he couldn't understand why he'd gone to Liao. What could he do in the Liao Kingdom?

Forced to guess, he could only believe it was for revenge. The Liao Kingdom alone could give him the requital he wanted. If he made a name for himself in the Liao Kingdom, he could avenge himself upon the emperor who had humiliated him, had disdained him.

But if that were the truth, he would really be as Mo Xi said—a person fighting only for his own ideals and vengeance, regardless of how much blood he shed.

Gu Mang buried his face in his palms, then clutched at his hair in confusion. "I don't know..." he mumbled. "I can't think of another reason either..."

"Neither can I. Gu Mang, you had your code of brotherhood and your unbreakable promise, and I have mine," Mo Xi said. "Since you chose revenge, then you and I—you and Chonghua—are destined for this sort of end."

Gu Mang sat disconsolately on his little stool without a word. He vacantly stared at the brick flooring in front of him through his fingers.

At last, Mo Xi stood up. "You should take two more doses of calming medicine today. His Imperial Majesty wouldn't want you to remember too many details about your defection. If you want to live a little longer, don't think on these things again."

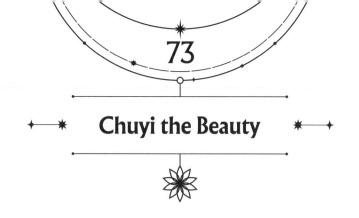

Chuyi the Beauty

INCE MO XI had put it like that, Gu Mang tried his best to avoid recalling details from before he defected. This was sometimes the way of things—after the momentary satisfaction of uncovering a secret, endless disappointment and frustration came in its wake. He wanted to enjoy his life, so it was best to remain obedient.

Mo Xi grew busier after the spring hunt in March. Overwhelmed with work, his routines disappeared and his appetite worsened. Seeing him neglect sleep and skip meals, Housekeeper Li ordered the kitchen to bring boxes of food to his desk. However, Mo Xi still often forgot to eat, or would find the food cold by the time he finally raised his head from his heap of scrolls, long after the sun had gone down.

"This happens every year around this time," Li Wei sighed. "There's no point in cajoling him. He eats cold food and drinks old tea all day—even an iron stomach wouldn't tolerate it. He's just asking to get sick."

Housekeeper Li seemed to have jinxed it: the day after he complained, Mo Xi fell ill. Never mind how ruthless Mo Xi was while at war—only the servants of Xihe Manor knew how high-maintenance he became whenever he got sick. It wasn't that he was fragile, or that he inconvenienced others, or made a big deal of his illnesses.

There was a much more insufferable issue: he was picky. He kept up his usual activities like attending court and annotating papers, but his temper worsened with his discomfort, and he became even more particular about everything than usual.

When Mo Xi's stomach issues flared up again, Li Wei went to Medicine Master Jiang for a prescription, and Medicine Master Jiang lambasted him with everything he had. "He's sick *again*? *Another* stomach bug? He's seen me for this problem since he was fourteen! I take such pains to fix him up, but *he* couldn't care less—he starts forgetting meals or eats nothing but cold food every year when military affairs get busy! If he keeps going like this, he may as well ascend and be done with it! Maybe he doesn't mind suffering, but *I* certainly mind him wrecking my reputation! Get *out*!"

Li Wei could only nod, sweat beading on his forehead. He somehow managed to extract the prescription between bouts of Medicine Master Jiang's ranting, but was met with one further command: "Keep an eye on that lord of yours! Make sure he eats his food while it's hot and has soup before each meal! And if he doesn't listen, don't come to Jiang Manor again, it's too fucking embarrassing!"

Thus Li Wei instructed the kitchen to make soup every day to aid Mo Xi's recovery. It was at this precise moment that Mo Xi's fussiness reared its head.

On the first day, the kitchens made white radish and pork rib soup. Mo Xi wouldn't drink it. "It's too greasy."

On the second day, the kitchens made pigeon soup instead. Mo Xi refused it. "There's a weird aftertaste."

On the third day, the kitchens tried making pig liver and spinach soup. Mo Xi wouldn't touch it. "Seeing offal turns my stomach."

And so on and so forth, until the seventh day. Li Wei walked dejectedly out of Xihe-jun's study with a pot of straw mushroom and chicken soup in his hands. The master cook who had accompanied him apprehensively asked, "How did it go?"

"He didn't touch it at all; he's too busy looking at his sand table." Li Wei rolled his eyes. "He said the smell of stewed chicken makes him nauseous and he doesn't have an appetite."

Sweaty and pale, the cook felt deeply chagrined. "That's not *my* fault. If the lord carries on like this, his appetite will only get worse. Didn't Medicine Master Jiang say so too? Healing that stomach of his is more about nurture than medicine."

Li Wei sighed. "Yes, exactly."

Mo Xi's appetite had indeed worsened over the past few days, but he didn't pay it much mind. As long as something was edible, whether it was hot or cold didn't matter to him, even if the food in question was a rock-hard bun. He'd have time to recover once this busy period was over.

While Li Wei and the cook were heaving deep sighs under the eaves, Gu Mang happened to walk past the courtyard with his arms tucked in his sleeves and the black dog Fandou at his heels. Noticing the worry creasing their faces, he asked helpfully, "What's up with you two?"

The cook gave him a scornful look. "Are you done chopping firewood? If not, get to it. Don't meddle in the business of others."

"I'm done," Gu Mang said.

The cook was about to retort when Li Wei was struck by inspiration—Gu Mang's cooking wasn't bad. Although Mo Xi hadn't offered any words of praise the last time he cooked, every plate had come back clean. They were in a dire situation, so why not fall back on their last resort? So thinking, Li Wei succinctly summarized Mo Xi's situation for Gu Mang.

"Oh..." Gu Mang glanced at the study. "No wonder his face has gotten thinner recently." He looked down and addressed the dog. "Fandou, soon he'll be even skinner than you."

Fandou barked twice, as though he resented the comparison.

Li Wei sighed again. "We've already tried anything and everything to convince him to eat. We've offered every kind of exotic delicacy, but the lord just never has an appetite, and he's never in the mood to eat either." He carefully watched Gu Mang's face as he said his next words: "Why don't you try?"

"This guy?" The cook interrupted, dripping disdain. "What can *he* possibly do?"

But Gu Mang nodded. "He can't keep starving himself. I'll give it a try."

Gu Mang planned to cook fish, so he needed the plumpest, freshest fish. Li Wei pointed him toward Peach Blossom Lake on the eastern outskirts of the capital. Not only was the lake flourishing with spiritual energy, which was good for cultivation, but the fish within it were known to be deliciously tender. So that afternoon, with his fishing gear in tow, a net strapped to his back, and his black dog at his heels, Gu Mang went to the city outskirts to fish.

Peach Blossom Lake wasn't difficult to find. When Gu Mang arrived, he found it profoundly quiet and calm. Due to the endless flow of spirit-energy veins, peach-blossom petals fluttered all year round, dyeing everything between the heavens and earth the rosy pink of clouds at sunset. Numerous craggy boulders protruded from the lake's surface, and though it wasn't large, it had a great many hidden nooks and crannies. Pavilions and walkways lined its shores, and every errant breeze sent flowers drifting across the steps.

"Nice place," Gu Mang said. "No wonder Li Wei said it was good for baths." He turned to the dog. "Fandou, do you want to take one?"

Fandou excitedly wagged his tail and leapt into the water like an arrow loosed from a bow.

It was yet late spring, but the days were already warm with the sun shining so brightly. Gu Mang had planned to disguise himself with a hat and cloak, but since he was alone and it would be difficult to catch fish while bundled up, he took off his shoes, socks, and cloak, then rolled up his pants to wade into the clear lake water.

"Arf!" Fandou barked loudly in excitement. He gamboled and scampered around Gu Mang in the shallows, splashing water everywhere.

Gu Mang brought a finger to his lips. "Behave," he warned the dog. "Go catch a fish for the poor princess Mo Xi."

Fandou barked and yelped as he cavorted about with even greater enthusiasm, chasing all of the fish from the shallows into the depths. Gu Mang was rendered speechless.

"Arf arf arf!"

"If you keep making a nuisance of yourself, I'll make you into dog soup, see if I don't."

A gentle approach was useless. Fandou fell in line as soon as Gu Mang got tough, the way he remembered he used to be. Fandou whimpered and tucked his tail between his legs, trembling with fear as he scrambled ashore. He vigorously shook the water from his fur and sat on the banks to soak up the sunlight, tongue lolling and beady eyes fixed on Gu Mang.

Gu Mang's martial arts had recovered a great deal, but his spiritual energy could never return to its level at the peak of his abilities. Nonetheless, thanks to his improved martial skills, he caught three plump and meaty grass carp in no time at all.

Grass carp were big, but they weren't the best for cooking. After some consideration, Gu Mang took up his net and made his way around some rocks that loomed out of the water to look for fish in

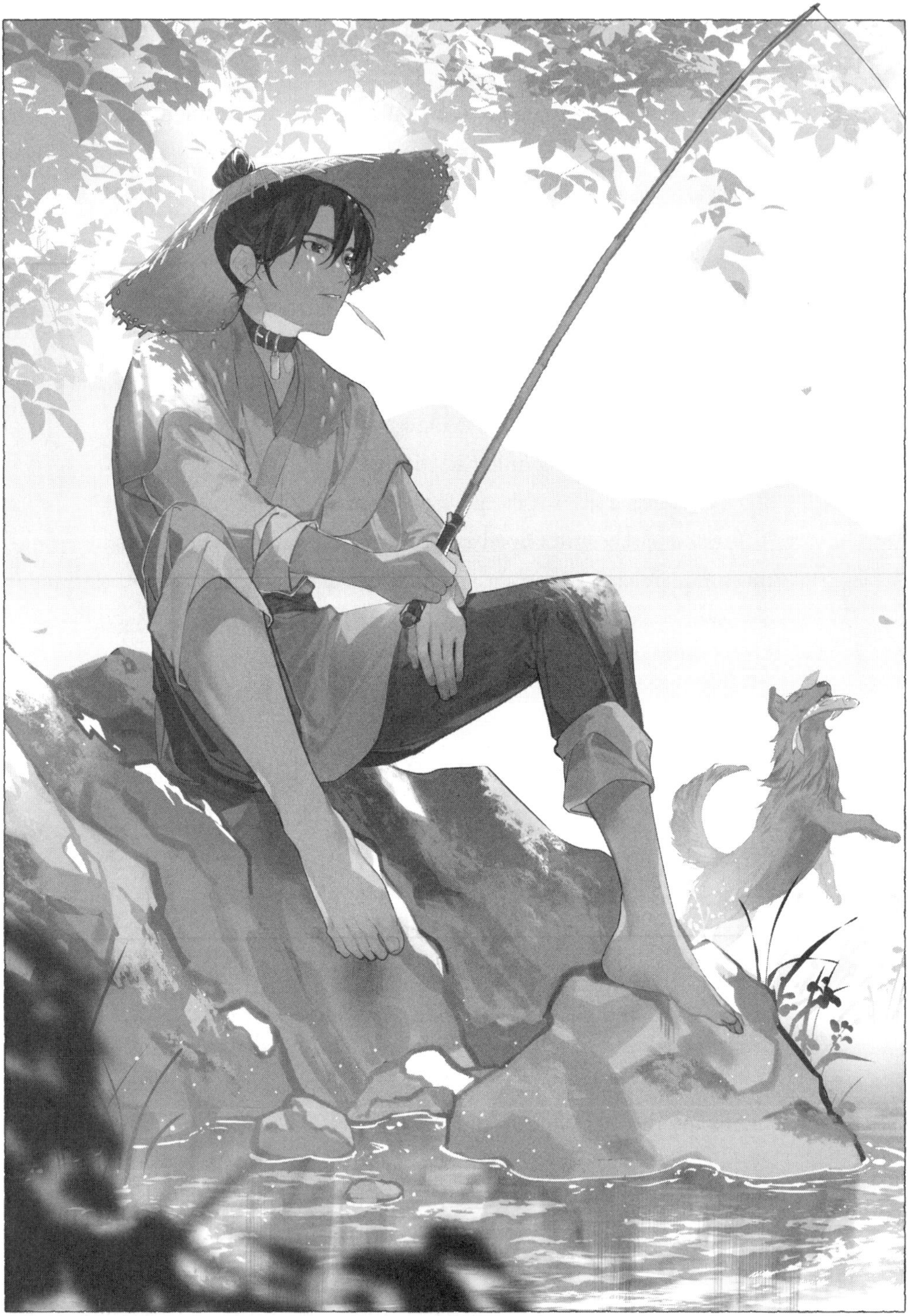

other parts of Peach Blossom Lake. His mind could be quite sharp sometimes, but it could be dull indeed at others. For example, at this moment, his thoughts turned sluggish and simple-minded. He yelled, "Fish! Fish! C'mere fishies," splashing through the water at every step. Even the fish in the distance vanished when they heard his clumsy movements. Gu Mang brushed away some green vines dangling over the rocky crags and turned a corner. "Fish, come quick—"

"Who's there?"

The voice that called out was as beautiful as Kunshan jade and richly melodious, yet with a vicious note of threat. Gu Mang jumped in fright and turned unthinking to look toward the speaker. He saw a flash of golden light the instant before a spell exploded on the water's surface, inches from his knees.

Amid the haze of its thunderous splash, a white-clad silhouette soared over the waterfall. Beads of water flew up to join the crashing cascade. When the pillar of water thrown up by the spell finally dispersed, Gu Mang, still coughing, heard that crisp, menacing voice say: "Look up."

Gu Mang mopped the water from his face and squinted in the direction of the speaker. If the memories he'd regained to this point were anything to go by, people who flew into an embarrassed rage upon being caught bathing in the depths of a peach-blossom pool were generally great beauties. Gu Mang's strong and innate sense of chivalry hadn't diminished a jot, so he hastily said, "Miss, I'm so sorry, I didn't do it on purpose, I just came to catch fi—"

Before he could finish the word, a stream of water shot out and slapped him squarely across the face. Caught off guard, Gu Mang was knocked straight back into the lake by the force of that purported-beauty's stunning blow. After swallowing several mouthfuls of lake water, he managed to stagger upright once more.

The beauty's voice was bone-chillingly cold. "Open your damn eyes and take a good look at whom you are speaking to."

I do want to look, Gu Mang thought, *but it's inappropriate for men and women to get too close; it's better if I don't.* But then he thought, *No—you're the one who invited me to take a look, so I'll seem guilty if I don't.* Only then did he wonder, *Huh? Why does this voice...sound familiar?*

Bracing himself against the wet stone wall, Gu Mang shook his dripping head much like Fandou. Then he opened his clear blue eyes and looked toward the boulder outside the waterfall's cave.

He was rendered wholly speechless. The speaker was beautiful to be sure, but unfortunately, it was a man—and not only that, one Gu Mang knew.

Murong Chuyi.

This man had the same hang-up as Mo Xi: he didn't like to fully disrobe when bathing and preferred to enter the water wearing a bathrobe. By now, he had already draped a second white robe over his sodden garment. Beneath his sharp, inky brows, his phoenix eyes were lowered, his gaze colder than the waters of Peach Blossom Lake.

After a few beats of silence, Gu Mang cupped his hands in greeting. "Sorry, Dage. Pardon me."

"Hold it," Murong Chuyi said, tone frosty.

"...Is there something else, Dage?"

Murong Chuyi raised a hand and tapped a finger upon his clothes. A fiery glow sprang to life at the tip of his pale, slender finger. Under this brilliant light, his wet clothes were dried in a flash. Murong Chuyi sat on a boulder and shot Gu Mang a glance. "Come here."

"We're both men here, and it was just a look. No one got taken advantage of." Gu Mang faltered. "If you're upset, why don't I...

Why don't I..." After racking his brains, Gu Mang tentatively offered, "Why don't I strip and let you see too?"

Murong Chuyi glared with his phoenix eyes. "Who wants to see you? Come here."

Gu Mang had little choice but to do as he was bid. His qinggong wasn't as good as Murong Chuyi's, so he was compelled to climb the tall and slippery stone platform on all fours. He slipped a couple times before pathetically clambering upward. At no point during this process did Murong Chuyi offer him a hand.

Once he reached the top, he approached Murong Chuyi. It wasn't until he was up close that Gu Mang noted how pale Murong Chuyi's face was—even his lips were bloodless. Gu Mang couldn't help but stare. "What happened to you?"

Murong Chuyi closed his eyes. "Go—go to Jiang Manor."

Gu Mang was utterly lost. "Why would I go to Jiang Manor?"

"Ask Jiang Fuli for some heartbalm. Bring it back to me."

Not even a *will you?* or *please*—Gu Mang took this to mean that the errand was another one of his chores. He nodded once and turned to leave. It was only after walking quite a distance that the other shoe dropped, and he turned in puzzlement. "Wait a minute— why do you want me to do this?"

"Because you happened to pass by," Murong Chuyi replied.

This man spoke like those crazy Daoists in the stories who would say upon bumping into a youthful warrior, "Young friend, fate has brought us together. Come to the mountains with me and learn cultivation," before dragging the hapless youth with them over all protestations. Gu Mang sulked. "It's not like I owe you anything, *and* you just hit me. Why should I help you?"

Light sparked at Murong Chuyi's fingertips. His expression was ferocious, as if he was about to lash out with another ruthless strike. He glared icily. "Are you going or not?"

Gu Mang shook his head. "A true man can be corrupted by neither wealth nor power—huh, what's wrong?"

The light at Murong Chuyi's fingertips had winked out. Murong Chuyi lowered his head and held his sleeve to his mouth as he coughed up bloody spittle.

"You're sick?" Gu Mang exclaimed.

Murong Chuyi was obviously struggling to maintain his poise, but when he tried to speak again, he choked on a great mouthful of dark blood. "You... You must not tell Yue Manor..." Pausing, he panted a few times, eyes flashing with stubbornness. "That I...was cultivating here..."

"I must not tell Yue Manor?"

Murong Chuyi was thoroughly weakened, but his expression and bearing were still as keen as ever. "Never," he gasped.

Gu Mang was silent.

"Promise me."

Gu Mang seemed to be stupefied by this man's imperious air. His head moved to nod before he realized he was doing it.

The second Gu Mang gave his assent, Murong Chuyi collapsed like a bow drawn too taut, his willpower dissolving the moment he had Gu Mang's word. Eyes fluttering shut, he crumpled atop the damp, frigid boulder and passed out cold.

Speechless, Gu Mang stared blankly at him. After a long while, he bent down and prodded at Murong Chuyi's cheek. His pale, thin visage was cool as stone to the touch, unnerving yet pitiable in a way that was difficult to describe.

Gu Mang swallowed nervously. "I'll go get you medicine right now, okay? Don't—don't just faint like that, bro."

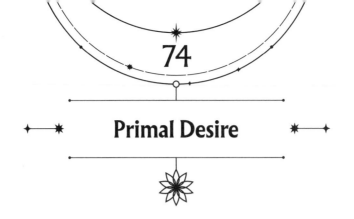

Primal Desire

"**H**EARTBALM?"

Inside the medicine master's manor, Jiang Fuli set down the scroll in his hands and raised his almond eyes to study Gu Mang, who was soaked to the bone and still had a fishing net strapped to his back. "Who do you want this for? Mo Xi or Murong Lian?"

"Murong..." He stopped himself, remembering the request Murong Chuyi had made right before passing out. Gu Mang knew a gentleman's word was gold. He had nodded to Murong Chuyi, so he had to do as he promised. "Not gonna tell you," he said instead.

Jiang Fuli narrowed his eyes. "Do you know what kind of substance this is?"

"Yeah. It's for healing."

"It can heal, yes, but it can also harm," Jiang Fuli said. "Heartbalm is a plant that's half-demonic in nature. Although it can be used to dull pain, its toxicity cannot be underestimated. I have piles of it in my storerooms—it's not particularly precious, so I don't mind giving you some. But..."

Gu Mang raised his hand. "I swear I won't use it to poison people."

Jiang Fuli scoffed. "Poison people? While I'm right here in Chonghua? If you dare get up to trouble where I can see, I'll respect you as a man of courage."

"Then what did you say *but* for?" Gu Mang asked.

"But—I will tell your lord Xihe-jun that you asked me for heartbalm."

Gu Mang thought it over. Murong Chuyi was still unconscious, so saving him was of utmost urgency. Once Gu Mang brought him back to life, he could explain all of this to Murong Chuyi. So he assented. He followed Jiang Fuli to the storeroom to fetch the herb, waited as Jiang Fuli prepared it, then took the jar of medicine back into the recesses of Peach Blossom Lake with all speed.

Murong Chuyi was still lying where he'd fallen. He didn't look well at all. His elegant face was devoid of color, and his skin was ice-cold to the touch. Gu Mang lifted him into a sitting position, opened the jar, and slowly began to pour the medicine into Murong Chuyi's mouth. This process proved difficult. Although unconscious, Murong Chuyi still coughed from time to time. He got half the medicine down and choked on the other, brows knitted as he muttered unintelligibly. Gu Mang heard him call for his older sister, then say Yue Chenqing's name, his expression pained throughout.

Gu Mang wasn't close with Murong Chuyi, but his compassion still won in the end. He stroked Murong Chuyi's hair and soothed him with gentle words.

"Jiejie..." Murong Chuyi murmured.

To which Gu Mang said: "Jiejie's here. There now, there now."

"Chenqing..." Murong Chuyi muttered.

To which Gu Mang said: "Yep, I'm that little white bird. There now, Fourth Uncle. Here—there's still a little medicine left."

Toward the end, Murong Chuyi's colorless lips trembled, as if he were gripped by a nightmare. He clutched Gu Mang's sleeve, his eyes flickering restlessly beneath their lids, long lashes fluttering like the wings of a swallowtail butterfly. "No... Don't..."

"What?"

"You..." Murong Chuyi's entire arm was spasming. Tendons stood out in his elegant hand. "You bastard... How could you...you..."

Stunned, Gu Mang rubbed his own nose in dejection. "I'm obviously trying to help; why are you being so mean and cursing at me?"

But Murong Chuyi was still trapped in his nightmare. His pale knuckles grew paler still, and he suddenly let out a muted grunt—as if he'd endured some pain or humiliation in the dream. The outer corners of his tightly shut eyes reddened. "Bas...tard..."

Gu Mang looked at him and sighed. "Who are you cursing? Your sister or the little white bird?"

Of course Murong Chuyi didn't answer. Gu Mang stayed with him for a while longer. Eventually, Murong Chuyi's mumbling died down. In the time it took to burn a stick of incense, he stopped speaking altogether. The heartbalm medicine had begun to take effect; his features slowly relaxed, and the crease between his brows smoothed.

Gu Mang half-carried and half-dragged him to a dry patch on the stone platform and laid him down so he could rest more comfortably. Then he put his chin in his hands and sighed in boredom. "I fed you the plant, so when will you wake up?"

Murong Chuyi gave no response.

Gu Mang continued waiting for another long interval. Murong Chuyi's eyes remained firmly closed; he showed no sign of waking. Gu Mang sighed again, face propped in a hand as he studied Murong Chuyi.

Murong Chuyi was a rare beauty indeed—refined and handsome, with stunning looks. Gu Mang wasn't well-read; he didn't have the words to describe what he saw in detail. He just felt that, despite the severe lines of Murong Chuyi's features and his dauntless and intimidating air, there was an ethereal quality about him. He was like those dragon ladies in the picture books, or billowing snow in human form. In short—he was good-looking. In more detail—he was well worth looking at. Gu Mang patiently watched him for an hour with his cheek still pressed to his hand.

But no matter how worthwhile his face, Gu Mang found that he could not keep looking at it after that hour had passed. He turned to Fandou. "Do we really need to keep watching over him like this? I don't mind...but Princess is still at home, waiting for me to cook fish for him."

Fandou barked exuberantly.

Gu Mang nodded. "You're right, Dragon Lady is an outsider, but Princess is one of us. We should catch the fish first. Anyway, I've already fed him the plant. It's not our fault if he doesn't wake up."

Fandou barked again.

And so Gu Mang went back to catching fish in the pond. The three fat grass carp he'd caught had escaped when Murong Chuyi's water strike knocked him over. His luck this time wasn't so good—despite extensive hunting, all the fish he netted were small and bony. Sunset was drawing near, and smoke was rising from the chimneys of the capital. Gu Mang couldn't help but feel glum. He hadn't imagined he would return empty-handed after so much effort. He stood by the lake, leaning on his net. The setting sun was like rouge rinsed from the boundless sky, shimmering across the ripples on the water.

"No way," Gu Mang sighed. "Don't all the books say that kindness is rewarded? I've saved the little dragon lady,[2] so why aren't there plump fish jumping into my hands in gratitude?"

---

2   Xiaolongnü (小龙女), literally "little dragon lady," is a character from Jin Yong's classic wuxia novel Return of the Condor Heroes who is described as ethereally beautiful and dressed in white.

As Gu Mang pondered this, a voice crisp as clinking jade came from behind. "What are you babbling about?"

Gu Mang jumped in surprise. He whipped around and skittered backward in one jerky motion. "You're awake? Why are you always sneaking around so quietly?"

The man who had soared over the waters was, of course, Murong Chuyi. His manner was back to normal and betrayed not a hint of his recent fainting spell. Gu Mang remarked: "That heartbalm sure was effective. You recovered so quickly."

Murong Chuyi snorted softly and gracefully flew ashore. Those phoenix eyes swept Gu Mang from tip to toe. Noticing that his clothes were still soaked, Murong Chuyi lifted a finger and golden light flashed once more. When it dimmed, Gu Mang touched his newly dried clothes in surprise and delight. "Thank you very much," he said with a grin. "You're a very kind person."

Murong Chuyi wasted no more breath. "You came to catch fish today?"

"Yes, the princess at home is sick and can't eat anything, so I wanted to catch a fresh and plump fish for him." Gu Mang rubbed his nose. "Family needs to help each other out, after all."

Murong Chuyi's sharp brows dipped slightly. "Princess?" He paused briefly. "Princess Mengze?"

Gu Mang waved his hand no. "It's Princess Mo Xi."

Murong Chuyi fell speechless. So this amnesiac Beast of the Altar wasn't being nasty calling him a "little dragon lady." Apparently, he'd somehow bestowed the ruthless god of war Mo Xi with the nickname "Princess."

Murong Chuyi looked away from Gu Mang, his features betraying nothing. He stood at the edge of the lake with his hands behind his back, facing the wind head-on. "Come ashore," he commanded.

Confused, Gu Mang waded out the water, using the pole of his fishing net for leverage.

"What kind of fish do you want?" Murong Chuyi asked.

Gu Mang was still lost, but sincerely responded: "Perch."

"How many?"

"The more the merrier."

"Too many would be wasteful," Murong Chuyi said. "I think five is sufficient."

"What are you doing?" Gu Mang wondered out loud. "Helping me nab some fish?"

Nab was honestly an insulting descriptor for what Chonghua's Ignorant Immortal Murong Chuyi was about to do. He was a master artificer after all, whose command of the art could not be fathomed by even the likes of Yue Juntian. With a gentle swish of his sleeves, a silver arrow materialized from thin air and shot into the water. It vanished into the depths of Peach Blossom Lake. When it broke the water's surface again and returned to shore, it was over ten feet long, with five fresh, plump peach blossom perch strung upon it.

Gu Mang's eyes widened, clear as blue glass. He looked at the fish, then turned to look at Murong Chuyi. After a long beat, he uttered one simple, crude phrase to express the reverence he felt. "Holy shit..." Of course it would be one of the vulgarities formerly favored by General Gu. Seriously... All his hard work had been out-done by a single sweep of the sleeves and flick of the fingers from Murong Chuyi.

With a crook of Murong Chuyi's finger, the fish flew into the basket on Gu Mang's back, and the silver arrow vanished. "If there's anything else you want, speak now," Murong Chuyi intoned.

Gu Mang shook his head as he stared at this beautiful, white-robed man with his face to the wind in the golden light of dusk.

Gu Mang was a frank person; he said whatever he thought. "No wonder Little White Bird worships you."

Murong Chuyi's brow furrowed slightly. "White Bird?"

"I mean Yue...Yue...Yue something." Vexed, Gu Mang clutched his head, "Ah, I forgot his name again."

"Yue Chenqing?"

"Mm-hmm! That's the one!" Gu Mang clapped and smiled. "No wonder he chases after you all the time. Dage, you're so awesome! Could you teach me how to go *swoosh-swoosh-swoosh* and catch fish like that?"

After a moment's pause, Murong Chuyi sighed softly. "Give me your hand."

Gu Mang did as he was told. Murong Chuyi summoned a handful of silver needles from who knows where and placed them in Gu Mang's palm.

"What's this?"

"Voice-Obeying Arrows," said Murong Chuyi. "I've given you fifty. This arrow can change size at will and obeys spoken commands. Will that be enough for you to fish with?"

Overjoyed, Gu Mang thanked him profusely. "Yes, yes! You're so generous! And such a nice person too!" He cautiously tipped the needles into his qiankun pouch, then carefully put the pouch in his robes, like a puppy working awfully hard to hide a meaty bone. Once the arrows were safely stowed, he said again, "Thank you, kind person!"

Murong Chuyi didn't reply—he wasn't used to being thought of as a kind person. The people of Chonghua saw him as standoffish and aloof, merely Chonghua's infamous Ignorance who pursued artificing with single-minded fervor. His expression became stiff and unnatural, and after a brief silence, he changed the subject:

"You mustn't tell anyone about what you saw today. Especially Yue Chenqing. Do not tell him."

Gu Mang nodded. "No problem, no problem. But there's one person I'm afraid I can't hide it from."

"Who?"

"Mo Xi," Gu Mang replied. "Medicine Master Jiang said heart-balm can be used as poison, so he'll definitely tell Mo Xi that I asked him for it."

Murong Chuyi considered this for a moment. "That's fine. I'll explain things to Xihe-jun myself. Think no further on it—just remember to tell no one else."

"What if Mo Xi asks me before you tell him?"

"You may respond with the truth."

"Okay," Gu Mang agreed. Still, he couldn't help but ask, "You're okay now, right?"

"I'm fine. The spiritual energy of Peach Blossom Lake is usually enough to suppress my symptoms. Today's episode was unexpected."

"Oh... But...Little White Bird and the others... They don't know about your sickness?"

"They know a little, but not much," Murong Chuyi replied blandly. "It's not a major issue—Yue Chenqing will inevitably ask a bunch of questions, and I don't want to deal with it. So I'm asking you to keep it a secret."

Murong Chuyi's story was full of holes, and his rationale behind the secret-keeping was so flimsy only a fool would believe it. But as things stood, Gu Mang was pretty much a fool; he swallowed it without question. He raised a hand and solemnly swore to Murong Chuyi that he'd never tell another soul.

By the time Gu Mang took his leave and returned to the manor, night was approaching. Li Wei stood in the doorway, scanning the horizon. When he saw Gu Mang return at last, evening light like a red cloak upon his shoulders, he rushed over in exasperation. "What's the matter with you? Were you catching fish or looking after them as pets? What kept you so long?"

Gu Mang took the basket from his back and showed it to Li Wei, smiling. "I caught five fat fish. There's still time—let me use the kitchen."

Gu Mang had never prepared fish in all the time he had lived at Xihe Manor, but he knew what to do. The scraps of memory he'd recovered included plenty of instances where he'd cooked fish. After he'd worked his way through those particular recollections, Gu Mang swiftly prepared several dishes and arranged them neatly in a box.

As he stepped out of the kitchen, he saw Li Wei waiting outside. "Is he still in the study?" Gu Mang asked.

"Yes, he went straight there as soon as court concluded and hasn't eaten a thing."

"Watch this," Gu Mang said, food box in hand. "Shidi-coaxing is my specialty."

"Wow..." Li Wei replied happily. But a second later, he realized Gu Mang's form of address wasn't right—he was being insubordinate again. He snorted in disapproval, but Gu Mang had already walked to the end of the corridor with the box of food.

A lantern glowed in silence, its oil pooling on the copper base plate. Mo Xi's sharp profile shone in its halo of light.

Although the northern frontier was stable for the moment, it wouldn't remain so. The armistice between the Liao Kingdom and Chonghua was a matter of necessity, not desire—the two nations had weakened each other through long conflict to the point that neighboring countries had begun to stir in action. If they continued waging a war of attrition, both would end up as easy prey for a third party. Thus, it was an armistice in name only; in truth, both countries remained at bitter odds, each eying the other to see who would recover first and most completely. The emperor had kept close watch over the Liao Kingdom's movements this year. The imperial report Mo Xi held was full of information gathered by Chonghua's spies, including intelligence on many demonic plants and objects from the Liao Kingdom. The contents were morbid, and Mo Xi's brow furrowed deeply as he read.

Just as he came to some detailed notes about the "Flower of Eightfold Sorrows" left behind by the demon race, the candle flame flickered. Gu Mang pushed open the door and strode right up to his desk. "Mo-shidi, it's time to eat."

After a pause, Mo Xi looked up. "You can leave it there. Also, you're not allowed to call me that. How many times have I told you? Why can't you remember?"

Gu Mang ignored him entirely. Reasoning with this person was useless; it was better to meet force with force. Feigning deafness, Gu Mang opened the food box and lifted the dishes out one by one.

Mo Xi frowned. "What are you doing *now*?"

"I'm not doing anything," Gu Mang said. "You read your books, and I'll eat my food. I'll just leave half for you."

Another pause. "You want to eat dinner with me?"

Gu Mang blinked at him. "Haven't we eaten together before?"

Mo Xi was silent. It was true that they had eaten at the same table in the great hall, but that was obviously different from sharing dishes from the same food box.

"Ah, it's not like I have much choice," Gu Mang said carelessly, mimicking how he spoke in his memories. "There's nothing tasty left in the kitchen, so I have to steal some of yours. Xihe-jun, have a little mercy—be magnanimous and share with me, okay?"

Mo Xi seemed rather stunned, so Gu Mang redoubled his efforts and added fuel to the fire. "Also, I personally cooked all the dishes here tonight. Aren't you worried I might have poisoned it? I'll humbly go first and be your taste-tester. That way you'll be able to properly enjoy your meal, your safety one hundred percent guaranteed."

Mo Xi stared at him. "What are you even talking about?"

Still, he let Gu Mang do as he pleased. Gu Mang cheerfully plunked the simple meal he'd made—four side dishes, plus soup—onto Mo Xi's spotless red sandalwood desk.

The dishes were still piping-hot, steaming and fragrant. Although they were uncomplicated stir-fries, nowhere near as sophisticated as the cook's usual handiwork, they smelled wonderful and looked bright and appealing. There was a dish of crystal pork terrine served with Zhenjiang vinegar and fresh-ground ginger; the meat was sliced very thinly, and the pork rind was soft and tender. Another plate held water caltrop and lotus root stir-fried with slices of celtuce, the delicate texture of the caltrop striking a refreshing harmony with the jade-green celtuce. There was also a dish of braised bamboo shoots, crisp and gleaming and generously coated with a glossy, savory sauce. In contrast, the soup was simple: a light and nourishing broth of three types of mushrooms, garnished with fresh greens and slivers of cured pork to add richness.

The final bamboo steamer lifted from the food box boasted a platter of sweet-and-sour perch. The fish had been sliced and prepared with a generous handful of julienned ginger to remove any odor. A splash of sizzling oil added a burst of flavor to the steamed fish, leaving the skin crisp-golden and the fat meltingly tender. The dish was finished with a drizzle of a sauce made with simmered sugar syrup and vinegar. At the touch of one's chopsticks, the rich, translucent flesh shimmered and trembled beneath a delectable veil of sweet-and-sour sauce...

"Yum." Gu Mang's chopsticks darted about in delight. He spoke aloud for the sake of Mo Xi, who was still reading with his eyes downcast. "All the fish belly's mine now," he proclaimed, and continued to apply himself to his meal.

As he reached to carve off the rest of the fish belly, which had the fewest bones and the most succulent flesh, Mo Xi finally couldn't stand it anymore. He shut the bamboo scroll as his fingers closed around Gu Mang's wrist.

"Whatcha doing?" Gu Mang asked, his cheeks bulging.

Mo Xi glared at Gu Mang as he wrested the chopsticks from his hand and grabbed a bowl of rice. He picked up the prized piece of fish and dropped it into his own bowl.

Secretly rejoicing, Gu Mang affected an exasperated expression. "Why d'you have to steal *mine*?!"

Mo Xi returned the chopsticks to Gu Mang with ill grace and grabbed his own pair. "What did you expect? Am I supposed to wait for you to finish, then gnaw on the bones?" With that, he took a vicious bite of fish.

Somehow, his white teeth and ferocious movements, coupled with this vaguely suggestive language, made Gu Mang shiver as he sat on the other side of the table.

To tear you apart, to drink your blood...

His domineering manner and forceful gaze made Gu Mang's head throb. Memories of the two of them pressed skin-to-skin flashed through his head, making his blood pulse so rapidly it sounded like a bow had snapped right next to his ear. As if his body was desperate to tell him that yes—there had been a time when this man, who looked so cool and aloof, had bared his teeth like a feral beast and possessed him entirely, devoured him whole...

Gu Mang stared at Mo Xi's handsome face, his gaze sweeping from the high bridge of his nose down to his pale yet sensual mouth. His heart skipped a beat, surprising even himself. The revelation roused a strangely disagreeable feeling in Gu Mang's chest. It was hot and uncomfortable, as if a pile of spent firewood had been kindled back to life, or a patch of new seedlings had been gently uncovered by the spring winds of April. He suddenly thought back to those memories from the night Mo Xi came of age. Mo Xi's lips had been pressed to his own—such a gentle touch, but it had left the old version of him shaking...

Mo Xi didn't notice the unusual glimmer in Gu Mang's gaze. Focused on eating his fish, he absentmindedly licked a bit of sauce from his lower lip.

Gu Mang's chest erupted with scalding heat; he was filled with an indescribable urgency and primal desire. For some reason, he wanted to inch closer and gently touch Mo Xi's cheeks, his mouth. He had no understanding of what this desire implied. He felt that this fire had sprung to life in his chest like an instinct, and only by acting on it could he soothe his own agitation.

Gu Mang swallowed and inched closer, like a cub sniffing for danger. Cautiously, he leaned in toward the wholly oblivious Mo Xi.

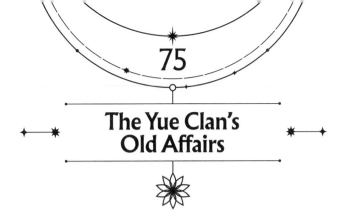

75

The Yue Clan's Old Affairs

"**B**Y THE WAY." Mo Xi looked up, interrupting Gu Mang's surreptitious approach. "The third of next month is Yue Chenqing's birthday."

"Ah?" Gu Mang jumped, sweating with fear. He hadn't heard a single word Mo Xi said. Like a dreamer startled awake, he looked away in panic, refusing to meet his eyes. "Oh...okay..." he murmured, touching his reddened earlobes.

His heart was still pounding. What had he meant to do? Why did he suddenly feel such pressing need? Between wolves, biting each other signaled dominance and submission—but what did it mean between him and Mo Xi? Was it the same? He wondered if he longed to overpower Mo Xi, but he discovered he didn't know what would count as "overpowering." Did he want Mo Xi to kneel to him? No. Not that, he wasn't interested in that at all. Or did he want...

"Are you listening?"

Gu Mang came back to his senses. "What? Yep! I'm listening, I'm listening."

Mo Xi looked at him and frowned. "Why are your ears red?"

Gu Mang scratched at them. "I-it's because I'm hot."

Mo Xi eyed him. He didn't know what Gu Mang's problem was, but he was almost finished with dinner anyway. He set down his chopsticks and said, "We need to send Yue Chenqing a gift. I'm busy and can't get away from my responsibilities, so you and Li Wei can handle it."

"Mn..." Gu Mang paused. "Why are we giving presents to Little White Bird?"

Mo Xi's face darkened. "Didn't you say you were listening?"

"...Must've missed it."

"The third of next month," Mo Xi repeated, grinding his teeth, "is Yue Chenqing's birthday."

This time, Gu Mang finally understood. His eyes widened. "It's Little White Bird's birthday?"

"Mn."

Mo Xi saw the sparkle in Gu Mang's eyes and was somewhat taken aback. He knew Gu Mang was fond of other people's celebrations. No matter if it was a birthday or a wedding, he loved nothing more than to join the fun. When Luoli-jun's son got married recently, the majestic bridal procession had wound its way through the city. Gu Mang wasn't allowed to come and go as he pleased, but upon hearing the clamor of gongs and drums, he climbed onto the roof and sprawled on the tiles to eat melon seeds and watch the procession. He clapped and cheered with the passersby, adding his voice and applause from the rooftop. After nightfall, Mo Xi allowed him to go outside, and he happily hunted for peanuts, pine nuts, and dried longans that had fallen between the cracks in the brick pavement during the day. Full of delight, he brought back an entire pocketful and even offered to split some with Mo Xi.

"I know what you're thinking," Mo Xi told the big rat Gu Mang. "But I'm afraid you'll be disappointed."

"Huh?"

"Yue Manor never arranges a great banquet for Yue Chenqing's birthday, so there won't be any candy or snacks tossed on the ground for you to collect."

Sure enough, Gu Mang wilted. "Oh..." he murmured. After a pause, he curiously inquired, "But Little White Bird is clearly very pampered by his family. Why don't they hold a banquet?"

Mo Xi took a sip of the hot soup. "It's due to the circumstances of Yue Chenqing's birth," he replied. "Yue Chenqing's mother was from the imperial family, and she passed away due to complications in childbirth."

Gu Mang was taken aback, but he quickly put it together. "So Yue Manor doesn't arrange a banquet for Little White Bird because Little White Bird's papa still hasn't forgotten Little White Bird's mama?"

"Since when was Yue Juntian so faithful? There's no chance he would do such a thing out of respect for his deceased wife," Mo Xi responded blandly. "But whether he would or not, Murong Huang was still of royal blood. Even if she died years ago, Yue Juntian still has to honor the imperial family. That's why he keeps his own son's birthday as spartan as possible."

"So that's how it is..." Gu Mang mumbled. He ticked the names he knew off on his fingers and suddenly exclaimed, "So Murong Chuyi is also part of the imperial family?"

"He doesn't count," Mo Xi replied.

"Wh-why? Isn't his surname also Murong...?"

"All of Chonghua's nobles have gold trim on their robes, but Murong Chuyi's clothes are trimmed in silver," said Mo Xi. "Why do you imagine that is?"

"Because white and silver suits him best, so he looks more handsome that way," Gu Mang responded in earnest.

Mo Xi glowered. "Do you think this is a beauty contest?"

"Well, why then?"

"Murong Chuyi isn't of royal blood. He's an orphan who was taken in by Murong Huang...Yue Chenqing's birth mother, that is. In her youth, Murong Huang visited a temple on Mount Han, outside the city. She came across a child on the way who had been abandoned on the steps of the temple. She felt they were fated to meet, so she took him in as a little brother. She even petitioned the late emperor to bestow the imperial surname upon him."

Under his breath, Gu Mang repeated a few snatches of Mo Xi's explanation to himself several times before finally understood. His blue eyes widened. "So Little Dragon Lady was adopted?!"

"Stop giving people random nicknames." Mo Xi felt a headache coming on. "You might get away with it for Yue Chenqing, but if Murong Chuyi heard you call him Little Dragon Lady, he'd shred you alive and use the pieces as raw material in his artificing forge."

Gu Mang waved a hand. "He's not that bad. Little Dragon Lady is a great person. Today, I ev—"

He cut himself off mid-word, realizing his tongue had slipped. He glanced apprehensively at Mo Xi, hoping he hadn't noticed what Gu Mang just said. But fate never bowed to the whims of man. General Mo had the eyes of a hawk and the ears of an owl, so how could he have missed it? He stared at Gu Mang through narrowed eyes. "You saw him today?"

Knowing he couldn't conceal this adventure from Mo Xi, Gu Mang helplessly crossed his arms and said in sycophantic tones, "Nothing can get past you, Xihe-jun. You're so wise."

"Don't try flattering me. How did you meet him?"

Gu Mang had no choice but to tell Mo Xi how he had bumped into Murong Chuyi at Peach Blossom Lake. Remembering

Murong Chuyi's warning, he kept the story brief and spared the details.

He had expected Mo Xi would be at least a little surprised by the revelation of Murong Chuyi's condition, but Mo Xi only frowned and sighed. "How pointless."

"What do you mean?"

"Yue Chenqing came to see me a few days ago and asked to borrow a copy of the Liao Kingdom's *Compendium of Plants Demonic and Divine*. He said he was searching for a cure-all herbal medicine," Mo Xi explained. "Unfortunately, I lent the book to the overseer at the cultivation academy two weeks ago. I'm not sure if Yue Chenqing would ask him for it."

Gu Mang blinked. "So Little White Bird has known about his uncle's symptoms for several days already?"

"Longer than that," Mo Xi said. "He's known for a few years that his fourth uncle's had some health issues. One of the reasons he came with me to the northern frontier was to seek a cure beyond Chonghua's borders. But Yue Chenqing also knows Murong Chuyi can't stand the meddling of others, so he's done all his research secretly, behind his uncle's back."

Gu Mang was stunned. "So Little White Bird has known for ages. But then why did Murong Chuyi say he only knew the gist of it?"

"Murong Chuyi isn't wrong. Yue Chenqing knows his uncle is sick—he doesn't know what manner of affliction he suffers from. He can't find the specific cure, so he's looking for a panacea."

Gu Mang was baffled. "Why does Murong Chuyi want to keep hiding it from him…?"

"They've never had a very good relationship." Mo Xi sighed. "The Yue Clan's family matters are a total mess."

Gu Mang sat in silence and considered the tangle between Jiang Yexue, Yue Chenqing, and Murong Chuyi for a good while. In the end, he could only clutch his head and sigh. "Too confusing— I give up."

Mo Xi looked askance. "What's too confusing?"

As he spoke, Gu Mang counted on his fingers. "I'm trying to figure out why their relationship is bad. First, look at Murong Chuyi— he was a child taken in and brought up by Little White Bird's mama, so why would he dislike his sister's son?"

In the past, Gu Mang innately understood the ways of the world when it came to matters like these. But now, in his ignorance, he needed Mo Xi to explain it to him. "It's very simple," said Mo Xi. "To Murong Chuyi, Murong Huang was both a teacher and a sister. Although Murong Huang called him her brother, she treated him and cared for him like he was her son. When she married into Yue Manor, she specifically asked His Imperial Majesty to allow Murong Chuyi to accompany her. That's why Murong Chuyi lives with the Yue Clan."

Gu Mang nodded vigorously. "I get it—in other words, Little White Bird and Little Dragon Lady are technically uncle and nephew, but are in truth more like big brother and little brother."

"Correct," Mo Xi said. "Murong Huang was Murong Chuyi's benefactor. When she was alive, Murong Chuyi accompanied her day and night, listened attentively to her every word, and regarded her with the utmost love and respect. Naturally, he wanted her to have only the best home to return to as well. But Yue Juntian..."

Mo Xi pursed his lips, unwilling to elaborate on his opinions of this person. But Gu Mang spoke clearly: "He's a bad person."

"Back then, Yue Juntian had a bad reputation, romantically speaking," explained Mo Xi. "His parents and Murong Huang's had arranged their children's marriage long before, but Yue Juntian was profligate by nature. By the time he was sixteen, he had already gotten a qin player with child, taken her as a concubine, and sired a son."

"Impressive," Gu Mang mumbled. "Before he even married Murong Huang, he already had a concubine, and a child on top of that." He pondered for a moment. "Was that child Jiang Yexue?"

"Mn." Mo Xi was uncomfortable discussing other people's dalliances. "It was him."

"Then I understand why Little Dragon Lady doesn't like Jiang Yexue," Gu Mang said. "Yue Juntian took two wives. Murong Chuyi is the little brother of the first wife, Murong Huang, and so he's on the first wife's side. Jiang Yexue is the son of the concubine, and so he's on the concubine's side."

Mo Xi had no wish to debate matters of wives and concubines. Lowering his lashes, he sighed softly. "Yes. Although such things aren't uncommon in noble families, it's just as you said: Murong Chuyi revered his foster sister and was greatly displeased with the marriage. Furthermore, with his disposition, Yue Juntian would often make Murong Huang sad or angry... So Murong Chuyi has always had very complicated feelings toward this nephew of his, whose blood is half Yue Juntian's." Mo Xi poured another two cups of hot tea, pushing one toward Gu Mang and holding the other in his hands.

Still perplexed, Gu Mang said, "I still don't really understand... Even if half of Little White Bird's blood is from someone he doesn't like, at least he's Murong Chuyi's sister's son. Don't people say, 'love both the house and its crows'? Why doesn't he like a child his sister must have loved dearly?"

"Because he thinks his sister wasn't happy. He believes that this child's birth was a mistake on top of a mistake."

Steam rose from the tea in spirals, twisting like the old grudges they discussed. "On top of that, there is another, more important, reason..."

"What's that?" asked Gu Mang.

"The complications with the birth didn't come out of nowhere," Mo Xi replied. "From the moment Murong Huang married into the Yue family, she often fought with Yue Juntian and lived in a state of constant worry. On the day she went into labor, a woman whom Yue Juntian had an affair with came to the manor to cause trouble and said plenty of vulgar things. Murong Huang was already frail and on the verge of collapse. After this disturbance, her qi and blood circulation were badly affected. In the end, she lost all faith and passed away."

Gu Mang let out a low sound of surprise.

Mo Xi sighed. "So you see—both the marriage and its issue were mistakes. In the end, these events stole the most important person on earth to Murong Chuyi. This is something he can't let go of even after so many years. Now that he's a master artificer, Yue Juntian has tried to break the ice with him many times, but Murong Chuyi won't even give him the time of day. As for Yue Chenqing...Murong Chuyi has never known how to face him." After a pause, Mo Xi concluded, "That's pretty much the story."

Gu Mang still couldn't quite make sense of this complicated drama. Bewilderment showed in his azure eyes. After a long while, he spoke, puzzled: "But Murong Huang's death isn't Yue Chenqing's fault—he was only a baby..."

"Of course Murong Chuyi understands that Yue Chenqing is blameless in all this. But understanding is not the same as forgiveness."

Rubbing his chin, Gu Mang repeated Mo Xi's words under his breath. "Understanding is not the same as forgiveness..." His eyes flashed with confusion. "Why does this sound familiar?"

"You said it to me once."

"Really?" Gu Mang exclaimed in wonder. "Wow, I'm so amazing."

Mo Xi said nothing. Seeing the pleased and self-satisfied look on Gu Mang's face, Mo Xi decided not to tell him that he had gleaned this entire analysis of Murong Chuyi's psyche from Gu Mang himself way back when. People's hearts were complex; Mo Xi hadn't understood this when he was younger. Nor could he easily make sense of the love and hatred between others, their affection and enmity. It was Gu Mang who carefully explained these things to him, who taught him the ins and outs of love and hate.

In memory, Mo Xi saw how Gu Mang, head pillowed against his arms as he lay on the riverbank, had once brought up Jiang Yexue as they chatted. Gu Mang had spat out the foxtail grass in his mouth and heaved a heavy sigh. "Jiang Yexue hasn't had it easy. To him, understanding and forgiveness are actually one and the same. See—after so many years, Murong Chuyi still treats Yue Chenqing so coldly because of his foster sister. Jiang Yexue's mama passed away too, but he didn't fight with the other two. He can let go of the past and treat the two of them with courtesy... Good heavens, what a saint. If I were in his place, I might have gone insane."

Mo Xi had turned to look at the stargazing youth lying beside him, his gaze full of tenderness. He knew that wasn't true; even if Gu Mang had been in Jiang Yexue's place, he would've also maintained his composure. He wouldn't have taken his anger out on anyone or blamed them unfairly. He would've treated everyone with kindness. After all, Gu Mang was bright and cheerful, like the sun.

If someone clung to Murong Chuyi and cried, Murong Chuyi would push them away and leave with a sweep of his sleeves. If someone did the same to Jiang Yexue, he would share in their sorrow and listen to them speak of their hurt.

But Gu Mang? If someone was clinging to Gu Mang and crying, Gu Mang would definitely make them smile through their tears. The one who brought laughter and light to others—that was the Gu-shixiong Mo Xi had always loved in his deepest heart.

Several days later, Mo Xi finally wrapped up all the military affairs that had descended upon him after the spring hunt. It was truly fortunate that Gu Mang was there to look after him toward the end. Although Mo Xi procrastinated before every meal, he at least ate regularly and didn't put the medicine from Medicine Master Jiang to waste.

On this particular day, Mo Xi had nothing to attend to. He considered if he should pay a visit to the cultivation academy and retrieve his copy of *Compendium of Plants Demonic and Divine* so that he could lend it to Yue Chenqing.

Mo Xi pondered as he got ready. Although Yue Chenqing had been lazy ever since he was little, he had always treated his fourth uncle as his guiding star. When it came to anything involving Murong Chuyi, Yue Chenqing would spare no earnestness or effort. The child might have seemed unfocused, but in truth, he could be blindly obstinate once he was convinced of something. In the fearlessness of youth, a chest full of passion could hamper one's judgment. Hopefully Yue Chenqing could stay out of trouble.

Just as he was about to step out, Li Wei rushed into the hall, his face full of worry. "My lord!"

"What happened? What's with that look on your face?"

"Something's happened at Yue Manor," responded Li Wei.

Mo Xi shivered, his heart pounding. *How could it be? Speak of the devil.* "Is it Yue Chenqing...?" he asked.

Li Wei's eyes flew wide. "It is! My lord, how'd you guess? Young Yue-gongzi has disappeared!"

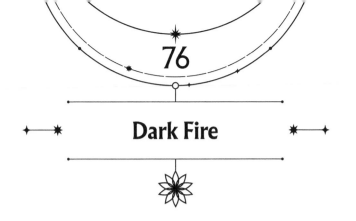

76

Dark Fire

THE EMPEROR SAT within the golden throne room, his chin propped in one hand as he toyed with a string of jade beads in the other, listening to Yue Juntian's sniveling sobs.

"Your Imperial Majesty! Your Imperial Majesty! This old subject has but one true-born son. He is of half-royal blood—Your Imperial Majesty can't ignore this! If something happens to my son, then this old subject...this old subject will..." Upon saying these sorrowful words, he wailed bitterly and pounded his fist against the golden brick floor, snot and tears leaking down.

The emperor found this sight rather distasteful. He wrinkled his nose and narrowed his eyes. "All right, all right, what use is crying?" he counseled. "We didn't say we'd ignore it."

Yue Juntian kowtowed repeatedly, his head thumping against the floor. "Many thanks to Your Imperial Majesty! Many thanks to Your Imperial Majesty!" he cried tearfully. "I ask that Your Imperial Majesty send for the invincible Northern Frontier Army to flatten the Dream Butterfly Islands and bring back my son!"

"Send for whom...? You think that the Northern Frontier Army can be dispatched at will?" The emperor was dumbfounded. "People ridicule the idea of a mounted soldier sent across the world to secure a concubine's smile[3]—surely you can't expect us to send a hundred thousand troops after a single man, can you?"

---

3   Quote from a poem by Du Mu, a Tang dynasty poet, criticizing the wasteful extravagance of Emperor Xuanzong sending military messengers to fetch lychees for his beloved concubine, Yang-guifei. "Concubine's smile" is a cultivar of lychee named for Yang-guifei.

Hearing this, Yue Juntian began to beat his chest and stamp his feet once more. "Your Imperial Majesty! This old subject has led a lonely and painful life!" he howled. "My first wife passed away early, and now my son—"

"Stop bawling! We've heard your spiel hundreds of times since you entered the hall!" The emperor pressed a palm to his forehead. "Listen, we will definitely rescue him. But forget about summoning the Northern Frontier Army. That's a truly preposterous thought..."

Yue Juntian, snot dripping, was about to break into more wailing. On the verge of losing his mind with disgust, the emperor hastily sat up straight and held up a hand. "Enough, enough! We're sufficiently alarmed, okay? We will appoint Xihe-jun to this matter. Surely that'll appease you?"

Yue Juntian stiffened for a moment, his nose running in silence. He sniffled loudly, forcing those clear droplets back into his nostrils. "But Xihe-jun is just one man," he mumbled. "What if he doesn't succeed..."

After enduring Yue Juntian's pestering for an entire day, the emperor had reached the limits of his patience. He couldn't believe Yue Juntian was still nitpicking his offer. "Can *you* handle it then? Why don't you go ahead and fetch him yourself?"

Yue Juntian was a grandmaster artificer, but he had been afflicted with a mysterious illness several years ago. Although he had survived, his mind and body were no longer strong. And now that he was getting on in years, he couldn't walk even a mile without needing to take a long break. The idea of him reaching the Dream Butterfly Islands was pure fantasy—he was more likely to get killed on the way. Moreover, the man was selfish and had no regard for others. Years ago, when Jiang Yexue had defied his will and made him lose face, Yue Juntian had kicked his son out and made trouble for him in a hundred and one ways. Yue Chenqing was much more pampered than Jiang Yexue, but how could he be more precious to Yue Juntian than his own life? He immediately shook his head, weeping. "It's not that this old subject isn't willing. If I were still hale, I'd go at once to rescue my son from those accursed islands myself! But, but..."

"But what? If you keep dawdling, your son's insignificant little life might just end!"

"Right, right! Just Xihe-jun then! I'll be troubling Xihe-jun then!" Yue Juntian could do nothing but agree.

Thus did the emperor summon Xihe-jun to the palace. Because Mo Xi had already heard Li Wei's report on this matter, he quickly grasped the situation as he listened to the emperor's cursory summary. Although Mo Xi's opinion of this unfaithful old radish Yue Juntian was poor in every regard, Jiang Yexue was one of his oldest comrades-in-arms and their brotherhood ran deep. Not to mention that Yue Chenqing had served as his deputy general for two years—of course Mo Xi wouldn't shirk this duty.

"It's just that the Dream Butterfly Islands are an archipelago. Do we have any definite news of Yue Chenqing's whereabouts?"

"We do—ah, fortunately, we do," said the emperor. "Otherwise, this problem would be even more thorny than it already is."

As he spoke, he summoned the last spiritual messenger bird that Yue Chenqing had sent. This was a fleeting creature of coalesced spiritual energy. The emperor had cast protective spells upon it to preserve the details of Yue Chenqing's call for help, so even now, the bird had yet to dissipate. As the emperor mouthed the words of the incantation, the messenger bird's beak opened and closed. Yue Chenqing's voice came through, weak and shaking. "F-fourth Uncle... Papa..."

At the sound of his son's voice, Yue Juntian burst anew into sobs, thumping his chest and stamping his feet.

"I-I'm stranded on the Dream Butterfly Islands! It's...it's dark everywhere... It's dark wherever I look... I...I'm starting to have dreams..." Yue Chenqing sounded tearful and terrified. "I don't know how long I can stay awake... I don't—I don't know what they want with me... Please save me... Fourth Uncle...Papa...save me..." He whimpered. "It hurts... My blood... They want..."

Mo Xi never heard what it was that they wanted. Yue Chenqing had exhausted his spiritual energy and couldn't record anything more.

The emperor wound his string of agate beads around his wrist. "Does Xihe-jun have any thoughts?"

After a moment of consideration, Mo Xi spoke. "The Dream Butterfly Islands are demonic islands uninhabited by humans. The monsters that live there are temperamental, and it's difficult to judge their powers. Under normal circumstances, cultivators wouldn't go there unless they had no other alternative.

"However." He paused. "According to folk tales, the Dream Butterfly Islands are composed of around twenty islands. Different types of demons live on each one, with a wide range of disposition and character between them. Yue Chenqing mentioned three pieces of information: first, it's dark everywhere; second, he's having dreams and might not be able to maintain consciousness; third, the demons seem to be interested in his blood."

The emperor was quite intrigued. Smiling, he stroked his chin. "So if Xihe-jun were to guess, which clan of demons has taken our Yue Chenqing hostage?"

"The bats," said Mo Xi.

Yue Juntian made a soft sound, his lips white as he trembled. "Bats... Bats... Yes...yes... There are records of a vampire bat island among the Dream Butterfly Islands..." He burst into tears. "Oh god! My son, my beloved son!"

"But this is just a guess. Our most pressing task should be to scout the Dream Butterfly Islands as soon as possible."

Taking this to mean that Mo Xi planned to depart soon, Yue Juntian hastily wiped his face and spluttered weepily, "Many thanks to Xihe-jun, many thanks to Xihe-jun!"

"I'm not doing this for you, but for your esteemed son," Mo Xi replied coolly. "There's no need to thank me."

Yue Juntian's lips moved without sound. He knew of Mo Xi's friendship with Jiang Yexue and understood his implication. Referring to Yue Chenqing as his "esteemed son" was a pointed reminder that he wasn't Yue Juntian's *only* son. There was also the son he had abandoned like an old shoe and harassed in every way: Jiang Yexue.

Seeing that the atmosphere between Mo Xi and Yue Juntian had become awkward, the emperor coughed. "This matter is an urgent one. Xihe-jun, return to your manor to make preparations and set out at once."

"Of course," said Mo Xi.

"One more thing. Keep this life crystal on you."

The emperor waved his hand, and a blue-and-white spirit stone appeared at Mo Xi's side. These life crystals were created from a drop of umbilical blood taken at the birth of some of Chonghua's prominent nobles. The stones would glow day and night with a unique light until their owners died. In Chonghua's oldest stories, it was said that such a crystal brought good fortune to the newborn infant, and so many nobles had their own.

"This is Yue Chenqing's. Right now, the light still looks all right, so there's no need to fear for his life," the emperor continued. "Keep it on hand; although it can't point the way for you, it can help all of you keep track of Yue Chenqing's status."

Mo Xi knitted his brows. "All of us?"

"Oh, we forgot to mention," said the emperor. "Two others requested to join this mission; they would not hear of staying behind. One is Murong Chuyi, and the other is Jiang Yexue."

Mo Xi's eyes widened abruptly. "They're coming too?"

At Mo Xi's expression, the emperor replied, "No need to worry about Qingxu Elder. He might not have use of his legs, but he's still a grandmaster artificer. His wooden wheelchair has many mechanisms for mobility; he won't slow you down."

"That's not what I meant. It's that...besides Gu Mang, who must remain under my supervision, I had no plans to take anyone else with me. The temperaments of these demons are strange and volatile. Many types of demons dislike any contact with humans; I'm afraid that the more people in the party, the harder they'll lash out in retaliation."

"It's just two more people," the emperor said. "You're making it sound like there's a whole army accompanying you. If we tell you to take them, you will. There's strength in numbers."

Mo Xi couldn't persuade the emperor otherwise. All he could do was return to his manor and prepare for the journey. He hadn't much to pack; other than some basic talismans and spirit stones, his most important baggage was Gu Mang. There was no way Mo Xi could leave this troublemaker behind. Gu Mang's memories were all jumbled lately; he might remember something he shouldn't at any time. If Mo Xi wasn't at his side when it happened, the consequences would be hard to predict.

He had to admit there was a second reason. Gu Mang's fall from grace and subsequent act of treason had both taken place when Mo Xi was absent. After all that had happened, deep down, Mo Xi very much feared the thought of a long separation from Gu Mang.

"Where are we going?" Gu Mang asked as Mo Xi packed his qiankun pouch.

"To rescue someone," Mo Xi responded.

"To rescue Little White Bird?"

"Yes."

"Just us?"

Mo Xi's hands stilled as he turned to look at Gu Mang. "No. Murong Chuyi and Jiang Yexue are coming as well." He could hear the apprehension in Gu Mang's voice; Mo Xi knew he didn't like interacting with strangers. "Are you afraid of them?"

"If it's those two..." After giving it some thought, Gu Mang said, "Then it's okay."

When Mo Xi and Gu Mang arrived at the roadside departure pavilion outside the city, they discovered Murong Chuyi and Jiang Yexue waiting for them. It was a truly bizarre situation—Jiang Yexue and Murong Chuyi were enemies who wanted less than nothing to do with each other. Murong Chuyi in particular refused to spare Jiang Yexue one glance more than necessary.

But right now they shared a goal: to carry out this rescue with Xihe-jun. One of them sat under the departure pavilion while the other stood under the pear-blossom tree beside it. Across this intimidating distance, they were talking. Mo Xi was too far away to overhear what they said, but the hostility emanating from the exchange could be felt ten leagues away. Especially Murong Chuyi—he was attired in his customary silver-trimmed white robes, standing with his hands behind his back. As his ethereal silk ribbons fluttered in the wind, his handsome and elegant features were cold as if covered in a layer of bitter frost.

As Mo Xi and Gu Mang drew near, the other two fell silent.

"Qingxu Elder, Murong-xiansheng."

Gu Mang copied Mo Xi's greeting: "Qingxu Elder, Murong-xiansheng."

In the few days since they had last met, Jiang Yexue's face had thinned considerably, and faint shadows were visible under his eyes. Ever since Yue Chenqing's disappearance, he had been so distraught he could neither eat nor sleep. "Xihe-jun," he said. He turned to give Gu Mang a small nod, which could be considered a greeting.

As for Murong Chuyi, he had never been bound by the conventions of etiquette. When his mood was poor, he ignored everyone without exception.

In this delicate atmosphere, the four set off on their journey.

The Dream Butterfly Islands weren't far from Chonghua. With two artificers in their party, there was no need to travel by sword. Jiang Yexue retrieved a tiny walnut from his qiankun pouch. When he tossed it onto the ground and cast a spell, it transformed into a swift boat that could sail among the clouds and traverse ten thousand miles in a day. Jiang Yexue invited Mo Xi and Gu Mang onto the boat, and then turned to Murong Chuyi, who still stood beneath the flowering tree. "Chuyi, you taught me to build this boat a long time ago; I've altered the design a little. Now, this ship can carry a hundred or more people. Come take a look."

But Murong Chuyi said stiffly, "I'll not take a single step onto your boat. No need to trouble yourself, Nephew."

Gu Mang, leaning over the ship's railing, pondered Murong Chuyi's words. A thought belatedly occurred to him. He pointed at Murong Chuyi, then at Jiang Yexue. "He calls him 'Nephew'?" He then pointed at Jiang Yexue, then at Murong Chuyi. "And he's his uncle?" Gu Mang turned to look at Mo Xi. "Right, I remember now—that's indeed their relationship. But I couldn't tell at all. This uncle looks to be about the same age as his nephew."

"Don't talk so much," Mo Xi admonished. "Let's go into the ship's cabin."

But it was evident that Muong Chuyi had already heard what Gu Mang said. For some reason, his face became even frostier than usual.

"Chuyi, you..." Jiang Yexue began.

"To whom are you speaking?" Murong Chuyi cut Jiang Yexue off, his sharp brows drawn severely together. "Jiang Yexue, you are born of Yue Juntian's concubine," he stated, tone chilly. "In terms of seniority, you should address me as Uncle. You and Yue Chenqing are both of the younger generation; when addressing me in this manner, don't you feel you've forgotten yourself?"

Jiang Yexue paused. "Yes. Xiaojiu[4] is right to teach me."

Murong Chuyi let out a snort and raised a hand to twirl a flower between his fingers. The pear blossom that had landed on his shoulder transformed into a beautifully decorated Jiangnan pleasure boat. This spiritual ship could also fly, just like Jiang Yexue's walnut ship. Murong Chuyi stepped onto the pleasure boat, his tall, upright figure disappearing behind a flaxen curtain.

Jiang Yexue was silent a moment. He turned back to speak to Mo Xi. "My apologies. I've embarrassed myself in front of Xihe-jun."

Mo Xi shook his head and murmured a few words of consolation.

As the two ships entered the sea of clouds, Mo Xi sat in the cabin, listening to the wind outside. Even now, he couldn't help but feel that something was amiss. The way Jiang Yexue spoke to Murong Chuyi was too odd, as if he were hiding some secret that onlookers wouldn't know. And whatever this secret was, it seemed to cause Murong Chuyi a great deal of consternation, to the point that he deliberately pressed the point of seniority despite usually paying no

---

4 Youngest maternal uncle.

mind to such worldly conventions. As a result, Murong Chuyi not only refused to enter Jiang Yexue's boat; his phoenix eyes had also flashed with some kind of unspoken warning—*I am the superior; you are the inferior. I am the respected elder; you are of the younger generation. I will not tolerate your trespass.*

Mo Xi furrowed his brow. Why would Murong Chuyi want to emphasize this boundary so pointedly?

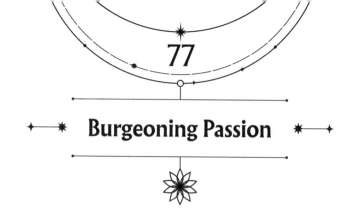

Burgeoning Passion

THE WALNUT SHIP soared through the cloud-dappled sky. The pleasure boat kept pace, but at a healthy distance. It was clear that Murong Chuyi was so averse to Jiang Yexue that he wasn't even willing to fly alongside him.

At dusk, the sun sank into the depths of the cloud sea, its brilliance lapping against the oars like the world's great river. Gu Mang had never seen such a sight and leaned over the ship's railing so as not to miss a moment. Reflected within those rain-washed blue eyes were the golden hues of eventide and the vast and distant lands below.

He was thoroughly engrossed in the view when something suddenly jabbed at his shin, twice. Gu Mang turned. At first, he saw no one. But after lowering his gaze, he saw that the culprit was an enchanted ceramic servant that could move under its own power. This servant was painted crudely, with uneven eyes and its nose and mouth squished together. Gu Mang found it incredibly funny and laughed out loud. "Who made this? Ha ha ha, it's so ugly!"

The bamboo curtain in the cabin rose and fell. Jiang Yexue emerged, clad in cream robes the shade of lotus root and seated in his wooden wheelchair powered by spiritual energy. He said to Gu Mang, "You made it."

Gu Mang was speechless.

At his shock and bewilderment, Jiang Yexue laughed. "It was a long time ago, when you were still in the army. You saw me making clay figurines, and of course you had to make one too. But you didn't have much patience back then. You always did things impulsively, starting off strong but losing steam toward the end. You sculpted half of it with me before you lost interest and half-heartedly drew on a face."

"So that's what happened..." Gu Mang sized up the ugly ceramic servant. When he considered how it had come from his own hands, he felt a little queer. The pottery figure bore signs of age, and some of its lacquer had already lost its color. It walked in circles around Gu Mang, its crooked mouth opening and closing as it recited clumsily, "Eat, eat."

Gu Mang reached deep into his sleeves and then said helplessly, "I didn't bring anything to eat. Also, you're made of clay—why do you want to eat?"

The ugly ceramic figure repeated stubbornly, "Eat, eat!"

Gu Mang thought that its obstinate expression, with its brows all scrunched up, was actually quite similar to Mo Xi's at times. But he had to keep such thoughts to himself. If anyone found out, whether it was the venerated Mo Xi himself or the droves of girls in Chonghua obsessed with Xihe-jun, Gu Mang would land himself in no end of trouble. He tried to shoo the figurine away. "There's nothing for you to eat, you can go."

The ugly clay servant reached out a tiny hand to tug on Gu Mang's sleeve. "Eat, eat!"

"It's not asking you for food," Jiang Yexue said with a smile. "It wants you to go into the cabin to eat."

Gu Mang had thought they would have to subsist on rations over this long journey and hadn't expected a sit-down meal. Curious, he asked: "Did you make the food?"

"No."

"Then forget it." Gu Mang shook his head like a rattle drum. "Whatever Xihe-jun makes is completely inedible."

"I've equipped this walnut ship with a couple of little enchanted clay figurines like this one," Jiang Yexue explained. "They did all the cooking. Just some simple dishes, but..." He paused and smiled, "It'll still be better than what Xihe-jun makes."

That brought Gu Mang a measure of relief. He turned to look at the pleasure boat sailing off in the distance. "We aren't asking Little Dragon—ahem, asking Murong-xiansheng to come eat?"

"Xiaojiu won't come." Jiang Yexue's expression dimmed, appearing gloomy and indistinct in the light of the setting sun. With a twitch of his fingertips, his wooden wheelchair turned and rolled toward the ship's cabin. "Let's go."

Within, two small clay people were busily arranging dishes and pouring tea. They were much more pleasant to look at than the one Gu Mang had made—their noses were noses, and their eyes were indeed eyes. One was a man and one a woman, both very endearing.

Although the dishes on the table weren't sophisticated fare, they were refreshing and tasty, and the tea was clear and sweet. Gu Mang didn't like to drink tea, so Jiang Yexue had warmed a jar of wine for him.

"Don't drink too much," Mo Xi said.

Jiang Yexue replied fondly, "This is fragrant snow wine; it's not easy to get drunk on it. If he likes it, let him do as he wants."

Gu Mang licked his lips, grinning artlessly. As the moist tip of his tongue darted out between his lips, Mo Xi swept a disapproving glance over it. "Qingxu Elder, he's a criminal. Why bother treating him with the same courtesy as before?"

Despite his words, Mo Xi still let Gu Mang have his way. It was indeed difficult to get drunk off of fragrant snow wine, but in the end, it was still wine. Gu Mang found its mild sweetness very much to his liking and ended up having a few cups too many. The food the little clay servants had prepared also contained some new and exciting flavors, and they were in charge of refilling all the dishes. Intrigued by their ungainly mannerisms as they served the food, Gu Mang wolfed down three more bowls than usual just so he could keep watching them.

When they finished dinner, each returned to their individual cabins to rest. Gu Mang's spiritual energy wasn't considered stable—he had, after all, gone berserk on Murong Lian's watch in recent memory—and they couldn't afford any risks with their walnut ship so high in the sky. Mo Xi had to monitor him as closely as possible, so he and Gu Mang were sharing a cabin tonight.

"So full..." Gu Mang groaned, holding his belly as he collapsed face-first onto his bed.

"Get up." Mo Xi, ever fastidious, hauled Gu Mang back to his feet. "Go bathe before you sleep."

Gu Mang refused. "I won't."

"If you won't bathe, then you can sleep on the deck tonight."

Gu Mang collected his blankets, clearly ready to go sleep on the deck in the wind. Mo Xi's sharp brows drew together in anger as he dragged Gu Mang back. "Who said you could leave?" he said severely. "Lie down."

Gu Mang's sleepy eyes were unfocused, their blue irises like a mist-veiled lake. "Can't I just not take a bath?"

"No."

Gu Mang frowned so intently his brows nearly touched. He slowly curled into a ball. "I really don't want to... I feel so weak... Why don't you help me wash?"

Mo Xi had worn a severe expression, but Gu Mang's response caught him off guard. He froze, and a hint of embarrassment surfaced on his features, instantly undercutting his intimidating aura. "Don't even think about it," he responded after a pause.

Gu Mang sighed and threw himself back onto the bed, sprawling across the blankets. He looked as though he could fall asleep just like this. Mo Xi's efforts to govern him were apparently fruitless; he was left to head to the washroom alone, where he took a bath and changed into clean clothes.

Mo Xi had assumed Gu Mang was acting out to avoid the bath. But when he returned, he found Gu Mang burrowed deep in the blankets, clutching his stomach. His brow was furrowed as he mumbled softly. At this point, there was no need for him to keep up the act. With a small jolt of surprise, Mo Xi realized he was truly feeling unwell. He dried his damp hair and came to the side of Gu Mang's bed. "What's wrong?"

Long lashes trembling, Gu Mang opened his eyelids a crack. His clear blue eyes were misty as he glanced weakly at Mo Xi. "Mn. Ate too much..." he grumbled. "So full, stomach hurts."

For a while, Mo Xi was silent. "Deserved," he said succinctly. But still he sat beside Gu Mang and gestured with a grim expression. "Roll over here."

Gu Mang hesitated. He generally couldn't afford to anger this person, and he could afford it even less when he was so weak. After all, a wise man knew better than to fight when the odds were against him. If he was told to roll, then he would roll. Thus he turned over twice on the bed, coming to a stop next to Mo Xi's hand. "Do I need to keep rolling?"

"Lie down and don't move," said Mo Xi.

So Gu Mang lay stiff as a salted fish. His clothes were in disorder, and his gaping lapels exposed an expanse of firm, scarred skin beneath. After a glance, Mo Xi reached over to pull Gu Mang's collar closed. Then he moved his hands to Gu Mang's stomach and slowly began to knead at it.

Gu Mang smacked his lips. "Are you punishing me for eating too much?"

"What do you think?" Mo Xi said curtly.

It wasn't Gu Mang's cynicism that was to blame, but Mo Xi's ornery personality. So often did he make life difficult for Gu Mang that Gu Mang had figured this somewhat ungentle massage was a new form of punishment. This punishment wasn't unbearable; although the kneading felt strange, the discomfort in his gut really did ease under Mo Xi's ministrations. Lying on the bed, Gu Mang heaved a sigh, his vision gradually dimming. Before he dropped off completely, he mumbled, "Then...you can punish me a little longer..."

In his last moments of consciousness, he saw Mo Xi's face go rigid as he registered these words, his eyes seeming to darken. Gu Mang's head lolled to the side. Face pressed to Mo Xi's arm, he fell into a hazy slumber.

That night, he dreamed once more, those lost memories glowing faintly.

He dreamed of a low tent, wind whistling outside as he breathed in the fragrance of pear-blossom white wine as well as Mo Xi's honey-eyed scent.

The world swam before his eyes. He realized this was the night of Mo Xi's coming of age, which he'd only half-remembered. On that night, he'd brought a porn booklet from an old book stall, his heart filled with mischief as he gifted it to his Mo-shidi on the eve of his adulthood. He hadn't realized he was playing with fire until Mo Xi finally pulled him down onto the bed...

The last dream had ended at this point, the memory broken off. He'd always been confused as to what exactly happened next, and why this scenario made him feel parched and uneasy. Perhaps it was due to the wine, and Mo Xi massaging his aching stomach in his bed—that regular, forceful rhythm recalling another kind of rhythm from his past.

Like clouds and mist dispersing, he remembered.

On the night of Mo Xi's coming of age, they'd fallen together onto the narrow little army cot. His thoughts were muddled, but he could remember with perfect clarity the passionate look on Mo Xi's face. His handsome, youthful, self-restrained features were drowned in the mist of love and desire. His dark eyes, usually so cool and controlled, looked slightly bewildered, like a young beast that had fallen into the trap of lust.

Youth meant inexperience and impetuousness, meant boundless power straining to break loose. Beastliness meant primal instinct and voracity, limitless desire threatening to spill out.

Those eyes stared fixedly and unerringly at Gu Mang. Clothes fell to the floor like the prying open of a clamshell, revealing trembling flesh beneath and the faint scent of the sea. Gu Mang's throat bobbed as he swallowed.

And now he was faced with the sight of Mo Xi undressed, which was exhilarating and terrifying in equal measure. His shoulders were broad, his waist slender yet well-muscled. Back then, Mo Xi had far fewer scars—especially on his chest. Back then, his chest was perfect and unblemished, clean of the wound Gu Mang had personally carved into his flesh.

In the dancing light and shadow, the bed swayed under the weight of their tangled bodies, emitting a strange chorus of creaks.

Gu Mang remembered how Mo Xi's motions had first been restrained as he pinned Gu Mang beneath him. As the night wore on, the young man's desire went to his head and his thrusts grew faster and harder. Gu Mang felt as though he had become clay in Mo Xi's hands as his wine-softened limbs were rearranged—half by his own will and half by Mo Xi's—into every sort of position as the two of them entwined.

He remembered Mo Xi's alluring lips, slightly parted as he panted; his low gasps as he pressed close to Gu Mang's ear; his body, surging ceaselessly in the murky light. An overwhelming sensation rushed through him. Gu Mang couldn't help but let out a hoarse moan, just like the one from his memories: "Sh-shidi... Ahh..."

Then, as though he had stepped into thin air, Gu Mang's eyes flew open.

His violent shudders gradually ceased, like the tide receding. He was soaked in sweat and still trembling minutely, panting through glossy lips. Those unfocused blue eyes looked up, right into Mo Xi's face, which was now tense beneath the candlelight.

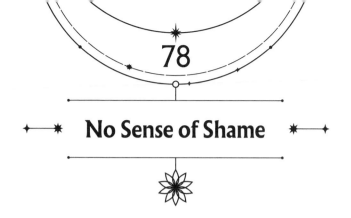

78

No Sense of Shame

"**W**HAT... What happened to me?" Gu Mang stammered in confusion.

He didn't describe his condition in more detail. But Mo Xi, with a downward flick of his gaze, immediately saw the messy stain on Gu Mang's underclothes and sank into an uncomfortable silence.

Gu Mang was unsettled by this reaction from his body. "I don't feel quite right... Am I sick?"

"You're not," said Mo Xi. "You're not sick."

Gu Mang's face was still flushed from the dream, and his breathing was rapid. He looked down at his own pants in helpless confusion. "Then what's going on here?"

His blue eyes were wide, giving Mo Xi the impression of a pure and innocent wolf cub. However, this wolf cub's questions were too embarrassing. The old Gu Mang had once charged at Mo Xi with an erotic booklet to give him a "coming-of-age lesson," but Mo Xi was too thin-skinned; no matter the circumstances, he could never do anything of the sort.

"You're just...having a normal reaction," Mo Xi replied. "It was only a dream, that's all."

Gu Mang quickly nodded. "It was just a dream. I dreamed of the night you came of age again. We...uh...we were sleeping together, and then we did...some very strange things."

Mo Xi said nothing.

"You looked like you really liked it... You seemed very happy..."

Mo Xi was especially adept at dealing out torment in bed—without fail, he pushed Gu Mang until he was choking back sobs, his body limp and his lips moving in pleas for mercy. Yet it was difficult for Mo Xi to say anything lewd if he wasn't pushed to the limit. Conversely, Gu Mang had always spouted the most mortifying things during their wildest entanglements, though whether he was trying to provoke Mo Xi or simply couldn't shut up was anyone's guess. Those words added fuel to an already raging fire, goading the youthful Mo Xi until he couldn't suppress his fervor. The world became firewood and flames, and the man in his arms the only source of water. He plunged repeatedly into the depths of this sweet spring, seeking to dampen the scalding heat in his heart.

Gu Mang blinked, his eyes watery and bewildered. "So you liked doing those things with me, right?"

Mo Xi wanted to say *no*, but before the word could leave his lips, Gu Mang continued pensively, "I think I liked it. It felt really good." He looked up, his face still tinged with the flush brought on by those memories. "It seemed like you needed me."

Mo Xi immediately stilled.

"It's good...to be needed by someone," Gu Mang said softly. "For someone to get happiness from me, not because of hatred or venting—that felt...so good."

"Do you know what you're talking about?" Mo Xi asked.

"How I felt back then," Gu Mang replied sincerely. "I'm talking about how I felt back then. On the night you came of age—I've remembered everything now. Some of those feelings, I don't understand and can't describe. But the others, I know I really liked them."

Mo Xi felt as if he'd been dealt a heavy blow to the heart. Ever since Gu Mang defected, Mo Xi had wondered what Gu Mang had felt toward him. He often thought that Gu Mang had been half-heartedly placating him, dealing with him, toying with him—or perhaps that he had been pestered into doing what Mo Xi wanted. When the word *liked* entered his ears after seven long years, he suddenly didn't know how to react.

"I've been living with you this whole time, without ever helping you out and always making you mad. Why didn't you tell me I could make you like me like that?"

Mo Xi jumped to his feet like a cat whose tail had been trod on. Swallowing hard, he glared through red-rimmed eyes. "Who—who said I liked you? Stop imagining things."

Gu Mang's eyes widened in puzzlement. "But you were clearly…"

"That was just a dream. Seems to me like you've had too much medicine; you can't even tell dreams from reality!"

Gu Mang wanted to speak, but he didn't know what to say. His tense, upright posture sagged slightly; he seemed disheartened, yet also unconvinced. After a moment's downcast thought, he suddenly stood and captured Mo Xi's lips with his own, pressing their mouths together.

Mo Xi's ears buzzed; all the blood in his body rushed toward his brain. For a split second, the world flashed white.

It was just like the past, like the days Mo Xi remembered in his dreams—Gu Mang looping his arms around his neck, pulling him down, his tongue pressing in between his teeth, lingering and tangling, making soft, wet sounds.

Gu Mang felt a sudden sharp pain at the tip of his tongue. Mo Xi was shoving him away. "You…" Mo Xi panted, his lips, usually cold and colorless, flushed red by their passion, making for a singularly arresting sight. But this beauty's brows were drawn tight in fury, glaring daggers that pierced clean through Gu Mang. Mo Xi was so angry he couldn't speak. Only after a long while did he yank at his lapels which Gu Mang had pulled into disarray, drawing them closed. "You really...have no sense of shame!" he snarled.

Gu Mang rubbed at his lips. Mo Xi had bitten him so viciously he had drawn blood, like an anxious beast trapped in a dead end. But there was something Gu Mang had finally confirmed.

"You're lying to me."

Mo Xi was silent.

"That wasn't a dream. It was real." Gu Mang swept a glance over the lower half of Mo Xi's body. "Just a moment ago, I felt you against me."

Mo Xi could muster no response. At last, he flung aside the door curtain and strode out of the room, his expression black as pitch. When Gu Mang hurried after him, Mo Xi turned and furiously jabbed a finger at his chest. "Stay where you are! Tell anyone about what happened tonight and I'll send you back to Luomei Pavilion the minute we return!"

"Where are you going?" Gu Mang asked.

"None of your business!"

"But aren't you sleeping with me?"

"Listen up, asshole," Mo Xi bit out through gritted teeth. "A gentleman knows what to do and what not to do. I will excuse your inappropriate actions today because I know your mind isn't clear. But I've told you now, so if you still dare—" Mo Xi choked on his words for a moment; this "gentleman" couldn't bring himself to describe Gu Mang's scoundrel behavior. He snapped, "If you still dare do anything like that again and seduce me, I'll see that you pay for it!"

His tone was fierce, but when paired with the parting of those fresh-kissed, suggestively pinkened lips, he inevitably became less imposing. Not only did his threats fail to quell Gu Mang, they conjured up the image of the Mo-shidi who had flown into an embarrassed rage at Gu Mang's teasing all those years ago. Even if many of the details from back then still eluded him, this feeling was like an unsealed jug of fine wine, suffusing the air with its rich scent. Gu Mang lowered his head and couldn't hold back a puff of laughter, just like in the past.

It would've been all right if he hadn't laughed. Now, Mo Xi's expression immediately grew darker, and his knuckles cracked as he clenched his fists. But although Gu Mang had recovered some of his memories, he at least wasn't quite so much of a troublemaker as he had been. That burst of laughter was pure reflex; upon seeing that Mo Xi was upset, he restrained his amusement and obediently knelt on the bed. "I'm sorry," he said earnestly. "If you don't like it, then I won't do it again. Please don't send me back to Luomei Pavilion."

Only then did Mo Xi leave the cabin, anger still etched in every line of his face.

Out on the deck, he bumped into Jiang Yexue in his wooden wheelchair. He looked up at Mo Xi in astonishment. "Xihe-jun, who provoked you? Why are you so angry?"

Mo Xi pressed his lips into a thin line and said tersely, "No one provoked me. What are you here for?"

Jiang Yexue smiled. "I was on my way to bring you quilts. Do you need any?"

"No."

"What about Gu Mang?"

"He's plenty warm. It would be better for him to sleep on bamboo mats."

"You fought with him again?" asked Jiang Yexue.

Mo Xi flicked his sleeves angrily. "It's his own fault."

"You two are really..." Jiang Yexue smiled faintly. "Long ago, when Gu Mang was stubborn and mischievous, he loved nothing more than to make you mad. How does he still anger you so, even when he's like this? But...upset or not, you should still give him an extra quilt. His health isn't as good as it used to be, and now he's weak to the cold. If he caught a chill, it would cause even more problems on this journey. You shouldn't bicker too much with him."

Mo Xi fell silent. At length, he reached out to take the quilt Jiang Yexue offered. "Many thanks."

When morning came, they found themselves hovering above the Dream Butterfly Islands. Jiang Yexue took out his compass and silently recited an incantation. The little object gleamed with brilliant light, then pointed toward a small island in the southeastern portion of the archipelago. "Bat Island is there," he said.

79

Chattery Little
Pig Monster

THE TWO SHIPS soared through the cloud cover and descended in tandem. As the black clouds thinned, the earth loomed below. They could now easily make out the details of Bat Island. It wasn't large, and they spotted buildings hidden here and there among its forests. A demon tower stood tall at its center, with lofty eaves and a dazzling golden roof.

In the cultivation realm, such towers were often built to suppress demons; soul-subduing copper bells would hang from their eaves and the bricks would be painted with talismans and sigils. However, this tower in the middle of Bat Island was not so. It had seven floors, with human heads hanging where copper bells should have been. Those heads were rotted to the bone, swaying eerily in the island's coppery wind.

Jiang Yexue and Murong Chuyi both modulated the flow of their spiritual energy to set the pleasure boat and the walnut ship down directly in front of this central tower. When they had all disembarked, the boats and oars shrank to their original size and were stowed in qiankun pouches.

The tower and its surroundings were dark and silent before them. Upon taking a closer look, they discovered thousands of bats clustered densely under the roof tiles. Because it was midday, these bats were sound asleep.

"Human sacrifice tower..." Jiang Yexue murmured.

"What's a human sacrifice tower?" Gu Mang asked. "I've only ever heard of demon-suppressing towers."

"It's a similar concept," Jiang Yexue explained. "People build towers to suppress demons, while demons build towers to trap people. This is a bat demon island, so of course the master of the island is a bat monster rather than a cultivator. This tower was built to imprison live humans in preparation for some future use."

"What kind of future use?"

Jiang Yexue paled. "Hard to say," he said softly. "Some monsters eat people, so they store them as food. Some monsters drink blood, so they..."

Jiang Yexue was still speaking when Murong Chuyi strode ahead of the group. Without a moment's hesitation, he flung a paper talisman onto the great doors of the human sacrifice tower. The doors, scarred with the traces of spells, rumbled open.

With a wave of his horsetail whisk, Murong Chuyi brushed away the miasma that rushed out of the tower. Then he turned, dark-brown eyes glancing coldly behind him. "Jiang Yexue, are you here to perform a rescue or give a lecture?" He then strode into the tower without a backward glance. Within seconds, the darkness had swallowed his pure white silhouette. Jiang Yexue and the others hastened to follow.

The great hall on the first floor of the human sacrifice tower was dark and empty aside from eight strange and imposing stone pillars. They looked to be carved with complex designs, but upon closer examination, it became clear that they were in fact constructed from many individual bones. Thousands upon thousands of bats hung upside down from their surface.

These bats were nothing like common bats one might see in the wild. Each was as tall as a person, and their wings weren't dark gray but a translucent white. Under these layers of white membranes, many of their bodies were visibly humanoid. Some had transformed greatly, while others retained their bestial features. The former were indistinguishable from regular humans but for their membranous wings, while the latter had only grown human legs, remaining otherwise batlike. These bat monsters seemingly in the process of metamorphosis blanketed the entire tower above them; they numbered several thousand, if not a full ten thousand.

Afraid to wake them, Gu Mang asked softly, "Are they asleep?"

Mo Xi shook his head. "They're cultivating in seclusion. There are ancient records about these monsters; they're fire bats."

Gu Mang had always been pragmatic. He swept a glance over the fire bats hanging from the seven floors of the tower like braised ducks and asked Mo Xi a second question. "Are they hard to fight?"

Mo Xi didn't answer directly. "Fire bats come from a half-demon, half-immortal tribe on Jiuhua Mountain known as the feathered tribe."

"They're actual immortals?" Gu Mang sized up these furry monsters with their prominent breastbones. *They must be hard to fight!* he marveled. Then, *These guys really don't look how I imagined immortals would at all.* Muttering to himself, he shot a glance at Murong Chuyi, who stood at the head of their party. In his opinion, immortals at least had to look like this man: graceful in gait and elegant in demeanor, as if their robes and ribbons would flutter even in the absence of a breeze. These half-rat, half-human creatures didn't compare in the *least*.

Fortunately, Mo Xi had more to say, promptly saving Gu Mang's impression of immortals: "Fire bats can't be considered half-immortal. Like I said, they're the offspring of the feathered tribe. The feathered tribe are half-immortal and half-demon; some of them with stronger demonic traits degenerate and become depraved enough to couple with beasts. The monsters resulting from this union are the fire bats you see."

Gu Mang diligently attempted the math on his fingers. "So they're...half-immortal, half-demon, half-beast?"

"They hardly inherit any immortal blood," said Mo Xi. "It would be simpler to say they're half-beast and half-demon."

Gu Mang brought the conversation back to its start. "So—are they easy to fight?"

"They're strong in terms of spiritual energy, but they're quite dull-witted, so not very difficult. But this is the gathering place of all fire bat demons. If possible, it'd be better not to engage. Don't go bothering them." He turned back to Jiang Yexue. "Qingxu, can you tell if Yue Chenqing left any tracks here?"

"Let me try to see," said Jiang Yexue. He produced a paper talisman from his qiankun pouch and gently blew on it. The talisman transformed into a spiritual sparrow that danced into the air on swift wings. "Seek out Chenqing's breath."

After receiving its order, the sparrow fluttered toward the top of the tower. Just as it reached the third level, it let out a screech. Its wings burst into formless flames, and it vanished in a wisp of gray smoke.

Eight large scarlet words materialized in midair:

YE OF FOREIGN CLAN, OFFER SACRIFICE OF BLOOD.

Jiang Yexue frowned. "It looks like anything that wishes to ascend the tower—whether it's us or our spiritual butterflies or beasts— must first offer fresh blood." He turned to look at a pool of blood in the center of the demon tower and sank into contemplation. "Do we drip blood into it?"

"Let's try it and see," said Mo Xi.

The four approached the blood pool. Mo Xi unfastened the

dagger hidden in his sleeve and sliced open his palm, then passed the dagger to Jiang Yexue. After everyone let a few drops of fresh blood fall into the pool, the scarlet within began to surge.

Blood splashed, and a hair-raising snarl emanated from the pool. A blazing red beast burst from the depths.

"What the hell?!" Gu Mang exclaimed.

Through the blood misting his vision, he saw that the beast had the body of a man but the face of a boar. Tusks protruded from his snout, which was covered in fiery scarlet fur, and his eyes glowed red as the setting sun. He swung a massive hatchet, flinging off blood from the pool, then sneezed violently.

The creature immediately launched into a stream of profanity. "The fucking fuck's going on these days? People keep tryna trespass. You so fucking tired of being alive, you're here to be snacks for Her Highness the Bat Queen?"

Jiang Yexue's eyes widened. "It's a shangao..."

This was a monster well-known throughout the Nine Provinces. Gu Mang, however, had lost his memories; he hadn't the slightest clue. The fact that the others clearly understood what was going on made him anxious, yet he was also embarrassed to ask. "What's a shangao?" he whispered to Mo Xi.

"An ancient evil beast," Mo Xi answered. "It's red as fire, looks like a pig, and has no interests beyond cursing people out."

This pig's interests are quite similar to yours, Gu Mang thought. *If the two of you start squabbling, I don't know who will win.*

Breathing noisily, the shangao stared through his piggy eyes at each of them in turn, then immediately cursed them out as expected. "Lamelegs, Deadface, Blue-Eyed Monster, and Missy—you four bastards have trespassed into Bat Tower and woken me up. You stupid assholes have got some nerve!"

Gu Mang assigned each of these insults the second he heard them. Silently, he ticked them off on his fingers: *Lamelegs would be Jiang Yexue, Blue-Eyed Monster is me. Princess and Little Dragon Lady both look like their faces are frozen like that, but Princess is pretty tall and built, so Missy would probably be Murong Chuyi, who's half a head shorter than Mo Xi. So Mo Xi is Deadface for sure.*

"What are you doing here? You'd better 'fess up quick!"

The creature *was* an ancient spiritual beast, so Jiang Yexue made obeisance and said, "My younger brother came to the Dream Butterfly Islands a few days back, but there's been no sign of him since. The only information we have led us to this Bat Island. This is why we've trespassed in your hallowed territory."

"Your brother?" The shangao squinted at him. "Ha ha, you're a big cripple, so is your brother a little cripple?"

Jiang Yexue had a good leash on his temper; his face betrayed nothing. "This one's younger brother is healthy and whole."

"Oh, a non-crippled brat then... I did see one a couple days back. Does he wear white robes with gold trim and chirp and chatter when he talks? Looks like a slacker with a pig's brain?"

Murong Chuyi's and Jiang Yexue's expressions shifted slightly. Although the shangao was crude, his description matched Yue Chenqing to a tee. Jiang Yexue bowed again. "Xiansheng, may I ask where this youth is now?"

It was impressive that Jiang Yexue could call this pig *xiansheng* without blushing. But the shangao didn't buy it. "Damn cripple, flattery won't get you anywhere," he snorted. "You still haven't answered the question I asked. I'll ask you again: Is your brother a chattering slacker with a pig's brain?"

Jiang Yexue paused, unwilling to endorse the shangao's unfavorable description of his brother. As he hesitated, he heard Murong

Chuyi's icy voice. "Correct. Stupid and long-winded, white clothes with gold trim. That's him. Do you know where he is?"

"Heh, little brat, at least you admit it frankly." The shangao's beady little eyes turned toward Murong Chuyi. "Although—you're a grown man, yet you're more like a fairy with that tiny waist and pretty face. That womanish look really makes you so *ugly*."

"I asked you where that youth is now." Murong Chuyi did not like to wait; he was already running out of patience, clipping each word as he interrogated the pig.

The shangao froze for a second, perhaps caught by Murong Chuyi's electrifying gaze and imposing manner. "If I answered just because you asked, wouldn't that be a huge embarrassment for me?"

Murong Chuyi narrowed his eyes. "What do you want?"

"Of course everything must go by Master Shangao's rules!"

Murong Chuyi's dark brows drew together in rage. "What rules."

The shangao snuffled. "That's a long story! First, I'll ask you all a question—do you know the original purpose of this tower?"

"It's a human sacrifice tower, used to imprison live humans for future use." Jiang Yexue replied.

"The cripple is right, but our Dream Butterfly Islands have plenty of spiritual energy, and the monsters have gradually learned to cultivate through inedia. The Bat Queen sincerely wants to ascend as an immortal and has hardly killed any living creature in the past hundred years. She has no need to capture humans to consume. This tower was gradually abandoned and now has become a haven for bat spirits cultivating in seclusion."

"In that case, there's no use in keeping my brother on the island," Jiang Yexue said gently. "Is it possible to beg magnanimity from your esteemed ruler and let my brother return with us?"

"Heh, keep dreaming, Lamelegs. The Bat Queen doesn't kidnap cultivators, but your pig-brained brother threw himself into our hands and violated Her Majesty's taboo. Let him go? Tsk tsk, you think it's so easy?"

"What taboo did he violate?" Jiang Yexue asked.

The shangao snickered. "Same thing. You ask, but do I have to answer? Everything according to Daddy's rules."

Murong Chuyi was at the end of his rope. Furious, he snapped his horsetail whisk. He didn't yet intend to strike, but his eyes sparked with rage. Brows drawn low, he snapped, "We've already asked for your rules, so why haven't you explained them?"

The shangao sneered, his tusks protruding, "Missy looks so delicate, but his temper's worse than mine—how spicy! Fine, Daddy will tell you." He paused dramatically. "Daddy guards this tower for the Bat Queen and doesn't usually hurt anyone. When you cultivators drop in to ask things, I can choose to be good and answer three questions—but if you receive the answer to a question, all must pay a similar price. So, you must think it through. Only three questions may be asked, but the cost of an answer can be as low as one hair or as high as your three ethereal and seven corporeal souls... How about it? You sure you want to do this?"

Murong Chuyi didn't even blink. "Question one. Where is Yue Chenqing right now?"

"Oh, that was quick, asking right off the bat." The shangao raised one finger. "Your first question isn't worth much, and Daddy doesn't swindle people. How about this? We can make a trade, and I'll tell you his whereabouts."

"What do you want to trade?"

The shangao licked his thick and greasy lips. "Daddy likes to dine on human suffering. The more painful the past, the better it tastes."

He glanced maliciously at the four. "If you're willing to stand right here and let me take some painful secrets to nourish myself with, then I'll answer your first question."

Since this matter involved the others, Murong Chuyi turned to look at them instead of immediately accepting.

The shangao could answer three of their questions. Mo Xi thought they absolutely shouldn't give him everything he wanted on the first one—otherwise, what would they have to barter with for the second and third? But before he could say so, Gu Mang spoke up. "Pig-xiong, aren't you being a bit unfair?"

The shangao widened his eyes. "How so?"

"Look," Gu Mang said, "we've only asked you one question, but you want to take painful memories from each of us. You're acting really greedy."

The shangao disagreed. "How's Daddy being greedy?!"

"You just said you're making a trade with us. One thing should be offered in exchange for another, so for each question we ask, you should only get to absorb one person's memories. Isn't that right?"

The shangao was quiet.

"So for each question you answer, you can choose the memories from one person, not all four of us," Gu Mang continued. "You're an *ancient deity*—shouldn't you be more generous and stick to your word?"

"You—!" The shangao choked on his anger, his piggish face flushing red and purple. This was his honor at risk. Although he wanted to expel these foreigners as quick as possible, he could sense that the four individuals present were all victims of suffering. Their anguish was sure to taste mellow and rich, a delicacy beyond compare. Why should one let go of ducks that had waddled into one's mouth?

The shangao roared, "All right, all right! One question for one taste of suffering! But it's not for you to volunteer yourselves— Daddy will pick among you!"

Gu Mang mimicked his tone and echoed cheerfully, "All right, all right, if you want to pick, then step right up. Come now, do you want Lamelegs, Deadface, Missy, or Blue Eyes?"

The shangao sized them all up with care, his piggy nose sniffing out the bitterness in the depths of their souls. The more he scented the greedier he became. Gu Mang was born a slave and was short two souls. Mo Xi's father had died early, his mother had betrayed him, and he'd been stabbed by someone he loved dearly. Murong Chuyi was abandoned by both parents in his youth and became an orphan. As for Jiang Yexue, no words were necessary: he led a life of eternal loneliness. The shangao swallowed hungrily. He wanted to go back on his words and gobble down all their memories at once.

But just as trees needed bark, people needed to maintain face; even the shangao had his self-respect. These humans smelled exceptionally delicious, but he hadn't lost all self-control. He cleared his throat and made a decision: "It'll be you. Yes, you. The damn cripple, you come up."

Jiang Yexue smiled lightly. "Why's that? Is it that Xiansheng thinks I've endured the most suffering?"

"You're maimed, you're the one. Are you unwilling?"

"What wouldn't I do to save Chenqing?" Jiang Yexue said. "But Xiansheng wants to eat secrets; naturally, these are things I don't want anyone else to know. I can provide painful memories for you to absorb, but you must not let them out. Xiansheng, will you accept this?"

"When memories enter my mouth, they become my food," said the shangao. "Why would I ever spit them out? Don't worry, don't worry—Daddy absolutely won't let them out."

Jiang Yexue was amiable but far from stupid. "Words are empty. Will Xiansheng swear a demonic oath?"

The shangao was once a pig after all. He was extremely greedy. He was merely in a hurry to swallow the suffering of others, and had no interest in broadcasting the secrets he absorbed. Without hesitation, the shangao raised two fingers to swear a demonic oath. "Can we get on with it now? Damn cripple, such a pain in the ass!"

Jiang Yexue smiled warmly. "Then I invite you to collect your dues."

Gu Mang and Mo Xi had no objections, so the shangao, standing in the middle of the blood pool, raised his head and opened his mouth. It emitted a whistling hiss. Wind whipped up around them, and dense wisps of black smoke soared out from Jiang Yexue's chest.

Everything rushed into the shangao's stomach.

When the gale subsided, the shangao opened his eyes wide. He licked his lips, far from sated.

"Oh, not bad, very tasty. You're just a damn cripple—I can't believe your painful memories actually involve—"

Jiang Yexue cut the shangao off with a smile. "Xiansheng, did you forget your promise?"

The shangao fell silent. But for some reason, once he finished chewing on Jiang Yexue's suffering, he peered over at Murong Chuyi, his shiny little eyes dancing with malice.

Murong Chuyi swept his sleeves back. "You've received our payment. Now speak—where is Yue Chenqing?"

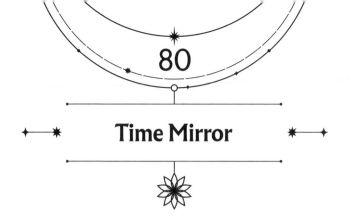

80

Time Mirror

"**H**IM?" The shangao snorted through his pig's snout. "As of now, he's locked in the fourth dark room at the top of this tower. There are two high-level bat demons guarding it, and twelve ancient bloodsucking vines on him. If the four of you are going to try rescuing him alone, heh heh, you'll have a bad time."

Murong Chuyi scoffed. "It's just two monsters and twelve chains—what's there to fear?" With a wave of his hand, the horse-tail whisk in the crook of his arm lengthened into a gleaming silver longsword. Lightning crackled and hissed around the blade. Murong Chuyi pressed two fingers together and called, "Zhaoxue, ride the wind!"

The longsword Zhaoxue flickered splendidly, brightening Murong Chuyi's face as it floated before him. Zhaoxue was slender and light, so Murong Chuyi used an unorthodox method to ride his sword. He didn't step on Zhaoxue—rather, the blade transformed into glowing orbs of sword glare. The silver lights encircled Murong Chuyi like gently drifting snow as the concentrated sword qi helped him ride the winds.

Seeing this, the shangao's tiny eyes widened, from the size of red beans to soybeans. "You—you're leaving? Aren't you going to ask the second and third questions?!"

"No need."

The shangao grew agitated. "You don't want to know what taboo the little pig-brain violated?"

Murong Chuyi's focus had turned entirely toward rescuing Yue Chenqing. "I don't care anymore," he said bluntly.

How could this be? The shangao flew into a rage. "How dare you! Wouldn't Daddy be taking a big loss? One person's painful memories aren't enough to fill the gaps in my teeth! No! None of you are allowed to leave! You better ask those questions! You need to stay and offer me two more sets of memories, otherwise Daddy definitely won't spare you!"

"Xiansheng, how have you taken a loss?" Jiang Yexue patiently responded. "We agreed on three questions at most, but we didn't promise to ask all three. Since Chuyi feels that one answer is sufficient, then of course—"

He was only halfway through his thought when the shangao brandished his massive hatchet and swung it down in uncontrolled fury. The blood pool's scarlet waters surged outward, spraying coppery waves in all directions. Jiang Yexue was closest to the shangao; just as the blade was about to strike him—as Mo Xi was still summoning Tuntian as a barrier—they heard a deafening explosion.

A golden talisman paper hissing with spiritual energy landed before Jiang Yexue and burst into a powerful protective barrier that deflected the force of the shangao's hatchet strike.

Mo Xi's eyes flew wide. "Gu Mang..."

The one who had deployed the talisman was neither Jiang Yexue nor Murong Chuyi. It was Gu Mang who had reacted fastest among the four. The protective talisman glowed with a blinding brilliance, and Gu Mang stood against the light, his clothes whipping around him in the gales of spiritual energy.

At that moment, it was not only Mo Xi but also Jiang Yexue who turned to stare at Gu Mang's figure in astonishment. They seemed to see the silhouette of that General Gu who had fought alongside them many years ago.

Give me another chance. This time, I won't disappoint you.

Gu Mang's beseeching words on Warrior Soul Mountain echoed in Mo Xi's ears. Mo Xi studied Gu Mang's figure as it melded with the golden light. The beating organ in his chest felt as if it were seized by a thorn-covered hand; it throbbed in bitter agony. All this time Gu Mang really had been trying to draw closer to his former self. To draw closer to the Gu Mang who hadn't yet committed treason, to the General Gu who had shared in life and death with them...

"Pig-xiong, if you want to eat painful memories, just say so. Why fight?" With a wave of Gu Mang's sleeve, the golden barrier vanished. "Come, you can have mine too. Will that satisfy you?" Gu Mang took a few steps forward, planting his feet on the cracked stones beside the blood pool. He pointed to his own head. "Have at it."

The shangao's greed was like a snake that wanted to eat an elephant. He jabbed a finger at Mo Xi and at Murong Chuyi, who was still ringed by sword glares. "What about them? I want theirs too!"

Gu Mang raised his eyebrows. "I'm not the boss of them. Why don't you ask them yourself?"

Their group was now on an isolated island in a tower filled with monsters. It would be better not to provoke them if they could help it. Murong Chuyi swept back his long sleeves, his expression wintery. "If you want them, then take them. Hurry up."

Afraid they would change their minds, the shangao wasted no time and sucked in a great breath of air. He first absorbed wisps of rushing black smoke from Murong Chuyi's chest, swallowing them into his stomach. Then he seized upon the accumulated suffering within Mo Xi's heart.

But the fretful fire in the shangao's heart didn't dissipate after these servings of misery were consumed—instead, he grew more insatiable. Because of his contract with the monster tribe, he had been stuck here guarding the tower for thousands of years. The previous Bat King ate people and took lives, so the shangao had plenty of suffering to feast on in his wake. But this current Bat Queen was obsessed with leaving her monstrous body behind and ascending as an immortal; she'd gone a century without taking a human life. The only cultivator the shangao had come into contact with in all this time was Yue Chenqing, who had scampered over a few days ago. The carefree and laid-back Yue Chenqing, who lacked for nothing and was always in a good mood, contained no great bitterness or hatred. He was exceptionally uninteresting to the shangao's palate.

But today was different. As Mo Xi and Murong Chuyi's suffering entered his gullet, the shangao was like a man on the verge of starvation tasting savory, piping-hot meat. He wasn't willing to let this meal go.

But despite everything, the shangao was still an ancient beast; he possessed *some* self-restraint. Hardening his resolve, the shangao moved his piggy eyes away from the two turned toward Gu Mang. "All right! Delicious!" he yelled coarsely. "I'll eat yours last, then Daddy will let you all go!"

Gu Mang smiled. "Aiya, then I really must express my gratitude for your leniency and grace."

His tone and mannerisms were uncomfortably close to the Gu Mang of the past. Truth be told, Mo Xi had recently felt that Gu Mang had been pressing closer and closer to the specter of the former Gu-shixiong. As he watched Gu Mang smilingly negotiate with the shangao, time seemed to have flowed backward.

The shangao was a simple-minded beast. He didn't hear the mockery in Gu Mang's words and thought he was earnestly being praised. He snorted and waved a haughty hand. "Well, of course. Daddy's word is his bond—when have I ever backed out of a deal?"

He began to absorb Gu Mang's suffering. Black qi rushed out from the depths of Gu Mang's chest, transforming into a wide curl of black smoke that hung in midair before rushing into the shangao's open mouth.

The shangao took a gulp, then suddenly closed his mouth. His eyes grew round as he stared at Gu Mang in disbelief, then flashed with a strange and avaricious brightness. Meeting those glinting eyes, Gu Mang had the feeling that this pig wanted to swallow him whole. He unconsciously took a step back. "Bit off more than you can chew?" he smiled tentatively.

The shangao huffed and puffed through his snout. Drool started running as he opened its mouth before he even spoke a word. How could this creature have imagined that a suffering equal to the accumulated grief of thousands would be contained within this young man, who looked to be barely over thirty? But strangely enough, the shangao couldn't explore all of his memories. He could feel the anguish there but couldn't get at the true reasons behind the suffering. For the greedy pig, this was like scenting the aroma of a sumptuous feast that constantly remained at a distance. Unable to satiate himself, his stomach rumbled with hunger, all his other organs tensing in sympathy.

"You've lost many memories..." the shangao muttered. "What a pity, what a pity. There's such pain there even when lost. If you were to remember them...that flavor...would be..." He sucked back a mouthful of drool, his eyes gleaming with a wicked light.

Seeing the shangao's expression grow sinister, Mo Xi felt a chill. "Shuairan, come!" he snapped.

In the same moment, the shangao tossed aside his previous proclamation about his word being his bond. He leapt from the blood pool, an evil beast pouncing on its prey. Face twisted and trailing spittle, he charged toward Gu Mang.

"Watch out!" Mo Xi shouted. Tossing out a talisman, he enclosed Gu Mang within a barrier.

A beam of fiery light crackled to life, illuminating the hall of the ancient tower. Shuairan arced into the air as Mo Xi raised the whip. He stood before the shangao, his gaze ruthless. "Beast—your greed knows no bounds!"

The shangao looked up, laughing maniacally. "Greed? So what!" His vicious scarlet eyes looked past Mo Xi and fixed upon Gu Mang standing behind him. The shangao licked his lips. "I hadn't expected such a prize to be delivered to my doorstep! I was tricked by the bat tribe, confined to this blood pool for thousands of years to guard the tower on behalf of the Bat Queen! If I can flashback your memories, exploit your suffering, and devour you piece by piece—then I... Then I... Ha ha ha! Then I would be free! I would be *free!*"

Mo Xi's heart juddered. Flashback his memories? What did that mean—could it be that...this beast could recover Gu Mang's memories? But how could that be?! Gu Mang was missing two souls. This was no ordinary case of amnesia, so how...

His mind was still racing when the shangao flung out an arm. An explosion boomed. The blood pool churned, as if hidden dragons and colossal whales stirred beneath the surface.

As the battle threatened to shake down the building, a bloody object as tall as ten men rose from the depths of the pool. It broke the surface, waves of blood spreading out to batter the shore as if thousands of hydrangeas had scattered their petals upon the stones.

A fall of scarlet droplets hit the earth, and the object became visible within the vermilion haze. Mo Xi was immediately stupefied, all the blood in his body seeming to freeze in an instant—

"The Time Mirror?!"

When the blood dripped away, the mirror emerged, emitting a magnificent golden light. Its frame was carved with ancient talisman seals, and its surface reflected none of their figures, instead veiled in an opaque fog. Within it flashed the light of time and space, gleaming intermittently.

It really was the Time Mirror...

Mo Xi had only read of this mirror in the academy's texts. It was linked to the three forbidden techniques—Rebirth, the Zhenlong Chess Formation, and the Space-Time Gate of Life and Death. Over the course of the boundless river of time, legends about the Rebirth technique were numerous and widespread, with tales of the Zhenlong Chess Formation coming in close behind.

Yet the Space-Time Gate of Life and Death remained mysterious. According to legend, if one were to grasp this last forbidden technique, they could rip apart space and time, returning to the past and changing the future. But this technique had too many strange pitfalls, and the scrolls that told of it were not whole; only fragments of text were extant. Whether this technique had ever truly existed or was simply a story was impossible to determine. Furthermore, it was said that any who tried to use the Space-Time Gate of Life and Death would meet brutal, sudden, and grisly ends. Thus, other than madmen with intense obsessions, no one would pursue this particular forbidden technique.

But the Time Mirror was different. Many ancient records across the Nine Provinces made mention of this legendary object.

According to myth, the Exalted God Fuxi had left it behind when he created the Space-Time Gate of Life and Death. Its function was similar to the Gate in that it could transport someone to the past, but the mirror was just a prototype—although it could construct an illusion of the past, it was impossible to actually change anything within it. Cultivators who entered the world of the mirror could make amends for past regrets, but their efforts had no effect beyond the world of the illusion. The instant the cultivator left the mirror world, any deviation from reality would be erased. The past in the mirror was like a dream; when the dreamer awoke, the world would be just as it was—perfectly unchanged.

Thus, this Time Mirror bore a more fitting name: Mirror of Fleeting Dreams. All the past it contained amounted to no more than three thousand dreams of golden millet.[5]

Jiang Yexue and Murong Chuyi were grandmaster artificers; they of course also knew of the Time Mirror. Even the usually calm and indifferent Murong Chuyi was ruffled. "The Time Mirror is a treasure from the divine race... What is it doing *here*?"

"I'm afraid it's not the full mirror," Jiang Yexue remarked. "Look at the left side."

They followed his lead and peered at the left side of the mirror. Indeed, there were clear signs of breakage—this mirror the height of ten men was just a fragment of the real Time Mirror.

But even such a scrap was more than enough to leave them stunned. The shangao roared: "Hatred indelible, even beneath the Yellow Springs—array formation!" He pointed his giant hatchet,

---

5   A metaphor for dreams that cannot come true, from Tang dynasty writer Shen Jiji's story "The World Inside a Pillow." In the story, Lu Sheng takes a nap on a celadon porcelain pillow in an inn while the proprietor steams millet cake. He dreams of a life of wealth and glory, but when he wakes, everything in his dream is gone and the millet cake is not yet cooked, symbolizing the illusory and unobtainable nature of dreams.

and the black smoke he had just inhaled from Gu Mang struck the mirror's surface.

As the wisp of smoke entered the mirror, the dense fog within began to churn, surging like clouds blown by the winds of time. A blinding golden light burst forth. "Sufferer, fall within!" the shangao howled.

This call was like a soul-summons; those unconnected to these painful memories were entirely unaffected. Only Gu Mang cried out and fell to his knees, coughing up a great mouthful of blood.

"Gu Mang!" Mo Xi called out, urgent.

Gu Mang's limbs seemed bound like a puppet on strings. He hooked his fingers into the cracks and gullies of the brick floor with such force that tendons and veins protruded from his arms, yet some shapeless force pulled him inexorably toward the mirror of light.

At the same time, the shangao emitted several piercing and bizarre shrieks. Murong Chuyi looked around, his sharp brows furrowing. "Watch out!"

The dark recesses of the tower suddenly glowed with flickering red light. From a distance, it looked like thousands of lanterns aglow in an endless night, or a splendid river of stars. However, this magnificent sight was nothing so elegant—it was the sign that the bat spirits perching at the corners of the tower had awakened.

Low, rustling cries swirled around them, growing gradually louder and more frequent until they crested like high waves on a stormy sea. Countless bat spirits flew toward them.

Killing intent rose in Murong Chuyi's eyes. With a wave of his hand, he shouted, "Zhaoxue, Destroy a Thousand Mountains!"

The light of the longsword encircling him at once transformed into a billowing, snow-flecked wave of spiritual energy that crashed toward the approaching bat demons. With a deafening collision, the white spiritual tide broke against the black sea of bats, leaving in its wake a vicious tangle of blows.

At the same time, the Time Mirror's pull on Gu Mang strengthened relentlessly. Gu Mang dove for the ground and wrapped his arms around the bone pillar next to him, but still couldn't resist the mirror's terrifying summons.

Since time immemorial, entering this mirror was known to be a death sentence. Jiang Yexue had been helping Murong Chuyi against the wild onslaught of bats, but as he turned and saw how poorly Gu Mang was faring, he moved to lend his aid.

Before he could do so, Mo Xi's Shuairan lashed out and bound Gu Mang tightly. "No need," Mo Xi said to Jiang Yexue. "I'm here!"

With these words, Mo Xi yanked back the snake whip Shuairan and wrapped his arms around Gu Mang. The instant he did, he understood how fearsome the call of the Time Mirror was—no mortal body could withstand the invisible pull of a mirror of godly make for long. Holding Gu Mang, Mo Xi too was yanked bodily toward the mirror.

"Mo-xiong! Gu-xiong!" Jiang Yexue cried.

It was an address Jiang Yexue had used on their military expeditions together. But since he had lost the use of his legs, he could no longer take part in remote campaigns. Later yet, one of this group of comrades became Xihe-jun, and another became Qingxu Elder. They had grown used to these polite and cold titles when they met. But in this moment of peril, the names that came to Jiang Yexue's lips were those from their youth.

The golden light grew brighter, its pull becoming stronger and stronger. They were about to be dragged into the mirror and into Gu Mang's excruciating past. It was a death sentence—a near-certain death sentence. How many people had returned from this mirror unscathed?

Although Gu Mang had no knowledge of this mirror, he had been thoroughly tempered by the Liao Kingdom and possessed an animal intuition. As the two drew near its swirling surface, Gu Mang struggled in Mo Xi's arms. "Let go!"

Mo Xi didn't make a sound. He commanded Shuairan to bind the two of them even tighter.

Gu Mang looked up, his eyes glinting with an unusual brightness. "If you stay outside, you can help them!" he snapped. "Let me go!"

Mo Xi gritted his teeth. "You'd better...shut up!"

"Let go—you shouldn't come with me—!"

"Shut *up*!" Mo Xi roared, thoroughly enraged.

The golden light grew so bright it blinded them. By now, even Shuairan anchoring them to the stone pillar couldn't resist the Time Mirror's power. The spiritual whip disintegrated into motes of red light, like rosy clouds dancing at sundown, and vanished back into Mo Xi's body.

Without Shuairan's protection, the two skidded toward the Time Mirror. At almost the same moment, the thousands of bats that had burst out of the darkness overwhelmed Murong Chuyi's holy weapon Zhaoxue. Murong Chuyi pulled out a dagger, its snowy blade illuminating his determined phoenix eyes. He slashed open his own palm without hesitation, then raised his hand, sending drops of blood flying into the air. He was attracting those bloodthirsty bats with spirit-infused blood, using himself as bait...

"Chuyi!" Jiang Yexue couldn't help but cry out.

Murong Chuyi sent a barrier crashing down, trapping himself within. His powerful spiritual blood drew the bats like a magnet; they swarmed to attack, surrounding the barrier. The entire barrier, and his snow-white figure within, was instantly engulfed. Only his harsh voice rang out: "Jiang Yexue! Stop that damn mirror, hurry up! I can't hold them for long!"

They were beset by troubles—here was Murong Chuyi wildly besieged by vampire bats, his thin protective barrier about to shatter at any moment. There were Mo Xi and Gu Mang, dragged to the very brink of the Time Mirror's realm, both seconds away from falling into the ancient godly mirror.

Jiang Yexue's face was pale as paper, but Mo Xi cried angrily, "It's not that easy! Help Murong drive off the fire bats and the shangao! Then come back and try to do something about this mirror!"

With that final instruction, Mo Xi and Gu Mang could hold out no longer. A final violent tug hauled them into the time that billowed within the mirror's depths.

The last thing Mo Xi saw before the mirror swallowed him was Jiang Yexue steering his wooden wheelchair to Murong Chuyi's side and opening his qiankun pouch. A dozen-odd bamboo automatons fell to the ground and transformed into warriors armed with swords.

Then he tumbled with Gu Mang into the abyss of time and space as his vision went black.

81

Return to Eight Years Ago

MO XI OPENED his eyes. Dark blue-green curtains patterned with clouds hung above his head. The bed-canopy fluttered gently in the wind, throwing dappled shadows across the hazy daylight coming in.

He was momentarily at a loss. Where was he?

Then he swiftly realized—he and Gu Mang had been sucked into the Time Mirror. This was the past that the ancient godly artifact had conjured. Although they hadn't truly traveled through time, the world within the mirror was an exact replica of reality. Mo Xi should be able to converse with the people of the past and even alter the course of events... So in that sense, there was little difference between truth and illusion.

Moreover, this must be a part of the past that Gu Mang found extremely painful. The knowledge made Mo Xi's heart race. He sat bolt upright, his inky hair dark as black jade falling loose around his shoulders as he yanked back the canopy.

He was in his own bedroom in Xihe Manor. Mo Xi looked around; the room's decor wasn't much different from his current one. The weapons rack was merely missing some blades, and a painting of Guangling peach blossoms still hung on the wall. He stepped over to the sundial placed by the windowsill. It was of Yue Manor make and glowed year-round with golden spiritual energy. With the tap of a finger, it showed the year and time of day. Mo Xi raised a hand and lightly pressed the sundial's glowing surface, and a small line of seal script appeared on the dial's face like ripples cascading outward.

Mo Xi looked at the date displayed on the sundial. The organ within his ribs beat more and more ferociously, his face growing more and more ashen.

As expected, it was *that* year.

As expected, they had returned to that particular time...

Mo Xi closed his eyes, his lashes fluttering. He swallowed.

He would never forget the events of this year—the year when Gu Mang had been stripped of his power and his rank in the wake of his great defeat at Phoenix Cry Mountain, when Lu Zhanxing had been beheaded, when the Wangba Army's surviving soldiers had been taken into custody.

It was the year Gu Mang defected.

And it was on this day that... Mo Xi's pale, slender fingers stroked the spotless sundial, caressing the text flowing over its surface. The pain in his heart crushed him like clouds smothering the sun; he could barely breathe.

On this day, he had been appointed to the northern frontier and left the capital. Gu Mang at the time had already had his fill of misery and passed his days grinning and giggling in a brothel. Mo Xi's attempts to persuade him were of no use; he could only wait for time to heal Gu Mang's wounds.

He had been so naive back then. He'd thought Gu Mang would pick himself up as he had in the past, that he'd persist through all the pain and suffering. He was so sure that such a day would come.

But he had been wrong.

Gu Mang didn't pull through. By the time Mo Xi completed his mission and returned to the capital, Gu Mang had already left Chonghua. A few months later, news came from the front lines that Gu Mang had committed treason and gone over to Liao.

He never noticed Gu Mang's change of heart. He never got the chance to understand how Gu Mang had felt, to have a proper conversation with him. He never even got to say more than a few words to Gu Mang or ask him to stay one last time before he stepped into hell.

But now Mo Xi had returned to this particular year, to this particular day. He had returned to the period he had dreamed of countless times, to...to this moment that, perhaps, could reverse destiny.

Despite knowing the Time Mirror couldn't actually change the past, Mo Xi's chest still burned as if scalded. He rushed out the door without even bothering about his appearance.

The bright sunlight from eight years ago shone fiercely onto his face, its piercing rays stinging his eyes. But he refused to close them. He fought back the urge to tear up as he gazed greedily at each plant and tree, each brick and stone.

From around the corner came a quiet exclamation of shock, swiftly followed by: "This one greets my lord!"

Mo Xi turned, and his heart churned strangely again—

Back then, Li Wei hadn't yet come into his employ. The one greeting him was a young servant girl named Shuang Qiu whom Xihe Manor had taken in. A pitiable beggar whom Mo Xi had seen on the streets, whom he took into his estate because he could not bear to see her disgraced by malicious men. He found her to be clever and intelligent, and had once considered appointing her head housekeeper of Xihe Manor. Shortly after, however, he discovered that she was a spy sent by Murong Lian with orders to seduce and sabotage him. He had expelled her from his residence.

Holding a water basin, Shuang Qiu bowed gracefully. "My lord woke up early from his nap today. I'll arrange for tea and snacks to be brought to you at once."

Back then, Mo Xi had been sympathetic of her predicament and was extremely courteous to her. But with what he knew now, he only felt a deep disgust. He swept his sleeves back. "There's no need."

"Does my lord not have an appetite? I brewed some refreshing plum wine a few days back, so if my lord is willing..."

"I said there is no need," Mo Xi stiffly said.

Shuang Qiu finally noticed there was something odd about Mo Xi. She didn't dare press the issue, so she conceded and made obeisance. "Yes," she murmured softly. After a pause, she persevered. "But I—I...was only acting out of care. I ask my lord not to blame me."

Mo Xi found her rather irritating, but he wasn't a vindictive person, nor did he care to argue with a woman. Besides, he had more important things to do. "Prepare a set of military robes. I need to go out."

"Does my lord mean to travel out of the city?"

Mo Xi paused. "I mean to enter the palace."

According to the remaining fragments of the ancient scrolls, those who entered the Time Mirror would return to their past self—their appearance, features, and thoughts would all be reconstructed. Mo Xi likely only retained his memories because he had been pulled into the mirror at Gu Mang's side. He wasn't the target but had entered by mistake.

As for Gu Mang... He had probably made a full return to his past state. He would have no idea that he had come in from outside the mirror, to say nothing of what would happen later.

Which meant that the person Mo Xi would encounter upon going into the city would be the General Gu from back then—that Gu-shixiong who had hit rock-bottom and was in the direst of straits.

Which meant he had a chance to talk to Gu Mang before he turned traitor.

Mo Xi's hands began to tremble at the thought—his current self had traveled through time and was about to meet Gu Mang from eight years ago. He could ask Gu Mang about so many things. He could get a clear look at Gu Mang's mental state before he defected. He could learn what kind of mood he was in and the details of what happened before he defected... He might even discover what, if anything, he could have done back then to prevent Gu Mang's treason.

This kind of experiment was of no practical use—as soon as Jiang Yexue rescued them from the mirror, any change he made would dissipate like smoke and clouds. Even so, Mo Xi could see himself on the cusp of receiving an answer to the questions, exhaustion, pain, and confusion that had plagued him for eight long years.

But before he could speak to Gu Mang, he needed to first visit the imperial palace.

"Xihe-jun!"

"This one salutes Xihe-jun!"

As he entered the palace, the imperial guards lowered their heads and crossed their arms to perform obeisance. The scarlet pheasant feathers on their helmets rustled, and their armor reflected the dazzling morning sun. It was an incredibly peculiar feeling: even though Mo Xi had much on his mind, he couldn't help taking note of some familiar faces.

In eight years, the soldier in the corner of the corridor would become a defense elder at the academy. The imperial guard standing to the right of the stone beast at the palace stairs was gifted to Wangshu Manor by the emperor and became Murong Lian's personal guard. The youth with seven beaded red tassels on his helmet eventually died rescuing civilians from a demonic inferno in Chonghua's capital.

Mo Xi himself had bestowed the ribbon of heroes upon him in his coffin. There were also soldiers here whom Mo Xi had later picked to join the Northern Frontier Army.

Whether they were destined to rise or fall, live or die, in the years to come, none knew their fates at this moment. Only Mo Xi walked among these living men of the past, as if strolling through a dream he'd had year after year. Seeing those faces, Mo Xi seemed to look upon lost souls from eight years ago, so unreal and indistinct were they as he passed.

Finally, he arrived at the imperial throne room.

The newly ascended emperor reclined on dragon-embroidered pillows, his cheek pillowed in his hand as he closed his eyes in meditation. The beaded veil on his imperial crown swayed gently before his elegant features, fracturing the lines of his face and making his expression all the more inscrutable.

Compared to his current self, the emperor of eight years ago seemed a great deal thinner and surlier. It was little wonder—in the months after the late emperor passed, the nation had been unstable. The internal problems and external threats facing Chonghua were thorny and difficult to deal with. The irascible temper latent in the emperor's features had likewise been much closer to the surface back then.

"This one greets Your Imperial Majesty."

"Oh, Xihe-jun's here." The emperor's eyelids fluttered open. His gaze was dark and cold as it alighted upon Mo Xi, who had come to stand before the throne. No matter how he tried to conceal it, that gaze betrayed a predatory air, containing vigilance, malice, and viciousness within its depths.

As this ice-cold look pierced Mo Xi, he felt a sense of familiarity. It was a feeling that brought him anger as well as pain. Back then, the emperor always betrayed this kind of attitude when speaking to him, whether intentionally or not. It was only after Mo Xi swore the Vow of Calamity, making it impossible for him to betray Chonghua or the power atop the throne, that the emperor gradually relaxed his guard around him.

But at this moment, the version of Mo Xi standing before the throne hadn't yet sworn this oath. When the emperor looked at Mo Xi, his eyes were those of a wild beast that had never been chained, like a ferocious wolf or tiger. Eight years ago, Mo Xi had been younger and his senses less keen; facing the emperor with the insight he had now, the wariness in that gaze made him feel a chill.

"Today, Xihe-jun should be setting out toward the fiefdom at the northern frontier, to teach and learn magic," the emperor drawled. "But you've come to the palace at this time to see us instead—could it be that there's some issue?"

Mo Xi performed an obeisance. "Yes. There is an issue. I would like to defer my departure for the northern frontier by a few days."

"Oh?" The emperor narrowed his eyes. "Why?"

"I'm feeling unwell."

No other excuse would work when dealing with this foxlike emperor. Only if Mo Xi said he was indisposed would His Imperial Majesty struggle to reject his request. Especially considering the fact that Mo Xi never lied back then—he always spoke the truth and never begged illness when he was well, so his words were entirely trustworthy.

As expected, the emperor was somewhat taken aback. After a moment, he sat up straight, eying Mo Xi from his high dais as he muttered, "Is that so... Is it severe? Why don't we select a skilled healer from Shennong Terrace and send them to Xihe Manor to examine you?"

"It's exhaustion and excessive dreams, no more, along with some difficulty sleeping," said Mo Xi. "I'll be better with a few days' rest. There's no need to trouble Shennong Terrace."

"I see." The emperor looked thoughtfully at Mo Xi, then asked with feigned carelessness, "How long does Xihe-jun propose to postpone for?"

Mo Xi had counted the days until Gu Mang would leave the city to defect: it should be a week after he himself left the capital. He didn't want the same thing to happen this time, with him away. "Ten days."

The emperor didn't immediately respond. Those eyes like deep, icy pools silently watched Mo Xi's face. At length, he chuckled softly. "Xihe-jun's been on campaign for so many years. There have been many occasions where you didn't balk at donning your armor and heading back into battle after serious injury. How is it that you now want to postpone the assignment we've given you for ten whole days on account of a touch of insomnia? This is rather too long."

Mo Xi didn't argue with him. "If I could push through it, I wouldn't have come to Your Imperial Majesty to request a deferment."

"It's rare indeed for Xihe-jun to ask for rest after fighting so many battles. It would be unspeakably cruel of us to refuse." The emperor toyed with the string of beads encircling his wrist, speaking slowly. "But as Xihe-jun is an important subject of Chonghua, the heavy responsibilities we place on your shoulders are naturally numerous. If you were to delay for ten days to rest, we're afraid that later affairs would prove difficult to manage." He paused, smiling. "What do you think of a three-day postponement?"

Mo Xi fell silent. *Three days?* Lu Zhanxing was due to be beheaded at the eastern market in three days. Why was the emperor insisting on that day in particular? Gu Mang was sure to have an extreme reaction to Lu Zhanxing's death. Yet the emperor wanted him to leave on that day... "I would implore Your Imperial Majesty to grant an extension of a further two days," said Mo Xi. "Will five days be acceptable?"

"No. We can give you three days at most." The emperor offered him another small smile. "Any more and we would be hard-pressed to deal with the urgent matters afterward."

"Your Imperial Majesty..."

Decision made, the emperor cut Mo Xi off. "Xihe-jun needn't continue. Since you're feeling unwell, go back to Xihe Manor and rest." After a brief pause, he said meaningfully, "To combat insomnia and restlessness, one must soothe the mind. In the next few days, it would be best if Xihe-jun sees less of certain people who may make him frustrated and discontent."

Mo Xi gazed up at the ruler sitting on his gilt throne. The emperor peered down through his swaying bead crown.

"Does Your Imperial Majesty mean Gu Mang?" Mo Xi murmured.

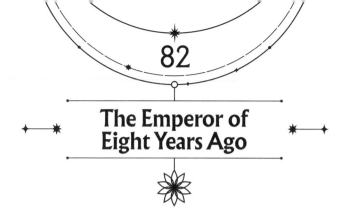

82

The Emperor of Eight Years Ago

M O X I H A D C U T right to the chase. The emperor didn't
beat around the bush either; with a chuckle, he said,
"As long as you take our meaning."

After a beat of silence, Mo Xi said, "Gu Mang is a true friend
of mine. Now that he's fallen from grace, would it not be bitterly
disappointing were I to discard him?"

"Mn. Of course, loyalty is an admirable thing. It's not as if we are
suggesting you never see each other again." The emperor's slender
fingers fiddled with the string of beads. "But he's a criminal now.
Shouldn't Xihe-jun avoid associations that might create misunder-
standings in such troubling times?"

"Those in the right fear no assumptions. I owe him. What's
improper about me persuading him a little? Besides, in Gu Mang's
current state, were he left alone, I'm afraid he would..."

"He would what?"

Mo Xi gritted his teeth. "Develop thoughts of treason."

Back then, he hadn't known Gu Mang's intentions. He'd never
suspected that Gu Mang could defect. But with the clarity of hind-
sight, he spoke now to remind the emperor not to push Gu Mang
too far.

The emperor's hands stilled. He smiled. "Is Xihe-jun so mistrust-
ful of his own true friend?"

"I only ask that Your Imperial Majesty not leave him with no other choice."

"No other choice?" The emperor snorted audibly. "All of his *choices* were his to make because the late emperor deemed him an exception. Otherwise, what right would a slave-born man like him have to don armor, step onto the battlefield, and achieve success? You speak of us leaving him no other choice... Has *he* considered what kind of choices would be available to him if not for the late emperor's grace? Would he not be no more than Murong Lian's dog?"

Mo Xi said nothing.

The emperor narrowed his eyes dangerously. "If Gu Mang has even a sliver of self-awareness, he should see that all of his former glory was bestowed upon him by the late emperor. Now that he's led an army to rout, we merely punish him in accordance with the law. What has he to complain about?!"

Mo Xi had come to the palace to ask the emperor to postpone his departure—he hadn't expected to trigger a conversation like this. This past version of the emperor was like a fox spirit who hadn't yet achieved human form; he couldn't effectively hide his motives from the Mo Xi of eight years in the future. Nor could he mask the great wariness in his eyes when he looked at Mo Xi. "What grievance could he have? What injustice could he feel? What right does he have to think of treason?"

The cruelty of these words chilled Mo Xi's blood. He had never heard such sentiments direct from the emperor's mouth. As these words registered in his ears, he felt a deep disappointment, even as a born noble—so how would Gu Mang have felt? Gu Mang, who had lost countless soldiers and seen his surviving forces taken into custody, who was denied gravestones when he asked, who had a brother about to be beheaded.

Mo Xi suddenly understood: back then, when Gu Mang had dragged him out drinking and cried out, deep in his cups, that he couldn't bear it anymore, that he was living a life worse than death—that wasn't a drunken impulse. Gu Mang really had been broken. Chonghua had sent him onto the battlefield in their name, but not out of a belief that Gu Mang and his ragtag army were safeguarding Chonghua. Rather, they considered this an act of grace; they, the powerful nobles, had bestowed this honor upon a slave. Hence his defeat could not be forgiven; to the emperor, Gu Mang wasn't a devoted general who had suffered a momentary defeat, but a slave who had failed to carry out his master's orders after being rewarded. He had frittered away the trust his master had graciously conferred.

Perhaps, upon realizing this, Gu Mang's heart had shattered. Perhaps it had broken into pieces from the inside out, crumbling to ash. It was only that back then, Mo Xi hadn't known. He had believed, so naively, in Gu Mang's apparently thoughtless laughter.

He hadn't understood Gu Mang at all.

Enduring the stabbing pain and trembling of his heart, Mo Xi swallowed thickly. "Your Imperial Majesty, you are not him," he said hoarsely. "You don't know exactly how he thinks, nor where his limits lie. If there were to come a day when he really defected..."

The emperor cut him off. "He doesn't dare."

Mo Xi held his tongue. How comical it was, to stand in front of the emperor from eight years ago and hear him say, so self-assuredly, that Gu Mang would never defect.

"He doesn't dare to now, nor ever. Where does Xihe-jun imagine he could defect to? In the past, when Hua Po'an betrayed Chonghua and founded the Liao Kingdom, he had a following of slave soldiers—but what does Gu Mang have? What's left of his army has been detained and locked in prison. Why don't you tell us what you think he could do as just one man?"

"Your Imperial Majesty thinks he couldn't leave Chonghua far behind as just one man?"

The emperor bared his teeth as he scoffed. "If he really can't get over himself, then he might as well go."

Mo Xi was stunned.

"He's of no use to us after his defeat at Phoenix Cry Mountain. If he wishes to defect for this, then he will become a scourge sooner or later if he remains in Chonghua." The emperor stared into Mo Xi's gradually paling face. "Xihe-jun, do you think that persuading him or accompanying him is useful? If he intends to defect, it is because he wants too much!" An emperor's heart was the cruelest of all. He said coldly, "What he wants, we can't afford to give."

Mo Xi's blood froze in his veins, as if his body were covered in ice. His hands clenched into fists as he said in freezing tones, "Your Imperial Majesty. What he wants are only gravestones bearing his men's names, nothing more!"

"Not just gravestones," the emperor replied. "Xihe-jun, what he wants from us is acknowledgment of their status. My apologies—we can offer them lenience, but we cannot give them glory."

Furious, Mo Xi snapped, "So then why is Your Imperial Majesty set on sending me away in three days? That's the day of Lu Zhanxing's execution—does Your Imperial Majesty desire to see if Gu Mang can remain loyal to Chonghua and its ruler after having yet another of his bones broken?!"

The emperor's expression darkened at once. "Xihe-jun. Do not be impudent."

"He can't bear Your Imperial Majesty's testing." Mo Xi was beyond caring, nearly trembling as he spoke. "I swear this in front of the hall today. If Your Imperial Majesty insists on this, Gu Mang *will* defect."

The emperor suddenly rose like a sword unsheathed; he slammed a palm down on the table. "What does it matter if he defects or not?! He's nothing but a dog! If he bites the hand that fed him and moves against Chonghua, will our nation collapse? Will it dissolve?! We *will* determine if this person is hiding treacherous intent—if he's cut from the same rebellious cloth as Hua Po'an!"

This emperor was young indeed—such naked rage was not something the current emperor would ever reveal.

"Three days. Three days from now, you *will* leave the capital." The emperor's breathing gradually slowed, but his gaze remained hard as he stared into Mo Xi's face. "You are dismissed."

Mo Xi had never clashed so spectacularly with the emperor. This conversation flashed like the edge of a blade, stabbing at his heart. Silent, he gazed up at the man on the throne. It was said that a ruler could see past falsehood, but when did this emperor ever let down his guard and ease off testing his own subjects? Especially those of Gu Mang's class, who had ever been regarded separately from the nobles. As the saying went, "those not of my clan are not of my heart." This was why the emperor was so wary of Gu Mang and so calculating, to the point that...

Wait! Mo Xi's heart pounded as he recalled something else. Back then, Mo Xi had clearly known when Lu Zhanxing's execution would be. Although he promised His Imperial Majesty to teach magic at the northern frontier, he had been set to return before Lu Zhanxing's beheading. In other words, if everything had gone according to plan, he absolutely would have had an opportunity to see Gu Mang one last time before he defected.

What had happened? The more he thought, the colder he grew...

There had been an incident on the northern frontier. Several monstrous beasts charged through the garrison, and he was forced to stay an extra few days quelling the invasion with the garrison troops. Back then, he had found it suspicious that so many monsters had descended upon them so suddenly yet hadn't given it much thought later. But now...

A hazy suspicion gave way to an even more horrifying idea. It was a thought that had never occurred to him before—

Back then, had the emperor purposely sent him away to test Gu Mang?

Mo Xi felt like a piece of ice had fallen into his chest, its insidious cold seeping into his bones. He was coming to a realization: his rushed departure, his delayed return—had this all been deliberately orchestrated by the emperor?

Perhaps the emperor had no intention of letting Gu Mang stay in Chonghua, which was why he wanted no one by Gu Mang's side during the days of his greatest pain and disappointment. This former slave general was no longer useful, and since the emperor couldn't find any suitable excuse to execute him, would it not be simply better to...force him to defect?

Could it be that the emperor had planned for Gu Mang's treason all along?

Mo Xi was so cold he was numb with it.

After taking leave of the imperial palace with its lofty eaves, Mo Xi worked for a long while to catch his breath so he could warm up a little. For a moment in the hall he had yearned to recklessly ask the question, to kick up a fuss—but he understood that if he wanted to uncover more secrets, he had to let the normal course of events unfold.

In this world within the mirror, he had one chance to unearth the truth. If he missed it, there wouldn't be another.

Mo Xi raised his head, blinking his slightly reddened eyes and doing his utmost to calm himself and rein in his impulses. Only when he had gathered himself did he continue toward the Apricot Mansion brothel in the north of the city. He knew he would find Gu Mang there—Apricot Mansion was Gu Mang's favorite pleasure house, filled with splendidly attired women and the harmonious trills of the sheng and the xiao. Gu Mang had once said with a smile how he adored the clever beauties there, that only their delicate charms could soothe the sea of suffering and hatred in his heart.

Mo Xi stopped before the brothel, which fluttered with red silks. He looked up at its wooden signboard, gold text on a red field. Eight years ago when he was leaving the capital, he had also passed by this building, fragrant with flowers, and stopped before it. But back then, he hadn't gone in. He couldn't endure Gu Mang's degenerate wasting, nor could he tolerate the sight of the man who had once shared his bed giggling amid a crowd of rouged and powdered women. The ache in his heart kept him from saying goodbye to Gu Mang before he left for the northern frontier. He missed his last chance to see Gu Mang before his defection.

But this time it would be different. This time, he wanted to have a sincere and genuine talk with Gu Mang. Just as he had imagined countless times, just as he had dreamed of night after night.

Mo Xi cleared his head, his nails sinking deep into his palms, and strode into the brothel filled with the chattering of women.

"Aiyo, Xihe-jun." The madam started at the sight of him. Remembering the last time Mo Xi came to the brothel to hunt down a particular man, she blurted fearfully, "What brings Xihe-jun here today?"

"Where's Gu Mang."

"General Gu...isn't—isn't here..."

"I know he's here." Mo Xi said, "Which room is he in?"

The madam shivered as she met his knife-like gaze. *My apologies, General Gu,* she thought to herself. *This little shop is a shoestring business—we can't handle what Xihe-jun would put us through.* She pulled on a greasy grin and forced a laugh. "Xihe-jun, what is my memory these days! Yes, yes, I recall now. General Gu is upstairs. Third floor, turn left at the end of the corridor. It'll be the third room—the Boudoir of Lingering Fragrance. Xihe-jun, please go ahead."

Mo Xi turned toward the stairs without a backward glance.

Before he even reached the door, Mo Xi could hear the fluid plucking of a pipa, as well as a singer's clear voice: "Our sons went forth with swords held brave, their blood and bones in distant grave. Last year this self was yet intact, last night this body spoke and laughed. Your loyalty I safely keep, your valiant deeds I freely speak. For when these heroes' souls come home, throughout the land shall peace be known."

It was Chonghua's soul-calling song.

The singer had clearly never performed such a weighty piece in a brothel. Though she sang without a single mistake, each faltering note betrayed her hesitation. A song used to console the dead played on the pipa like "Song of Courtship"[6]—what a stark contrast in tone.

Mo Xi walked over and stopped by the red lacquer door, which stood ajar. The singer played the final phrase, the last echoes of those delicate notes fading, followed by the peals of Gu Mang's lazy laughter. Such a soft sound, but it made Mo Xi's heart stutter in his chest.

"Jiejie's voice is as sweet as a yellow oriole, but there's a section you played too quickly. The tune lost its shape."

"It's my first time singing this," the girl simpered. "I can't play it well—I've embarrassed myself in front of General Gu."

---

6 "Phoenix Seeking Phoenix," a famous love song written by Sima Xiangru for Zhuo Wenjun, with whom the latter eloped.

Gu Mang chuckled. "So what? In the vast country of Chonghua, you girls are the only ones willing to have fun with me these days and sing the soul song with me in secret... Come, I'll teach you how to play that part correctly."

"General Gu, do you know how to play the pipa too?"

"The fingering is too hard for me," Gu Mang said. "But I can play other instruments."

The room was silent for a moment. Then Gu Mang casually said, "Fengbo, come."

Fengbo... Mo Xi closed his eyes. His fingers, suspended before the door, trembled. Suddenly, the bright notes of a suona sounded, shrill and comical... It was almost ridiculous. Yet tears brimmed behind his lashes. This was the sound of the holy weapon Gu Mang later couldn't summon ever again—Fengbo, its cry full of unsung regrets.

Mo Xi felt a stubborn lump in his throat. He couldn't speak for a long beat, filled with the anxiety of a traveler who feared returning home as much as he yearned for it. In the end, he heaved a deep sigh, and, enduring his dizziness, reached out to gently push open the red lacquer door.

Sunlight poured in. In this dreamlike chiaroscuro, he saw Gu Mang. Gu Mang from eight years ago.

Despite all Mo Xi had done to ready himself, the sight of this man felt like an unseen dagger tearing through his old scar. The agony spread from his heart to his limbs, a pain that made him tremble and go numb.

He saw Gu Mang once more—clear-headed, black-eyed, wearing the robes of Chonghua. Whole, healthy, not yet a traitor, bearing in his unbroken mind their shared memories...

General Gu of the empire.

His Gu-shixiong.

83

Gu Mang of Eight Years Ago

I<small>N THE BOUDOIR OF LINGERING FRAGRANCE</small>, smoke rose in spirals. The floor was covered in soft red carpets, and the eight-grid bamboo door to the balcony had been flung open, revealing the rich red lacquer of the engraved banister beyond. Below the balcony a foxglove tree stood in full bloom, its branches wreathed in a smoky haze of pink and purple.

His Gu-shixiong was perched atop the wooden railing, one knee bent, holding a suona the color of weathered copper. That suona gleamed with a muted patina, the white silk ribbon tied to its shaft fluttering gently in the evening breeze.

The holy weapon Fengbo.

Surrounded by flowers, Gu Mang brought Fengbo to his lips. After testing out a few notes, he closed his eyes and played a throaty tune.

"Our sons went forth with swords held brave, their blood and bones...in distant grave."

Gu Mang had always used to prefer jaunty little folk tunes, but the melodies he now drew from the suona were heartrendingly sorrowful. Cheeks puffed and lashes trembling, he tilted his head back in the fragmented sunlight streaming through the flowers and played his suona.

"Last year this self was yet intact, last night this body spoke and laughed..."

The notes soared into the sky.

Mo Xi said nothing; the world's bitterest olive seemed to be stuck in his throat. He stood at the door, gazing at Gu Mang's distant silhouette as if into a dream of a past lifetime.

Hearing movement, the pipa girl turned in his direction. Her eyes widened, and she moved to kneel before Mo Xi waved a hand at her, indicating that she should remain quiet.

Gu Mang was engrossed in his playing. The lips wrapped around the reed were red and wet, and his cheeks were endearingly puffed in concentration. As the setting sun fell on his handsome face, it gilded his black hair in rich gold. He sat crooked on the red railing, turning to soak in the sight of the drifting petals and luminous dusk as he played. By his hands, the silk ribbon tied around the suona swayed like the tide.

"Your loyalty I safely keep, your valiant deeds I freely speak."

Slender fingers pressed down on the mottled suona, dancing smoothly as the world's softest breeze.

"For when these heroes' souls come home, throughout the land... shall peace be known."

Only when the song ended did Gu Mang slowly open his eyes, turning to smile. "Look, this way we didn't lose the melody, so..."

Halfway through his explanation, he noticed the pipa girl's rigid and fearful expression. He turned and noticed Mo Xi, who had appeared at the door when he wasn't looking. His smile froze.

After a beat of silence, Gu Mang amended his expression and adjusted his manner. He twirled the instrument in his slender fingers as he teased Mo Xi. "Xihe-jun, how refined your tastes are today— somehow you're at this pleasure house as well."

Mo Xi heard a frighteningly hoarse voice. It was a moment before he recognized it as his own. "Get out," he told the pipa girl.

"At once."

"Hold it," Gu Mang said.

The girl fell still. Gu Mang smiled as he cocked his head. "How bossy, Xihe-jun. How could you shoo away the girl I paid to spend the night with? Have you asked my permission?"

"Gu Mang," Mo Xi rasped. Emotions swept violently through his chest. "There are some things I want to discuss with you. Alone."

"What's there to discuss?" Gu Mang asked. "Two single men sharing a room is rather suspicious, don't you think? Especially since you're a rising star and I'm doomed. What could *we* have to discuss?"

"Gu Mang!"

Gu Mang raised a hand to disperse Fengbo, and the suona scattered into motes of glimmering light that merged back into his body. He leapt off the railing with his arms crossed, then looked down and chuckled. "Stop fussing, gorgeous. Now that you're on the up-and-up and have caught Princess Mengze's eye to boot, it would be terrible for your reputation to be seen in the company of an infamous libertine like me. We've been brothers for so many years, haven't we? Gege would feel bad."

The familiar cloying tone echoed in Mo Xi's ears. It wasn't a dream or an illusion. This was Gu Mang in the flesh, a man he could see and touch. The Gu Mang of eight years ago. Who was doing everything he could to distance himself from Mo Xi, to mock him, argue with him. Perhaps this grinning man had already made his plans to defect and leave quite soon.

The realization birthed a violent impulse that pummeled Mo Xi in the chest. The rims of his eyes reddened. "I won't leave." He said once more to the pipa girl, "Get out."

Gu Mang's eyebrows rose. "Did you not hear me? I've already bought her for the evening. If you chase her away, who will keep me company through the endless night ahead?"

"I'll stay," Mo Xi said.

Gu Mang blinked his dark eyes. "Do *you* know how to play pipa?"

"...I don't."

"Do you know how to sing me songs?"

"I don't."

"Well then, why would I want you?" Gu Mang smiled. "You're hardly worth her price."

Mo Xi didn't bother arguing with him. "Gu Mang. I'm not going to the northern frontier today."

Gu Mang cocked his head again, a deathly infuriating smile lingering at the corners of his mouth. "Mm, how nice for you. But what does that have to do with me?"

"It does have to do with you. Give me one more night. I have some things to say. If I don't say them now—" Mo Xi paused, looking squarely into Gu Mang's eyes. "I'm afraid I'll never get the chance to say them after."

Perhaps it was because he knew Gu Mang already intended to defect. When Mo Xi carefully observed the minute changes in Gu Mang's expression, he could see his features flicker slightly at this.

Gu Mang lowered his lashes. "I have no interest in dealing with military affairs tonight. I only want to lose myself in beauty. If you really want to talk, there'll be plenty of time in the future. We can talk when you get back."

"I can't wait until then."

More silence. The pipa songstress was caught in the middle, frozen like a wood carving or a clay figure, afraid to make a sound or move a muscle.

At length, Gu Mang lowered his head. His chuckle was like a long sigh. "Why are you still clinging to me? I no longer have anything left."

"I just want to talk."

Smiling, Gu Mang stabbed every cruel word deep into Mo Xi's heart. "What's there to talk about? Your shige has nothing left to offer you. *Please*, Princess, I just want to cheer myself up a bit, have a little fun. You should leave. Let me go."

If Mo Xi had heard these words eight years ago, he might've been deceived. He might've believed that Gu Mang was merely heart-broken and upset, that he'd make a full recovery after some time messing around. But the Mo Xi who stood before Gu Mang now had the knowledge of eight years. To hear Gu Mang speak of "fun" only filled Mo Xi with an indescribable heartbreak and irony.

"Just for one night," Mo Xi rasped. "Save tonight for me."

Gu Mang sighed. "Don't make it sound so indecent. You have a long road to walk in the future, you need to guard your purity..."

"Am I still pure?"

There was a deafening silence. Even the pipa girl's head had jerked up in shock. She swiftly turned her bloodless face back to the ground, trembling delicately.

Finally, Gu Mang laid down that detestable smile. He looked at the man standing before him, at Mo Xi's stubborn and furious expression, his gaze inscrutable. "Have you lost your mind?" he whispered.

"You know exactly what I mean."

Gu Mang said nothing. Before he had been tempered in the Liao Kingdom, Gu Mang had been wickedly sharp, seeming to possess a demonic sixth sense that told him precisely what his Mo-shidi was thinking. But today, as he looked at the man before him, Gu Mang felt a sense of unfamiliarity; he couldn't read him at all. Gu Mang had wanted to make Mo Xi furious with him before he left. But now, as Mo Xi glared at him fiercely from across the room, Gu Mang found those sharp eyes filled with a mix of emotions he couldn't understand. There was heartbreak there, and dread, and hurt.

Yes, he seemed to look hurt. Gu Mang observed this almost helplessly. The rims of Mo Xi's eyes were already red with unshed tears.

Mo Xi clenched his jaw, eyes stinging. In a rough yet determined voice, he continued. "I've long lost any purity I had; I don't care about these things. You can't chase me away."

Gu Mang had no retort. He felt more and more helpless, more and more uneasy. In the end, he conceded; he couldn't change Mo Xi's mind. He sighed and turned to the pipa girl. "Miss Feitian, my apologies. There's a madman here—I must ask you to withdraw."

Miss Feitian finally heard the words she'd been waiting for. She excused herself and practically fled the Boudoir of Lingering Fragrance. Only the two men remained in the richly appointed room perfumed with incense.

Gu Mang came in from the balcony. He waved his hand to close the wooden doors, then turned into the room. A gentle flick of his fingertip lit the candle on the copper crane rack. Only then did he approach Mo Xi, coming dangerously close without the slightest hesitation, until mere inches remained between them.

Gu Mang looked up, a question in his dark eyes and provocation in his gaze. Their breaths rose and fell in the space between them. He reached out to stroke the line of Mo Xi's elegant jaw. "Look at you," he whispered. "Well done—you made such a fuss even the girl I paid for left. Are you pleased with yourself?"

Gu Mang sized him up as he would a brothel girl, scrutinizing Mo Xi's face. After a moment, his gaze slid down to Mo Xi's pale lips. He brushed his thumb over the softness of his mouth, caressing it.

"Since you were so keen to rush over here and fight for my favor... I'll allow you to accompany me for one last night," Gu Mang murmured. "After tonight, Princess, we'll keep to ourselves—no more of this."

He grabbed Mo Xi by the lapels and pulled him into a kiss.

There came a muffled groan. Wet lips captured cool ones, and a clever tongue snuck into Mo Xi's mouth to dance like a butterfly tasting nectar, drinking in his breath, his scent.

This same Gu-shixiong who spoke with cruel indifference was always the one to make the first move when they kissed. He enjoyed it, caressing Mo Xi with those soft and glossy lips, seducing him with those dense lashes, passionately pressing his tightly muscled abdomen against Mo Xi's, almost as if he wanted to become one with him.

But it was only ever *almost*, wasn't it. Gu Mang's forwardness was the cause, first for Mo Xi's misunderstanding, then later, his intoxication. In the end, the largest part of what was left for Mo Xi was heartbreak. He remembered vividly their first union on the night he came of age. His heart had felt steeped in honey—he'd assumed Gu Mang loved him back. He'd assumed that from then on, he could lock his shixiong to his side with assurance and take him for himself.

But in the light of day, Gu Mang had told him the events of that night were but a momentary impulse.

After that, they shared many such momentary impulses. He drove Gu Mang into delirium so many times, melted him into soft spring waters until Gu Mang, in his tent, couldn't help but say that he liked him. Until Gu Mang, in his arms, couldn't help but say that he wanted this. Until Gu Mang, in his stare, couldn't help but say that he loved him.

But once the storms of passion cleared, Gu Mang would change, waving it all off as a moment of indulgence. So Mo Xi had managed to lay claim to his body again and again, taking for himself all of the softness hidden within that chitinous shell. But these repeated entanglements, impossibly intimate yet impossibly sorrowful, only left Mo Xi ever more lost and heartbroken. He waited for Gu Mang to believe him, hoped for Gu Mang to treat him with sincerity.

But no matter how many times they lost themselves in each other, no matter what nonsense Gu Mang babbled as he shivered with passion—when day broke, never would Gu Mang acknowledge the feelings between them. Mo Xi couldn't understand this. He couldn't understand why Gu Mang would curl so close if he didn't love him back; why Gu Mang would tumble with him between the sheets if he didn't plan on spending a lifetime with him.

He understood even less why Gu Mang could now embrace and kiss him so freely when he intended to defect. Clearly Gu Mang already wanted to leave. He already *knew* he would leave, that they would be torn apart by their loyalties and meet next with blades drawn. How could he be so calm and composed...

Gu Mang abruptly hissed and pushed Mo Xi away. Pressing a hand to his lip, he stared at Mo Xi in shock. "Were you born in the year of the dog? What are you biting me for?!"

The rims of Mo Xi's eyes were wet and red, his expression betraying shame and anger, hatred and sorrow. In the glow of the lamplight, he stared into Gu Mang's eyes. Only after several seconds did he brusquely ask, "What do you take me for?"

"You're the one who wanted to take Miss Feitian's place and keep me company." Gu Mang paused; he had more to say, but the hurt on Mo Xi's face brought him up short. As he watched the young man standing before him—his chest heaving as he tried yet failed to stay calm—Gu Mang's resolve suddenly wavered.

Would Gu Mang really bed a man for no reason other than pleasure? He who was known as the Beast of the Altar, who commanded countless troops—would he willingly lie with a man three years his junior and allow himself to be fucked into delirium with no reservations?

No. He hadn't made a carnal mistake because of a silly impulse, nor did he repeat it just to chase a fleeting pleasure. In truth, Gu Mang had long since developed a fondness he barely recognized; from this rose the impulse, and from this the pleasure. His heart had stopped belonging to himself long ago—it was just that he was unwilling to admit or accept it.

Gu Mang looked into Mo Xi's reddened eyes and sighed. He lifted a hand, wanting to touch his young and handsome face. "Oh, you... If I'm not here in the future..."

Mo Xi's eyes filled with tears. He couldn't hold back any longer. He reached out and wrapped his arms around Gu Mang, hugging him so tightly, so forcefully, so deeply, as if he wanted to break Gu Mang apart and smuggle him into his bones, as if he wanted to use his own flesh to imprison Gu Mang's. Only then could he keep this man with him forever. Only thus could he prevent that future betrayal, that future confrontation and the dagger in his heart.

Gu Mang sighed in his arms. "What's gotten into you today?"

"I just want you to be well." Mo Xi rested his chin on the top of Gu Mang's head as he held him tight. "If there's any sadness or grievance in your heart, won't you tell me?" Mo Xi asked hoarsely. "Could you let me share the burden? Could you not overthink it? Don't bear it all alone..."

"Mo Xi..."

Mo Xi cupped the back of Gu Mang's head with a large hand, folding him even more tightly, even more deeply into his embrace.

The pain of regaining what was lost, only to soon lose what he'd regained, set every inch of him to shaking, reawakened every piece of him. Mo Xi held this Gu Mang of eight years past like he was embracing a wandering ghost that had finally come home. He closed his eyes, his straight brows drawing together as he murmured, "Shixiong...if there's something on your mind, could you not hide it from me?"

The person in his arms stiffened slightly but remained silent.

After a time, Gu Mang pushed him away. He pressed a hand to Mo Xi's chest, keeping them at arm's length. Those eyes, black as night, calmly met Mo Xi's.

"Xihe-jun," he asked lightly, "what is it you think I've hidden from you?"

84

Lu Zhanxing of Eight Years Ago

A S GU MANG ASKED this question, an indescribable apathy came over his face. His mischievous smile had disappeared, but the sharp viciousness within him was yet to be unsheathed. He looked at Mo Xi the way he'd look at a stranger.

Of course Mo Xi couldn't ask if he had thought of defecting. He closed his eyes and murmured, "I know you're still greatly displeased with Chonghua and His Imperial Majesty. I—"

"Don't." Gu Mang raised a finger to Mo Xi's lips. He stared at Mo Xi, then broke into a grin, a touch of sweetness surfacing on his features, along with a profuse danger. "Sleeping around is one thing, gorgeous, but running my mouth is another entirely. Now that I've lost my rank, my remaining soldiers are imprisoned, and my brother is set to be executed at the eastern market in three days' time—*now* you come ask me whether I'm displeased with His Imperial Majesty? Do you want to saddle me with yet another sentence and see me even more hopelessly damned?"

"I've never wanted to do that to you."

"You don't want to now, but that doesn't mean you won't in the future. A beauty's favor always comes with danger, to say nothing of one as beautiful as you." Gu Mang traced Mo Xi's lips with a finger, then down to his chin to tilt his face upward. "I can't help but be wary."

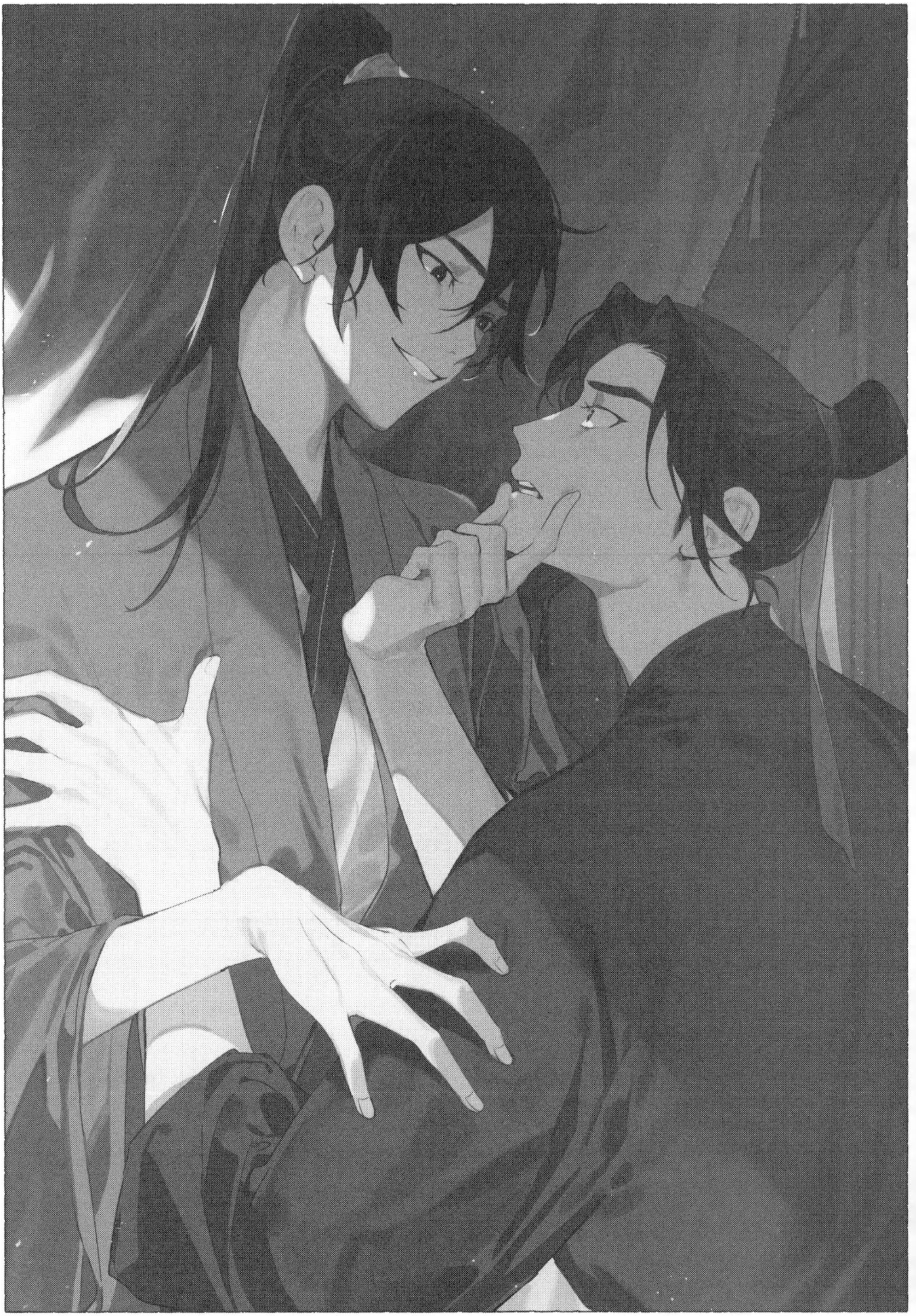

"Gu Mang." Mo Xi looked at him through somber, sorrowful eyes as he said roughly, "My feelings for you are sincere."

"You nobles have gotten too used to doling out rewards. You gift jewelry to please women and power to please men. When that no longer works, you decide to make a gift of your sincerity as well. How could I dare accept it?" Gu Mang sighed. "People's hearts are ever-changing. Even His Imperial Majesty was devoted to me once. Back when I was fighting to expand Chonghua's borders, I never imagined that the next ruler would treat me like this after taking the throne." He paused. "I can't understand you people."

"Including me?"

Another pause. The corners of Gu Mang's mouth deepened into a smile. He had an uncanny ability: when he was happy, the traces of his smile made others feel they were bathed by a warm spring breeze. But when he was upset, that spring breeze became a wintry rain.

He patted Mo Xi's face. "Including you, darling."

Mo Xi grasped his fingers before he could move them away. Gu Mang looked up slowly, lashes fluttering. "Let go."

But Mo Xi didn't. He was undoubtedly hurt and despairing. But these emotions were like darkening storm clouds, lending his aura a deep stubbornness and shadow.

"How would you like me to prove it?" Mo Xi tightened his grip on Gu Mang's fingers, light flickering unsteadily in his eyes. "Gu Mang, at this point, are you only willing to believe people of common birth like you? Would you listen if Lu Zhanxing were the one standing before you?"

Gu Mang's expression didn't change. "Surely Xihe-jun jests," he said lightly. "I am no more than a lowly slave. You're all the ones who never believed my words—when was it my choice to believe or not?"

As Mo Xi studied him, it dawned on him that, right now, Gu Mang already wore the same expression as the traitorous general who had turned on his nation. In the depths of his eyes, his departure was a sure thing. He was like a man standing at the edge of a cliff, ready to throw himself into the boundless dark below at a moment's notice.

Mo Xi swallowed—it turned out that there had been many signs. He had just been too young to understand Gu Mang's true feelings, to the point that he'd missed all these hints that foretold the future. He closed his eyes and slowly released Gu Mang's hand. "I'm sorry," he murmured.

"Why are you apologizing to *me*?"

"For not being at your side the day you and your troops returned."

Gu Mang said nothing for a moment, then smiled. "You were still fighting on the front lines at the time, so I understood. Anyway, what would you have done even if you'd been there? Could you have changed anything?"

He sat down at the table covered with vibrant Shu-style embroidery and poured two cups of tea. Gu Mang's arms were still golden and firm with muscle, not bone-pale as they would later become. He pushed one cup toward Mo Xi and took a sip from the other. "Xihe-jun, this punishment was the new emperor's idea. It's not something you could change by pleading on my behalf. I've never resented you for not being there that day. But to be honest, our paths were never the same. Different people walk different roads, that's all. You don't owe me an apology."

"This apology isn't for you alone," Mo Xi said. "Will you let me finish?"

Gu Mang tossed him a careless smile. "Sure, go ahead. If it's not just for me, who else is it for?"

"The seventy thousand souls at Phoenix Cry Mountain."

Gu Mang fell silent.

"I'm sorry, Gu Mang. Chonghua owes you seventy thousand named graves."

The smile on Gu Mang's face faded. His lashes fluttered, then lowered as he sighed. "It's been so long since that happened, Mo Xi. I've already gotten over it. Why bring it up again?"

Mo Xi looked at this man who spent his days in a brothel making songstresses play the soul song, this man who claimed to have "gotten over it." After a few beats of silence, he said, "I will petition His Imperial Majesty for the gravestones you asked for."

Gu Mang had been toying with the cup in his hand, but his head shot up when he heard this. For some reason, a change came over his face. "Who asked you to meddle?"

"I'm not meddling," Mo Xi said.

Gu Mang scowled, a look that gave every impression of a wary beast. "Listen up, Mo Xi. Even if my army's been disbanded, they're still men that *I* led. Dead or alive, they are my people, not yours. You have no right to act on my behalf!"

"It's what they deserve, what each martyred hero is due. You were right to ask for them. If your plea goes unanswered, I will ask in your stead."

The room was silent, like they had sunk to depths of the sea. Gu Mang glared at Mo Xi, but he didn't utter a word.

After a moment, he lowered his head and closed his eyes. For the first time since Mo Xi entered the room, he saw a crack in Gu Mang's cold mask, the sorrow behind it surging forth like a tide. Cast in shadow, Gu Mang hung his head and chuckled. "Xihe-jun, you must be kidding. What martyred heroes...? They were no more than ants."

Mo Xi made no reply.

"How could ants be worthy of gravestones? Even if they were erected, it would be an awful joke. Who would make offerings to them? Who would honor them?" Gu Mang gripped the cup in his slender fingers. He stared at the tea inside, at the reflections on the surface. "Even if they were erected, they would be glorified heaps of rubble. I've long stopped demanding it."

Mo Xi watched him carefully.

"There's no need for you to involve yourself. This is a matter for us lowborn; it's nothing to do with Xihe-jun."

"Gu Mang..." There seemed to be something stuck in Mo Xi's throat. After a long interval, he asked, "What can I do so you stop being like this?"

"You don't have to do anything at all." Gu Mang set the cup back down on the table. "Just be good and leave me alone. Time heals all things."

But time can't heal hatred. Time can't unpick the knot in your heart, nor can it stop you from staking it all and tossing yourself off the cliff. It will only wear you down into something unrecognizable, bleach your black eyes to blue, cover your body in scars, and grind your reputation into the mud.

Time can only bring me your ruins. Gu Mang, I've come from the future. I've already seen how this ends.

Each breath pained him like the twist of a knife. Mo Xi endured the agony, his nails sinking deep into his palm as he whispered, "What about, after..."

"After?"

"What are you going to do after?"

"What else can I do? Revel in the pleasures of the flesh," Gu Mang said. "His Imperial Majesty stripped my rank, but he at least let me keep my money. From now on, I'll live however I please. It's not a bad deal."

"There's nothing else you want?"

"Nothing at all."

Mo Xi parted his lips but didn't speak. He wanted to recklessly blurt out: *Stop lying to me. I know everything that happens in the next eight years. I know what kind of doomed path you'll take if I leave you be.* But he couldn't. The ancient books recorded that if a traveler in the Time Mirror were to reveal they had come from the future, they would be trapped there forever, unable to escape.

Mo Xi wanted so very much to understand the truth of the past and what Gu Mang had been thinking then. He wanted to know what he could have done to stop Gu Mang from stepping into the darkness.

How many weights pressing on Gu Mang's heart needed release? His Imperial Majesty's cruel words, Gu Mang's own despair. What else was there? Were there other burdens Mo Xi didn't know of, or that he had overlooked—

In the warm, dimly lit room, Mo Xi stood beside Gu Mang from eight years in the past, mind racing like a trapped beast.

Weights on his heart... Were there any others he didn't know of...?

Realization dawned, striking cold into Mo Xi's heart. He suddenly recalled an old matter he had forgotten.

Back then, when he had returned from the northern frontier and heard of Gu Mang's treason, he couldn't believe it. As if mad, he had questioned anyone who might know anything. Someone had told him this: "After you left, His Imperial Majesty summoned Gu Mang to the palace. He saw Gu Mang idling in such low spirits and thought it a shame to waste someone like him, that he could still be of use. So he gave Gu Mang a mission. Gu Mang accepted and left Chonghua, but he never returned to make his report."

Mo Xi had made relentless interrogations, trying to uncover what the emperor had asked of Gu Mang. But no one knew for sure.

"I heard it was some minor matter, something about getting back on his feet, but Gu Mang didn't want to listen and left quite quickly. He didn't even stay in the hall for the time it takes a stick of incense to burn."

"It should have been a very small assignment, really."

In the end, the only answers he got were about how the emperor wanted Gu Mang to pull himself together, but Gu Mang turned a deaf ear. Mo Xi had taken note of this at the time, but as the years passed, that detail gradually faded from his memory. Yet now, as he recalled it, his hands grew sweaty, fingers curling into fists. He had just witnessed for himself His Imperial Majesty's attitude; the emperor meant to test Gu Mang's loyalty. Why would he so solicitously ask after Gu Mang's welfare at a time like this? It couldn't possibly have been the real reason behind the mission.

Mo Xi examined Gu Mang's face in the rosy candlelight. If Gu Mang hadn't yet decided to defect, then Lu Zhanxing's death and the emperor's assignment could very well be the two things that finally pushed Gu Mang to jump into the abyss of vengeance. His heart galloped in his chest. The more he spoke with these people of the past and considered the course of events, the more he sensed strange clues everywhere. Something else must have happened back then—there must have been a piece he had missed. What was the last mission the emperor had given Gu Mang?

The only stroke of luck was that time passed differently in the Time Mirror. One or two days in the Mirror corresponded to a much briefer period on the outside. Murong Chuyi and Jiang Yexue couldn't defeat the shangao and rescue them that quickly.

He still had time. He could investigate what happened eight years ago.

In the end, Mo Xi left the brothel. Despite how deeply he longed to talk with Gu Mang in his right mind, his rational judgment still won out. He stepped back into the street, seeking out a third person from the past.

Within a cell in the deepest recesses of the imperial prison, a single oil lamp burned, its flame a dark blue glow. There was no other source of light. Lu Zhanxing lay on the icy stone bed with one leg jauntily propped up, humming as he tossed a pair of dice he'd gotten from who knew where. He wore a set of loose, clean prisoner's robes, the snowy-white lapels setting off his tanned and chiseled face.

Possibly because his execution was at hand, or perhaps because he had a knack for making friends, the jailers hadn't abused him. The cell was furnished with a little table, on which a pot of wine had even been placed. By the look of it, it was likely the flower wine issued to all the jailers in Chonghua.

The first person Mo Xi had needed to see when he entered the Time Mirror was the emperor—an inexperienced new ruler. The second person was Gu Mang—an old friend who hadn't yet lost his souls.

The third person he had to see was Lu Zhanxing—a dead man from his memories.

Mo Xi stopped outside his cell and turned to the warden who led him there. "You may go."

"Yes sir."

Lu Zhanxing hadn't yet recognized Mo Xi's voice. He thought the prison guard had gotten bored and come to chat with him, so he pulled himself up to a sloppy seat on the bed. He propped a cheek on one hand, tossing the pair of dice in the other. "Divination[7]

---

7   Divination (zhanxing, 占星) sounds similar to Lu Zhanxing's name (展星).

and fortune telling, the journey of fate—the words of a man on his deathbed always strike true. Your Lu-ge can part the veil of the heavens with just two dice. Twenty silver cowries to have your fortune read, double if you're asking about your fated other half."

As Mo Xi entered his cell, he pulled back the hood of his black cape. Lu Zhanxing flicked a lazy glance up, only to freeze at the sight of Mo Xi's face. He missed the dice as they fell; they tumbled to the edge of the bed. "Xihe-jun?"

Mo Xi swept a glance over the dice and the wine on the table. After a pause, he said, "This is the first time I've seen someone imprisoned in such conditions."

Lu Zhanxing lay back down on the bed, limbs askew, and grinned. One hand groped for his fallen dice. "Would you like your fortune told? This stall of mine is closing up for good in three days' time. You'd better not miss this chance."

Mo Xi sat down across from him. "Why don't you read your own fortune?"

"I already have." Lu Zhanxing waggled his stinky feet. "I, Phony Prophet Lu, am a general whose successes cost ten thousand withered bones,[8] but I can wither ten thousand bones even in failure. I've spent most of a year in this cell and have read my fortune hundreds of times. Nothing much to see there."

Mo Xi raised a hand and cast a soundproof barrier in the cell.

"What are you doing?" Lu Zhanxing asked.

"I've come to ask you a question."

As usual, Lu Zhanxing never took things seriously. "About your fated match?"

"About injustice."

---

8   A line from the poem "Two Poems in the Year 879," by Cao Song, which laments the countless soldiers that must be sacrificed for a great general to be awarded his accolades.

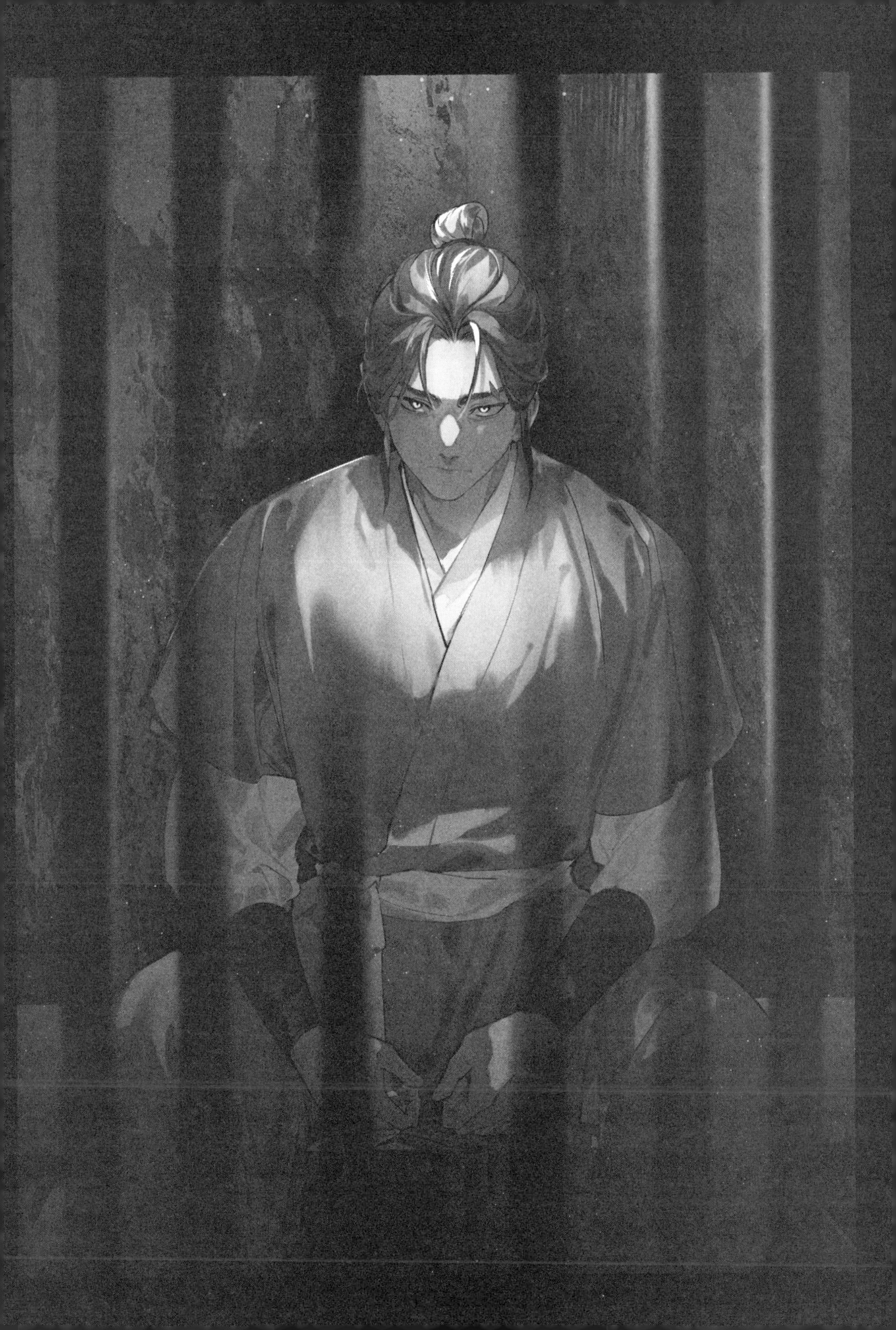

Lu Zhanxing fiddled silently with the dice in his hands. Only after a long beat did he chuckle. "How noble of you."

"Gu Mang doesn't want to see you go. So I'm here to ask— Lu Zhanxing, is there some injustice regarding the battle at Phoenix Cry Mountain that you wish to make known?"

Lu Zhanxing tossed the dice onto the stone bed. Displeased with the result, he picked them up and tossed them again. Only after many repeated tries did he finally roll a pair of sixes and stop. Looking up, he bared his teeth at Mo Xi in a grin. "Yes. His Imperial Majesty arrested me because I killed the envoy. I'll fucking take the blame for what I did, but because of my mistake, Chonghua punished Gu Mang and thirty thousand survivors. Why is that, if I may ask?"

There were not many people who could stir Mo Xi to anger with a few words, but Lu Zhanxing was one of them. What did he mean, *take the blame*? This impertinent man only understood instant gratification; he'd never cared for strategy or collaboration. He did as he pleased, and his last hotheaded impulse had sent Gu Mang into impossible circumstances. Mo Xi gritted his teeth. "Why couldn't you control yourself? Regardless of how improper or suspicious that envoy's actions were, did *you* have the right to execute him?"

85

The Plan of Eight Years Ago

L U ZHANXING SMILED. "What's done is done—I've already killed him. What else is there to say?"

"Lu Zhanxing!" Mo Xi snapped, dark brows drawing together in anger. "Do you know what things are like on the outside?"

"What are they like?"

"After the defeat at Phoenix Cry Mountain, where your seventy thousand comrades died in battle, the remaining thirty thousand were taken into custody and await their sentence even now. The dead are without gravestones, and the living have no way forward! And Gu Mang...all his achievements have been erased. His Imperial Majesty will never again use him for matters of importance. Almost everything he cares for has been destroyed, yet all you can say is 'what's done is done'?"

Lu Zhanxing listened in silence, though his rough fingers never stopped moving the dice. After a moment, his mouth split into a mocking grin. "Isn't it a good thing, to never again be used by the emperor for important matters?"

Mo Xi stared in shock. What did Lu Zhanxing mean?

Lu Zhanxing and Gu Mang had grown up together and were thus inseparable, but Mo Xi understood little about this brother of Gu Mang's. Countless times, he had seen Lu Zhanxing embrace Gu Mang and ruffle his hair as the pair of them laughed uproariously.

He saw, too, that Gu Mang would regularly help Lu Zhanxing dress his wounds. It bothered him. No matter that it was proven again and again that Lu Zhanxing adored women and Gu Mang harbored no feelings beyond friendship for him, still Mo Xi was bothered. The sight of Lu Zhanxing made his skin crawl with irritation.

Likewise, Lu Zhanxing had a poor impression of Mo Xi. From his perspective, his childhood buddy had suddenly, for some inexplicable reason, gained an aristocratic young master as a bosom friend. Of course the intrusion displeased him; plus, this little aristocrat constantly monopolized Gu Mang's free time. Oh, he needed Gu Mang to accompany him while patrolling or cultivating. And sometimes, when Lu Zhanxing was wounded, that rich young master would promptly also get hurt, forcing Gu Mang to rush back and forth between them. The first time it happened could be chalked up to coincidence, but when it kept on happening, Lu Zhanxing began to suspect that the Mo brat was doing it on purpose.

And so Lu Zhanxing's initial courtesy toward Mo Xi turned chilly. When the two crossed paths, they would pretend not to see each other. If Gu Mang was watching, they would halfheartedly nod in greeting.

Given this standoffish relationship of theirs, Mo Xi's understanding of Lu Zhanxing remained entirely superficial. Mo Xi had presumed Lu Zhanxing would at least feel regret or shame for the disaster he'd brought down on his brother's head—never had he imagined that Lu Zhanxing would look as if he'd gotten exactly what he wanted.

At the sight of Mo Xi's bloodless face, Lu Zhanxing stretched his limbs into a more comfortable sprawl and continued to toss his dice. "In any case, I'm a dead man walking. There's no harm in saying what I truly think."

Mo Xi gritted his teeth. "What other disgraceful last words do you have?"

"They're not so disgraceful." Lu Zhanxing snickered. "I think I've been awfully clever—it's just that I had to sacrifice a bit more than I should have. But I've more or less achieved my aim."

"What do you mean?"

Baring his teeth like a wolf, Lu Zhanxing shot Mo Xi a glance designed to provoke. Eyes never moving from Mo Xi, he said, "Do you all think I killed that envoy because I felt him suspicious? That I was further enraged by his disrespect, so I beheaded him on impulse?"

Mo Xi's lips parted. "Is that not so?" he asked softly.

Lu Zhanxing swung one leg over the other and scoffed. "Xihe-jun, do you think so little of me and Mang-er?" He spoke lazily, his expression open and uninhibited. "Mang-er and I grew up together. Did you think he would appoint me his deputy general were I really so stupid and reckless? He's a demon of war, not an idiot who lets his emotions call the shots."

The candle within the cell silently shed its waxen tears. Lu Zhanxing's words almost made Mo Xi tremble in fear. "You did it on purpose..."

"I've fought with him on so many battlefields, for so many years. When have I ever done anything so irreversible on impulse?" Lu Zhanxing said casually. "Yes. I did it on purpose."

Air whipped through the cell as Mo Xi yanked Lu Zhanxing from the bed and shoved him against the stone wall. Two lamps guttered out and the cell sank into gloom, but Mo Xi's eyes seemed only brighter. In the darkness, they glimmered with flame, sparking with disbelieving wrath. His knuckles strained; he was on the verge of simply snapping Lu Zhanxing's neck. "Lu Zhanxing! Are you fucking insane? Do you have any idea what you've done? You've ruined his life!"

Lu Zhanxing's face flushed red in Mo Xi's grip. He looked down at Mo Xi with a single breath remaining in his lungs. Even so, he still plastered a mocking smile onto his face. "Having me ruin his life is still better than seeing him ruin his own and the lives of others." Lu Zhanxing ground each syllable between his teeth as light flashed in his eyes. "Still better than...letting him lead a flock of idiots, driven by a dream doomed to fail...to risk their lives on behalf of you people..." Mo Xi was choking him so hard that vessels stood out on his forehead, but he still he said contemptuously, "Risking their lives...like fools! His Imperial Majesty was right to strip him of his power!"

Upon hearing that honest shout, Mo Xi dropped him as if bitten by a wild dog. He stood there panting, hands shaking in fury. He felt cold all over. How many truths from eight years ago were hidden in bloodshed and death?

The instant Mo Xi let go, Lu Zhanxing doubled over and coughed violently. Only after many great, gasping breaths did he turn his face up.

Mo Xi's voice sounded hollow and empty. "You ruined him on purpose?"

"Wrong." Lu Zhanxing licked his lips and rose slowly. "I saved him."

Mo Xi looked at him as if he'd heard the most absurd joke. "Saved him?"

"Yes," said Lu Zhanxing. "How could a noble young master like yourself, born into the lap of luxury, understand our circumstances? Ever since the late emperor made an exception for Mang-er, started making use of him, he's fought countless battles without ever tasting defeat. But the higher he flies, the more inexplicable the criticism slung at him. I wonder, Xihe-jun, if you've heard the things they say?"

Mo Xi fell silent. He didn't know whence those slanderous rumors had originated, but they were like innumerable demons and monsters dancing wildly behind the curtain of night. How could Mo Xi not have heard them? When Gu Mang had been only a minor officer, there were a few comments and jabs. But as he gained more valor and distinguished himself further, those cold and malicious words turned into a swarm of snakes, slipping from unknown tongues to wrap themselves inextricably around Gu Mang's limbs.

"He's just biding his time, hiding who he really is."

"Beast of the Altar? What real ability has he got? And don't you think his strategies and illusions feel a bit...dark? He's too opportunistic; I've heard he even dabbles in black magic spells of the Liao Kingdom."

"He's a slave after all, not a proper cultivator born of a noble house. Of course he'd have dishonest ambitions. If His Imperial Majesty keeps trusting him so—pardon my disrespect—ill will befall Chonghua sooner or later."

There were even those who directly compared Gu Mang to that villain from the past.

"He's just the next Hua Po'an!"

"The nation's inviting disaster upon itself!"

Watching Mo Xi's expression, Lu Zhanxing laughed, his slender lips curving. "It seems Xihe-jun isn't totally deaf to it all."

Stepping over to the little table, Lu Zhanxing sat down. He tossed the pair of dice onto its surface, then poured a measure of wine for himself and took an unhurried sip. "Mang-er has pretty much heard it all. It made me furious, but he would always say there was no need to take these words to heart. He would say that as long as we proved ourselves, these voices would falter by and by.

More and more people would understand that not all slaves would be like Hua Po'an. There were those like him, Gu Mang, and me, Lu Zhanxing."

Lu Zhanxing smiled bitterly. "He's just naive. Or maybe it's not that he's naive. It's that he always sees the best in things—despite living in the mud, he still insists on raising his head to look up into the boundless sunlight."

"Yes," Mo Xi said softly. "He's always been like this."

"You probably understand why he's a war god," Lu Zhanxing continued. "He's never faltered. No matter how difficult the battle, he always made it seem like it was no big deal. He had an endless, inexhaustible passion, more than enough..." He sneered. "More than enough for the leech that is Chonghua to suck from him till bloated."

It was a cruel thing to say. "That's what *you* think!" Mo Xi fixed Lu Zhanxing with an icy glare. "That's why *he's* the war god, and not you. He's the one who wanted to take new territory; he's the one who wanted to prove himself."

Lu Zhanxing smiled grimly but said nothing.

"Not everyone who steps onto the battlefield imagines that their blood is being drained," Mo Xi said. "Gu Mang had his own ideals— he said he chose this path for himself with no regrets."

"Ha ha...ha ha ha... No regrets, no regrets..." Lu Zhanxing threw his head back and laughed. The chains on his wrists and ankles clanged as they swayed. "That's why I said he's stupid! Look at him! So many years of merits and honor, and what has he proved? Did those voices pecking at him stop? All he's done is make those old nobles fearful as they see a face that looks more and more like Hua Po'an's with each passing day. After so many years of him constantly proving himself, I've never seen anyone who hates him change their tune. I've only seen those who once tolerated him begin to suspect him at every turn.

Tell me, Xihe-jun, what did he prove? Didn't he merely prove he can mobilize troops just as well as Hua Po'an?!"

Mo Xi couldn't contain his fury any longer. "Then what do you want?! To prevent him from continuing on this stupid path by giving him no other choice but to follow in Hua Po'an's footsteps in actuality?"

Lu Zhanxing slapped the table. "I just hoped he would stop!"

Wine splashed over the rim of the cup, and the dice tumbled on the stained old table.

"...I just hoped he would stop." Lu Zhanxing repeated. These words seemed to have struck something tender in that coarse heart. His eyes lost focus, and his voice softened as he mumbled, "I just wanted him to wake up...to stop...to not be so naive."

Lu Zhanxing closed his eyes. His face was flushed with emotion, but his voice had gone hoarse with the helplessness of despair. "It's been so many years... His future seemed so bright. You saw him taken off the slave registry, you saw his fame spread throughout the land as he was showered in praise—but when I look at him, I see him standing on an iceberg about to melt, surrounded by sharks waiting to tear him apart the instant he touches the water."

He looked up at Mo Xi. "Power threatens kings. Not just for him—this goes for you too. Xihe-jun, can you afford to have these words applied to you?"

Mo Xi said nothing.

"But he refused to take it seriously." Lu Zhanxing took up a white and red die again, slowly spinning it on the table. "You see, he's gone undefeated—his army's gone undefeated. No one could find a real reason to act against him. But he can't go a lifetime without defeat. And the consequences of defeat for him are destined to be more tragic than that of any other general with the power to pose a threat."

Mo Xi tensed.

Without a shred of courtesy, Lu Zhanxing said, "Because, from the beginning, he was no more than a dog you people picked off the streets."

If someone had dared to say these things to Mo Xi before he entered the Time Mirror, he would have roundly denied it. But he'd just heard the emperor himself speak those words: *Gu Mang is nothing but a dog.* He had no way to refute what Lu Zhanxing was saying. The more truths he uncovered, the more his heart ached, and the more his blood chilled. That fire in his chest seemed to be slowly guttering out.

Lu Zhanxing sighed. "The new emperor has recently ascended; Mang-er hasn't angered him much. At this point, his defeat because of my actions only resulted in him being stripped of his power and dismissed from his position. His life isn't under threat. If he had continued to behave so recklessly—if he had suffered defeat at the pinnacle of power—he would die mutilated and scorned."

Mo Xi's throat was raw. "So you did it on purpose..."

"Yes." Lu Zhanxing smiled lightly and crossed his arms. "I have divine omniscience; I can see heaven's will. Yes, I made him lose on purpose. I wrecked his future on purpose. Reality has proven the accuracy of my guess—look. Sure enough, he has nothing left."

Mo Xi's fingertips were trembling; he stared into Lu Zhanxing's face. Today he had finally gained some understanding of what kind of person Lu Zhanxing was.

A madman. A madman who risked it all.

Mo Xi forced out each word from between his clenched teeth. "Lu Zhanxing! Don't you know...seventy thousand soldiers died because of you?"

"Better than seven hundred thousand to come."

"Don't you see that you destroyed Gu Mang's life's work?"

"Better than for him to end up drawn and quartered, tortured to death."

Wrathful fire gripped Mo Xi; his heart throbbed violently. Fingertips trembling, he grabbed Lu Zhanxing and slapped him fiercely across the face.

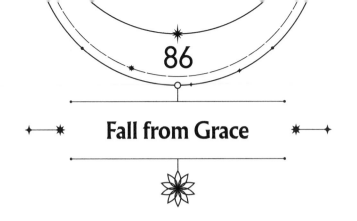

86

Fall from Grace

THE SLAP LANDED with an audible *crack*, with Mo Xi's full strength behind it. Lu Zhanxing's cheek swelled almost instantly, and blood ran from the corner of his mouth.

Mo Xi stared at him viciously, the rims of his eyes a bloody red. His voice shook with every syllable: "What right do you have to decide for him? What right do you have to choose for him? Do you know what desperate straits he'll be in after your death, after the deaths of his seventy thousand comrades who can never return? Are you trying to push him into the abyss, Lu Zhanxing?" Fire blazed in his eyes. "You wanted to preserve his life," he howled, "but have you ever really understood his heart?"

Lu Zhanxing's voice rose as well, his bloodstained lips parting. "His heart soars too high! Sooner or later, it'll have him strung up! What do you know?!"

Their exchange was like the clashing of two swords, or a battle between beasts.

"You were born to a life of luxury; your so-called 'troubles' were nothing more than some family drama! What have you experienced of the hopelessness that comes from your life hanging by a thread at another's whim? Do you know how hard it's been for Gu Mang to make it this far?" Lu Zhanxing seemed to choke with anger and despair. "He's just a stupid donkey; you people took the slave collar off his neck and dangled rank and fortune as carrots in front of him, but did anything change? He's still shedding blood and sweat, pulling the grindstone for you, but somehow he's stupidly delighted about it..."

At this point, Lu Zhanxing helplessly tilted his head back and covered his eyes with an arm as he rasped, "But a donkey is still a donkey. One day, when he gets lazy or tired, when he can't walk anymore, he'll still be consigned to the slaughterhouse!"

He let out a long sigh. "What he can't see, I'll help him understand. What he understands but can't let go of, I'll force him to give up! He thought he owed the old emperor a debt, so I waited. I waited for the new emperor to ascend before making my move, so that he wouldn't be scorning the old emperor's favor. What *haven't* I thoroughly considered for his sake?"

"Lu Zhanxing..." The emotion Mo Xi was suppressing in his throat surged like lava. "You're insane..."

"I'm not insane. He is." Lu Zhanxing lowered his arm. His eyes were faintly red, but the softness in them had been completely cast away, leaving only a ruthless hatred. He stared at Mo Xi. "How crazy does Mang-er have to be to believe he can singlehandedly change the opinion of all the people of Chonghua and the Nine Provinces when it comes to slaves? How crazy does he have to be, how *insane*, to think there's hope for any of this!"

"You'd rather he lose the fire in his heart so he can live the life you chose for him?" Mo Xi asked hoarsely.

"What's so bad about living in poverty, away from the whims of the court? A person is no more than a drop of water in the sea, yet he believes that a mayfly can shake the skies. Look, now he understands how this will end—all it takes is the emperor opening his mouth for his castle in the sky to crumble to nothing. For the price of seventy thousand lives, neither Gu Mang nor those poor, stupid slave culti-vators will ever again sacrifice their lives for Chonghua!"

Lu Zhanxing's lips twisted in a smile. "Whoever rules the nation should guard the nation. Please, noble gongzi Xihe-jun, *please* stop meddling. Just let his laughable army fall apart. We'd rather a grace-less life than an honorable death."

We? We? Ever since his academy days, Gu Mang had said, his voice filled with longing, that he wished for a day when the world would change—that he wished he himself could change the ways of the world, even if just the slightest bit. As long as he could ignite a single sunbeam, he was willing to burn himself up in exchange, skin and bone. And here was Lu Zhanxing saying that "we" would rather a graceless life than an honorable death. What right did he have?!

Mo Xi felt a flare of staggering rage, but this conflict with Lu Zhanxing had already intensified to the point that a momentary slip would result in bloodshed. He didn't want to throw the events within the Time Mirror into chaos, so he forced himself to close his eyes.

Only after some seconds did his overwhelming anger recede. Mo Xi slowly opened his eyes, black pupils fixing upon Lu Zhanxing once more. He wanted to have a proper conversation with the man, but Lu Zhanxing struck out at him yet again.

"Xihe-jun, leave him alone. I won't be able to keep him company in the future. Please, sir, have some mercy. Don't give him any more fatal hope."

Mo Xi realized he couldn't look at Lu Zhanxing another second; even one glance would fan the embers of the rage he had just suppressed. He jerked away to stare at the swaying candle flame beside him.

"Stop leading him down that road," Lu Zhanxing continued.

Fingers curling silently into fists, Mo Xi's gaze wandered from the candle to the two dice Lu Zhanxing had been playing with. He wasn't really interested in the dice; in his pain and anger, he just wanted to find something to focus on, somewhere to rest his gaze. He stared at those two white dice with red lacquer for a long time. Presently, he sensed that something wasn't quite right—the hairs on the back of his neck prickled as he was hit with a sudden realization.

Mo Xi's spine stiffened. These dice...

These dice were white with red lacquer, carved from rosewood, with an unremarkable little lotus motif in place of the sixth dot. Could they be...Gu Mang's wooden dice?

Indeed—back in the army, Gu Mang had liked playing yezi cards and dice gambling. He'd envied the insignia of the Mo, Yue, and Murong Clans, so he cleverly and sneakily invented one for himself. What he came up with was a Buddha's lotus. He didn't want to be mocked, so he only carved it on this set of dice he tossed with his brothers—it would be too vainglorious to put it anywhere else.

Back then, Lu Zhanxing had teased, "You're a grown man; why are you using a little red lotus as a symbol?"

"A lotus blooms for seven days," Gu Mang explained with a grin. "Even though it's not long, its gentle fragrance can fill the skies. What's wrong with that?"

Later yet, when Gu Mang and Mo Xi secretly set their blood seals and marked their necks with a sigil, they used the symbol Gu Mang had chosen.

As Mo Xi realized all this, Lu Zhanxing's voice sounded as if it were coming from an ocean away. Mo Xi paid no heed to what he was saying; his fingers were shaking, itching to grab the dice and examine them thoroughly.

"Xihe-jun."

Mo Xi ignored him.

"Let Mang-er go," Lu Zhanxing continued. "If you really care for him and see him as a person, stop stringing him along, forcing him to slaughter and sacrifice for your sakes. Let him go."

Swallowing thickly, Mo Xi managed to rein in his impulse. After some silence, he turned away from the dice, face pale. Looking back at Lu Zhanxing, he murmured, "With this plan you've made for him, are you so certain he'll walk the path you've arranged, living the rest of his life free as a wild crane?"

"What other path is open to him?"

Mo Xi stared dark-eyed into Lu Zhanxing's face. "Have you never thought he might defect?"

Lu Zhanxing looked at him in confusion. He seemed to find the idea almost laughable. "What nonsense are you talking? Mang-er, defect? Do you not know what kind of person he is?"

"Then surely you know how important you and those hundred thousand cultivators are in his heart?"

Lu Zhanxing's face went pale. After a momentary silence, he looked up in clear disbelief. "There's no way," he said stiffly.

Mo Xi assessed every inch of his face, taking in Lu Zhanxing's reactions.

"I know him," Lu Zhanxing said. "It doesn't matter what state he's in, he would never do that... He...he..."

"Is that so?" Mo Xi asked. "You've never heard of him acting strangely in the six months you've been in prison?"

Lu Zhanxing took a step back, a strange panic visible in his eyes.

Just as expected... Lu Zhanxing seemed to know something he didn't. This man was hiding a secret. Into this strained silence, Mo Xi said carelessly, without preamble, "Lu Zhanxing, you've seen Gu Mang since entering prison, haven't you."

Lu Zhanxing jerked as if struck by a hidden arrow. His head snapped up and his face drained of color; he quickly turned away. After a long beat, he asked, "What is Xihe-jun thinking? Mang-er is a criminal now; how could he come visit me? Of course I want to see him again and talk about old times. But..." He chuckled, smiling as if to mock himself. "Better to dream it instead—it would feel more real in a dream."

Mo Xi said nothing more. He'd gotten his answer in Lu Zhanxing's reaction. His eyes darkened. He was almost certain that Gu Mang had met with Lu Zhanxing in the past six months. But this made the whole thing even more bizarre. How could Gu Mang, a demoted official monitored by His Imperial Majesty's spies, manage to get past all the guards in the imperial prison and enter Lu Zhanxing's cell?

"I'm going to ask you one last time," Mo Xi said. "Lu Zhanxing, Gu Mang really hasn't come to see you?"

A pause. "He hasn't."

"And you haven't endured the slightest injustice?"

"I haven't."

Mo Xi knew he wouldn't get a reasonable answer however he asked. In the end, they failed to have a meaningful conversation; neither would convince the other, nor cede to him. Mo Xi strode out of the dim and cold inner cell of the prison. The door clanged shut behind him, enchanted iron chains sealing Lu Zhanxing's cell once more.

Before Mo Xi left for good, he turned to take a final look at Lu Zhanxing. The man sat in the murky halo of the oil lamp, his head bowed and eyes closed. As Mo Xi turned to go, Lu Zhanxing looked up once more. "Wait a minute!"

Mo Xi pursed his thin lips and gazed sidelong at him. "What is it?"

Lu Zhanxing gritted his teeth. "One more thing. Since you're here, I also have a question for you."

"Go ahead."

Lu Zhanxing hesitated. This question had been bottled up in his heart for a terribly long time, so long it had practically rotted there. If he didn't ask it now, he would never get another chance. Finally, clenching his jaw, he said, "It's been so many years, I've always wanted to know. You...and..."

Mo Xi could guess from Lu Zhanxing's expression and tone what this was about. He stood motionless, calmly waiting for him to continue.

"You and him... You and Mang-er... Are you two..." What he wanted to ask was too unspeakable, and it involved his childhood friend no less. No matter how brazen Lu Zhanxing was, he couldn't help but stammer. "Are you two..."

"Yes," Mo Xi said.

The confirmation from Mo Xi's own mouth seemed to deal a blow to Lu Zhanxing. None of their prior exchange had made him as dizzy as that single *yes* from Mo Xi.

He and Gu Mang had served together for many years; in truth, Lu Zhanxing had clued in to certain things long ago. It was just that, out of respect for Gu Mang, he was too embarrassed to ask about it outright. But just because he'd never asked didn't mean he was stupid, or blind. He'd seen how Mo Xi and Gu Mang looked at each other too many times. If it had been once or twice, he could've blamed his own overactive imagination. But with the frequency of these gazes, he could never convince himself there was nothing between them. He had too often seen Mo Xi wait for Gu Mang to patrol together, and when the two of them returned, the outer corners of Gu Mang's eyes would frequently be a little red, his voice slightly husky. Once, by the light of the bonfire, he had even seen the telltale mark of a bite on Gu Mang's neck.

But conjecture was conjecture. Lu Zhanxing still felt a little short of breath to hear Mo Xi directly admit as much in front of him. He took a few steps back and sat heavily on the stone bed. "Mang-er is insane... He was doing just fine, why did he have to get mixed up with you..." He sounded exhausted. Lu Zhanxing slumped over, burying his face in his hands and rubbing his cheeks. "Doesn't he know his own station...?" he rasped. "Why... Why does he always insist on striving for the most unattainable... What a lunatic... He was crazy for real..."

He paused, bone tired. "What point is there in chasing self-destruction like a moth flying into flame? Why is it that...all his life's desires, whether goals or people, are all so...so..." He swallowed, the final syllables falling from between his lips: "absurd."

In the flickering light, Mo Xi looked at him. At last, he said, "Don't blame him. Between the two of us, it wasn't that he was striving for me. I'm the one who was seeking my own destruction—it was I who clung to him."

With that, he turned on his heel, black robes billowing as he strode up the stairs and disappeared into the corridor's darkness.

Night had fallen hours ago. Mo Xi returned to Xihe Manor, but he tossed and turned, unable to sleep. Finally, he snapped upright in bed, draped a robe over his shoulders, and opened the door.

The sky was clear as water, stars like loose diamonds filling the dark blue dome of night. He shrouded himself within a hooded cape and went straight back to Apricot Mansion.

It would be unwise for him to again show his face to Gu Mang if he hoped to uncover more buried secrets. Still, he still couldn't stop himself from yearning for a few more glimpses of Gu Mang from eight years ago.

87

Mysterious Visitor

THE HOUR WAS LATE; the chatter of women and plucking of strings rose and fell without cease within Apricot Mansion. Mo Xi headed straight for the balcony where Gu Mang resided; he wasn't worried about being seen by others. Yue Chenqing's paternal grandfather had made the cloak Mo Xi wore using feathers of the traceless bird. Though these feathers were known to lose their effectiveness when plucked from the bird's body, the late Yue patriarch was a grandmaster artificer who had successfully preserved some properties of the plumes. This cloak could render its wearer invisible thrice.

Mo Xi jumped down from the eaves of the roof and landed soundlessly upon the balcony flourishing with flowers. The eight-grid tortoiseshell and bamboo door was open wide. Gu Mang hadn't called Miss Feitian the pipa player back; he was alone in the room.

Gu Mang sat at the table with his eyes closed, elbow propped on the table and cheek pressed in one hand. He looked as if he were asleep, yet also seemed keenly alert, his long lashes fluttering with every exhale. Smoke rose in spirals from the incense burner at his side, blurring and gentling his features. Mo Xi looked him over, inch by inch, from the tails of his eyes and the tips of his brows to his lips and chin. The candlelight's glow was like orange butterflies alighting on the tip of his nose.

Wrapped in the invisibility cloak, Mo Xi approached him with his breath held and attention rapt, staring down at his too-familiar face. He suddenly understood how Murong Lian could depend on ephemera so deeply despite knowing it was a poison that he shouldn't touch—knowing it could dissolve one's willpower and erode one's strength, yet still choosing pleasure over life.

His addiction to Gu Mang had sunk into his bone and marrow, deep as intoxicating smoke.

There came a knock at the door.

Mo Xi and Gu Mang snapped out of their trance at nearly the same time. Mo Xi took a step back; Gu Mang stood to open the door.

Mo Xi thought it would be another little pipa-playing minx. But when the door opened and Gu Mang turned to let the newcomer in, Mo Xi found it was no songstress at all, but rather a figure in a black cloak much like his own.

This person wasn't using an invisibility cloak, but they had hidden their face completely behind a gold and silver mask. The only detail to be gleaned from their tall and upright figure was that this individual was likely male.

Who?

Mo Xi had scarcely finished the thought when the cloaked man spoke. His voice was obviously distorted by a voice-changing spell. It came out as an uncanny rasp.

"Did anything strange happen today?" the man asked.

Gu Mang was silent for a moment, then answered: "No."

"Is that so?" the cloaked man replied thoughtfully. "No one came to visit?"

"No," Gu Mang said again.

At his insistence, the masked man dropped the matter. He placed a bundle wrapped in cloth on the table. "I brought this for you. You should change into it."

Gu Mang turned down a corner of the bundle, but then quickly folded it back up. "What do you mean by this?"

"If you're going there, you'd best prepare, hadn't you?"

Gu Mang's fingertips hovered over the package. At these words, he tensed, his fingers curling around the cloth. This only left Mo Xi more perplexed. Gu Mang had always been the picture of steady composure. If the sky should fall on him, he would probably use it as a blanket. Yet the cloaked man had made Gu Mang blanch with just this handful of words.

"If I tell you what's there, I doubt you'll believe it," the cloaked man said. "Tonight, I'll take you there in person, so you can see the truth with your own eyes."

However warm and soft the candlelight, it brought no color to Gu Mang's pale face. He seemed to suppress some complicated emotion, until even his lips were bloodless. He lowered his lashes, his shoulders trembling. In the end, he took the cloth bundle and disappeared behind the screen.

When Gu Mang stepped out, he was wearing clothes indistinguishable from those of the cloaked man. A dark cape embroidered in pale gold with a swirling cloud-and-thunder pattern obscured his form completely. "Let's go."

The two departed the Boudoir of Lingering Fragrance one after another. Mo Xi followed in their wake.

This brothel played host to all sorts. The madam and maidens working here all had three *don'ts* engraved into their hearts: *don't look, don't ask, don't listen.* When two conspicuously dressed men walked through the corridors of the brothel, the servant girls didn't show the slightest hint of surprise. They merely lowered their heads and made obeisance, and kept their heads down until the men were gone.

Gu Mang and that black-garbed man didn't speak as they walked; the two kept the distance of strangers. The black-garbed man walked in front, with Gu Mang wholly silent as he followed behind.

If the black-garbed man had any martial abilities, they weren't obvious, and he kept his aura well concealed. Mo Xi couldn't probe his spiritual energy flow any further without exposing his own position; he could only tail them to see where they were going.

When they had walked for the time it took to burn an incense stick, their direction became clear, and the doubts in Mo Xi's heart deepened. This was...the way to Warrior Soul Mountain?

As he expected, they eventually stopped at the foot of Warrior Soul Mountain. There were no guards at the entrance eight years ago. Nevertheless, the graves of generations of Chonghua's heroic dead stood at the summit of the mountain—there was still a formless barrier at the gate to denote respect and reverence. This barrier could disperse almost every disguise or invisibility spell. Mo Xi could track them no farther.

Gu Mang lowered the hood of his cloak and gazed at the winding stone path. Pines and bamboo swayed on either side, and bright moonlight shone through the tips of their branches to scatter over the ancient limestone steps.

"What is it?" asked the black-garbed man.

"Just thinking about how I'll be leaving soon, and my hands will be stained with the blood of Chonghua's soldiers. I..."

He said no more, but Mo Xi's heart clenched. Sure enough, Gu Mang had been lying when they'd talked. He had already decided to defect. He was already certain that in the future, his hands would be stained with the blood of his former comrades.

Gu Mang... Gu Mang... Why did you do it? Who is this mysterious black-clothed man at your side?!

Mo Xi's eyes burned red with the desire to snatch away that man's mask. He squashed the impulse down. Mo Xi had a feeling that, were he to remove this mask, many questions might be answered, and many mysteries explained. But the trail would end there—he would be unable to discover more. What he learned would not make up for what he would lose.

Swallowing thickly, Mo Xi endured the rushing impatience in his heart. He heard the black-garbed man speak:

"Chonghua's current state is as you've seen. You experienced it yourself after Phoenix Cry Mountain. When you and your army fell from grace, all you found were those who would kick you when you were down, none who would offer help in your hour of need." The black-garbed man noticed Gu Mang about to protest and waved a hand. "You don't need to tell me that if Xihe-jun were here, he would side with you. His support is useless. You're a clever person; you understand that Chonghua has always been ruled by the nobles. You cannot change anything with your power alone."

Mo Xi's ears seemed to ring. This person was clearly encouraging Gu Mang to defect—he was describing Chonghua's current attitudes, telling Gu Mang *other than Xihe-jun, no one would support you...* Was this man from the Liao Kingdom?

No, that was impossible. How could anyone from Liao move so easily through Chonghua to enter this deserted place? How could anyone from Liao so openly stand in front of Gu Mang without stirring up his intense disgust and reproach?

Unless...

Unless Gu Mang trusted this black-garbed man more than the nation of Chonghua. But how could such trust be built in a couple of months, with just a couple of words? Had Gu Mang already had dealings with some Liao Kingdom spy since long ago? How could this be?

"It's come to this," the man said. "The pieces are already in place for your treason; this move cannot be taken back."

Mo Xi's throat seemed to be filled with cloying blood. On this one short day eight years ago, on the eve of Gu Mang's defection, so much had happened that was buried by the sands of time—His Imperial Majesty's cold ruthlessness, Lu Zhanxing's stubborn devotion to his aim, Gu Mang's many worries...as well as this black-garbed man undisguisedly pushing Gu Mang onto the path to hell.

Gu Mang heard every word the man said, but he showed no reaction. The night wind blew harder, buffeting Gu Mang's wide sleeves like fallen flowers in the grip of a sudden gust. The cold evening seemed to chill him, his fingers curling as if he wanted to tuck them into his cuffs.

The black-garbed man reached out from beneath his dark sleeves and wrapped one fine-boned hand around Gu Mang's.

Mo Xi wasn't the only one stunned by this movement—Gu Mang's head whipped around, dark eyes wide in shock. He wanted to pull away, yet didn't move.

"General Gu," the black-garbed man said gravely, "none who seek to blaze a new path have hands unsullied by blood." As he spoke, he lowered his lashes to carefully examine Gu Mang's fingers and palm. "You know what the nobles of Chonghua are like. As I said, you're a clever person—I don't need to say much. Go up the mountain and take a look." The black-garbed man paused. "It is my hope that after you've seen it, you'll understand what can and cannot be believed, and what is and is not worth the price."

Gu Mang closed his eyes. His cloak snapped in the night wind as it whipped past. In the quiet night, Mo Xi wished so deeply that Gu Mang would flatly refuse; that he would push the black-garbed man away and say *I don't want to defect.* Even *Let me think about it* would be enough.

But Gu Mang said nothing. In this heartbreaking, bone-shattering silence, Mo Xi's heart chilled.

"I understand," Gu Mang said. "Let's go."

With that, he strode through the barrier on Warrior Soul Mountain, his black robes billowing like clouds of ink as he ascended the mountain without looking back.

Mo Xi didn't know how long the pair spent on Warrior Soul Mountain. He was numb all over. A single day in the Time Mirror had opened a box stuffed with eight years of secrets; they came tumbling down on him like an avalanche. This man, who had always stood so tall and upright as if he could bear any burden, found himself leaning against the stone wall just to keep on his feet. Though he managed to stand, his vision flashed dark. These events of the past tore at his tendons, ground his bones into dust. In the end, Mo Xi slid slowly to the ground, doubling over beside the limestone mountain path.

He raised a trembling hand to cover his face. The sheer number of threads he was trying follow had him tangled in a mess. How cold-blooded and detached would he have to be to maintain his composure after suffering such a shock?

As dawn began to peek through the clouds, Gu Mang and that black-garbed man descended the mountain. Just as before, the man walked in front, with Gu Mang trailing behind. An exhausted Mo Xi looked up through eyes spiderwebbed with blood vessels. He faced the faint light of dawn as he watched those two draw near, then pass back through the barrier.

Mo Xi's mind had been thrown into disarray; he felt utterly destroyed. At that moment, even this darling of the heavens wouldn't have been able to recite anything from the book *Legends of Divine Catastrophe* he'd memorized in childhood.

Despite it all, in the hazy mist of morning, he could tell from a single glance that Gu Mang had been crying.

Gu Mang was an indomitable man, but a strong spirit wasn't necessarily contained in a strong body. Gu Mang's body was warm and soft, his black eyes as gentle as a queen of the night blooming amid darkness, easily shedding tears from sorrow or stimulation. Mo Xi had explored Gu Mang's body as thoroughly as he'd explored his own mind; engraved upon his memories was Gu Mang in all his moods. The instant he saw the faint redness at the delicate outer corners of Gu Mang's eyes, Mo Xi knew Gu Mang had wept.

For whom, or for what, was he crying? For the past he was helpless to change, or the future on which he had staked everything?

The two men came to a stop at the foot of the mountain. The black-garbed man looked up at the sky. "It's late. If we stay longer, we'll be discovered."

"Yes." Gu Mang's voice was slightly hoarse. He performed an extremely formal obeisance toward the black-garbed man. "I've seen all that I should. Many thanks for tonight's accompaniment. Farewell."

"No need to thank me. You as well… Take care."

In a flash, the black-garbed man leapt up with qinggong and vanished into the breaking light of day. Gu Mang turned to take one last look at Warrior Soul Mountain, wreathed in mist. Then he tightened his black cloak around his shoulders as if it were hiding some precious secret. He lowered his head and strode away.

Mo Xi had no need to hide after Gu Mang left. He removed the concealment spells and walked up Warrior Soul Mountain alone to search for clues. He made for the restricted area. Since Gu Mang had told him it seemed familiar, Mo Xi could believe he had most likely gone there.

The restricted area on Warrior Soul Mountain was built with the strength of the imperial family, but it was simply a prototype at this point. It wouldn't be difficult to break the barrier. Mo Xi stood outside the deserted mountain area, his fingertips brushing the glowing light array. It was high-level, but still no more than an ordinary blocking barrier, nowhere near as impenetrable as the one eight years hence. But here in the Mirror, as an uninvited guest no less, his spiritual energy and magical abilities had been greatly impaired. The array wasn't perfect, but he couldn't break it. The barrier glowed relentlessly in front of Warrior Soul Mountain's restricted area, as if in mockery of this wandering soul who had come from the future.

"Chonghua's current state is what it is. You cannot change anything with your power alone."

"General Gu, none of those who seek to blaze a new path have hands unsullied by blood."

"You know what the nobles of Chonghua are like."

"The pieces are already in place for your treason; this move cannot be taken back."

Who was the black-garbed man? His words were intended to remind Gu Mang that Chonghua held bloodlines sacrosanct above all, to convince him to pledge allegiance to a new ruler. He sounded exactly like a Liao Kingdom agent trying to convince Gu Mang to defect.

But did Gu Mang really collude with those from the Liao Kingdom so early? Mo Xi could think of one other possibility. The restricted area on Warrior Soul Mountain was built according to the imperial family's instructions. Perhaps some rebellious noble saw something within it, realized what the emperor was planning, and developed treasonous intentions. So he brought Gu Mang here to witness it for himself—all the better to cause him anguish and shatter his resolve, prompting him to make a clean break with Chonghua's nobility and blaze a dark path.

But this line of reasoning also had its holes. Many factions jockeyed for power in Chonghua's imperial court, but which noble would truly want to see the system that honored bloodlines above all overturned...?

His heart was battered by one question after another. Mo Xi felt he was trapped in a dense and disorienting fog; he groped about within it but had no way of capturing the truth. In the end, he couldn't uncover the secret on the opposite side of the barrier. The only thing he was sure of was that Gu Mang's defection was far from the simple matter it seemed.

By the time he returned to Xihe Manor, Mo Xi still hadn't completely recovered. Shuang Qiu, holding a plate of tea and snacks, carefully approached. "My lord," she said tentatively. "My lord, did you not sleep well last night?"

Mo Xi didn't make a sound. He knew how unsightly and ridiculous he looked.

He used to think that the ancient notes regarding the deadliness of the Time Mirror were preposterous, but he now realized they were no exaggeration. Gu Mang had been completely hypnotized by the illusion, while Mo Xi couldn't escape the torment of the Mirror even as a bystander who had been pulled into the past.

Everyone had regrets in life, and all manner of secrets were concealed within the twists and turns of a lifetime. When faced with these regrets, wouldn't anyone who returned to the past want to try and mend it? When faced with these secrets, wouldn't anyone from the future be astonished?

When someone traveled back in time within the Mirror, they would realize that seas could rise or mountains could fall by the whims of a single word or misstep. Or they might end up like Mo Xi, learning that the reality he'd assumed true was but a shoddy facade that had fooled him for eight long years. And yet the truth eluded him.

Mo Xi felt as if his head were splitting; the pain was about to drive him mad.

"My lord," Shuang Qiu started. "You..."

He was gripping his teacup too hard; it shattered with a sudden squeeze of his fingers. Shuang Qiu screamed as blood ran from the cuts, streaming over the pale skin of his hand. "M-my lord," she stammered, "I'll help you at once—"

"Get out."

"My lord?"

Mo Xi's dark eyes were so bloodshot, they looked to be veiled in red clouds. He stared at the blood trickling without pause from his hand and rasped, "Get lost."

Shuang Qiu didn't dare talk back; she hastily tidied the plates and cups and scurried out. Mo Xi didn't wipe the blood from his hand, hoping the mild pain could help clear his head.

He desperately needed to clear his head.

There were two days until Lu Zhanxing's execution. He could still bear it; he wouldn't disrupt the past inside the Time Mirror over a momentary impulse. He hoped Murong Chuyi and the rest wouldn't defeat the shangao and rescue them from the Mirror so quickly. The present had already buried this past he was in; he wanted to stay longer in this world of eight years ago.

Gu Mang once said he would choose to burn brilliantly even if the fire reduced him to ash. Mo Xi didn't have such a grandiose dream. But even if the agony should grind him to dust, he would choose to dig out the truth.

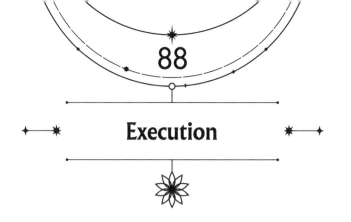

88

Execution

I N A BLINK, three days passed inside the Mirror.

Mo Xi sat in the side room of a small lodge in the city outskirts, watching the water clock by the window in silence. In
accordance with the emperor's demands, today he should have been
on the road to the northern frontier. But he hadn't left. He raised a
hand to look at his palm; it had a translucent sheen. And it wasn't
only his palms, but everything in this world—even the blades of
grass were beginning to lose color.

The Time Mirror was weakening.

Murong Chuyi and the others were in the real world, where time
flowed quickly. Perhaps Murong Chuyi or Jiang Yexue was merely
performing one spell or reciting an incantation on the outside, while
several days had passed in the mirror. If his current state was anything to go by, Mo Xi estimated that he and Gu Mang would leave
this world in another two or three days. Thus, he didn't care if the
emperor discovered he hadn't left for the north—he just wanted to
learn a few more secrets before the dream shattered.

Another drop of water fell.

The time on the water clock neared the hour of wu—nearly
noon. Mo Xi rose and walked up to the bronze mirror. He altered
his features with a simple illusion spell, then pushed open the door
to leave.

"Let's go, let's go! Hurry over to the eastern market to watch the beheading!"

"Deputy General Lu's about to get his head chopped off. Who would've thought—ah, times really do change..."

"His rash action killed so many people; if you ask me, not even death is enough to clear his sins!"

The street bustled with raucous activity as people hurried toward the eastern market. Some of their faces showed anticipation, others elation; some were sobbing, others terrified. Whatever emotions they experienced, the eastern market seemed to draw them all like piping hot blood-buns[9] fresh from the steamer, luring vultures that craned their necks toward the execution platform.

Mo Xi silently joined the flow of people and arrived before long at the gate of the eastern market. At its center were the officials carrying out the execution, as well as a crowd of spectators like soft dumpling skins, wrapped around and around the platform.

Lu Zhanxing, in a spotless white prison uniform, sat barefoot and cross-legged on the platform. His expression was serene, without any of the panic of one about to die. The execution official brought him wine and meat; Lu Zhanxing grinned and thanked him with a laugh. He pulled a chicken leg from the plate and bared his pointy canines as he tore into his meal. Swiftly he finished all the meat and started on the wine, gulping down the gallows brew with bravura. At last, he wiped his mouth on a sleeve. "Sir, your little wine pot is so dainty, so girlish—can't you just bring me a jug?"

The official looked at him strangely. "How are you still eating so happily? You're about to die."

---

9   Buns steamed in human blood. The concept originated from old superstitions that eating one could cure tuberculosis, or from Tang dynasty doctor Chen Zangqi's book Lost Writings of Herbs and Plants, which stated that people would go up to the executioner to buy buns dipped in the blood of the executed to cure sickness.

"Exactly." Lu Zhanxing bared his teeth, laughing as though his true form were a hungry wolf. "It's the last meal of my life. Did you want me to cry as I eat it?"

The official glared at him, perhaps wondering how shameless a person must be to snicker like this after making the kind of trouble he had. "There's no jug of wine for you," he said stiffly. "That's the whole last meal. No refills."

Lu Zhanxing sighed. "A shame. I could've set off drunk."

The official scoffed. "So you're not actually that calm. You're just looking for some liquid courage so you won't feel it when your head comes off."

"Not quite." Lu Zhanxing clapped and smiled. "My head coming off will only make a wound the size of a bowl. This officer just wants to set off for the Yellow Springs drunk and borrow some courage from the wine to admire the beautiful scenery on the banks of the Wangchuan River.[10] Perhaps I'll even compose some poems that'll make me famous in the underworld."

The executioner was rendered wholly speechless. At this moment, a clear voice called out from the bustle below the platform. "What poem do you want to write now? Is it 'two orioles sing in the green willow, one's uglier than the other though,' or 'I was born like this to have some means, nights of pleasure aren't just dreams'?"[11]

The crowd turned to see that Gu Mang had appeared in their midst. He was wearing a pin-straight set of Chonghua's formal military robes. Though stripped of the tassels of rank, they still accentuated the length of his legs, the slimness of his waist, and the solemnity of his features. From two slender fingers hung a loop of

---

10   In mythology, the river separating the Yellow Springs from the rest of the underworld. To cross it, souls must go over Naihe Bridge, which requires them to drink Meng Po's soup of forgetfulness.

11   The first halves of these couplets come from famous Tang dynasty poems; the second halves are original. The poems are "Four Quatrains, No. 3" by Du Fu and "Qiang Jin Jiu" by Li Bai.

twine attached to a wine jug sealed with clay. Under the merciless noontime sun, he walked toward the execution platform.

"Aiya, it's General Gu... Pah, pah, pah, I misspoke. It's not General Gu. It's Gu Mang, Gu Mang."

The audience gathered for the execution slowly parted to make way for him. Countless pairs of eyes stared in open curiosity. Everyone knew of Lu Zhanxing and Gu Mang's lifelong friendship. Everyone also knew Lu Zhanxing's mistake precipitated Gu Mang's fall from the pinnacle of society to its very gutter, becoming a wastrel who spent his days lazing around a brothel. Now that these two were finally meeting again, how would they treat each other? Would Lu Zhanxing look ashamed before Gu Mang? Would Gu Mang spit on his former friend and curse him in rage?

Few things were more exciting than the drama of jealous competition, antagonism between a wealthy man's wives, or brothers turning on each other. Absent the first two, the crowd at least hoped to see these brothers at each other's throats. The noisy execution platform gradually fell silent.

It was too quiet. Hidden in the crowd, Mo Xi could almost hear the rhythm of his own pounding heartbeat. He sought Gu Mang's silhouette, that tall and elegant figure clad in the old robes of Chonghua. Today Gu Mang didn't appear listless at all. He was like refined bamboo standing in a cool breeze, as if the past half-year's dissipation hadn't eroded his strength a bit.

In this silence, Gu Mang walked onto the platform alone. Once, he'd had multitudes at his beck and call and was never without an escort. But of those hundred thousand comrades, only he remained. All the rest had been sacrificed or detained. There was nothing else he could bring—just one man, one jug of wine, one set of military robes stripped of all honors. Their past glory like a fleeting dream, leaving behind a pitiable ruin.

Lu Zhanxing tilted his head back to watch him approach. After a moment, he bared his teeth in a grin. "Mang-er, you still remember the poems I wrote?"

Gu Mang glanced down, his thick lashes casting shadows under his eyes. He sat down with the jug of wine in his arms. "You slapped those lines on so poorly, I couldn't forget them even if I tried."

Lu Zhanxing chuckled, scratching his foot as he laughed. "I knew you'd come send me off today."

Gu Mang snorted and removed the clay seal on the wine. He took a sip and pushed it at Lu Zhanxing. "Have some."

"Ah, the Soaring Swan's fifteen-year pear-blossom white?"

"What else?"

These two didn't come to blows, nor did they argue. The spectators below weren't the only ones surprised—even the execution official standing nearby was stunned speechless.

Although Lu Zhanxing had been sentenced to death, Gu Mang hadn't yet defected. He'd been stripped of his rank, but his past merits remained. The official didn't want to openly make things difficult, nor did he dare to. He hesitated. "Gen—ahem, you see, the rules around the execution meal..."

"We were brothers, you know. I'm here to send him off." Gu Mang looked up. "Sir, allow me this small mercy."

Regardless of all else, Gu Mang was still Chonghua's Beast of the Altar, the ever-victorious god of war. Even at the peak of his influence, he had never been a bully or held grudges. Before those eyes, dark as black jade, the official quailed. He stepped aside with a sigh.

As the sun climbed in the sky, the shadow cast by the sundial grew denser, darker than ink. Lu Zhanxing drank and laughed as he chatted with Gu Mang. Perhaps because talk of hatred was futile on the brink of death, neither brought up the defeat at Phoenix Cry Mountain.

The hour of the execution drew closer and closer. The blazing sun burned with white heat, and the air was filled with the scent of death approaching. The spectators swallowed as they stared at the sundial, slowly growing anxious. Yet the ones most at ease were the man about to die and the friend here to see him off.

At last they finished the wine. "Do you have any last wishes?" Gu Mang asked.

Lu Zhanxing smiled. "Too many."

"Which of them can I help you with?"

"Taste more pear-blossom white for me," said Lu Zhanxing.

"I will."

"Look at more beautiful people and beautiful scenes for me."

"Okay."

Lu Zhanxing thought for a moment. Finally, he reached up to touch Gu Mang's military uniform. "Mang-er...don't wear these anymore, all right?"

The charcoal in the firepit crackled. Gu Mang lowered his lashes, his expression dark and thoughtful. No one at the scene would understand what this expression meant, other than Mo Xi, who knew Gu Mang had already decided to defect. Lu Zhanxing's final wish was for Gu Mang to lay down his armor and return to a life of peace, away from the butchery of the battlefield. How could he know that Gu Mang would indeed never wear the military robes of Chonghua again—instead, he'd replace them with the black battle armor of the Liao Kingdom and step onto a blood-soaked path of no return.

Gu Mang paused, head low. His lashes seemed to quiver as he smiled faintly. "Okay. Never again."

Lu Zhanxing's eyes brightened, a smile stretching across his face. "You mean it?"

"When have I ever lied to you?"

Lu Zhanxing burst into laughter. "You've made pretty promises ever since you were little." As he chuckled, the smile that had unfolded in his eyes like spring leaves faltered slightly.

"Is there anything else you want to say?" Gu Mang asked.

Lu Zhanxing's gaze shone with tenderness—the first time Mo Xi had ever seen such a gentle look on his sharp and predatory features. "Mang-er," he said, "you should get married and settle down."

Gu Mang stared.

"You've always been a free spirit, but we've been brothers all these years. I know you've always wanted a place to call home." There was a meaningful note in Lu Zhanxing's voice. "You're not getting any younger. If you're done having fun, you should rein it in, so I can..."

Gu Mang cut him off. "Uncle Lu, how old *are* you?"

Lu Zhanxing widened his eyes and pursed his lips. "I'm saying this because I care. Why don't you know what's good for you?"

He was about to say more when there came a sharp whistle. The cultivator standing at the corner of the high platform had begun to blow his yak-horn bugle, its clarion call piercing the skies. "The time has come!" the crier shouted.

The time has come.

The blinding sun had reached its zenith; its white light streamed onto the confounded multitudes, onto the one about to leave and the one left behind, onto the darkly massed spectators.

This would be the end for these two brothers from childhood.

Gu Mang gazed calmly at Lu Zhanxing, so calm it was as if they were only a general and his soldier splitting up for a battle strategy and would soon regroup.

"I'm heading out," Gu Mang said.

Lu Zhanxing smiled. "Think about what I said."

Gu Mang cast him a long glance. After a pause, he said, "Okay, I will." With that, he descended the high, narrow stairs of the execution platform, long robes brushing the ground.

The execution official stepped forward, raising a copper mallet wrapped in red cloth to strike the gong. Its metallic tone was clear and carrying as the man cried, "The time has come—prepare!"

It wasn't like in the storybooks, where a mounted soldier would charge in shouting to spare the prisoner, an imperial edict held aloft as he spurred his horse through the crowd. Lu Zhanxing didn't put up a struggle; there was no sudden rescue. Hardly any escaped the jaws of death. Those who received the grace of fate were a scant few indeed.

Lu Zhanxing and Gu Mang looked at each other, one upon the platform and one below. Both struck by the memory of what Lu Zhanxing had said when he enlisted years ago:

"I don't want to die at all. I wanna be an ancient geezer who takes a handful of wives and sires a bunch of kids. That's the good life for me."

Back then, Gu Mang had laughed. "Now that you've stepped onto the battlefield, your life's in danger every minute. How are you going to become an ancient geezer?"

But Lu Zhanxing feared nothing. He stroked his chin, half joking and half serious. "You're right. Then I might as well think about what kind of death would suit me."

"What would?"

"It would be best if I got stuck in a Liao Kingdom dreamscape, one filled with peerless beauties all chasing me for you know what"—at this, he waggled his eyebrows—"and of course, I couldn't be so rude as to refuse, so I'd end up dying from loss of *essence*." Lu Zhanxing grinned lasciviously, kicking his feet. "Aiya, what a way to go."

Back then they were fearless. In their mouths, matters of life and death were no more than fodder for jokes.

"Or beheaded by an incomparably gorgeous Liao Kingdom demoness," Lu Zhanxing continued. "Hopefully she first takes a fancy to me, and I'd rather die than submit, so she defiles me first, then kills me—wow, how thrilling—"

"Can't you come up with something normal?" Gu Mang heckled.

"Normal is boring." Lu Zhanxing licked his lips and grinned. "Normal would be a horsehide burial, my brothers weeping around me, faces streaked with tears. It's a horrifying thought."

Who would've guessed that the worst death Lu Zhanxing could imagine for himself was far better than his destined end? As a soldier, his final rest was no horsehide burial, but a pointless death as a disgraced criminal on Chonghua's chopping block. No one cried for him; no one wept with their face streaked with tears. Of his imagined "brothers," only Gu Mang remained.

The executioner stepped forward, raising the curve of that snow-bright blade high into the air. The wind ruffled Lu Zhanxing's bangs. He looked down at Gu Mang standing below, the corners of his lips lifting in a smile of relief.

"Down!"

Farewell came as that word rang out, life and death forever sundered.

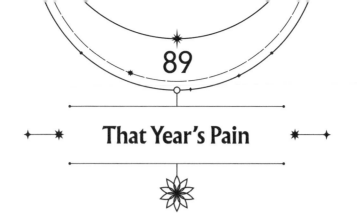

89

That Year's Pain

CRIMSON BLOOD SPLASHED and the onlookers cried out. Amid gasps from the crowd, it slowly soaked into the grain of the high platform's wood.

The noon sun was so bright as to be unnerving. Gu Mang stood ramrod straight, his face devoid of emotion as he looked on, watching as the head fell and rolled, watching as the body collapsed.

His best friend's body lay cleaved in two. Lu Zhanxing's head rolled forward, finally coming to rest at the edge of the platform. Open eyes stared at Gu Mang. As if trying to say, *Mang-er, turn back. It's all over. Let my death become the end of this dream—don't go on. There's no way forward, only the mirage of a castle in the sky. Turn around. Give up.*

The executioner's blade dripped scarlet, warm blood running across the floor in rivulets.

Go home...

The execution official cried, "Execution complete—"

After the initial excitement and awe had passed, the frozen crowd gradually thawed, like a sleeping beast waking from hibernation within a dark cave. Most wanted a look at Lu Zhanxing's broken corpse, but few dared. Some of the women gathered their courage and snuck a peek, only to immediately bury their eyes in their palms with a yelp, shuddering with fright at the mess of blood and flesh...

"How terrible."

"Don't look, it's really scary. If you see it, you'll probably have nightmares tonight."

The crowd bustled, their focus gradually shifting to Gu Mang. Some began to notice Gu Mang's expression and started to whisper among themselves: "Why hasn't General Gu reacted at all...?"

"He really hasn't, he hasn't even paled... Does he really hate Lu Zhanxing? Lu Zhanxing did ruin him, after all."

"Why did he come to send him off, then?"

"Probably just to keep up appearances. Ah, people like this keep all their fights private—they're not going to air their grievances in public."

Gu Mang hadn't defected yet; at this point, he was still an honored subject of the nation. Someone else immediately shot back, "Nonsense, General Gu isn't that kind of man! Deputy General Lu was an old friend. Even after making such an awful mistake, General Gu sent him off out of friendship. He's keeping calm for propriety's sake. After all he's done, what more do you want from him?!"

The other bystander wasn't to be outdone. They snorted disdainfully. "To share in life and death, in good and ill—*that's* what brotherhood is. If I were Gu Mang, I would've broken Lu Zhanxing out ages ago or gone directly to His Imperial Majesty and begged him to exchange my own life for my brother's. I wouldn't have done what he did at all!"

"How do you know General Gu didn't beg?"

"Just look how indifferent he is. Gu Mang only pretends to be a good person—he's cold-blooded and heartless!"

Perhaps Gu Mang had heard these words, or perhaps he hadn't. He was still staring at the execution platform. The executioner had left, and the execution official was directing the cleanup. Gu Mang stood in the harsh noon sun, his back straight as pine and bamboo, elegant and upright without the slightest hint that he'd been struck by heartbreak. He watched unblinkingly as Lu Zhanxing's corpse was bound and his head strung up high, watched as the bloodstains were washed away.

The execution official unrolled an imperial edict of yellow silk and read in dispassionate tones, "Let it be known throughout the nation that the guilty subject Lu Zhanxing failed to control himself on the front lines, decapitating an envoy and causing the defeat at Phoenix Cry Mountain, greatly disappointing His Imperial Majesty's heavenly grace. After today's execution, his corpse will be exposed for three days."

The voice echoed through that cloudless sky. Everything had come to an end. The execution was over.

Gu Mang didn't stay long; beneath those watchful eyes, carrying that jug of pear-blossom white he shared with Lu Zhanxing, he turned and left without looking back.

Of those hundred thousand comrades, he alone remained.

Gu Mang returned to his own dwelling. Mo Xi, under the invisibility cloak, followed.

This former first general of Chonghua was so poor he didn't even have his own manor. This was little wonder: recruitment and weapons cost money, provisions and equipment cost money, and making connections also cost money. His soldier's pay was only so much, so after his slave collar was removed, he had rented a little house in a quiet area near the eastern market. This humble abode had a firewood hut and a single bedroom with one bed, one set of blankets, a desk and chair, and a couple of dilapidated wooden boxes.

These were all the possessions this famous general had to his name.

When Gu Mang returned to his house, he set the jug of wine on the desk. He then went to the firewood hut. It was lunchtime, so he made a fire and boiled water to heat up the leftovers he kept in the muslin cabinets.

He was eating. His last brother was dead. Everything he had was irrevocably lost. But he was eating.

On the little wooden desk sat the red clay jug that Lu Zhanxing had drunk from before his death, a large bowl of white rice, and a dish of vegetables and tofu. Like a starving man, Gu Mang shoveled food into his mouth, scraping his chopsticks against the bowl. The food vanished quickly—not a single grain of rice remained. He rose once to refill his bowl and continued to eat.

It was as if an endless void had opened in his heart, and he could only stave off the chilling emptiness by eating. He ate, head down, cheeks bulging. Eventually he couldn't swallow as quickly as he shoved food into his mouth. He slowed down, but still choked. He tried his best to swallow that mouthful of rice in silence, as if trying to absorb some words he couldn't say, a pain he couldn't voice.

He swallowed miserably, face upturned and eyes wide. Staring at the ceiling, he suddenly let out a sob. It was like a groan of indigestion, so comical was the sound. But the rims of his eyes were red.

Mo Xi was right by his side, mere inches away, but he couldn't speak a word, nor touch so much as a strand of Gu Mang's hair. He watched, helpless, as Gu Mang's eyes filled with tears.

Gu Mang kept his head tilted back, as if trying to keep the tears from spilling. He swiped at his lashes and sniffed.

He had stopped himself—or at least he thought he had stopped himself—so he lowered his head once more and picked up the chopsticks to return to that plain and flavorless white rice. The same white rice he and Lu Zhanxing had used to eat with vegetables and tofu, back when they were small at Wangshu Manor.

He attempted a few more bites, but the agony of loss was like the belated fall of a blade—it stabbed deep into his belly, finally thinning his breath and breaking down his flesh, shattering that falsely composed facade. His hand shook as he held the chopsticks, and his lips began to tremble as he scooped in rice. He tried to keep still through his shuddering, but to his dismay, tears started to squeeze their way out of his eyes. One after another, they streamed down his cheeks to drip onto the desk.

He moved his chopsticks in silence while wiping away his tears. His throat tasted bitter; all his sobs were trapped within, and he forced them down along with the rice. But the point came when his shaking hand could no longer pick up the tofu. He tried once, it slipped; he tried again and it fell apart...

This man, burdened with the weight of seventy thousand souls, was broken by this tiny tableside defeat. Gu Mang flung the chopsticks down. Rising to his feet, he swept everything off the desk with an almighty crash. Plates and cups smashed on the ground, and most completely shattered of all was the empty wine jug Gu Mang had brought back with him.

He panted, his chest rising and falling as he stared blankly at the mess. He had smashed that red clay jug into the broken splinters of an old dream. Gu Mang stared and stared. Eyes red and teary, he walked over and squatted in a daze, reaching out to try tidying it—but he retracted his hand before even touching the shards.

He looked like someone waking from a dream, a kind of awakening that left him absolutely shattered. It was the first time Mo Xi had witnessed this kind of shattering in him. If Gu Mang dared to show such a face in front of his comrades in the military, their admiration and trust in him would fall to pieces. He was no war god but mere soft mud, a lonely and helpless ant, a scattered handful of sand.

Gu Mang sat weakly. He was wearing a neatly pressed and spotless military uniform, yet he seemed to have been stripped of all strength as he crumpled to the dirty floor. He stared, trembling, at the mess on the ground.

A small whimper issued from his throat, like that of a lost wolf pup. The whimpers became sobs, struggling out of his mouth, one after another.

"I'm sorry... I'm sorry..."

Mo Xi watched him: Watched as he slowly curled in on himself on that ice-cold floor, hugging his knees as he tried to resist with all he could but failed to hold back the flood of tears. Watched as he desperately bit his own lips till his teeth were bloody but couldn't keep those soft sounds from escaping his mouth.

The deity had finally shattered. The god of war had been completely defeated.

Gu Mang's lips parted. He had bitten himself viciously; he was on the edge of madness. He panted, the rims of his eyes scarlet, his gaze despairing as he looked around the room—as if hoping someone would suddenly appear, whether god or ghost, to save or to slaughter him.

Someone to save him. Someone to stay with him.

It hurt... It hurt so much.

How was the world so vast yet it wouldn't hold on to seventy thousand heroes? How was hell so deep yet it wouldn't take him, a single living ghost?

He was the only one left.

Gu Mang finally wailed aloud—he wept and clutched at himself desperately, as if trying to embrace his comrades, his brothers, through the barrier between life and death. As if his deceased friends had possessed him, martyred souls crossing the Yellow Springs to hold their General Gu.

Sobs leaked from those bitten lips. In the end, his cries became breathless, his pain beyond reckoning.

"I'm sorry..." Gu Mang kept saying. *I'm sorry...*

Mo Xi watched in agony. His heart had hurt as if cut up by a knife since he watched Gu Mang desperately try to eat as he shed silent tears. Gu Mang's pain felt like his own pain. Gu Mang's helplessness felt like his own helplessness. Only now did he see with his own eyes how much it hurt Gu Mang to lose Lu Zhanxing, so much that he felt his whole heart being wrung dry of blood.

He watched Gu Mang's face carefully. Gu Mang was almost delirious; he looked as if he could see ghosts, or as if he *wanted* to see ghosts. He looked around the small house in despair. He wanted someone to be with him. Even if they wanted his life, even if they blamed him, he hoped for someone to come to him.

A knife was twisting in Mo Xi's heart. When Gu Mang had voiced his grievances in the palace hall, Mo Xi wasn't by his side. When Gu Mang's pain grew deeper, still he wasn't by his side.

And now...

Despite knowing that nothing could be changed within the Mirror, despite knowing that impulsive action was dangerous, Mo Xi's anguish—like Gu Mang's—was too much to endure. Before Gu Mang had defected, *he* was the one who had failed Gu Mang... He was the one who didn't accompany Gu Mang, didn't see the cares weighing on Gu Mang's heart. He was the one who treated Gu Mang like an invincible god, forgetting that beneath the war armor lay a mortal's body made of flesh and blood.

A mortal body, still struggling despite its wounds...

A person's heart was not stubborn stone and cold steel—the silent sufferance of eight years collapsed like an anthill. Mo Xi couldn't bear it anymore; he lifted the invisibility spell on his cloak. Brows drawn low, he knelt by Gu Mang, who had curled into a ball. "Gu Mang," he choked out. "Look at me. I'm still here."

I'm still here.

But perhaps Gu Mang was too heartbroken, or his mind had been strained to its limits and finally collapsed. He didn't react at all to Mo Xi's voice, nor his sudden appearance.

Mo Xi was in such pain that he couldn't speak; his hands, too, were shaking. He reached out, wanting to take hold of his beloved— clad in a military uniform stripped of that fathomless glory—and gather him into his arms. In this moment, he stopped caring for consequences. Really... Over the eight years of pain and longing, in the upstream flow of the Time Mirror, he'd finally lost his mind.

"Gu Mang... Gu Mang..." Mo Xi whispered, unintelligibly hoarse. "It's okay, I'll stay with you... I'll stay with you..."

He reached out to take him into his arms, hugging Gu Mang from behind. But where his shoulder would have touched Gu Mang's back, a faint light flashed. Mo Xi found he had passed right through Gu Mang's body.

He looked at his own hand in shock. His face paled, his expression slowly transforming into one of panic.

They were out of time. Murong Chuyi and Jiang Yexue's spell to break the Mirror must have reached its final phrases. He didn't know how much longer he could stay in the Mirror's world. At this moment he had already become insubstantial.

He couldn't interact with this world. He couldn't show himself. He couldn't comfort Gu Mang, nor could he turn Gu Mang from his path.

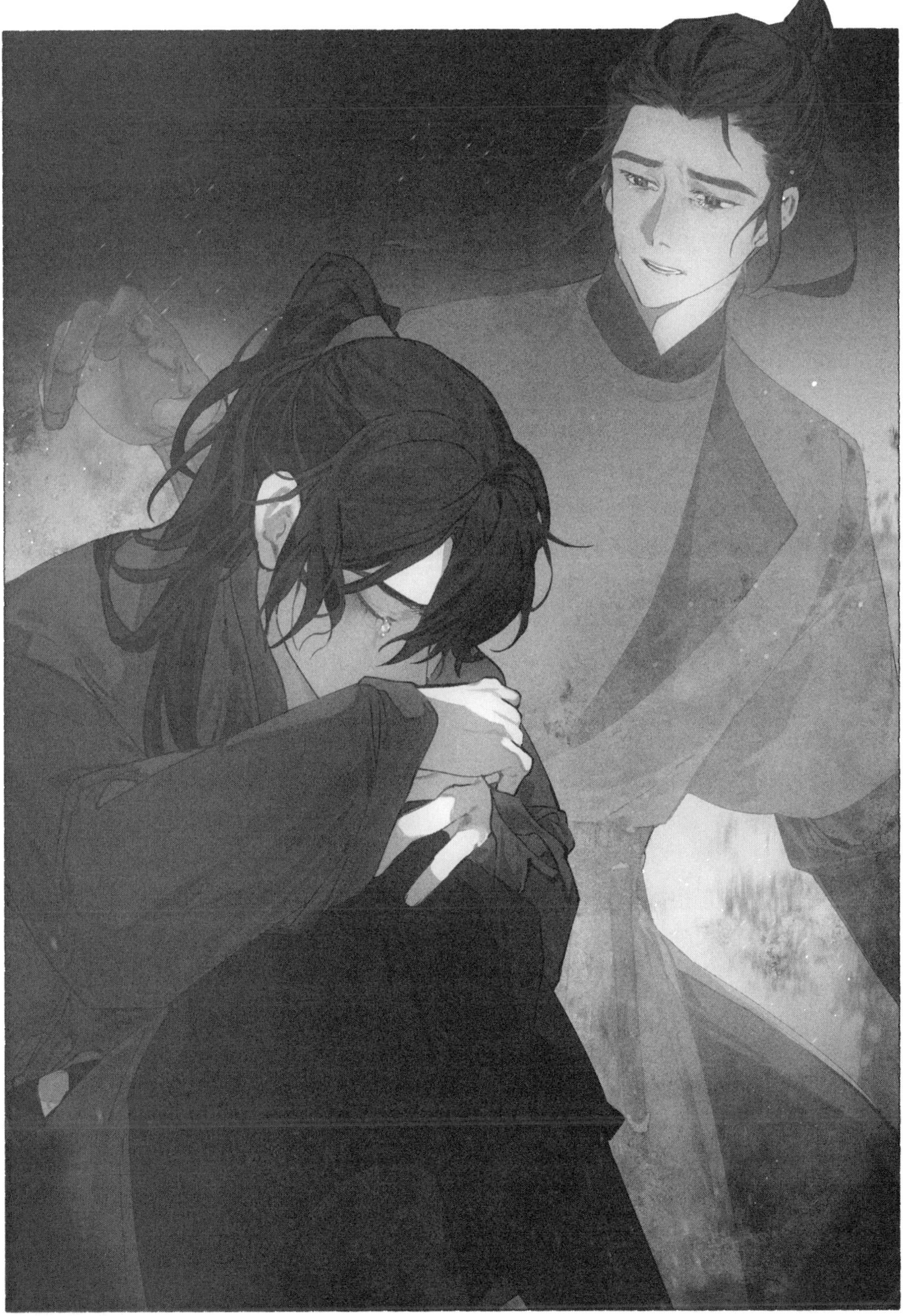

That day, Gu Mang huddled amid the broken crockery, hugging his own knees as day turned to night.

When darkness fell, he leaned against the icy wall. Like a beast separated from its pack, he slept curled in a tight ball. His eyes were yet red, his nose was red, and even the ears hidden in his inky hair were flushed a pitiful red.

Mo Xi sat by his side all night. Even asleep, Gu Mang whimpered with unconscious sobs. Mo Xi raised his hand, but he couldn't wipe away a single one of these tears that had been shed eight years since.

This was the nature of time—there was nothing he could change. Even within the illusion, the two of them had still ended up like this.

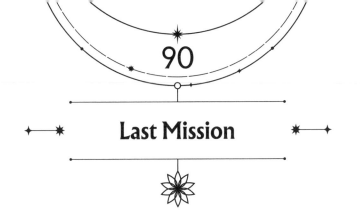

90

Last Mission

L U ZHANXING'S CORPSE was left in the sun for three days.
Over their course, Mo Xi's surroundings within the Mirror
gradually lost their color, and people's voices became so indistinct, they seemed to be speaking from across an ocean. Mo Xi no
longer needed the invisibility cloak to walk about freely, but he had
already run out of time. It was impossible for him to talk to anyone
from eight years ago or draw out any more buried truths.

He sank into passive waiting.

In these three days, Gu Mang didn't go out, nor did anyone come
to visit him. Lu Zhanxing had been Gu Mang's closest friend, as
well as the deputy general of the Wangba Army. Many had believed
Lu Zhanxing would earn a reprieve, that the emperor might pardon
him at the last minute. But the emperor took neither Gu Mang's
feelings nor reputation into account, and Lu Zhanxing was beheaded. Anyone could see the writing on the wall: Gu Mang had
truly fallen from grace. He'd never again recover his former standing.
It was the end of the Gu army.

No one would commiserate with someone downfallen and discarded. No hoofbeats stopped outside the door of the former general.
For company, he had only Mo Xi, who had come to him across eight
years of time, but whom Gu Mang could not see. Gu Mang stayed
in his house, lying dazed in his bed, only eating if he had to, only

moving if forced to, as if time had come to a standstill. But Mo Xi knew that time flowed ruthlessly on. Mo Xi would look at his own hands from time to time. When he spread his fingers, they were almost transparent. He suspected just a few shichen remained until they'd leave the world of the Mirror. He didn't even know if it would hold until the evening.

"General Gu."

A knock, and someone calling from the doorway. Gu Mang opened his eyes and stared blankly before stumbling to his feet. He hadn't eaten or stood up in too long; he was dizzy, and tripped as soon as his feet touched the ground. Mo Xi instinctively reached out to help him, but he couldn't—Gu Mang crumpled pathetically to the floor. He hastily clambered to his feet. The door opened; a herald from the palace stood outside.

"His Imperial Majesty commands you to present yourself in the throne room."

Gu Mang seemed exhausted. "Did something happen?"

"Um..." The herald paused. "This official isn't sure either. General Gu just needs to go."

Mo Xi understood—the emperor was about to give Gu Mang his final assignment. He prayed he could stay a little longer in the Mirror, that he wouldn't be torn away in this last moment. He wanted badly to learn of this assignment Gu Mang received before he defected.

After sending the official away, Gu Mang walked to the dull bronze mirror. He changed into a set of clean, coarse robes and splashed his face with water. Droplets streamed down his cheeks, washing away the exhaustion writ there. But they couldn't wash away the redness of his bloodshot eyes. In a bid to make himself look more alert, Gu Mang pulled his hair into a high ponytail. He moved out of habit to fasten the hair crown that represented his military rank, but his fingers closed around empty air.

He'd stopped being a general long ago.

Gu Mang stood silent for a time, then fumbled for a silk ribbon to secure his hair. The ribbon was white as a lotus root—as if he were mourning someone in secret rebellion.

He entered the palace. When the imperial guards saw him, the red feathers on their helmets rustled as they moved to perform obeisance, then quickly realized that they oughtn't and straightened their heads.

In the deep and forbidden recesses of the palace, the emperor's heavenly power lay solemn over the halls; the imperial guards couldn't openly gawk at Gu Mang. But there wasn't a soul among them who didn't watch covertly from the moment he appeared at the end of the long corridor until he vanished into the depths of the palace.

Over the years, Gu Mang had walked this corridor countless times, his rank constantly rising, his admirers constantly growing. Now he was a commoner once again, attired in blue clothes and cloth shoes, with no one by his side. For half his life he had spent all his passion, exhausted all of his sincerity. He'd weathered so many tribulations only to return to square one, not so different from the first time he entered the palace as a slave.

He approached the majestic throne on the high dais. Court wasn't in session, and three pale-yellow veils hung in front of the throne, hiding everything behind from view. The sovereign's appearance was not so easily glimpsed.

Gu Mang paused. He didn't lift his gaze; he kept his lashes lowered, his head bowed. He knelt, then kowtowed. "The commoner Gu Mang greets Your Imperial Majesty."

The throne room was still. No answer came.

Gu Mang was silent for a while, then raised his head and kow-towed once more. "The commoner Gu Mang greets Your Imperial Majesty."

This time a response came, but not from the throne. A voice floated over from behind Gu Mang, light as smoke. "You bastard Gu, so you do know you're a commoner now. Why would His Imperial Majesty want to see *you*?"

Mo Xi and Gu Mang both turned to see Murong Lian, wearing a malevolent smirk as he stood in the doorway with his arms crossed and his hands tucked in his sleeves.

Eight years ago, Murong Lian hadn't yet used ephemera. He was in visibly better condition, not yet so weary and weak. He wore a noble's robes, blue with gold trim. Though he looked, as ever, the picture of a rich and spoiled scion, his shoulders were straight, and he stood upright on his long legs. It was a far cry from the indolence he'd later display, looking as if he'd fall over wherever he went.

Gu Mang stood up. "Why is it you?"

"Why shouldn't it be?" Murong Lian scoffed. "General Gu is *so* forgetful. You spent so many years serving in my manor, giving me massages and fawning over me in every possible way—what's changed? You've forgotten your roots after a few years as a general?"

Gu Mang made no reply.

"Besides, now you're a commoner, and I'm still nobility. To receive a message from me on His Imperial Majesty's behalf is already an honor for someone like you." Murong Lian's sharp chin tilted up, mockery showing on his fair face. "Why don't you kneel to accept the edict?"

Gu Mang was silent for a time, but in the end, he lowered his gaze and knelt on the ground, the hem of his light blue robes brushing the floor.

Mo Xi, who had grown used to the armored General Gu, saw now how thin and weak his unarmored body was. The wide collar of his robe exposed a bare neck that looked so defeated, a gentle pinch might snap it entirely.

Murong Lian spread his glittering gold-trimmed sleeves with a loud snap and produced the emperor's order. "As heaven's will and the emperor commands," he said in languid tones, "the casualties at the battle of Phoenix Cry Mountain were a result of Commander Gu Mang's misjudgment. Deputy General Lu Zhanxing showed lack of discipline before the troops and beheaded the envoy from Rouli, dooming our soldiers and souring Chonghua's relations with this nation. The guilty subject has been beheaded and the corpse displayed to the public. The former General Gu is charged to take the head and personally present it to Rouli in apology. End of edict."

When this scroll had been read, Gu Mang wasn't the only one stunned—Mo Xi stared as well. The emperor meant for Gu Mang to personally take Lu Zhanxing's head, leave for Rouli, and apologize for the offense of Lu Zhanxing killing their country's envoy.

As the sound in the Time Mirror grew fainter, Mo Xi felt the ringing in his ears grow louder. The emperor wanted Gu Mang to personally go to the neighboring country and offer them Lu Zhanxing's head... He clearly didn't care at all for Gu Mang's feelings, didn't care whether Gu Mang fell apart or defected. He truly was testing Gu Mang's limits, heedless of the price of pushing this man away.

Murong Lian narrowed his sultry eyes. "Hm? Does General Gu not accept the edict?"

Mo Xi shook his head. *No. Don't accept it... Don't...*

But judging from Gu Mang's expression, he seemed to have long recognized the emperor's cruelty. After the first moments of shock,

Gu Mang's features turned cold and indifferent; he became calm, revealing only an undisguised weariness.

Don't accept it...

"The commoner Gu Mang," those low words issued from Gu Mang's mouth. "...accepts the edict." He raised trembling hands to take the scroll from Murong Lian.

An endless fall. A foregone conclusion.

And so it was that, in the late autumn of that year, many people came into new fates—Chonghua's only slave army met a terrible end after past glory, while Lu Zhanxing was executed at the eastern market, his corpse strung up for three days. To humiliate the once unyielding Gu Mang, the emperor ordered him to personally bring Lu Zhanxing's head to Rouli as a formal apology for the disrespect of killing their envoy.

Gu Mang set off carrying his brother's head on his back.

Dusk should have come with a lustrous splendor, but in Mo Xi's eyes, it was so pale as to be transparent. The power of the Time Mirror thinned, and the world within began to overlap the world without. From time to time, Mo Xi could hear chanting: Jiang Yexue's voice, reciting the incantation.

"Cross o'er the abyss of suffering, chase no more the past,

Wake thou from these fleeting dreams, return, return..."

As Mo Xi listened in his daze, Jiang Yexue's voice faded. Only the sounds of the Mirror world remained.

Gu Mang, prepared for a long journey, adjusted the cloth sack on his back. He arrived at the entrance to Chonghua's eastern market and looked for a stall selling meat pies. "Boss Lady, could you get me five?"

The pastry-seller was a pretty married woman. When Gu Mang had visited her stall in the past, she would shout and laugh, her voice carrying, eager to ensure everyone knew General Gu ate their meat pies. But today, when she lifted her cheerful face from the stove, her smile froze.

Gu Mang thought he hadn't been clear and repeated, "Five pastries, the same kind as always."

The woman instantly flushed. On one hand, she was eager to break off all connection with this man—it might prove troublesome even to take him as a customer. On the other hand, she found herself ashamed, her conscience at odds with her self-interest. Torn, she stood frozen until her husband came over. "Nope, nope, we're closing up shop!"

Gu Mang was startled, eyes widening. "But the night market has just opened..."

"Nope!" the man snapped brusquely.

Gu Mang understood. He looked at the woman for a moment; her face was scarlet with shame. Her conscience seemed to have suffered a shattering blow, the blood from the breakage rushing to her face and dyeing it red. He remembered the first time he came here to buy pastries. She had been single, a delicate maiden who grew so flustered at the sight of him that she'd stammered with it. Her cheeks had been rosy as a sunset then, as they were now.

Unfortunately, as time passed, many things changed—the maiden was now a madam, and the reason for her blush was likewise different.

Gu Mang sighed. "Never mind. I just wanted to buy some for the road. Your stall's pastries are really similar to ones I've had on the northern frontier; they're both delicious. Thank you for letting me taste them all these years."

He turned to leave. The lady thought she might die of embarrassment. As she watched his retreating silhouette, she couldn't help shouting, "General Gu—!"

Her husband turned pale with fright and immediately clapped a hand over her mouth. "What are you doing? Do you want to get yourself killed!"

The lady trembled; after one shout, she had lost all her righteous courage. She looked down, too afraid to make another sound. Gu Mang's steps paused for a moment before continuing into the bustling crowd. When she raised her head again, eyes teary, he'd already disappeared.

Mo Xi followed at Gu Mang's side, watching as he walked. Gu Mang seemed to have wanted to take some snacks from the capital with him. He hovered longingly in front of a little stall that sold Chonghua paper cutouts, but he was too conspicuous; the longer he stayed in the eastern market, the more people stared. The stallkeepers who were eagerly trying to attract customers lowered their heads and averted their eyes in silence when he walked by, wishing they could disappear together with their stall.

Gu Mang was an understanding person. He didn't blame them. These simple stallkeepers were guarding their livelihoods; if they served him today, they'd have it hard in the future. He had once lived in the lowest stratum of society, so he understood how it hurt to be disdained, to be left starving. When he looked at these little shops all avoiding him, his eyes held no blame. He just hadn't expected it would be so difficult to buy some mementos from his homeland on the eve of his departure.

In the end, Gu Mang left the bustling eastern market empty-handed. As he walked, he sighed. "Sorry, Zhanxing. I won't be able to buy that pear-blossom white you like for a while. I can't drink it for you."

Of course, the head in his knapsack couldn't respond. Gu Mang adjusted his burden again and walked on.

He quickly passed the guards and left the city gates behind. He made his way to an old bridge carved of white jade stone known as Chonghua Bridge, which spanned the wide river that protected the city. One end connected to the road he had taken out of the city, the other to a path winding through wild grassland to the roadside departure pavilion and the capital outskirts.

At the end of the bridge was a disheveled old man, about seventy years of age. His legs were ruined, and a swarm of flies and mosquitoes picked at him. Gu Mang knew this person; he always sat here, leaning crookedly against the bridge, begging for money or food from the people flowing in and out of the city.

The beggar was old, and he never moved from his spot. The city guards had driven him away countless times, but he would always roll his rheumy eyes, propping his arms on the ground and cursing them as he crawled away. After a couple days, he would crawl right back like a stubborn, bone-deep infection, lurking about here to beg.

Gu Mang had once asked around as to why this old fellow insisted on staying at the city gates and never left Chonghua Bridge. An aging cultivator had told him that this old fellow was once a soldier; when his entire troop was wiped out on the battlefield, he'd fled in cowardice and survived. But the geezer's conscience wore him down; after a time, he could bear it no longer and went to confess his crime to the late emperor. The emperor had been taken by benevolent governance at the time and refused to have him executed; instead he stripped him of his rank, shattered his spiritual core, and left him as a commoner.

The man tried drowning his sorrows in wine and tried becoming a monk, but nothing could absolve him of his guilt. It gnawed at him with each passing day, until his mind slowly broke. The young cultivator became an old cultivator, and the old cultivator became a madman. Every day he'd recall the moment he left his comrades behind and fled. The memory drove him insane. In his madness, he hacked away at his own legs, thinking this could change the past and prevent his former self from running. But it was useless. The old lunatic's state only worsened.

He was almost eighty, and for so many years, he did nothing but wait by Chonghua Bridge, day in and day out. He waited on the road that the army would take to return, his rheumy eyes forever gazing at the distant horizon.

No one knew what he was waiting for.

Until the day Gu Mang returned victorious as a commander for the first time, armor shining beneath his scarlet cape as he rode astride a pegasus with golden wings, weaving through myriad troops and trampling the billowing dust. That dirty old man at Chonghua Bridge suddenly seemed livelier than Gu Mang had ever seen him. He dragged his broken limbs to sit upright, straining to wave to them as his eyes overflowed with hot tears. "You're back! You finally came back!"

"Who's that old guy talking about?" one of the soldiers asked, baffled.

Gu Mang looked to his left and his right, but it was just him, and his comrades and brothers in the dust behind him. He thought it over briefly and realized with a jolt whom the old man had been waiting for.

He had been waiting for those brothers he once abandoned to pass through the decades and return to the city in blazing colors astride their prancing horses. All these years, he had been waiting.

Gu Mang had dismounted and walked over to him. The old man looked up at the young general, the sun blinding his dulled eyes.

Then he burst out sobbing, crying as he kowtowed to Gu Mang and crawling forward to try to hug him.

Lu Zhanxing had clicked his tongue. "Mang-er, that's dirty!"

"It doesn't matter," Gu Mang replied, stroking that old man's head. Everyone had their moments of weakness; everyone made mistakes. This deserter had spent most of his life suffering for his split-second decision. It was enough, Gu Mang thought.

The old man wept hysterically, missing teeth showing in his open mouth. First he called Gu Mang "Xiao-Zhao," then "Xiao-Chen" and "Xiao-Donggua." Gu Mang answered to all of them.

After that, the old man seemed to have found peace. He was still mad, but he stopped staring so fixedly at the horizon. He acted more like a proper beggar; he would smile at passersby, offering his dirty, broken bowl and singing his folk songs.

Gu Mang tightened his hold on the bag holding Lu Zhanxing's head and walked to the end of the bridge. Today might be the last time he passed by this old beggar.

"Uncle."

The beggar's catch was good today. In his broken bowl lay a great big steamed bun, and a pastry was tucked into his lapels.

Though Gu Mang himself had been the one to lift the weight on the old man's heart with his victorious return all those years ago, the man had forgotten Gu Mang completely. He was elderly, after all, and had been tormented by his obsession for so long; he didn't remember which general it had been who had dismounted to forgive him back then, to act as his Xiao-Zhao, his Xiao-Chen, his Xiao-Donggua. He looked up, chuckling mindlessly and watching Gu Mang with languid eyes. "Sir, spare some change?"

Gu Mang lowered his head to look at this stinking beggar. After a time, he smiled, too. "Now you're the only one who'll talk to me."

So saying, he emptied all his valuables and cowries from his qiankun pouch and handed them to the old man. "I'm off," said Gu Mang. He stood to leave, but the old man grabbed his wrist. "What is it?"

The beggar seemed to have come to some realization...or perhaps he hadn't realized anything at all. He reached up to take that dirty pastry from his robes and held it out as if presenting a treasure, the wrinkles on his face overflowing with his smile. "Here, here."

"For me?"

Perhaps, in his advanced age, the old man had some sensibility others lacked. He determinedly shoved the pastry into Gu Mang's hands. "Take it, you and your brother, eat it on the road... Eat it on the road..."

Gu Mang was stunned. Perhaps the eyes of elders and children really could see ghosts, as well as the future. He looked into that wrinkled face, so deeply creased it resembled a walnut. After a moment, Gu Mang slowly arranged his face into a smile and accepted that meat pie of his homeland from the old beggar's hand. "Thank you. I can take a memento of home with me after all."

The old man nodded vaguely at him, his lips quivering. "You two must come back, must come back..."

Gu Mang's smile froze, but it didn't fall. Lashes fluttering, he rose to leave. "Goodbye."

Adjusting the cloth parcel on his back, he turned to take one final look at the city gate with its towering eaves. The word *Chonghua* was emblazoned there in solemn seal script. In the setting sun, it gleamed splendidly. Gu Mang looked for a long time and mumbled—as if to himself, or as if to someone else. He said once more, "Goodbye."

Goodbye.

The last soldiers of the Wangba Army were imprisoned by the emperor, and what remained of Lu Zhanxing's corpse was in Gu Mang's knapsack. No one had come to see him off. He turned, a lonesome figure stepping onto Chonghua Bridge. The river flowed beneath it like yesterday's glory, vanishing into dust.

The old man beside the bridge suddenly called out, his voice clangorous. He craned his neck to watch Gu Mang disappear into the twilit horizon. Hoarsely, while smacking that beaten bowl of his, he began to sing a verse of the folk song he knew best—

"Time as swift as the shuttle does fly
Yet before it I think two paths lie:
In bygone days was I envy of all,
Careless years passed in careless thrall.
Alas, today is my purse light;
Each hour, minute a yearlong blight.
I, too, once rode a splendid horse,
My flag bid thousands on their course;
One cry dispersed the demon crowd;
Godlike, before my feet all bowed.
Today none mark my glories past,
Men once called friends all turn their backs;
By day I starve, my nights lack sleep,
Streetside I sing here for my keep.
Too high a flight, too far a fall;
I blame not heaven nor kin for't all.
But knowing now my bitter end,
I rue th'demons I once called friends.
And now that naught can change my state
I beg you all to avoid my fate."

I, too, once rode a splendid horse, my flag bid thousands upon their course.

I, too, once wore dark armor and bore a jade token amid arrows that shot to the sky.

And now...

Mo Xi gazed at Gu Mang's retreating silhouette without blinking. Even a blink would mean one less glimpse of him, so he watched Gu Mang leave with his eyes wide open, tears streaming down his cheeks. He had always known it caused Gu Mang pain to defect, but knowing it in his heart and seeing it with his eyes were not the same. The sight of it burrowed through his heart and his bones, seeking to shatter his soul.

Why did he end up like this... Why did he have to end up like this?

This man, who had once been a youth in blazing colors astride a spirited horse, was now like a delirious beggar, a wild and wandering ghost, as he walked down that ancient road into the distance. Mo Xi knew this departure marked a five-year-long farewell to Chonghua. When he returned, it would be with two souls missing, a mind broken, and a body covered in bloody filth—a chasm that could no longer be bridged.

When he returned, regardless of what known or unknown webs had been spun eight years ago, all the mistakes would be set in stone—neither Mo Xi nor Gu Mang could change anything that had happened.

"Gu Mang..."

Mo Xi felt his heart impaled by sharp awls. He wanted to follow, but Jiang Yexue's singing grew ever clearer, and the colors within the Time Mirror became ever more indistinct.

Gu Mang's silhouette seemed so insubstantial it might disappear at any moment. Mo Xi yearned to cross the seas and cliffs of time to take that lonely figure into his arms. To wade through oceans of blood and redeem that man who would never again turn back. But as the release incantation neared its end, Mo Xi lost the ability to move. He would leave this world behind at any second; he could only look on as that tiny, lonely figure, with no one to accompany him, set off alone—

Mo Xi's organs felt like they were being ripped apart. He wanted to tell Jiang Yexue to wait a little longer...to stop chanting...

Wait a little longer, give him one last moment. Let him accompany Gu Mang to the end of this path, or at least let him stay a few more seconds.

"Cross o'er the abyss of suffering, chase no more the past..."

Let him keep him company just a bit longer, bearing neither hatred nor grudges. Even if for only one moment.

"Wake thou from these fleeting dreams, return, return..."

Stop chanting...

Racked by the agonizing pain of farewell, Mo Xi watched as Gu Mang was swallowed by the horizon's light. An endless darkness fell. His heart convulsed and struggled; it twitched, beating so relentlessly, so fast. The pain came for his mind and sought to destroy it. He almost didn't want to return to the present—to return would hurt more. He would have to face the shattered remains of the man Gu Mang had been; he would have to contend with a world in disorder.

How could he face Gu Mang? How could he look upon the emperor? How could he ignore the sins Gu Mang had committed, or suppress the heartbreak he felt for him?

The Time Mirror was naught but a fleeting dream, drowning so many within its depths. The descriptions the past academy elders had left were not wrong...

In the throes of this stabbing pain, Mo Xi struggled to breathe as a ruthless force yanked him viciously forward. Countless colorful and twisted reflections flashed before him—the smile at the corners of Gu Mang's eyes, the anger in Gu Mang's gaze, that too-radiant youth from their time at the academy, that traitorous general who vowed never to turn back aboard a ship at the battle of Dongting Lake; the happiness, the anger, the sorrow, and the joy they had shared over half their lives all rushed into his head, only to splinter in the setting sun over Chonghua Bridge...

"Xihe-jun!"

He heard Jiang Yexue's voice.

Mo Xi tumbled onto the icy floor of Bat Tower, his wide eyes unfocused, his chest heaving. He couldn't catch his breath... He was like a fish dragged ashore; the pain of waking up to find himself thrust again into a position of helpless passivity strove to tear him asunder. As he lay panting on the ground, he saw Jiang Yexue come over amid the chaos to kneel by his side...

"Gu Mang..." Mo Xi was almost sobbing. "Gu Mang... Don't go... Don't go any farther..."

Jiang Yexue grabbed his wrist and checked his pulse: Mo Xi was on the verge of death. The agony was such that his heart had all but stopped—a heartrending pain, a bone-breaking pain, stripping flesh from his bones... His heart seemed to be wailing in despair, as if crying out that it really didn't know how to face love and sin. Might as well just kill him... Might as well just let itself stop beating.

It hurt too much.

To look on helplessly as his most important person walked into hell... No, no...was forced into hell...tempted into hell... And this time, just as before, he could neither redeem him nor accompany him. Just as before, he never discovered the true reason Gu Mang turned traitor...

"Xihe-jun!" Jiang Yexue called to him anxiously. "Mo Xi! Mo Xi!" *Don't go... It's a dead end...*

At this moment, a beam of golden light spilled from the Time Mirror. Gu Mang had also been freed—he was thrown out, skidding to a stop on the floor of the demon tower.

Mo Xi dragged himself forward. The Time Mirror had nearly worn his body to the breaking point. "Gu Mang..." He crawled, stumbling and falling toward that figure who had crumpled to the ground. He reached for Gu Mang's hand, the hand he hadn't taken eight years ago, neither in reality nor in the Mirror. "Gu Mang..."

His fingertips were shaking badly. Just as they were about to touch Gu Mang, the man on the ground twitched. Mo Xi's fingers curled back as he unconsciously withdrew.

Gu Mang slowly, slowly sat up.

Silence reigned. Gu Mang closed his eyes, his brows knitting and lashes fluttering, then slowly opened them once more. His face was pale, his lips bloodless.

He turned to look at Mo Xi, and for a long while, remained silent. His gaze went from confused to clear, from broken to focused. All the color and emotions he had lost returned to his face like ink spreading on paper. Little by little, they traced out his countenance and character.

A familiar face emerged as Mo Xi watched. As confusion gave way to awareness, it was as if he saw a long-dormant queen of the night flower bud finally stretch its petals in bloom. Gu Mang was no longer that vacant and ignorant shell, no longer a shackled slave who couldn't distinguish past from present. His eyes remained that tempered blue, but the blank expression on his face gradually shifted to one that was calm, strong, and untamed, clear and unyielding.

There was no need for any explanation, no need for a single word; all it took was a glance for Mo Xi to recognize that this was certainly not the Gu Mang whose mind had been shattered. Rather...the man who had returned from the Time Mirror was Gu Mang with all his past memories.

Chonghua's Beast of the Altar, the former General Gu. Gu-shixiong.

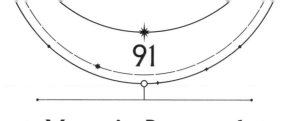

91

Memories Recovered

HOW WAS IT POSSIBLE?

The two souls that governed memory and mind had unmistakably been stripped from Gu Mang. By all accounts, the Time Mirror only allowed someone to return to an image of the past; it couldn't change anything about the real world. So how had Gu Mang regained his memories after his trip through the Mirror?

But Mo Xi had no time to devote further thought to this. There was a sharp cry from the upper reaches of the tower, and a bat monster came diving straight for Gu Mang. With a flap of its wings, a storm of fireglow arrows shot toward the ground.

"Watch out!" Jiang Yexue shouted.

Mo Xi wanted to shield Gu Mang, but the arrows flew too swiftly—there wasn't time to react or evade. As the arrows were practically upon him, a paper talisman flashed, expanding into a barrier that crackled with lightning. With a *boom*, the fireglow arrows crashed uselessly into the outside of the barrier.

The one who tossed out the talisman was none other than Gu Mang.

Even if Gu Mang had a million things on his mind, General Gu was General Gu. He leapt forward, his movements sharp as a blade unsheathed on a winter's night, gleaming with cold frost.

Moments later, rustling came from behind—a tide of rat monsters scurrying toward them. Jiang Yexue was instantly overwhelmed by this two-pronged attack. Gu Mang had no time to comb through his mess of memories nor think too deeply about his circumstances. Most wouldn't be able to jump into battle after such a mental shock, but Gu Mang was exceptional. He was a general who could direct ten thousand soldiers with a clear head after three days without sleep; he seemed to have been born with an innate readiness and capability for the battlefield.

Blue eyes scanned their surroundings, swift and decisive, ignoring all distractions as he surveyed their situation:

First was the Time Mirror, which had already sunk back into the blood pool.

Second was the shangao, who had been sealed by a tremendously complicated talisman. It had fallen into deep sleep and been discarded in a corner.

Beyond this, there was a golden demon-summoning token stuck in the ground, which the shangao had apparently managed to toss out before it succumbed. Innumerable demons were now pouring forth in answer to its summons.

As for their injuries, Mo Xi was in a bad state, and Jiang Yexue wasn't much better. He'd suffered several wounds, leaving his lotus-pale robes soaked in blood. As for Murong Chuyi...

Gu Mang frowned. "What about Murong Chuyi? Where is he?!"

"Chuyi's..." Jiang Yexue coughed. "He went to the top of the tower to rescue Chenqing."

Which was to say that they couldn't count on Murong Chuyi's support for the time being. Gu Mang swiftly weighed their strength against the enemy's. As the tide of rats surged toward them, he stood and faced the roiling crowd of demon beasts with a shout. "Fengbo!"

A beam of gold and silver light flashed in his palm and coalesced into the shape of a holy weapon suona. In the darkness, the white ribbon tied to its end glowed like the Milky Way.

"Come!"

Mo Xi's handsome face was completely drained of color as he watched Gu Mang's silhouette from behind. A distant, muffled cry issued from Gu Mang's former holy weapon, and it exploded in a dazzling halo—but in the next moment, that blazing light of the summons fractured. Before it could fully materialize, the holy weapon Fengbo became motes of scattered light drifting down around them.

Gu Mang sighed. It'd been a risky attempt, but there were too many beasts. A wide-range weapon was their best bet, but the only such weapon he had was Fengbo. He wasn't surprised that the summons had failed. His spiritual core had been shattered long ago. After regaining his memories in the Time Mirror, he could recall the incantation to summon Fengbo—but holy weapons were linked to the core and resided in the soul. Without a strong spiritual core and soul, he'd never be able to summon Fengbo for real.

The tide of demon rats drew nearer; Gu Mang's eyes darkened. In the end, what he shouted was, "Yongye, come!" Before the sparkling remains of Fengbo fully faded, an intense burst of black magic qi swarmed from his palms and coalesced into a wicked black dagger.

It was the demonic weapon the Liao Kingdom had forged for him upon his defection—the demonic weapon that nearly murdered Mo Xi at the battle of Dongting Lake. The dagger Yongye.

Gu Mang flicked his slender fingers, spinning the dagger nimbly in his palm. He shot forward like an arrow loosed, his movements swift and vicious as he slaughtered his way through that tide of demon beasts. This demonic weapon was imbued with soul-sucking power—so long as its formation was activated, it would attract the bats like fresh blood, then absorb all of these demons into itself.

In moments the rat beasts had him completely surrounded. A dense shroud of demonic energy enveloped him; his silhouette disappeared into it. All one could see within the horde was the intermittent fiery flash of magic as beast corpses and black blood spewed forth.

Unlike Mo Xi, Jiang Yexue only now recognized the change in Gu Mang. Face pale, he turned to Mo Xi. "Has...has Gu Mang somehow recovered?"

Mo Xi didn't answer, his reddened phoenix eyes fixed upon the center of that mass of black qi. But his expression told Jiang Yexue everything he needed to know. "When the shangao said it would 'flashback' Gu Mang's memories, did it mean 'repair'?" he asked, stunned. "The Time Mirror...could it have patched his memories even when he's missing two souls?"

Mo Xi wanted to reply, but when he opened his mouth, only black blood spilled out.

"Xihe-jun..." Jiang Yexue gasped.

Mo Xi's injuries were much worse than Gu Mang's. Gu Mang had entered the Mirror directly; although it had affected him, the Time Mirror was, after all, an ancient godly artifact, not some monstrous relic. One who entered and left it as designed shouldn't suffer serious harm.

But it was different for Mo Xi. He had been sucked into the Mirror while stubbornly trying to protect Gu Mang. He was essentially an uninvited guest, a trespasser. Hence, even though he hadn't exerted himself much inside the Time Mirror, the trip had exacted a great cost on his spiritual energy. When he emerged, his body was mortally weakened.

But as Mo Xi watched Gu Mang fight hand-to-hand with demons, watched him wield the demonic weapon Yongye encircled in black mist, he suppressed his discomfort. Swallowing the bloody tang in his mouth, he stretched out his hand: "Tuntian, come."

The tall scepter Tuntian appeared at his summons, glowing a pristine white.

As Gu Mang slashed through the horde with his Liao Kingdom blade, Mo Xi closed his eyes, enduring the dual exhaustion of heart and body. He lifted the scepter and pointed it into the air. Wind and waves swirled, and the sound of oceanic tides surrounded them. "Swallowing Leviathan!"

A beam of silver light rushed out, and a colossal spirit whale burst into being in midair. Its song seemed to resound through the ages as a wild gale whirled to life, its irresistible pull drawing all the attacking beasts into the air. With an explosive toss of its tail, the whale soared toward the tower's peak. Those monsters were swept along in its wake, only for the giant whale Tuntian to beat its tail in another vicious stroke.

Black blood filled the sky, plummeting toward the earth in a torrential downpour. Every one of the beasts had disintegrated.

Amid the bloody storm, Gu Mang whirled in astonishment, his clear blue eyes wide as he looked behind him. "Mo Xi..."

Mo Xi's hand around the scepter was shaking. He hadn't created a barrier, and those drops of still-warm blood fell upon his shoulders and hair, running past his pitch-black eyes to stream down his pale cheeks like gory tears.

He stood in this scarlet downpour, exhausted and helpless, and slowly closed his eyes. The Mo Clan bloodline ran with ferocious power, and this holy weapon Tuntian was the most terrifying of his birthrights. It was impossible to moderate—if the killing move was made, its wide swath left no survivors. Mo Xi had sworn never to use it regardless of how dire the situation their army found themselves in. He'd always kept himself under tight control, refusing to let himself summon Tuntian, to say the words "Swallowing Leviathan."

Not only would this move make him look monstrous in the eyes of onlookers, but more importantly: Mo Xi didn't wish to exterminate his opponents. He hated the battlefield. He enlisted in order to protect, not to conquer, and least of all for revenge. Whether his opponents were humans or beasts, good or evil, Mo Xi's instinct was to spare them whenever possible, to give them a chance to retreat. This power that could destroy thousands of living souls in an instant was one that he possessed, but never let himself use.

But now...

To put an end to the sight of Gu Mang killing with the Liao Kingdom's demonic weapon, to put an end to the strife as quickly as possible; on the verge of utter collapse, he unleashed this forbidden fatal blow.

"Mo Xi..." Jiang Yexue murmured.

Mo Xi didn't seem to have heard him. He was still haloed in Tuntian's fury, its power instantly piercing the barrier Jiang Yexue tried to erect over him. He stood silent, alone in the pouring blood rain.

The dagger in Gu Mang's hand retracted, becoming a cloud of black mist that disappeared into his body. He walked over to Mo Xi.

Mo Xi stood fixed in place like a broken statue; his face was pallid, his expression drained, eyes empty. He seemed submerged in the falling blood.

Gu Mang came to a stop before him, looking up at Mo Xi's figure, drenched to the skin. This proud man seemed to have been reduced to an abandoned dog—so deeply lost and injured that he didn't know where to go.

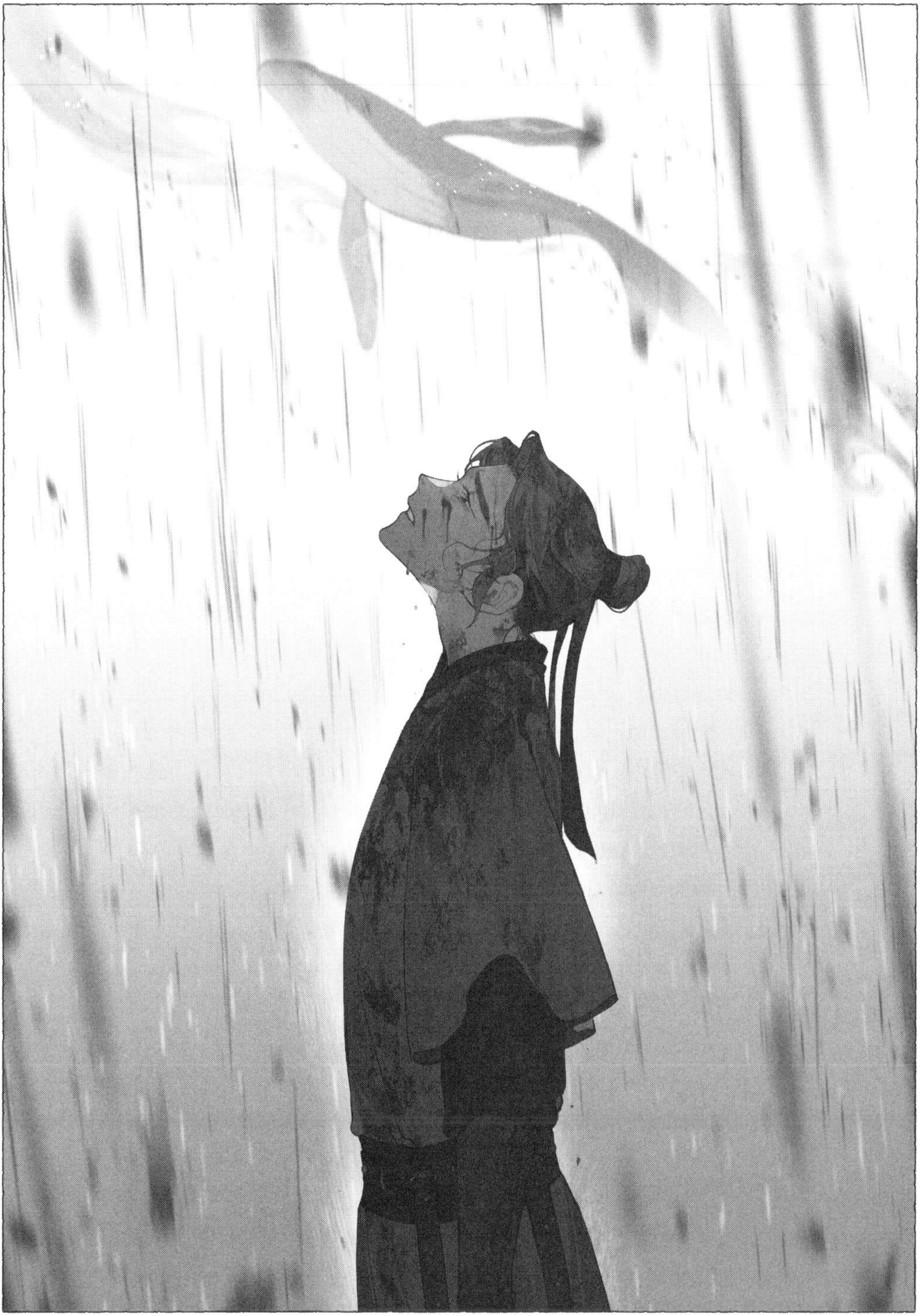

But Gu Mang's thoughts were also a mess. Although his returned memories granted him clarity, they also brought him a terrible unease and disorientation. His body had gone back in time within the Mirror and recovered the memories from before he'd defected. Once out of the mirror, those memories hadn't dissipated. Instead, they connected in his mind to the events after he'd returned to the city as a prisoner of war.

To him, it felt as if he'd left Chonghua bearing Lu Zhanxing's head on his back in one instant, and he had awoken in the next to find himself a traitor in the prison wagon of his own motherland. Gu Mang retained nothing of what had happened in between— nothing that happened in the five years he defected. Lacking this crucial information, Gu Mang regarded many things with suspicion and confusion. He felt profoundly lost and was all the more wary as a consequence.

Gu Mang deliberated for some time before he said to Mo Xi, "My thanks to Xihe-jun for the assistance."

Only Mo Xi's dark eyes shifted at the sound of Gu Mang's voice, his vacant gaze landing on his figure. After a beat of silence, he managed one word. "You..." His throat tasted bitter, and the next words he spoke were bitter too. "...remember everything now?"

Gu Mang was silent a moment. "Not everything. But...most of it."

Mo Xi made no reply.

"My mind is clear at least. I'm a functioning person now."

"Then...what happened in the Mirror... You still..."

"Mn," Gu Mang said. "I remember it all."

Mo Xi fell silent, eyes fluttering closed as he swallowed. He seemed to want to maintain a nonchalant, serene expression, but his mouth wobbled dangerously. He closed his eyes, his throat tight and acrid. "I'm glad."

His heart was in chaos, his body breaking down. He was nearly as weak as when he'd collapsed in a pool of blood at Dongting Lake, and just as physically and mentally worn. He didn't know how to approach Gu Mang, so he muttered hoarsely once more: "I'm glad..." After a pause, he continued. "Are you leaving?"

"Hm?"

"You wouldn't want to stay in Chonghua as a prisoner. Up till now, you've stayed because you didn't remember, but now you do," said Mo Xi. "Are you going to leave?"

Gu Mang was silent for a beat. He reached up to yank his collar open, exposing the black hoop around his pale neck.

No one spoke.

"Slave collar. The one you gave me." Gu Mang watched Mo Xi as he spoke. "I'm your slave. If you don't let me go, I'll never be able to leave."

The bland phrasing seemed to deal Mo Xi a piercing blow. He swayed. Not just because he had learned many new secrets inside the Mirror and felt a complex mixture of emotions toward Gu Mang, but because of the expression Gu Mang wore as he said it.

He'd seen Gu Mang in many moods: grinning, compassionate, earnest, bewildered, sorrowful, dazed. If Gu Mang had cried, laughed, or raged at this moment, it would have been a relief. At least then Mo Xi could believe Gu Mang was still a living person, someone he could chase down, someone real and tangible.

What he feared most was Gu Mang's apathy. Gu Mang had only worn such a light and emotionless expression on the handful of occasions they'd met after his defection. Seeing it swept Mo Xi without warning into those darkest bygone days: Gu Mang, standing on the deck, wielding a dagger, the bloodstained ribbon around his head fluttering, telling Mo Xi that nothing could be changed.

Mo Xi tried to speak, but the old scar on his chest flared with pain as if newly gouged by a knife. Or perhaps it was the spasming of the organ beneath as it slowly tore itself apart. His vision flashed dark. He seemed to see a vague hint of sorrow betrayed in Gu Mang's blue eyes. He wanted to get a better look—to see if that sorrow was real, or if, in his obsession, he had simply imagined it. He took a step forward...

But his legs felt full of lead. He crumpled.

The violent convulsions in his chest brought up another mouthful of blood. Surprised, Gu Mang instinctively reached out to catch him, the same way he had when Mo Xi was young and still called him Gu Mang-shixiong.

Jiang Yexue's voice rose anxiously from nearby: "He's at his limit. Put him down. I have spirit-concentrating powder. Give him a dose, quick."

Mo Xi didn't care. He felt very light, as if his soul might struggle free of his body and fly away at any moment. Strangely, the feeling of nearing death was one of release. Perhaps he should have died that year, on that ship in Dongting Lake. If he had, he wouldn't have lived through so many years of torment. He wasn't a person forged of steel and iron. Constrained by his circumstances for so long, he'd slowly been driven insane.

Harming Chonghua, harming Gu Mang, hurt him too. Every time he said something to wound Gu Mang, it hurt him too. Every time he told himself to hate Gu Mang, to not be selfish—every time he reminded himself of what Gu Mang had done and what Gu Mang had suffered—every time he tried to strip away the past, he felt like he was being flayed and torn open—*it hurt him too!*

But he had to live. Without him, the Northern Frontier Army would have ended up disbanded and destroyed. He had to use that body of his, which had already lost a decade of life, to bear the weight of the shadow his old friend left behind. Without him, Gu Mang would have to return to Luomei Pavilion. He had to use that manor of his, which would never be filled with merry reunion, to shelter the broken ruins a hero had left behind.

Jiang Yexue's voice seemed to grow more and more distant. "Mo Xi...wake up... Mo Xi..."

He was so tired. He studied Gu Mang's blue eyes. He wanted to reach out, but he couldn't even move his fingertips. "How nice..." he whispered. "How nice would it be...if your eyes were black."

If they were still black, I could lie to myself and pretend nothing's happened—that it was all just a ridiculous nightmare I had while we were stationed at the frontier. I could lie to myself and say, once I wake up, you'll be that brilliant, smiling youth with a heart full of joy, and I can stay by your side and listen to your jokes. We would still be in the barracks, our ranks not so high and our pay so very low. All the people you loved—your comrades, your brothers, your childhood friends—none of them had left you yet. I could hold your hand with a heart full of sincerity, gaze at your face with nothing but love, see how every inch of you seemed to be wreathed in sunshine.

Mo Xi's eyes fluttered shut.

Gu Mang, if your eyes were still black...how nice that would be. Back then, our biggest worry was whether Lu Zhanxing would lift the tent flap and come bursting in.

Back then, I could still look toward our future with boundless imagination and hope.

How nice.

Or perhaps, Mo Xi thought, not without sorrow, if he had truly died at the battle of Dongting Lake, that would be nice, too...

For someone as strong and unyielding as he to develop such a wish, it could only be that he'd suffered too many blows.

Before he completely lost consciousness, the last thing Mo Xi heard was the humming sound of a sword in motion. A voice as elegant and cold as jade spoke from afar: "I just went to the top of the tower to rescue one person; what are all of you doing, standing around in this river of blood?"

92

Scoundrel Shixiong Comes Online

A DROP OF WATER dripped from a crack in the stone cave and landed on the tip of Mo Xi's nose.

Mo Xi's lashes quivered as he slowly opened his eyes.

His gaze was unfocused; he couldn't tell if he was in the past or the present. The mess within Bat Tower swayed before his eyes, interspersed with glimpses of Gu Mang's meager silhouette walking into the dusky distance.

His heart was still beating, muffled by his flesh, after having nearly faltered, pushed to the limits of what it could bear. Mo Xi took a moment to breathe. Once his vision had cleared somewhat, he stretched his stiff neck and looked around.

He was lying inside a shallow cave, the starry sky visible beyond its mouth. A fire crackled merrily, and three people sat by the firepit: Gu Mang, Jiang Yexue, and Murong Chuyi. Yue Chenqing lay not far off with Jiang Yexue's coat draped over him.

Mo Xi's head ached atrociously; he had to close his eyes. The memories from before he lost consciousness sparked like flint in his head. All the past events within the Time Mirror, Gu Mang slowly walking toward the horizon with Lu Zhanxing's head on his back, the old beggar and his mournful folk song—*I, too, once rode a splendid horse, my flag bid thousands on their course. One cry dispersed the demon crowd; godlike, before my feet all bowed. Today none mark my glories past, men once called friends all turn their backs...*

And the coldness on Gu Mang's face when they finally came out of the Mirror, as he stood in the storm of blood.

Mo Xi sat bolt upright.

The movement alerted the group chatting around the fire. Gu Mang was first to notice; he turned and met Mo Xi's eyes. They looked at each other in silence.

The first thing Gu Mang said wasn't directed at Mo Xi. He stared at Mo Xi for a moment, and then turned to Jiang Yexue and Murong Chuyi. "He's awake."

The remaining two looked over. Jiang Yexue wheeled his wooden chair to Mo Xi's side. "Xihe-jun, how do you feel? Is anything bothering you?"

Mo Xi didn't respond. Heart pounding, his eyes never strayed from Gu Mang where he sat by the fire. He was still stunned and bewildered by Gu Mang suddenly regaining his memories. He even thought it might be a dream, but when he closed his eyes and opened them again, he was still in this cave, with these people. It was real.

The Time Mirror had shocked Gu Mang's brain when it brought him back to the past, and somehow repaired his mind.

Mo Xi's dry lips parted, his voice shockingly rough. "You..."

Gu Mang glanced at him, but his blue eyes quickly turned aside, indifferent. The expression he wore was nearly identical to that of the youth from eight years ago, only that there seemed to be a thin layer of frost over it.

Jiang Yexue saw that Gu Mang hadn't responded and was afraid Mo Xi would feel awkward. "Gu Mang's fine. Also...while you were unconscious, he told us about recovering his memories, so you don't need to worry."

Mo Xi stared past Jiang Yexue to the silent Gu Mang. He lay sprawled casually, an elbow propped on his knee. His lapels were even somewhat loosened, just like the roguish soldier he'd been.

Again and again, Mo Xi had been shocked upon entering the Mirror, but this final blow was beyond anything he could imagine. When Mo Xi realized Gu Mang had recovered his memories, he'd felt a flash of pathetic, short-lived ecstasy, thinking that they finally shared the same past. But the joy only lasted an instant. As he looked at Gu Mang now, the fervor in his heart slowly cooled. That brief flutter was crushed by unfamiliarity, anxiety, helplessness, and confusion. In that moment, he came to several realizations, but all were numbed by the tortuous mental beating he'd received.

After a long, dull pause, he finally settled on this: Gu Mang had regained his memories, but he acted much less like the Gu-shixiong he remembered. On the contrary, he was incredibly cold and removed. He had been first to notice Mo Xi was awake, but rather than get up, he was content to let Murong Chuyi and Jiang Yexue deal with it. He'd even turned away to take a leisurely sip of hot tea. Mo Xi examined Gu Mang's face in profile and the heaviness in his heart deepened.

At the sight of him staring silently at Gu Mang, Jiang Yexue asked with concern, "Xihe-jun, are you okay?"

Mo Xi paused a moment, looking away from Gu Mang and doing his best to sound calm. "I am." And because he didn't want Jiang Yexue to pick up on anything else, he changed the topic. "Where... are we?"

"Still on Bat Island," Jiang Yexue answered. "It's become a bit of a sticky situation. Wuyan sealed off the entire island and we've sustained too many injuries, so we can't leave just yet."

"Who?"

"The island's Bat Queen. Her name's Wuyan—*yan* as in swallow."

"Isn't she a bat?" Mo Xi asked wearily. "Why does she call herself a bird?"

"Yes, it's an odd name for sure," Jiang Yexue said. "When we entered the tower, Wuyan was at a critical point in her secluded cultivation within the underground palace, so she didn't emerge even with all the ruckus we made. After you destroyed her tribesmen in the tower, Chuyi..." Jiang Yexue paused, feeling uncomfortable, and corrected himself. "Xiaojiu rescued Chenqing from her prison. When you were passed out, she finished her qi circulation and broke seclusion to come after us. Fortunately, we had Gu Mang."

As he spoke, Jiang Yexue glanced at Gu Mang. He was being perfectly polite to the others, and grinned at Jiang Yexue as if he'd never defected. Jiang Yexue didn't know how to respond; he looked away. "Gu Mang stepped in to handle it, which is how we managed to escape and find this cave. But Wuyan is crazed with fury. At this point, she's covered all of Bat Island with alarm spells—a moment's carelessness and she'll find us. I've set up a concealment talisman here; we'll be fine for a while, so you don't need to worry just yet."

Mo Xi massaged his pulsing temples. He turned to look at Yue Chenqing, who was curled up within Jiang Yexue's greatcoat, fast asleep. In the dozen-odd days since they'd last crossed paths, Yue Chenqing had lost a good deal of weight; his once-round cheeks had become sunken, the lines of his face pathetic and helpless.

"How is he?" Mo Xi asked.

As Jiang Yexue took a breath to respond, Gu Mang cut in. "Why not come over here to talk? Come warm up by the fire and have something to eat."

Mo Xi's scarred and callused heart beat faster at these vaguely gentle words. He looked up at Gu Mang. Just as he was about to say a word of thanks, Gu Mang lazily continued: "Or is Xihe-jun so delicate that he can't walk? Do I need to come give you a piggy-back ride?"

Mo Xi's words lodged in his throat, choking the breath from him. He had thought they could at least mend their relationship somewhat after coming out of the Time Mirror. He wanted to make amends, at least: to properly apologize for his absence back then and try to ask Gu Mang for the truth one more time.

But Gu Mang didn't seem to share these sentiments. The hostility in his words was no different than when he was the Liao Kingdom's loyal subject—he sounded absolutely unrepentant.

"Gu Mang..." Mo Xi said softly.

"Hm?" Gu Mang scoffed. "You *do* need me to carry you?"

Mo Xi's eyes dulled, like a candle extinguished after guttering too long. Gu Mang had put out the last glimmer of light in his eyes. Gu Mang's attitude seemed to mock him—*Oh Mo Xi, what's the point? The two of us are already like this. Whatever the truth is, whatever happened in the past, let's just be enemies. What other choice do we have?*

Mo Xi clenched his jaw and rose; despite his injuries, he managed to make it to the firepit unassisted. He cast Gu Mang a meaningful glance, as if he wanted to say something, but in the end, he turned away. He silently sat next to Murong Chuyi, as far as possible from Gu Mang.

Naturally, Gu Mang noticed. He smiled without saying a word and focused instead on turning the meat over the fire.

An uncomfortable silence descended. After a moment, Mo Xi turned to ask Murong Chuyi, "How is Yue Chenqing?"

Murong Chuyi's face was wan. Eyes downcast, he said simply, "I've taken care of his injuries, so there's no threat to his life. However, he's been poisoned by the Bat Queen's gu worms, and I don't have an antidote."

Mo Xi stared. The shangao had said Yue Chenqing was locked in the cell and covered in bloodsucking vines. It hadn't mentioned anything about a gu worm. "What kind of poison is this gu worm?"

"I've never seen it before; there's no record of it in any cultivation realm texts. I interrogated two of the bat demons guarding his cell, but they didn't know much either. The only thing they said..." Murong Chuyi paused. Frowning with disgust, he coughed quietly.

Jiang Yexue came over and offered him a cup of hot tea. "Xiaojiu, have some."

Murong Chuyi gave him a withering look. He shoved the tea aside, spilling it all over Jiang Yexue's sleeves. Jiang Yexue fell silent.

After waiting for his breathing to steady, Murong Chuyi continued. "The only thing they said was that this gu worm could take a body drained of blood and create an undead puppet in the form of an individual of the poisoner's choosing. It could reconstruct everything about that person, from their appearance to their voice, memories, and feelings."

With nothing better to do, Gu Mang had summoned his demonic dagger to play with. He poked it into the fire like a pair of tongs, stoking the merrily burning flames. At Murong Chuyi's words, he asked, "So it kills someone and then uses their corpse to construct someone new?"

"Precisely."

"What is the demoness after?" Gu Mang nimbly spun the blade in his slender fingers. "Who does she want to reconstruct using Yue Chenqing's body?"

"I don't know," Murong Chuyi responded wearily. "Those two bat guards were loyal to the end. When I pressed them, they shattered their own cores and killed themselves. After I recover, I'll trap a suitable monster here on the island and ask some questions." He coughed again. "If we want to cure Yue Chenqing of this poison, the more we know, the better."

"All right then," Gu Mang said decisively. "How about this? I have a slave collar around my neck, so I can't run away no matter what. You guys haven't yet recovered. Why don't I go grab a likely demon for you to interrogate?"

Murong Chuyi looked at him. "How kind. Why?"

Gu Mang smiled at Murong Chuyi. "I'm just looking out for myself. In exchange for helping save him, I would ask you sirs to do a kind deed. Do me a solid: don't tell anyone I've regained my memories once we return to the capital."

No one had expected this, and all three of them fell silent.

"Why are you looking at me like that?" Gu Mang gave the dagger one last twirl. With a flourish, the blade became a wisp of spiritual energy that sank back into his palm. "Is my request so strange?"

"Gu Mang," Jiang Yexue said, "this is the crime of lying to one's emperor."

Gu Mang smiled. He was antagonistic and cold to Mo Xi, but there was friendliness in his expression when he spoke to the others, "Sorry 'bout that, I know I'll be troubling you all. But I don't have much choice. If the rest of Chonghua knows I've recovered, I'll probably be sent back to Luomei Pavilion, and those with grudges will come swarming. And His Imperial Majesty too—he'll take me for black magic experiments and interrogate me about the Liao Kingdom's secrets."

Murong Chuyi's expression was cold as ice and snow as he asked, "Do you not deserve such treatment?"

"I'm not saying I don't," Gu Mang said shamelessly. "But can't I fear that fate, at least? Who'd want to spend their days waiting to get offed or get fucked..."

Murong Chuyi paled at such vulgarity. "You!"

Jiang Yexue tried to compromise. "If you don't want to return to Luomei Pavilion, we'll help keep you safe. But we can't hide this truth. You *should* declare Liao Kingdom secrets to Chonghua."

"I can't divulge anything," Gu Mang said. "I've forgotten."

No one spoke.

At the expressions on the faces of these three noble sirs, Gu Mang added earnestly, "Sorry, I've really forgotten."

Mo Xi watched Gu Mang across the fire. That organ in his chest hurt so horribly it seemed to pulse with resentment at its neglect. He closed his eyes, biting out each word. "Did you not regain your memories?"

"I didn't say I remembered *everything*," Gu Mang said. "I'm missing two souls. No matter what I do, I'll never recover completely."

Mo Xi nailed Gu Mang with a stare. Hatred and heartbreak were clear in his eyes, but he exerted all his will to keep his delicate features composed. "And how, exactly, did you lose those two souls?"

The smile on Gu Mang's face disappeared. After a time he said lightly, "Oh, this is also something I've forgotten."

Mo Xi said nothing.

"Don't look at me like that; I really don't know. Believe me or don't. If you don't, you could use the Soul-Recording Spell or Draught of Confession to torture me as you like; if you can get the truth out, I'll admit defeat."

Mo Xi turned away, his grip slowly tightening around his own knee. He didn't reply.

Murong Chuyi had remained cool and calm. Unswayed by emotion, he considered Gu Mang's words and returned to the topic at hand. "If you're afraid of harsh treatment upon our return, why not just kill us and escape?"

"Good question, gorgeous." Gu Mang chuckled with a thoughtful hand to his chin. "Cold and beautiful men certainly are hard to handle. Xihe-jun is one example, and Murong-xiansheng is another."

Murong Chuyi and Mo Xi greeted this statement with identical silences.

Gu Mang laughed, but his blue eyes swept across each of them in turn. "Let's see. It does seem like I have a reasonable chance of killing you all and escaping. Look—Jiang-xiong is disabled, and he's used up much too much of his spiritual energy. Murong-xiong doesn't seem to be at his best either—he must've been injured saving his nephew. This Yue Clan kiddo isn't even awake, so I could kill him more easily than I would a sparrow."

His gaze fell next upon Mo Xi. It was a fleeting glance, like a dragonfly skimming water, before he looked indifferently away. He crossed his arms and grinned. "My god, at this rate, it'd be more absurd if I *didn't* kill you all and run."

"So?" asked Murong Chuyi.

With a flick of his fingertip, Gu Mang summoned the dagger Yongye once more. He lunged forward without warning—but Murong Chuyi had been watching the whole time. He summoned a gleaming gold talisman and instantly raised a protective barrier.

Gu Mang looked at the barrier and spread his hands with a smile. "You see? It'll end up like this, won't it? If I tried to kill anyone, you guys would retaliate. Even if demonic qi gave me an advantage, my core is still broken, and I might still lose. Plus, I certainly wouldn't make it out unscathed, and when the noise alerts that bat lady, what then? Should I lie here and let her mold me like a clay figurine?"

Murong Chuyi stared at Gu Mang for a moment. The golden light at his fingertips slowly extinguished, and he turned to glance at the unconscious Yue Chenqing. "I'll trust you this once. If you help us, I won't speak of your condition once we leave."

Gu Mang smiled. "Your word alone won't do. Can you guarantee your cute little nephews' mouths will also stay sealed?" He paused, his fluid gaze finally landing on the silent Mo Xi. "And Xihe-jun's mouth..." Gu Mang ran his tongue over sharp incisors, his mannerisms retaining their wolfishness. His gaze was dark with secrets as he stared at Mo Xi's pale lips, his voice a low, syrupy murmur. "The most stubborn of all. Murong-xiong, could you do me a favor and ask him the same question? See if he's willing to cooperate and keep those pretty lips of his...shut *tight* for me?"

93

Shixiong Won't Pamper You Today

GU MANG'S ARCH SMILE and relentless stare filled Mo Xi with an awkwardness he hadn't felt in a long time. He bit his lip and turned away.

Of course Murong Chuyi wouldn't plead with Mo Xi and Jiang Yexue on Gu Mang's behalf, but since he had shown where he stood on the matter, it seemed worth considering. Gu Mang casually clasped one shoulder, his back against the stone wall as he spun the dagger in his free hand. "How does that sound? Do we have a deal?"

Helping a criminal conceal important information would amount to the great crime of deceiving one's emperor. However, Gu Mang's assessment wasn't wrong; they were truly all in the same boat.

Jiang Yexue glanced at Murong Chuyi. "If Xiaojiu is willing to do this...then I won't say anything either. As long as you don't make things difficult for us in the future, I'll help you keep this secret."

Gu Mang smiled as he cupped his hands at Jiang Yexue. "Sensible. Thanks."

He then turned to look at Mo Xi, that slight smile dimming. "Xihe-jun, what about you?"

Mo Xi was silent for a beat. "I won't hand you over to the emperor."

"Perfect." Gu Mang smiled again lazily. "Everyone is a gentleman here—a man's word cannot be taken back. I'll help you with this, you'll help me keep my secret, and we're even."

"Do you plan to go trap a demon now?" Murong Chuyi asked.

Gu Mang sat down. "No rush. I used up too much spiritual energy escaping Wuyan's clutches. Let Gege have a bite first." With that, he turned the two skewers hung over the fire.

Only then did Mo Xi notice that there was a plump goose suspended over the firepit. Mo Xi was a proud person, but he'd just witnessed Gu Mang's past suffering. His heart ached bitterly; he still wanted to make amends. So he quietly asked, "Where'd you get the goose?"

Gu Mang ignored him.

Mo Xi shut his mouth.

Jiang Yexue noticed the awkwardness and warmly replied, "It was stored on my walnut ship."

He brought out the tiny ship he had used to ferry them to the island. Putting the thumb-sized ship on the ground, he tapped it with a fingertip. The vessel immediately grew a dozen times larger, to the size of a wooden basin.

Jiang Yexue called out in a gentle voice: "Boatwoman, could you please bring us some more tea and refreshments?"

"Coming!" From the inside of the basin-sized ship came a crisp and pleasant voice with a soft Wu-dialect accent, giggling, "There's fresh fruit and desserts, and we've got miaoyu tea from Lingshan and dancong tea from Wudong. Which would you like, my lord?"

"Some of each."

The tinkling voice laughed. "All right, coming right up."

The bamboo cabin curtain on the walnut ship swished, and a lifelike clay maiden emerged. On the ship, she was only half the height of a palm, but she transformed into a clay servant the size of a child as soon as she touched the ground. She carried a wooden tray laden with fruit and desserts, as well as two pots of hot tea.

Mo Xi watched the clay boatmaiden cheerfully settle the tray next to the firepit. "Why didn't we see this puppet on the ship?" he asked.

"She's cleverer than the other puppets; I spent a lot of time on her. When we were on the walnut ship, she was busy with the steering, so you didn't see her."

The clay boatmaiden looked up, revealing willowy brows and slender phoenix eyes. Jiang Yexue 's careful work was evident; she was merely a clay person, but her face was as detailed as a real human's. All her paints and lacquers had been attentively applied, and she moved more smoothly than her clay brethren.

The boatmaiden performed an obeisance and said in a charming voice, "If there's nothing else, I'll wait on the ship."

Gu Mang was watching with rapt interest and stopped her. "Hey hey, miss, don't be in such a rush to leave." He asked with a smile, "Do you have any lychee wood on your ship?"

"The mast is made of lychee wood, but unfortunately I can't give it to you."

"You know why I want lychee wood?" Gu Mang asked curiously.

The maiden chuckled and pointed to the crackling bonfire. "Meat roasted over lychee wood has an extraordinary flavor. Gongzi must have a craving."

Astonished, Gu Mang turned to Jiang Yexue. "How does she know that?"

Jiang Yexue lowered his gaze and laughed. "When I was refining her, I merged a copy of *Recipes of the Nine Provinces* into her head."

"Damn." Gu Mang clapped. "I've been away just a few years and Jiang-xiong's artificing skills have improved considerably. These constructs are not only lifelike but also clever."

Jiang Yexue glanced at Murong Chuyi. "I'm still not as good as Xiaojiu."

Murong Chuyi pretended to be deaf. He leaned silently against the stone wall with his arms crossed.

Despite Murong Chuyi's attitude, Jiang Yexue smiled faintly. He allowed the boatmaiden to return to the cabin and shrank the boat back to the size of a walnut. After he'd stowed the ship back in his qiankun pouch, he continued to warmly compliment Murong Chuyi: "My Xiaojiu is the greatest grandmaster artificer of all; he can transform a flower into a ship, a raindrop into a tower."

Jiang Yexue spoke with the intent to cajole, but it didn't work on Murong Chuyi. He closed his phoenix eyes as if repulsed.

Mo Xi and Gu Mang both stared. What kind of power, Mo Xi wondered, did this Ignorant Immortal have for both his nephews to praise him so? While Yue Chenqing praised him with fiery enthusiasm, gushing about his uncle to anyone he met, Jiang Yexue wouldn't necessarily mention him unprompted. But oddly, whenever the two of them were compared, Jiang Yexue would say without hesitation that Murong Chuyi was his better, despite being one of the best artificer elders at the academy himself.

Jiang Yexue's self-deprecating praise was different from Yue Chenqing's loud boasting. Murong Chuyi's indifference to Yue Chenqing only made Yue Chenqing look foolish. When Jiang Yexue praised Murong Chuyi so sincerely at his own expense and was still ignored, he seemed rather pathetic.

Sensing the tense atmosphere, Gu Mang spoke up. "Murong-xiansheng is of the older generation; it's natural that Jiang-xiong cannot compare. Come—the goose is almost ready, let's have something to eat. You haven't had my crispy roast goose before, right? Give it a try."

Although Gu Mang was an enemy of Chonghua, Jiang Yexue couldn't bring himself to hate him, while Murong Chuyi had no sense of patriotism to begin with. Besides, they all shared a goal at the moment, so they put aside any petty bickering.

The roast goose was ready, dripping grease that hissed when it fell into the flames. Gu Mang took it off of the spit, picked the plumpest part of the goose breast, and sliced it thinly, the skin crackling beneath his little knife. The savory fragrance of meat and char assaulted the senses, crisp golden-brown skin clinging to the firm, piping-hot meat. Gu Mang placed each slice on a banana leaf and sprinkled coarse salt over top, carving just enough for two servings before passing them to Murong Chuyi and Jiang Yexue.

As Jiang Yexue tried a bite, Gu Mang smiled. "How is it?"

"I didn't know you could cook."

Gu Mang laughed out loud. "If only we had some lychee wood and stuffed the goose with berries while it roasted. I guarantee the flavor would leave you speechless."

"When did you learn to make this?" Jiang Yexue asked.

"I taught myself; I'm a genius." As Gu Mang spoke, he carved some more goose meat. "Doesn't it hit the spot?"

"Why didn't you make this back then?" Jiang Yexue remarked.

Mo Xi, staring into that warm bonfire, murmured, "He did."

Jiang Yexue was startled, but still managed to smile warmly. "That's right, you two were close in those days. I remember Gu Mang really did take good care of you..."

But it seemed Gu Mang didn't wish to be associated with Mo Xi. He hastily waved a hand. "It was nothing. I wouldn't quite call it *care*." He turned to Mo Xi with a shallow smile. "It's been so long, but you still remember that goose. As I recall, it wasn't my best effort; it tasted like wax. Xihe-jun, however much you hate me, I'll ask you not to bring up my shortcomings right now." He rubbed his nose, unwittingly leaving a smear of soot. "I do have my pride, you know."

Across the fire, Mo Xi watched Gu Mang's smiling, callous face. There were torrents of words stuck in his throat, but it would be futile even if he could express them. He couldn't figure out how to talk to Gu Mang; he felt that he might do something extremely reckless at the tiniest impulse. Should he open his mouth and vent his feelings, he'd never be able to take it back.

And so, he stayed silent. Whether Gu Mang was purposefully distancing himself from Mo Xi or whether he genuinely viewed him as an enemy, Mo Xi chose to endure it without complaint for as long as he could.

Gu Mang spread the crisp and fragrant goose over another banana leaf. He retracted the knife and sat back down with his own leaf in hand.

Jiang Yexue was an observant man. He paused in the middle of his meal as he noticed something was amiss. Gu Mang had served him and Murong Chuyi, but not Mo Xi. This was already quite awkward. On top of that, Mo Xi was a pampered scion who never dirtied his hands with such tasks; there was no way he'd know how to carve roast goose. The atmosphere grew even more uncomfortable.

Just as Jiang Yexue was about to speak up to smooth things over, Gu Mang looked up. "Oh right. I forgot about yours, Xihe-jun."

Mo Xi was silent.

He continued: "Do you want me to help you cut some?"

But before Mo Xi could respond, Gu Mang went back to eating from his banana leaf with a smile. "Aiya, never mind," he said without a hint of sincerity. "Think how much blood I have on my hands; how could the noble and honorable Xihe-jun be willing to eat anything I've touched? You'd better do it yourself."

"There's no need," Mo Xi replied. "I'm not hungry."

Jiang Yexue knew Mo Xi was incredibly stubborn. He couldn't help saying, "Xihe-jun, you've only just recovered, you should really eat something—"

"It's fine." Mo Xi stood. "You guys go ahead. I'll worry about myself."

"But..."

"If he says he's fine, believe him." Gu Mang pulled Jiang Yexue back and smiled. "Xihe-jun isn't some fifteen-year-old brat who's just joined the army anymore—give him some credit. Jiang-xiong, do you want another drumstick?"

Jiang Yexue fell silent.

When they'd finished the goose and had some tea and refreshments, it was time for Gu Mang to go. He summoned the demonic weapon Yongye and prepared to set off. "You guys should sit in the cave and meditate, recover some spiritual energy. Wait a shichen for me; if I haven't found a suitable demon by then, I'll use the old way to tell you. Understood?"

This "old way" was via messenger butterfly. When they had been out on the battlefield in the past, their scouts had used them to pass intel from the front lines to their comrades.

"Yes, don't worry." Jiang Yexue said.

Gu Mang hid the dagger in his sleeve. "I'm off, then."

His silhouette vanished as he leapt swiftly into the darkness.

Mo Xi stood at the cave mouth. As Gu Mang had left, they'd brushed shoulders, but neither had looked at the other. Now that Gu Mang was out of sight, Mo Xi stared out toward where he had melted into the gloom.

Jiang Yexue came to Mo Xi's side. "What happened to you?"

Mo Xi's velvet lashes lowered. He said nothing.

"You've been acting strange ever since you came out of the Time Mirror. I asked Gu Mang about it a bit ago. He said the Mirror shocked his brain and repaired most of his memories, but he didn't say much more. I knew I wouldn't get anything else out of him, so I let it go." Jiang Yexue paused. "Now that he's gone, can you tell me what you saw in the Mirror?"

"We returned to eight years ago," Mo Xi replied.

Jiang Yexue's eyes widened. "Right after Gu Mang defected?"

"No. Before," said Mo Xi. "The days before he defected."

Seeing the way Mo Xi's face went ashen, Jiang Yexue hesitantly asked, "In the Mirror, did you try to persuade Gu Mang to change his mind?"

"Mn. I tried. But it was no use," Mo Xi said wearily. "That's not the most important part though. The most important is...I saw some things we didn't know about before."

The hand Jiang Yexue had laid on the arm of his wheelchair curled slightly. "What did you see?" he asked with concern.

Mo Xi paused for a moment. "I can't say yet. I'm missing a lot of context, and what I know is only the tip of the iceberg. I want to wait until we return to the capital. I need to investigate some events that happened eight years ago."

Jiang Yexue had opened his mouth to reply when they suddenly heard Yue Chenqing's faint, teary voice from the depths of the cave. He sobbed, "Fourth Uncle..."

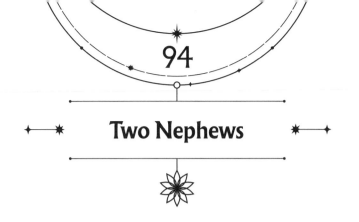

94

Two Nephews

AT YUE CHENQING'S CRY, Jiang Yexue whipped around to look toward Murong Chuyi, while Mo Xi turned to Yue Chenqing. "Is he having a nightmare?"

Curled up beneath the greatcoat, Yue Chenqing was still asleep with only a small wisp of black hair visible. His voice was choked with tears. "Fourth Uncle...don't be mad..." he sobbed. "Don't blame me, don't ignore me..."

Murong Chuyi wasn't one for emotional confrontations, so even though Yue Chenqing was clearly calling for him in his dream, he pretended not to hear. He closed his eyes and began to meditate where he was.

Yue Chenqing continued to mumble; the nightmare seemed to be torturing him. By the end, the confusion and heartbreak in his tone was almost tangible. "Fourth Uncle..." the still-childish youth whimpered tearfully.

Murong Chuyi knitted his brows and was silent a moment. When he could bear it no longer, he rose with a sweep of his sleeves and swiftly sat beside Yue Chenqing. He lowered his head to look at the young man. His elegant face, like moonlight on a frozen lake, showed an unmistakable reluctance and impatience, yet still he moved the coat aside and brushed jade-like, porcelain fingers over Yue Chenqing's forehead.

With that single touch, Murong Chuyi's expression changed.

"How is he?" Jiang Yexue asked.

"He has a high fever," replied Murong Chuyi.

Fevers and colds were little more than nuisances to cultivators; a single dose of medicine was usually enough to cure them completely. Nevertheless, Yue Chenqing's condition was dismaying.

Jiang Yexue maneuvered his chair over to them. First he carefully tucked the greatcoat around Yue Chenqing, then reached up to check his temperature. He was immediately alarmed. "So hot..."

"He shouldn't have a fever." Murong Chuyi gazed down at Yue Chenqing's ruddy face. "When I rescued him, I used the Sacred Heart Technique."

Mo Xi looked up at Murong Chuyi in surprise. Wasn't the Sacred Heart Technique—

Jiang Yexue was also aghast. "Xiaojiu, how could you..."

"What?" Murong Chuyi retorted coldly.

"That's a forbidden technique!"

"So?"

Jiang Yexue was silent. Expecting Murong Chuyi to abide by Chonghua's laws was like expecting a fish to live on land: completely impossible.

The Sacred Heart Technique was a forbidden healing spell. It could rapidly mend a grievously wounded body while ensuring that the patient would not catch any kind of cold or fever-like illness that might weaken them. It was a powerful, simple, and crude technique that a cultivator could easily grasp even without any specialty in medicine.

And yet such a miraculous healing technique was nowhere near commonplace. Just as no person was perfect, no spell was infallible. Sacred Heart had a terrifying drawback: it made extreme requirements of the spellcaster's mind. The wielder's so-called "sacred heart" needed to be pure and holy, free of any blemish. And while the cultivator was casting the healing spell, their mind must remain pure, without the slightest stray thought. A single faltering ripple and the spellcaster's heart vein would suffer damage. A mild case would greatly diminish their vital energy; a severe case would result in instant death.

Jiang Yexue knew any attempt to reason with Murong Chuyi to be futile, so he ventured hesitantly, "Then, your body..."

Murong Chuyi ignored Jiang Yexue's concern, instead lowering his head to check the pulse at Yue Chenqing's neck. After a few seconds, he opened his phoenix eyes and said, "The Sacred Heart Technique can prevent all common colds and illnesses, but Yue Chenqing still has a high fever."

"Is it because of the gu worm?" Jiang Yexue asked.

Although Murong Chuyi didn't respond, he frowned slightly. This couldn't be caused by anything other than the gu. However, a poisonous insect that even the Sacred Heart Technique couldn't suppress was sure to be enormously difficult to deal with. At the moment, they were completely in the dark as to the characteristics of the worm; all they could do was wait for Gu Mang to come back with some information that would help.

"Let's wait." Murong Chuyi laid his hand on Yue Chenqing's forehead, smoothing the mussed hair at his temples. "Wait for Gu Mang to return."

They had no other choice. The three of them stood guard over Yue Chenqing, meditating and recovering their strength as they silently sat inside the cave and waited for Gu Mang.

Mo Xi's innate power was the strongest in their group. On top of that, the Time Mirror had only consumed his spiritual and vital

energy; he hadn't been physically wounded. He had mostly recovered before a shichen had passed.

When Mo Xi opened his eyes, he found that Murong Chuyi and
Jiang Yexue were both still weak and nourishing their qi. Murong
Chuyi's condition seemed especially poor—his elegant face was like
frozen jade, his lips not merely bloodless but tinged a sickly green.

Something was wrong. Mo Xi rose and walked over to Murong
Chuyi, getting on one knee to look at him. "Murong-xiansheng?"

Murong Chuyi didn't respond. Spiritual energy clashed between
his knitted brows; he looked faintly pained.

Mo Xi extended a hand and started in shock—Murong Chuyi's
spiritual energy was so turbulent it showed signs of an impending
qi deviation. He reached out at once to press two fingers to Murong
Chuyi's temple, passing him spiritual energy.

A long interval passed before Murong Chuyi slumped forward
and hacked up a mouthful of filthy blood. Emerging from his
meditative trance, he slowly opened his eyes and found Mo Xi's face
with his unfocused gaze. Swiftly, he looked down and wiped at the
bloodstains. "Many thanks," he said, voice rough.

Mo Xi knew Murong Chuyi was cold and antisocial. He didn't
want to say too much, but he still pressed his lips together upon
seeing Murong Chuyi so unwell. "You should have felt it yourself.
When you attracted the fire bats singlehandedly and then used the
Sacred Heart Technique soon after, you damaged your heart vein.
If you recklessly meditate under these conditions, you'll fall prey to
inner demons. Why didn't you say something?"

"There's nothing to say," replied Murong Chuyi.

Mo Xi stared pointedly.

"I ask Xihe-jun not to speak of my injuries," Murong Chuyi
continued. "I don't want more people finding out, whether it's

Yue Chenqing, or..." He paused, shooting a glance at Jiang Yexue, who had entered an energy-gathering state. "Or him."

This was slightly strange. Everyone said the Ignorant Immortal was cold and aloof, unaffected by matters of the mortal world. He spent most of his days in seclusion, and rarely showed his face in public. Mo Xi had previously only understood that he treated both his nephews poorly. In these recent interactions, however, he'd realized there was a marked difference in how vicious Murong Chuyi was to Jiang Yexue in comparison to Yue Chenqing.

Murong Chuyi tended to ignore Yue Chenqing and didn't like to waste words on him. But if Yue Chenqing really clung to him, acted pathetic, and went overboard with praise, Murong Chuyi might spare him a glance or a few words as his elder. Furthermore, Murong Chuyi was willing to use forbidden techniques to save Yue Chenqing, even sustaining injuries in the process. Which was to say, when all was said and done, Yue Chenqing at least had a small place in Murong Chuyi's heart.

But it was different with Jiang Yexue. Jiang Yexue's mother had been married to the same man as Murong Chuyi's adopted sister, Murong Huang. So perhaps Murong Chuyi was hostile toward Jiang Yexue because Murong Huang had been mistreated on account of Jiang Yexue's mother. But there was more than hostility; there was also hatred. There was even... Mo Xi couldn't put his finger on it, but he felt there was some hidden adverse emotion filling Murong Chuyi's eyes.

"Fourth Uncle...it hurts..."

Yue Chenqing called again in a weak voice, muttering helplessly in his fevered delirium. "My head... It hurts..."

Murong Chuyi looked at the child curled up in the corner. Yue Chenqing called for him several more times, whimpering. Then he mumbled another hoarse name: "Mama... Mama..."

Murong Chuyi stiffened. He was always aloof and indifferent whenever Mo Xi saw him, unaffected by the vicissitudes of human feeling, whether in life or death, joy or fury. That face clear as white jade rarely showed a ripple of disturbance, but now, Murong Chuyi's face seemed to be tangled in a thousand emotions. He gritted his teeth, looking hateful and angry. "Always so disappointing and disobedient. What right do you have to call for her?"

But still he took hold of Yue Chenqing's trembling hand. The youth's temperature was terrifyingly high. Murong Chuyi grasped Yue Chenqing's fingers tight, his severe expression flashing with a hint of tender sorrow. In the end, he stiffly tried to soothe him: "It's all right, it's okay."

Yue Chenqing mumbled in his sleep, "It hurts..."

"I'm here, it'll be okay."

"It hurts so much..."

Murong Chuyi's swordlike brows drew together sharply in anger. His patience had reached its limit. "Bear with it!"

Mo Xi found himself speechless.

Time passed like this. Eventually, Jiang Yexue recovered most of his spiritual energy and woke from his trance. He looked around. "Has Gu-xiong returned?"

"Not yet," said Mo Xi.

Jiang Yexue went to Yue Chenqing as well, but with Murong Chuyi present, there was no place for him—nor was he the one who ought to be holding Yue Chenqing's hand. His status in the Yue Clan had always been thus. It was the same before he left the family, and it remained so now. Whether with his uncle or his brother, he was always the one pushed to the sidelines. He was the expendable one.

Jiang Yexue had long grown used to it. His wistful gaze paused only briefly on the hand Murong Chuyi was holding before he spoke up. "If his fever continues...why don't I use the Sacred Heart Technique this time? Maybe—"

Swift footsteps outside the cave trampled the rest. "We're back, we're back, we're back!"

Gu Mang charged into the cave. Following hesitantly at his heels was a half-transformed little demon, hiding behind Gu Mang and looking around in curiosity.

Unbelievable. When Gu Mang left, he distinctly said that he would catch a demon—but this little creature seemed to have *followed* him back instead. Not only was it trailing Gu Mang of its own volition, but it had even curled a fuzzy brown claw tightly around Gu Mang's sleeve, as if it had entered a tiger's den and Gu Mang was its trusted protector.

Were Yue Chenqing awake, he would've definitely asked, *Bro, did you drug it?*

But none of the three present would ask such a thing. Mo Xi stared at that delicate claw. He'd caught just a small glimpse of the little demon when it entered the cave—after that, it stuck close to Gu Mang, keeping its small body pressed behind him and refusing to show its face.

"Sorry for the wait," Gu Mang sighed. "There are many demons on the island, but only a few who know anything of importance. Wuyan is searching all over for us, so it took some time—how is our young Yue-gongzi?"

"He has a fever, probably caused by the gu worm." Murong Chuyi paused, eyes flicking to Gu Mang's back. "Who's this?"

"Oh." Gu Mang smiled, then waved a hand to show them the little claw hooked around his sleeve. "Rongrong, come out. These are the people I told you about."

After a lengthy silence, a little face peeped out from behind Gu Mang, then quickly shrank back. Gu Mang turned and said consolingly, "Don't worry, no one's going to hurt you."

Only then did this little demon slowly and shyly step out from behind Gu Mang. She was a young female demon—though her exact age was difficult to discern, her figure resembled that of an adolescent human girl. Upon closer examination, she wasn't a bat, either; the fuzz that covered her dainty little body was tawny bird down.

"Her name is Rongrong. She's a little bird spirit, not a demon," Gu Mang explained with a smile. "Rongrong, this is Murong Chuyi, Murong-xiong. This is Jiang Yexue, Jiang-xiong. This is..." He glanced at Mo Xi and held his gaze this time. "This is Mo Xi, Mo-xiong," he said, still smiling. "They're all good people. Why don't you say hi?"

Rongrong seemed to be very timid; she'd kept her head down all this time. Only after Gu Mang prompted her did she gently raise her eyes. Her features possessed a blossoming beauty, shaming flowers and moon alike. Upon her delicate face were a pair of beautifully soulful eyes and naturally scarlet lips; her pale forehead was marked with a red pistil.

"I-I'm A-Rong," she murmured bashfully. "I'm not a bird spirit, I'm just...a half-immortal from the feathered tribe of Mount Jiuhua..."

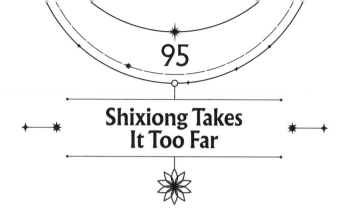

95

Shixiong Takes It Too Far

THE FEATHERED TRIBE of Mount Jiuhua?! Everyone stood in shock at these words.

Members of the feathered tribe were born with half-immortal bodies, and pure immortal blood ran in their veins. No matter how diluted by the currents of time, the feathered tribe was still the most mysterious race, and the one closest to the gods.

"The feathered tribe is reclusive and unpredictable; they reside in the immortal realm of Peach Blossom Springs and may go hundreds of years without setting foot in the mortal world." Murong Chuyi's eyes scanned Rongrong. "But you don't seem to conform to any of that."

Rongrong immediately flushed. "I-I was...very y-young when I was...was...brought here... I-I didn't grow up in the feathered tribe. That's why...I'm, I'm n-not really the same as other tribe members..."

"Who brought you here?" Jiang Yexue asked. "Was it Wuyan?"

At the name of Bat Island's ruler, Rongrong shuddered, swaying on her feet. At first, she shook her head in fright, but after a few moments, she remembered she was safe and hastily nodded.

Jiang Yexue turned to Gu Mang. "She seems to be terribly afraid."

Gu Mang patted Rongrong's head soothingly. "Why don't you go sit by the fire and rest a little? I'll talk to them."

Rongrong obediently went.

It couldn't be helped; some men had a natural charm when it came to the opposite sex. Gu Mang's comforting words were satin-soft, but if Mo Xi were to say the same, the girl would probably think he was threatening her, and that she'd be buried on the spot if she didn't comply.

Jiang Yexue watched Rongrong pick her way over to the firepit and asked Gu Mang, "Should we get her some tea and snacks?"

But Rongrong promptly sat next to the fire and stuck her hand in up to the wrist. She grabbed a handful of flames as if she were scooping out a watermelon, then lowered her head to take dainty bites.

Jiang Yexue stared in silence.

After a pause, Mo Xi turned to Gu Mang. "It's barely been two shichen and you've not only found such a useful individual, you've also won her trust."

Gu Mang smiled smugly and cocked his head. "Aren't I amazing?"

"How did you manage it?"

Gu Mang stroked his chin. "Maybe I look too deceptively kind and sweet? Xihe-jun, weren't you docile for me too? Aiya, men who smile easily make the best liars. People like you, Xihe-jun, you can't get away with it. You're a great beauty to be sure, but every day you're giving orders to beat or kill people—you exude viciousness. Forget two shichen, even if you had two days and nights you couldn't find anyone willing to come back with you."

Those gentle blue eyes blinked up at Mo Xi. They were the mild color of a clear sky after rain, but they shone with a provocative glint. "Shouldn't you do something about this? C'mon, you're already thirty, yet you still don't have a wife?"

This was clearly meant to get on Mo Xi's nerves. Gu Mang expected that Mo Xi would definitely fly into a rage, and indeed his eyes swiftly clouded over in anger. Gu Mang smiled insincerely and waited for him to blow up.

But Mo Xi only glared at him. As this tall man glared, he seemed almost wronged, the rims of his eyes growing red. Mo Xi silently turned away, biting his lip, holding himself back from speaking another word.

Neither Jiang Yexue nor Murong Chuyi caught the emotion in Mo Xi's eyes, but the awkwardness and hostility between Mo Xi and Gu Mang was something even a fool would see. Into this uncomfortable atmosphere, Jiang Yexue gently said, "Gu-xiong, why must you say that about Xihe-jun? Deep and abiding passion is a rare thing—it's not like you don't know why he hasn't yet wed."

"Hm?" Gu Mang blanched slightly, but his smile remained fixed. "Jiang-xiong, what...do you mean by this? What do I know about?"

Jiang Yexue didn't notice the cold sharpness beneath his sweet exterior. He replied frankly, "Princess Mengze has been sick for a long time, and even after so many years of convalescence, she still isn't suited for marriage. Xihe-jun has been waiting all these years because of deep passion, and not because of what you said—" He paused and sighed. "Exuding viciousness, and no one liking him."

The icy light in Gu Mang's eyes slowly softened; he gradually relaxed. He smiled, glancing meaningfully at Mo Xi. "Oh, so that's how it is."

Gu Mang began to examine Mo Xi with a new and clinical look in his eyes, as if they had never touched, as if he was distantly curious. He looked Mo Xi up and down several times, assessing this man's tall physique, his chiseled and straight nose, his strong and slender fingers, and his long, straight legs.

He was taking it too far. Gu Mang obviously understood Mo Xi best—understood the way his throat bobbed in the thick of passion;

understood how his brows knitted when he could no longer restrain himself, eyes flashing with light; understood how strong his hips were, how unbridled his motions when he let go his restraint; understood what positions he liked, and how long he could torment someone in bed.

Still Gu Mang smiled as if he had never felt Mo Xi's skin on his. "With Xihe-jun's physique, he really could take Princess Mengze's life."

Mo Xi's face was ashen. He stood silent for a moment. Finally, he could no longer endure it and turned to walk away.

Jiang Yexue eyed Mo Xi's silhouette standing at the mouth of the cave and frowned with a sigh. "Gu Mang, why are you constantly poking his sore spots ever since you recovered, making things unpleasant for him..."

Gu Mang hugged his knees and barked out a perfunctory laugh. "It's just a habit. I used to like teasing him. Back then he could handle it, but it seems he's lost the skill; what a shame. It's his own fault that his mind only grows narrower—Jiang-xiong, do you think it's because he only gets prettier as he ages, so he's become arrogant because of his looks?"

Jiang Yexue helplessly shook his head. As he made to respond, Murong Chuyi impatiently said, "Can't you two focus on the task at hand? Talk about this later."

"I want to, but it's not that easy." Gu Mang sighed. "Rongrong needs to recover some strength first—she'll have to assess his pulse before we can find out how to cure him."

As he spoke, he turned to look at the maiden from the feathered tribe still crouched by the firepit eating flames, then very fairly made a judgment: "Miss Rongrong is still weak. She can't do much, so we should let her rest properly."

Although Mo Xi had walked to the periphery of the cave, the space was small enough that he overheard Gu Mang. This was why he used to be a favorite among girls—he always sincerely, instinctively, deftly, and elegantly helped a maiden in distress. Even if the maiden in question was just a...

Mo Xi shot a glance at Rongrong and thought: *Just an ugly female bird demon whose feathers haven't even grown in.*

Murong Chuyi observed that Rongrong was truly in poor condition. He gave up insisting and turned to ask, "That Wu...whoever, why did she kidnap one of the feathered tribe?"

"You mean Wuyan?" asked Gu Mang. "Wuyan took her so she could cultivate into immortality."

"Cultivate into immortality..."

"Mn. Do you guys remember what the shangao said before it summoned the Time Mirror? It wasn't much, but it hid many strange facts. It said the Dream Butterfly Islands were abundant with spiritual energy, so the demons here had gradually started to cultivate by fasting. The Bat Queen wholeheartedly wants to ascend, so she's rarely killed in recent years and hasn't needed to catch humans for food."

"What was wrong with any of that?" Jiang Yexue asked.

"Too much," Gu Mang said. "Chonghua doesn't practice any kind of demonic cultivation, so its cultivators have little understanding of demons or evil spirits. But when I was in the Liao Kingdom..."

He paused. Probably out of consideration for Jiang Yexue, he lowered his voice when he mentioned the Liao Kingdom and didn't linger on it. "When I was there, I read many scrolls. Spiritual energy is split into two types, yin and yang. We cultivators take in yang energy and walk the path of gods and immortals, while demons take in yin energy and walk the path of devils," Gu Mang explained. "Which is to say, as a demon, Wuyan's body is undoubtedly more compatible with yin energy. Killing less often may decrease her yin energy, but it can't provide her with the pure yang essence needed to attain immortality."

Jiang Yexue thought this over. "So in other words, a demon cultivating into immortality would go against the natural order?"

"That's pretty much what it means," Gu Mang said. "A demon attaining immortality is like a mortal entering demonhood. Both are paths that defy the law of nature."

At these words, Mo Xi couldn't help but turn to glance silently at the sliver of Gu Mang's profile visible in the firelight. He considered that Gu Mang could be regarded as a mortal who had entered demonhood—even with his spiritual core shattered, he could still use demonic energy to summon demonic weapons. However, the price he'd paid was the loss of two souls and the repeated tempering of his body...

But Gu Mang cared for none of this and continued his explanation. "In any case, Wuyan is the queen of the bat tribe, and this tribe is descended from the offspring of the feathered tribe and demonic beasts. Although some adulterated immortal energy still flows within their bodies, they possess mostly demonic beast energy. If her cultivation technique is unsuited to her demonic nature, it would consume a great deal of spiritual energy before she becomes an immortal and accelerate her aging in the process." He then asked, "So here's a question for you—if you were Wuyan, what would you do at this point?"

"Find a way to slow down the consumption?" Jiang Yexue replied.

"Correct." As Gu Mang spoke, he glanced at Rongrong beside the bonfire. "The best way for Wuyan to slow down the rate of spiritual energy consumption is to increase the amount of immortal energy from the feathered tribe in her own body. That's why she took the risk of going to the feathered tribe's realm and kidnapping one."

Rongrong was still carefully eating flames out of her cupped palms. From time to time, she reached out a little claw to stir the fire, and then scooped up another handful of red-gold light and nibbled at it. Some color had already returned to her breathtaking face, but she was still visibly nervous and frail.

Murong Chuyi was a grandmaster artificer who never missed a detail. After looking her over from head to toe, his sharp brows furrowed. "What's that on her neck?"

Gu Mang sighed. "Those are bloodletting scars."

"Bloodletting?" Jiang Yexue's eyes widened.

Gu Mang nodded. "Correct. Since Wuyan is basically a leaking jug, she's been maintaining her own vital energies by taking regular pills made of Miss Rongrong's blood. I found her in Wuyan's pill-refining room."

Jiang Yexue frowned. "She's such an important resource, and Wuyan's pill-refining room must be strictly forbidden. No one would've pointed it out to you, so how did you think to look for it?"

Gu Mang smiled. "Who said no one pointed it out? The one who pointed me toward the Bat Queen's pill room is right here."

"Who?" Jiang Yexue exclaimed.

"Murong-xiansheng."

A beat of silence. Murong Chuyi stared coldly up at Gu Mang. "What do you mean?" Flames danced in those subtly imposing phoenix eyes. "Are you accusing me of working with these damn birds?"

"No no no—you're so beautiful, how could I?" Gu Mang waved his hands. "I meant..." He shot an apprehensive glance at Jiang Yexue, then turned to look at Mo Xi. He scratched his nose, embarrassed. "It all started that day at Peach Blossom Lake." Gu Mang cleared his throat. "Didn't I catch you bathing...?"

96

Legend of the Bat Queen

MO XI'S HEAD whipped around. With his handsomely chiseled face in profile, he stared at them with an interrogative air.

Jiang Yexue's warm almond eyes were wide with shock.

Murong Chuyi's expression darkened, and he squeezed a sentence between clenched teeth. "You caught me *cultivating*."

"All right, if you say so. It's not like you would've forgotten the circumstances. I know you wanted me to hide your illness from the rest of the Yue Clan, but the truth is young Yue-gongzi already learned of it long ago."

Murong Chuyi said nothing.

"He was looking for treatments for you, to help you. But since you always hid it from him, he had only a rough idea of what to do and didn't know how to proceed. His sole option was to collect and comb through all sorts of texts on medical cultivation."

"And how do you know so much about it?" Murong Chuyi asked.

This time, it was Jiang Yexue who sighed before Gu Mang could answer. "Yue Chenqing's interest in medical texts is no secret. If you showed a little more concern for him, you would know this too."

Murong Chuyi seemed extremely dissatisfied with Jiang Yexue's words. His eyes narrowed dangerously.

Gu Mang sighed. "So you see, even though Murong-xiansheng took pains to hide his ailment, young Yue-gongzi's care for you is such that he must have noticed long ago."

After a moment of silence, Murong Chuyi turned aside. "He's little more than a child. Why should I let him meddle in my business?"

"You're not wrong," Gu Mang said. "But even a blind man could see the reverence young Yue-gongzi holds for Murong-xiong. Even if you want him to stand back and do nothing, it's impossible for him. He's not a healer, but he wants more than anything to find some sort of miracle cure for your illness."

After a pause, he continued, "Let's return to the matter at hand. There are countless legends of miracle cures in the Nine Provinces: fruits from the Flame Emperor's sacred tree, the tears of the Xiangfei Empress, indigo woad root watered with the sweet dew from Guanyin's sacred bottle."

Murong Chuyi said nothing.

"But these are fairy tales. Of all of these legends, the only one with creditable records within the past few centuries is the Xueling Pill of the Dream Butterfly Islands."

"Xueling Pill? Why have I never heard of such a thing?" Murong Chuyi countered.

"Because it's not orthodox medicine. There aren't many who know about it in Chonghua. However, were you to flip through any of the Liao Kingdom's ancient texts—for example, the copy of *Compendium of Plants Demonic and Divine* Xihe-jun lent to the cultivation academy some days back—you would find it mentioned."

"Wait a minute," Murong Chuyi cut in.

"What is it?"

Murong Chuyi narrowed his eyes. "You seem very knowledgeable about the Liao Kingdom's records."

Heart pounding, Gu Mang's face paled.

As Murong Chuyi stared at him, his voice took on a predatory edge. "But as I recall, you've forgotten everything from the five years you defected."

Silence fell.

Jiang Yexue hadn't noticed, and Mo Xi's thoughts were in turmoil—but this statement instantly alerted them to something extremely obvious. Yes, Gu Mang had indeed said he couldn't remember anything about the Liao Kingdom. So why then had he mentioned the Liao Kingdom's records just now, and the Liao Kingdom's spells earlier? Sure enough...this traitor was still hiding the truth from them!

The atmosphere that had eased became strained again, the pressure in the air like a silk bowstring braced against flesh.

"Why did you lie?" Murong Chuyi's gaze was as vicious as a cheetah's, and the words that left his pale, thin lips were laced with murderous intent. "Speak up."

Even Rongrong could see that something was amiss. She stopped with her handful of fire suspended in midair, unsure if she should still be eating.

Gu Mang took in Jiang Yexue's frown, then Murong Chuyi's glare, and finally Mo Xi's face. Mo Xi stood at the mouth of the cave, leaning against the wall with his arms crossed, his expression inscrutable. But Gu Mang could see he was silently watching him from afar, waiting for his answer.

For a moment, Gu Mang was still. "Because I don't want to be dragged into anyone's black magic experiments." He glanced away indifferently, his fluttering lashes concealing all the mysteries within his eyes. "If you guys knew I still remembered so many things about the Liao Kingdom's black magic techniques, would you have agreed to keep my secrets so readily?"

Murong Chuyi said nothing.

"But I really didn't lie to you. I only remember disjointed fragments from those five years in the Liao Kingdom." He paused. "If you don't believe me, I'll swear an oath here and now." He raised a hand and said solemnly, "If I, Gu Mang, speak a single false word, let me live and die alone, shunned by men and women alike, while the person I love marries and finds happiness with someone else..."

It might've been a trick of the light. As Gu Mang said these words, Mo Xi seemed to see a faint gentleness come over his expression. As though he wasn't swearing an oath, but rather sorrowfully yet tenderly giving his blessing.

"Let me die of jealousy." In the end, the softness disappeared, and too the sorrow. When Gu Mang looked up, his eyes gleamed anew with cheerful light. "How 'bout that. You gotta believe me now, right?"

Jiang Yexue sighed and shook his head helplessly. Murong Chuyi looked as if he didn't believe a word of it, but neither did he want to waste more breath on Gu Mang.

Mo Xi knew without a sliver of doubt that Gu Mang was still hiding something. But given Gu Mang's temperament, no one would have a single true word from him if he didn't wish to speak it, even if they pried his lips apart with a knife.

In the face of their silence, Gu Mang spread his hands. "Now, are you three beauties willing to hear about the notes in the Liao Kingdom's ancient texts?"

Murong Chuyi was silent for a while. "Proceed."

"You won't regret it. Sirs, if you have coin to spare, spare it; if you have none, lend me your ears. This storyteller will spin you a tale!"

Silence.

Gu Mang cleared his throat. "It's like this. Legend has it that hundreds of years ago, the mother of a low-level Liao Kingdom cultivator was stricken by foul disease. The cultivator sought doctors throughout the land, but none could cure his mother's illness. One day, he heard of an immortal island, carried through the sea on the shell of the Xuanwu. All seasons were mild as spring on that island, and it was home to a wise immortal. The cultivator gathered his last strands of hope and boarded a ship for this legendary isle, along with his mother.

"The weather on the sea was changeable, and one night, a wild storm rose from the ocean. The oars of their ship were depleted of spiritual energy, and they drifted aimlessly on the waves for three days and three nights. To keep the boat afloat, the little cultivator expended almost all his spiritual energy, fainting from exhaustion. When he woke, he discovered that he had arrived on an island populated with thousands of bat demons—"

"This island..." Jiang Yexue muttered.

"Yes," Gu Mang said. "It's written in some of the more obscure records of the Liao Kingdom that when this little cultivator reached the demon island, he was certain they were doomed. Yet to his surprise, the demons on the island did not devour him immediately. Instead, they escorted him to the island's Bat Queen."

"Wuyan?"

"Quite possibly, yes."

"Then what happened?"

"Then? The records differ on what happened next. Some describe Wuyan as a peerless beauty with a heart of gold and claim that she bestowed a Xueling Pill upon the little cultivator's mother. After the declining lady took the medicine, she recovered to full health within the time it takes to burn a stick of incense. Not only that, but so effective was this medicine that the aged matron regained her youth and reassumed her radiant appearance from decades ago.

They thanked Wuyan for her grace a thousand times over, and mother and son happily returned home."

Jiang Yexue nodded. "And what do the other records say?"

"The others are all a little wild. I'll pick some of the slightly more promising ones to recount. In other legends, Wuyan was a wrinkled, white-haired hag who had never laid eyes on a man in her life. Thus she presented some terms to the little cultivator: she really did have a Xueling Pill made of fresh blood that she would furnish his mother to cure her illness, but in exchange, the little cultivator must stay on the island as her obedient little boy toy."

Murong Chuyi and Jiang Yexue stared at him in silence.

"How about that, isn't it disgusting?" Gu Mang said. "But in the end, whatever the truth, the fact is that there are more than a few records of the Xueling Pill on Bat Island."

"So you're saying Yue Chenqing came here for this pill?" Jiang Yexue asked incredulously.

"Most likely," replied Gu Mang. "A few days before young Yue-gongzi left for the Dream Butterfly Islands, I heard he was looking to borrow a Liao Kingdom book of herbal medicines. Once I made the connection, I thought it prudent to take a look in Wuyan's pill-refining room; perhaps I could find some clues." He glanced at Rongrong. "And found them I have."

"So the Xueling Pill is medicine refined from Miss Rong's blood?" asked Murong Chuyi.

Gu Mang nodded. "That's right."

Jiang Yexue sighed. "How awful."

"Right—this Bat Queen is quite the shady character; I'm more inclined to believe the second legend about the little cultivator. Wuyan doesn't seem the type to give out medicine after hearing a pretty story. If you ask me, she'd definitely demand a commensurate price."

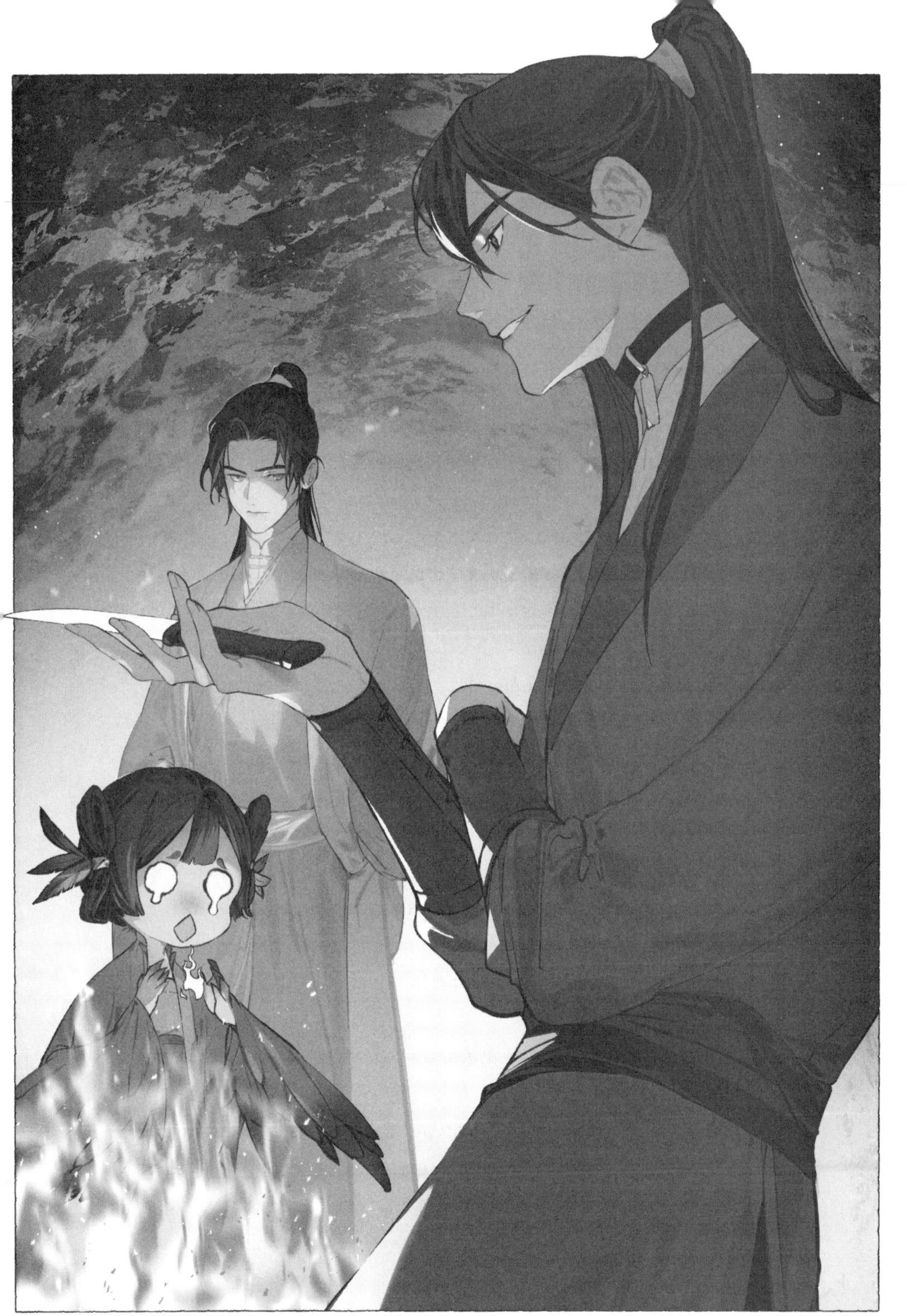

Murong Chuyi lifted his chin slightly in Rongrong's direction. "Why didn't you ask her for the truth?"

Rongrong had been quietly listening in, but as soon as they turned their eyes on her, she lowered her head in fright and resumed her meal.

"Of course I asked her. But Rongrong has been locked in the pill-refining room for years being used for medicine. She doesn't know much about what happens outside, so I couldn't get any concrete answers. But my guesses are usually correct."

"Then you have other guesses?" Murong Chuyi asked coolly. "Why not just share them all while we're at it?"

Gu Mang rubbed his palms together and smiled. "I do, actually. I also suspect the reason Wuyan wanted to keep the little cultivator as her plaything might not be because she's lived on the island for too long and has never seen a man. Perhaps it was because she had seen a *certain* man before and had never forgotten him."

A slight crease appeared between Murong Chuyi's swordlike brows. "What makes you say that?"

Gu Mang looked at the feverish Yue Chenqing. "The gu worm." After a pause, he continued. "The gu worm in Yue Chenqing's body can change someone's voice and appearance, as well as their memories and personality. If Wuyan merely wanted to snatch a man to keep as her plaything, why on earth would she go to so much trouble?"

Murong Chuyi pondered this and then said, "Makes sense, keep talking."

"The shangao said before that young Yue-gongzi had violated some taboo—most likely, that men are not allowed on this island. Young Yue-gongzi rashly landed here and was captured by Wuyan, just like that cultivator from hundreds of years ago, who was nurtured and transformed into the man Wuyan actually wants to possess. Of course," Gu Mang added, "perhaps there are other reasons we aren't aware of. But I can't think of a better explanation than this."

Murong Chuyi looked at Gu Mang thoughtfully. In the past, he and Gu Mang had almost never interacted. He only knew that, for a time, many in Chonghua believed they had nothing to fear so long as General Gu stood on the front lines, even if the sky were to fall. But he and Gu Mang rarely crossed paths; Murong Chuyi couldn't recall ever having spoken to him directly. Thus, he had never understood why people had that sort of superstition about a general. But as he listened to this sound analysis and observed Gu Mang's thorough and methodical reasoning, Murong Chuyi couldn't help but scrutinize his face in earnest. Slowly, he realized that Gu Mang did have a powerful charisma. When Gu Mang was taking things seriously, when his blue eyes were flashing with light, the vigor in his features was deeply compelling.

"So that's what I think," Gu Mang said, concluding his tale. "In any case, the fire bat tribe and the feathered tribe share a common origin. Jiang-xiong, Murong-xiong, you guys don't need to worry too much. I'm sure that Miss Rongrong will find a way to dispel the poison Wuyan used."

Gu Mang exuded an aura of competence; perhaps this was why, whenever he said there was nothing to worry about, it seemed to act as a soothing balm. A few words were all it took for them to believe that he had everything under control.

After a long moment of silence, Murong Chuyi replied, "All right."

Reality proved Gu Mang correct: as Rongrong ate more and more flames, the red marking between her eyebrows became darker and darker. In the end, she let out a little hiccup of flickering sparks and covered her face in embarrassment: "I-I-I'm done resting. I can help now!"

"Many thanks," said Jiang Yexue.

"Please don't thank me," Rongrong said anxiously. "If Gu Mang-gege hadn't rescued me from that pill-refining room... I would've been Wuyan's prisoner for a lifetime." As she spoke, she unfolded herself from the ground and approached Yue Chenqing. "This little gege who's been poisoned with gu... Would it be all right if I touched his face?"

"Go ahead," Murong Chuyi answered.

Rongrong performed a crooked obeisance at him and clumsily replied, "Then—I ask the beauty to please pardon my offense."

Seeing Murong Chuyi's expression, Gu Mang couldn't hold back a laugh. "She's been locked up since she was young; her only exposures to the outside world were a few bat demons and random books tossed in the pill-refining room to entertain her. She talks a little strangely; try to get used to it."

Rongrong pursed her delicate scarlet lips, realizing she'd said something wrong again. Her face flushed a rosy-pink and she spoke no more. Head drooping, she reached out and carefully placed a fuzzy little claw over Yue Chenqing's forehead.

After a while, she asked, "May I touch his neck?"

"You may," said Murong Chuyi.

Rongrong touched the side of Yue Chenqing's neck. After inspecting it for a while, she asked, "May I also touch his chest?"

Murong Chuyi preferred doing things simply and quickly, so he soon grew impatient with all her requests. "You may touch him wherever you like as long as you cure him."

Having received consent, Rongrong examined Yue Chenqing's chest, arms, and ankles.

"How is he?"

"He can be cured, but there's not much time. And I'll need to use a relative's blood for the antidote..." She glanced hesitantly at Murong Chuyi, "Isn't this xianjun his uncle? I-is Xianjun willing to give yourself over to..."

She shivered at the sight of Murong Chuyi's dark expression. "Is—is that how the phrase 'give yourself over to' i-is used?" she stammered.

"No." Murong Chuyi pressed his colorless lips into a thin line, the glint in his eyes turning stormy. "Besides, I'm not his real uncle."

"Y-you adopted him?" asked Rongrong.

Murong Chuyi's features were chilly. "I was the one who was adopted."

Rongrong was rendered speechless before this awe-inspiring cultivator.

At this moment, Jiang Yexue spoke up from nearby. "Miss Rong, does it have to be the blood of a relative?"

"Mn...it's best that way... Otherwise, it'll be very dangerous..."

"Then you can use mine," said Jiang Yexue.

Rongrong stared at him, taken aback. "You're...?"

"I'm his elder brother from the same father but a different mother." Jiang Yexue smiled bitterly. "Unfortunately, we don't have exactly the same parents—will my blood suffice?"

Rongrong had noticed the way these men had spoken earlier. She saw that Murong Chuyi always acted as Yue Chenqing's guardian while pushing Jiang Yexue aside so he couldn't get a word in edgewise. She had assumed Murong Chuyi was close to Yue Chenqing, and Jiang Yexue was the outsider. She hadn't expected that Jiang Yexue was Yue Chenqing's blood family, while Murong Chuyi had no blood relationship with him to speak of. Naturally, she didn't understand the difference between di and shu sons,[12] nor the twists and turns of harem infighting. The inexplicable ways of these humans made her head spin.

It wasn't until Jiang Yexue warmly spoke up for the third time— "Will my blood suffice?"—that Rongrong snapped out of it. She nodded repeatedly. "I-it will! It will!"

It would take time and effort to draw the gu out of Yue Chenqing, and the process was perilous and could not be disrupted. Jiang Yexue was wary. "Wuyan has had her prisoner stolen, her prized tower destroyed, and now we've taken Miss Rongrong too. She'll no doubt be furious. I set down invisibility barriers around the cave, but if she can't find us with magic, I'm worried her next step will be to send her people to comb the island in search of us. Can we find a more secure hiding place?"

Rongrong shook her head. She pointed at Yue Chenqing as she shyly turned down this request. "This little gege cannot be moved right now. He's had the gu worm in him for a few days already. If we delay, I don't know if I can destroy the worm... We can't afford to wait."

As Jiang Yexue hesitated, Mo Xi—who had been listening silently at the mouth of the cave—turned around. "You all stay here and guard Yue Chenqing while the gu is drawn out," he said. "I'll deal with Wuyan myself."

---

12   Born of the first or official wife, "di" sons are direct heirs in matters of inheritance. "Shu" sons, born of other wives or concubines, are ranked second if at all.

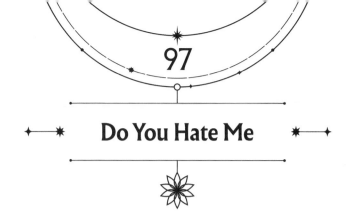

97

Do You Hate Me

MO XI DIDN'T HAVE TO spell it out; the others weren't stupid. They understood at once that he planned to find some far-off spot and expose his whereabouts, using himself as bait to divert Wuyan.

"Absolutely not, it's too dangerous," Jiang Yexue protested.

"If I can't even handle a flock of bats," Mo Xi said, adjusting the hidden weapon compartment on his wrist, "how could I hold my head up as the commander of the Northern Frontier Army?"

Jiang Yexue knew Mo Xi had always been stubborn. Seeing that he wouldn't be persuaded, he looked toward Gu Mang.

Gu Mang's face was a patchwork of shadow in the flickering light of the fire. It wasn't clear whether he would bestir himself for this. But after a long moment, he finally spoke. "What's Xihe-jun thinking, running off to meet that crowd of bats alone? Are you in such a rush to become a trophy husband for the Bat Queen?"

At these words, Mo Xi looked at Gu Mang and then turned away. "I'm ill-tempered and vicious," he said softly. "All I do is order people to beat and kill. No one would take a liking to me."

Gu Mang stared at him. They were the very words Gu Mang had just bullied Mo Xi with; he hadn't expected Mo Xi to commit them to memory and turn them back on him. No matter how thick-skinned Gu Mang was, he still felt abashed at that moment.

Mo Xi fastened the buckles of his hidden weapon compartment. "I'm leaving," he said over his shoulder.

"Hey hey, wait up!"

Turning halfway, Mo Xi paused. "What is it?"

Gu Mang rubbed his nose. "Humans wouldn't take a liking to you, but demons might."

Mo Xi's face was stony.

"I heard that demons only look at humans' skins. Your personality is a bit of a bore, but your face is pretty, I'll admit—you've got that innocent allure. You're absolutely perfect as long as you don't open your mouth. If that old bat doesn't take a liking to you, she must be blind; maybe she should go to Jiang Fuli's manor to get her eyes checked."

With a sweep of his sleeves and a stunned pallor in his cheeks, Mo Xi turned on his heel and strode off.

Gu Mang gazed at Mo Xi's retreating back and sighed. "You know, I didn't notice while my memories were gone, but now that they've returned, I can see his attitude really hasn't improved in all the years I was out of the country. No—it's gotten worse. Now he can't even take a joke."

At this, Mo Xi finally couldn't bear it anymore and whirled around. He looked as though he was about to fly into a rage, but he forced his anger down and only said with red-rimmed eyes: "Gu Mang, did you just discover my terrible temper today?"

Mo Xi stalked away without another word, striding into the distance beneath the swaying moonlight. As he was about to vanish out of sight, Gu Mang turned to the others. "Why don't I...go with him? Youngsters can't be trusted to do things properly. I'll keep an eye on him, and we'll lead Wuyan away together."

"Go, quickly," replied Jiang Yexue. "There's safety in numbers."

Gu Mang grimaced. "I'm just afraid he'll be angry if I tag along. Didn't you see his face when he left?"

Nevertheless, he still quickly followed after Mo Xi.

Mo Xi's steel-toed military boots crunched over dried branches and withered leaves. After walking alone for a while, he heard the rustle of footsteps behind him.

"Xihe-jun."

The sound of that voice made Mo Xi's heart ache unbearably. Instead of turning around, he quickened his pace.

Gu Mang caught up to him. "What are you walking so fast for?"

As if Gu Mang hadn't spoken, Mo Xi kept his head down and strode on.

"I'm asking you a question. Are you so mad you're ignoring me?"

It was some time before Mo Xi finally spoke up. "Why are you insisting on coming with me?"

"How long have you been in the army? You've fought too many battles not to understand the concept of strategic deployment of troops. Why else would I follow you?"

Gu Mang pulled a blade of foxtail grass and began fiddling with it. He smacked the wildflowers growing by the side of the path as he continued: "We can't let anyone interfere with Jiang Yexue and the others while they're dealing with the gu in the cave. The more of us on the outside attracting Queen Wuyan's attention, the better. To provide for all possible contingencies, there must be someone on guard in the cave, but Murong Chuyi is clearly the better choice to stay behind. He's Yue Chenqing and Jiang Yexue's uncle, so he's more suited to be their last line of defense."

After laying out his logic, he smiled at Mo Xi. "So why are you behaving so recklessly? Just because you don't want to see me?"

Mo Xi said nothing. The two of them trod over dead foliage, walking into the distance step by step. They hadn't yet removed the spells that concealed their spiritual energy, so they had no cause for worry even when they began to see bat demons here and there patrolling through the trees.

For a while they walked shoulder to shoulder like this, until Mo Xi suddenly said, "Gu Mang."

"Mm-hmm."

"There's no one else here now. So can you tell me the truth?"

"Hm?"

"Do you really hate me?"

A pause. "Why are you asking this out of the blue?"

"When I didn't want you to accompany me, it wasn't because I didn't want to see you," Mo Xi replied. "It's because I feel that you despise me, and I don't know how to face you."

Gu Mang was silent. Their surroundings were very quiet, filled only with cold moonlight and the rustle of leaves. Even the twitter of birdsong seemed remote.

Mo Xi hesitated. "Have you really resented me all along?"

"Why would I resent you?" Under the light breeze and pale moon, Gu Mang's white clothes fluttered, billowing like waves. He tucked away the careless and cavalier mask he'd worn in front of Jiang Yexue and the others, revealing a face that—having experienced too much death—seemed apathetic and unnaturally pale. "Would I resent you for not being able to stay with me back when I fell into trouble? Or for thinking that I was drunk and making a scene when I most needed someone to pull me back?"

Mo Xi failed to respond.

Gu Mang chuckled softly. "In the Time Mirror, you asked me

pretty much the same thing. Whether it was eight years in the past or eight years in the future, my answer is the same."

He raised those long lashes like willow catkins. As if a gauze veil had been lifted, bright moonlight poured into his azure eyes. Gu Mang gazed at Mo Xi with those irrevocably blue eyes and said, "Mo Xi, I've never hated you for this."

Mo Xi suddenly stopped in his tracks and lowered his gaze to Gu Mang's face. Ever since he and Gu Mang had reunited, he had nigh always been powerful and decisive in front of Gu Mang. But at this moment, facing Gu Mang with his memories intact, what did Mo Xi have left? Gu Mang had watched him grow up. Gu Mang had seen all of his suffering, misery, and struggle, had forgiven all of his recklessness and immaturity.

In front of Gu Mang without his mind, Mo Xi might've been his lord, his companion, or Xihe-jun. But in front of his Gu Mang-gege, Mo Xi was just Mo Xi. His armor and blades were stripped away, leaving behind a scarred and bloody heart full of sincerity.

Mo Xi's voice shook as he asked quietly, "If you don't hate me... why do you have to treat me like this?"

"Does there have to be reason? It's no different from how you treated me," Gu Mang said. "These are the choices we've made, just as you chose Chonghua and I chose the Liao Kingdom. The Time Mirror's release incantation says it best—*cross o'er the abyss of suffering, chase no more the past.* The past is in the past; there's no point dwelling on it. I've already let go of all our rotten history; you're the one who insists on clinging to it. What else can I do but be ruthless with you?"

Gu Mang's words felt like a scalding pipe pressed to the flesh of his chest. Mo Xi's heart strained to breaking. "You've let it all go?"

"Ages ago."

Mo Xi closed his eyes, his long lashes fluttering. "Gu Mang..." Swallowing hard, he sighed. "It's been seventeen years."

Gu Mang was taken aback. "What?"

"From the time you helped me complete my first assignment at the academy, I've known you for seventeen years. From my youth to my coming of age, from the classroom to the battlefield...you said you'd always stay with me. You said you'd always be at my side, for richer or poorer. You once said—"

You once said you loved me.

But how could Mo Xi speak those words now? They stuck in his throat, choking him with their bloodied sweetness.

He closed his eyes, forcing down the quaver in his voice. He heaved a sigh, but his voice still shook as he spoke. "Once upon a time, you taught me many things: you taught me to endure in silence, you taught me magic, you taught me the ways of the world, and you taught me the meaning of romance. Now, you want me to stop clinging to you. Okay. I'll do my best," he said. "But, before that, Gu-shixiong, I ask you to teach me one last thing. It's been seventeen years—half our lives so far. Teach me how to let go."

Gu Mang said nothing.

Mo Xi's eyes flew open as he jabbed at his own heart. "Can you teach me how to feel at ease?" His fingertips trembled faintly, and his eyes were red. "How do I lose two souls—can mine be missing instead? I still have my memory and my mind; I *can't* let go! I knew I couldn't change a thing upon traveling eight years into the past, but I still wanted to ask you not to defect; I still hoped for you to stay, even if you think it's all useless!"

"Mo Xi..."

"What *cross o'er the abyss of suffering, chase no more the past*—I've lived in the past for eight years! Since the day you left, I've lived eight years in the past. I wished so badly for you to recover your memories, but now that you've recovered them, you tell me you've let go... Gu Mang, Gu-shixiong...in those seventeen years, what was I in your heart?!"

As he choked out those last words, his voice went hoarse and broke off. They stuck in his throat, becoming sobs. He felt tears swimming in his eyes, but to let them fall would be too shameful. The rare times he cried had almost always been in front of Gu Mang. It could be excused when he was young, but how could he bear to appear so utterly defeated in front of the same person after all these years?

He turned abruptly away, striding forward on rapid steps. The white birch forest rustled as the night fog wove around the trees. Mo Xi walked through this hazy and indistinct mist; after a while, he heard Gu Mang catch up. Gu Mang's footsteps always followed close behind him. It had been like this, too, many years ago, when they had raided enemy camps and chased deer in the countryside. No matter where they went, as long as Gu Mang was present, he would always be just a sidelong glance away.

It had been the first thing in his life to bring him peace.

Then Gu Mang defected and left. When Mo Xi marched and fought on his own, he never again found this kind of tacit understanding with his comrades. When he galloped ahead too quickly, leaving all others behind, he couldn't hear the voices of those accompanying him—as if all that existed between the heavens and the earth was him astride his horse, galloping toward a glorious, solitary end. Dissatisfied, he commanded his soldiers to follow no more than a single step behind—but even when the sounds of footsteps and hoofbeats returned, the faces were no longer the ones he remembered.

From then on, Mo Xi understood that, although the death of an old friend was agonizing, it could not compare to the pain of an old friend irrevocably changed. When he thought how this person yet remained on this earth but could never return to the past; of how their deep emotion had decayed, how their shared path had split into two unlike roads, how his beloved had become his enemy—that was a suffering that brought agony with each breath.

"Useless!"

Up ahead came an angry scream, dragging Mo Xi's thoughts out of their morass.

"All of you, useless!"

Mo Xi stopped short. Gu Mang had heard too, and swiftly drew even with Mo Xi, peering through the dense fog. "Is it Wuyan?"

Their relationship was complicated and the atmosphere awkward, but they knew their priorities. They exchanged a wordless glance, then slowed their spiritual energy circulation and breathing to noiselessly approach the source of the voice.

They followed the sound to a tree so giant that three men linking arms would have barely girdled its circumference. When they silently looked around it, the sight that greeted them astonished them both.

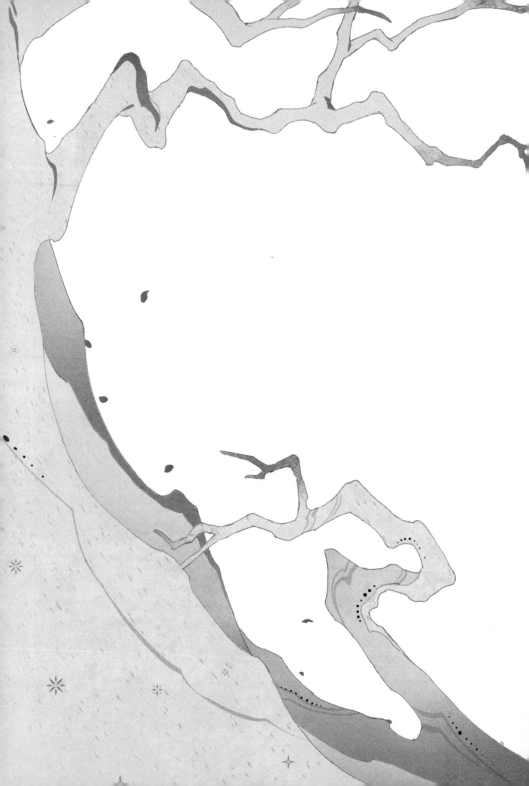

THE STORY CONTINUES IN
Remnants of Filth
VOLUME 4

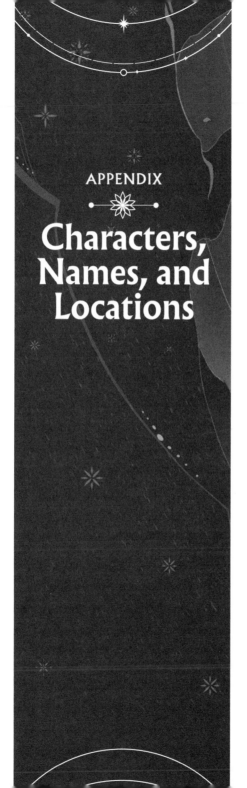

APPENDIX

Characters, Names, and Locations

Characters

Mo Xi

墨熄   SURNAME MO; GIVEN NAME XI, "EXTINGUISH"

TITLES: Xihe-jun (羲和君 / "sun," literary), General Mo

WEAPONS:

Shuairan (率然 / a mythical snake): A whip that can transform into a sword as needed. Named after a snake from Chinese mythology, said to respond so quickly an attack to any part of its body would be met immediately with its fangs or tail (or both). First mentioned in Sun Tzu's *The Art of War* as an ideal for commanders to follow when training their armies.

Tuntian (吞天 / "Skyswallower"): A scepter cast with the essence of a whale spirit.

The commander of the Northern Frontier Army, Mo Xi is the only living descendant of the illustrious Mo Clan. Granted the title Xihe-jun by the late emperor, he possesses extraordinary innate spiritual abilities and has a reputation for being coldly ruthless.

Gu Mang

顾茫   SURNAME GU, "TO LOOK"; GIVEN NAME MANG, "BEWILDERMENT"

TITLES: Beast of the Altar, General Gu

WEAPON:

Yongye (永夜 / "Evernight"): A demonic dagger from the Liao Kingdom.

Fengbo (风波 / "Wind and waves"): A suona used by General Gu.

Once the dazzling shixiong of the cultivation academy, Murong Lian's slave, and war general to the empire of Chonghua, Gu Mang fell from grace and turned traitor, defecting to the enemy Liao Kingdom. Years later, he was sent back to Chonghua as a prisoner of war. His name comes from the line "I unsheathe my sword and look around bewildered" in the first of three poems in the collection "Arduous Journey" by Li Bai.

Murong Lian
慕容怜   SURNAME MURONG; GIVEN NAME LIAN, "MERCY"

TITLE: Wangshu-jun (望舒君 / "moon," literary)
WEAPON:

Water Demon Talisman (水鬼符): A talisman that becomes a horde of water demons to attack its target.

Gu Mang's former master and cousin to the current emperor, Murong Lian is the current lord of Wangshu Manor and the owner of Luomei Pavilion. He is known as the "Greed" of Chonghua's three poisons.

Jiang Yexue
江夜雪   SURNAME JIANG; GIVEN NAME YEXUE, "EVENING SNOW"

TITLE: Qingxu Elder (清旭长老 / "clear dawn")

Disowned son of the Yue Clan, Yue Chenqing's older brother, and Mo Xi's old friend, Jiang Yexue is a gentleman to the core.

Yue Chenqing
岳辰晴   SURNAME YUE; GIVEN NAME CHENQING, "MORNING SUN"

TITLE: Deputy General Yue

Young master of the Yue Clan and Murong Chuyi's nephew, Yue Chenqing is a happy-go-lucky child with a penchant for getting into trouble.

Murong Chuyi
慕容楚衣 SURNAME MURONG; GIVEN NAME CHUYI, SURNAME CHU, "CLOTHES"

Yue Chenqing's Fourth Uncle, Chonghua's "Ignorance," and all-around enigma, Murong Chuyi is a master artificer whose true motivations remain unknown.

SUPPORTING CHARACTERS
(IN ALPHABETICAL ORDER)

Changfeng-jun
长丰君 "LONG, ABUNDANCE"

An older noble worrying himself sick over his daughter Lan-er.

Chen Tang
沉棠 SURNAME CHEN, GIVEN NAME TANG, "FLOWERING APPLE"

Chonghua's legendary Wise Gentleman, who was once the head-master of the cultivation academy as well as guoshi of the nation. He perished in battle with Hua Po'an, a slave cultivator turned traitor whom he had personally taught.

The Emperor
君上

TITLE: His Imperial Majesty, "junshang"

Eccentric ruler of the empire of Chonghua. Due to the cultural taboo against using the emperor's given name in any context, he is only ever addressed and referred to as "His Imperial Majesty."

Fandou
饭兜 "BIB"

A loyal black dog and Gu Mang's best friend.

Guoshi of the Liao Kingdom
国师   "IMPERIAL PRECEPTOR"

A mercurial and immensely powerful Liao Kingdom official who conceals his true identity behind a golden mask.

Hua Po'an
花破暗   "FLOWER BREAKING THE DARKNESS"

Chonghua's infamous first slave general. After learning cultivation under the beneficence of Chen Tang, Hua Po'an turned on Chonghua and became the founding monarch of the Liao Kingdom.

Jiang Fuli
姜拂黎   SURNAME JIANG; GIVEN NAME FULI, "TO BRUSH AWAY, MULTITUDES"

Also known by his title of Medicine Master, Jiang Fuli is the finest healer in Chonghua, dubbed the "Wrath" of Chonghua's three poisons.

Lan-er
兰儿   "ORCHID"

A sweet little girl with a dangerously volatile spiritual core.

Li Wei
李微   SURNAME LI; GIVEN NAME WEI, "SLIGHT"

The competent, if harried, head housekeeper of Xihe Manor.

Lu Zhanxing
陆展星   SURNAME LU; GIVEN NAME ZHANXING, "TO EXHIBIT STARS"

Gu Mang's oldest friend, who grew up with him as a slave in Wangshu Manor. Later his deputy general of the Wangba Army.

Murong Mengze
慕容梦泽 SURNAME MURONG; GIVEN NAME MENGZE, "YUNMENG LAKE"

A master healer and the "Virtue" of Chonghua's three gentlemen, Princess Mengze's frail constitution and graceful, refined manner are known to all.

Su Yurou
苏玉柔 SURNAME SU; GIVEN NAME YUROU, "JADE, SOFT"

Known as the most peerless beauty in Chonghua. Jiang Fuli's reclusive wife.

Locations

Dongting Lake
洞庭湖

A real lake in northeastern Hunan, named "Grotto Court Lake" for the dragon court that was said to reside in its depths.

Luomei Pavilion
落梅别苑 "GARDENS OF FALLEN PLUM BLOSSOMS"

A house of pleasure where the nobility of Chonghua could have their pick of captives from enemy nations.

Feiyao Terrace
飞瑶台 "FLYING JADE"

A terrace in the imperial palace.

Shennong Terrace
神农台

The healers' ministry of Chonghua. Shennong is the deity and mythological ruler said to have taught agriculture and herbal medicine to the ancient Chinese people.

Warrior Soul Mountain
战魂山

Where the heroes of Chonghua are laid to rest.

Maiden's Lament Mountain
女哭山

Once Phoenix Feather Mountain, this peak was renamed due to the vengeful spirits of the maidens buried alive upon it.

Cixin Artificing Forge
慈心冶炼铺   "KIND HEART"

A shabby forge in Chonghua's capital where uncommonly humane spiritual weapons are refined.

Peach Blossom Lake
桃花湖

A lake on the eastern outskirts of the capital, known for its flourishing spiritual energy and delicious fish.

Dream Butterfly Islands
梦碟岛

An archipelago of demonic islands not far from Chonghua. The archipelago is composed of around twenty islands, and different types of demons live on each one.

Bat Island
蝙蝠岛

One of the Dream Butterfly Islands, Bat Island is inhabited by fire bats, demons descended from the feathered tribe of Mount Jiuhua. The bats on their island are led by their queen, Wuyan.

Name Guide

Diminutives, nicknames, and name tags

A-: Friendly diminutive. Always a prefix. Usually for monosyllabic names, or one syllable out of a two-syllable name.

DOUBLING: Doubling a syllable of a person's name can be a nickname, e.g., "Mangmang"; it has childish or cutesy connotations.

XIAO-: A diminutive meaning "little." Always a prefix.

LAO-: A familiar prefix meaning "old." Usually used for older men.

-ER: An affectionate diminutive added to names, literally "son" or "child." Always a suffix.

Family

DI/DIDI: Younger brother or a younger male friend.

GE/GEGE/DAGE: Older brother or an older male friend.

JIE/JIEJIE/ZIZI: Older sister or an older female friend.

-JIU/JIUJIU: Maternal uncle.

Cultivation

SHIFU: Teacher or master.

SHIXIONG: Older martial brother, used for older disciples or classmates.

SHIDI: Younger martial brother, used for younger disciples or classmates.

DAOZHANG/XIANJUN/XIANZHANG/SHENJUN: Polite terms of address for cultivators. Can be used alone as a title or attached to someone's family name.

ZONGSHI: A title or suffix for a person of particularly outstanding skill; largely only applied to cultivators.

Other

GONGZI: Young man from an affluent household.

SHAOZHU: Young master and direct heir of a household.

-NIANG: Suffix for a young lady, similar to "Miss."

-JUN: A term of respect, often used as a suffix after a title.

-XIANSHENG: A polite suffix for a man, similar to "Mister."

Pronunciation Guide

Mandarin Chinese is the official state language of mainland China, and pinyin is the official system of romanization in which it is written. As Mandarin is a tonal language, pinyin uses diacritical marks (e.g., ā, á, ǎ, à) to indicate these tonal inflections. Most words use one of four tones, though some (as in "de" in the title below) are a neutral tone. Furthermore, regional variance can change the way native Chinese speakers pronounce the same word. For those reasons and more, please consider the guide below a simplified introduction to pronunciation of select character names and sounds from the world of *Remnants of Filth*.

More resources are available at sevenseasdanmei.com

NAMES

Yú Wū

Yú: Y as in **you**, ú as in "u" in the French "tu"
Wū as in **woo**

Mò Xī

Mò as in **mo**urning
Xī as in **chi**c

Gù Máng

Gù as in **goo**p
Máng as in **mong**rel

Mùróng Lián

Mù as in **moo**n

Róng as in **wrong** / c**rone**

Lián as in batta**lion**

Yuè Chénqíng

Yuè: Y as in **y**ammer, uè as in **whe**lp

Chén as in ki**tchen**

Qíng as in ma**tching**

Jiāng Yèxuě

Jiāng as in mah**jong**

Yè as in **yes**

Xuě: X as in **sh**oot, uě as in **wet**

Mùróng Chǔyī

Mù as in **moo**n

Róng as in **wrong** / c**rone**

Chǔ as in **choo**se

Yī as in **ea**se

GENERAL CONSONANTS

Some Mandarin Chinese consonants sound very similar, such as z/c/s and zh/ch/sh. Audio samples will provide the best opportunity to learn the difference between them.

X: somewhere between the **sh** in **sh**eep and **s** in **s**ilk

Q: a very aspirated **ch** as in **ch**arm

C: **ts** as in pan**ts**

Z: **z** as in **z**oom

S: **s** as in **s**ilk

CH: **ch** as in **ch**arm

ZH: **dg** as in do**dg**e

SH: **sh** as in **sh**ave

G: hard **g** as in **g**raphic

GENERAL VOWELS

The pronunciation of a vowel may depend on its preceding consonant. For example, the "i" in "shi" is distinct from the "i" in "di." Vowel pronunciation may also change depending on where the vowel appears in a word, for example the "i" in "shi" versus the "i" in "ting." Finally, compound vowels are often—though not always—pronounced as conjoined but separate vowels. You'll find a few of the trickier compounds below.

IU: as in **ewe**

IE: **ye** as in **ye**s

UO: **war** as in **war**m

APPENDIX

Glossary

Glossary

While not required reading, this glossary is intended to offer further context for the many concepts and terms utilized throughout this novel as well as provide a starting point for learning more about the rich culture from which these stories were written.

GENRES

Danmei

Danmei (耽美 / "indulgence in beauty") is a Chinese fiction genre focused on romanticized tales of love and attraction between men. It is analogous to the BL (boys' love) genre in Japanese media and is better understood as a genre of plot than a genre of setting. For example, though many danmei novels feature wuxia or xianxia settings, others are better understood as tales of sci-fi, fantasy, or horror.

Wuxia

Wuxia (武侠 / "martial heroes") is one of the oldest Chinese literary genres. Most wuxia stories are set in ancient China and feature protagonists who practice martial arts and seek to redress wrongs. Although characters may possess seemingly superhuman abilities, they are typically mastered through practice instead of supernatural or magical means. Plots tend to focus on human relationships and power struggles between various sects and alliances. To Western moviegoers, a well-known example of the genre is *Crouching Tiger, Hidden Dragon*.

Xianxia

Xianxia (仙侠 / "immortal heroes") is a genre related to wuxia that places more emphasis on the supernatural. Some xianxia works focus on immortal beings such as gods or demons, whereas others (such as *Remnants of Filth*) are concerned with the conflicts of mortals who practice cultivation. In the latter case, characters strive to become stronger by harnessing their spiritual powers, with some aiming to extend their lifespan or achieve immortality.

TERMINOLOGY

COWRIE SHELLS: Cowrie shells were the earliest form of currency used in central China.

CULTIVATION/CULTIVATORS: Cultivation is the means by which mortals with spiritual aptitude develop and harness supernatural abilities. The practitioners of these methods are called cultivators. The path of one's cultivation is a concept that draws heavily from Daoist traditions. Generally, it comprises innate spiritual development (i.e., formation of a spiritual core) as well as spells, talismans, tools, and weapons with specific functions.

DI AND SHU HIERARCHY: Upper-class men in ancient China often took multiple wives, though only one would be the official or "di" wife, and her sons would take precedence over the sons of the "shu" wives. "Di" sons were prioritized in matters of inheritance.

EPHEMERA: In the world of *Remnants of Filth*, a drug from the Liao Kingdom. Its name is likely a reference to the line, "Life is like a dream ephemeral, how short our joys can be," from "A Party Amidst Brothers in the Peach Blossom Garden" by Tang dynasty poet Li Bai.

EYES: Descriptions like "phoenix eyes" or "peach-blossom eyes" refer to eye shape. Phoenix eyes have an upturned sweep at their far corners, whereas peach-blossom eyes have a rounded upper lid and are often considered particularly alluring.

FACE: Mianzi (面子), generally translated as "face," is an important concept in Chinese society. It is a metaphor for a person's reputation and can be extended to further descriptive metaphors. "Thin face" refers to someone easily embarrassed or prone to offense at perceived slights. Conversely, "thick face" refers to someone who acts brazenly and without shame.

FLAME EMPEROR: A mythological figure said to have ruled over China in ancient times. His name is attributed to his invention of slash-and-burn agriculture. There is some debate over whether the Flame Emperor is the same being as Shennong, the inventor of agriculture, or a descendant.

FOXGLOVE TREE: The foxglove tree, *Paulownia tomentosa* (泡桐花 / paotonghua), also known as empress tree or princess tree, is native to China. In flower language, the foxglove tree symbolizes "eternal waiting," specifically that of a secret admirer.

FOXTAIL GRASS: In flower language, green foxtail grass, Setaria viridis (狗尾巴草 / gouweibacao), symbolizes "secret, difficult yearning," often in reference to star-crossed love.

GENTLEMAN: The term junzi (君子) is used to refer to someone of noble character. Historically, it was typically reserved for men.

GU POISON: A legendary poison created by sealing many types of venomous creatures in one vessel until only one survivor remains, which would then possess the strongest and most complex poison. The term may be used as a stand-in for dark poisons of all types.

GUOSHI: A powerful imperial official who served as an advisor to the emperor. Sometimes translated as "state preceptor," this was a post with considerable authority in some historical regimes.

HORSETAIL WHISK: Consisting of a long wooden handle with horsehair bound to one end, the horsetail whisk (拂尘 / fuchen, "brushing off dust") symbolizes cleanliness and the sweeping away of mortal concerns in Buddhist and Daoist traditions. It is usually carried in the crook of one's arm.

IMMORTAL-BINDING ROPES OR CABLES: A staple of xianxia, immortal-binding cables are ropes, nets, and other restraints enchanted to withstand the power of an immortal or god. They can only be cut by high-powered spiritual items or weapons and often limit the abilities of those trapped by them.

INCENSE TIME: A measure of time in ancient China, referring to how long it takes for a single incense stick to burn. Inexact by nature, an incense time is commonly assumed to be about thirty minutes, though it can be anywhere from five minutes to an hour.

JADE: Jade is a semi-precious mineral with a long history of ornamental and functional usage in China. The word "jade" can refer to two distinct minerals, nephrite and jadeite, which both range in color from white to gray to a wide spectrum of greens.

JIANGHU: A staple of wuxia and xianxia, the jianghu (江湖 / "rivers and lakes") describes an underground society of martial artists, monks, rogues, artisans, and merchants who settle disputes between themselves per their own moral codes.

KOWTOW: The kowtow (叩头 / "knock head") is an act of prostration where one kneels and bows low enough that their forehead touches the ground. A show of deep respect and reverence that can also be used to beg, plead, or show sincerity; in severe circumstances, it's common for the supplicant's forehead to end up bloody and bruised.

LOTUS: This flower symbolizes purity of the heart and mind, as lotuses rise untainted from muddy waters. It also signifies the holy seat of the Buddha.

LIULI: Colorful glazed glass. When used as a descriptor for eye color, it refers to a bright brown.

MERIDIANS: The means by which qi travels through the body, like a magical bloodstream. Medical and combat techniques that focus on redirecting, manipulating, or halting qi circulation focus on targeting the meridians at specific points on the body, known as acupoints. Techniques that can manipulate or block qi prevent a cultivator from using magical techniques until the qi block is lifted.

MYTHICAL CREATURES: Chinese mythology boasts numerous mythological creatures, several of which make appearances in *Remnants of Filth*, including:

GUHUO NIAO: A mythical bird created by the grief of women who died in childbirth; their song mimics the sound of babies crying as the bird seeks to steal chicks and human infants for itself.

SHANGAO: An small piglike animal said to live in the mountains, vivid scarlet in color, with a decidedly foul manner of speech.

TAOTIE: A mythical beast that represents greed, as it is composed of only a head and a mouth and eats everything in sight until its death. Taotie designs are symmetrical down their zoomorphic faces and most commonly seen on bronzeware from the Shang dynasty.

TENGSHE, OR SOARING SNAKE: A mythical serpent that can fly.

ZHEN NIAO: Also known as the poison-feather bird, this mythical creature is said to be so poisonous its feathers were used in assassinations, as dipping one in wine would make it a lethal and undetectable poison.

NINE PROVINCES: A symbolic term for China as a whole.

PAPER MONEY: Imitation money made from decorated sheets of paper burned as a traditional offering to the dead.

QI: Qi (气) is the energy in all living things. Cultivators strive to manipulate qi through various techniques and tools, such as weapons, talismans, and magical objects. Different paths of cultivation provide control over specific types of qi. For example, in *Remnants of Filth*, the Liao Kingdom's techniques allow cultivators to harness demonic qi, in contrast to Chonghua's righteous methods, which cultivate the immortal path. In naturally occurring contexts, immortal qi may have nourishing or purifying properties, whereas malevolent qi (often refined via evil means such as murder) can poison an individual's mind or body.

QIANKUN POUCH: A common item in wuxia and xianxia settings, a qiankun pouch contains an extradimensional space within it, to which its name (乾坤 / "universe") alludes. It is capable of holding far more than its physical exterior dimensions would suggest.

QIN: Traditional plucked stringed instrument in the zither family, usually played with the body placed flat on a low table. This was the favored instrument of scholars and the aristocracy.

QINGGONG: Literally "lightness technique," qinggong (轻功) refers to the martial arts skill of moving swiftly and lightly through the air. In wuxia and xianxia settings, characters use qinggong to leap great distances and heights.

SEAL SCRIPT: Ancient style of Chinese writing developed during the Qin dynasty, named for its usage in seals, engravings, and other inscriptions.

SHICHEN: Days were split into twelve intervals of two hours apiece called shichen (时辰 / "time"). Each of these shichen has an associated term. Prior to the Han dynasty, semi-descriptive terms were used. Post-Han dynasty, the shichen were renamed to correspond to the twelve zodiac animals.

> HOUR OF ZI, MIDNIGHT: 11 p.m.–1 a.m.
> HOUR OF CHOU: 1–3 a.m.
> HOUR OF YIN: 3–5 a.m.
> HOUR OF MAO, SUNRISE: 5–7 a.m.
> HOUR OF CHEN: 7–9 a.m.
> HOUR OF SI: 9–11 a.m.
> HOUR OF WU, NOON: 11 a.m.–1 p.m.
> HOUR OF WEI: 1–3 p.m.
> HOUR OF SHEN: 3–5 p.m.
> HOUR OF YOU, SUNSET: 5–7 p.m.
> HOUR OF XU, DUSK: 7–9 p.m.
> HOUR OF HAI: 9–11 p.m.

SOULS: According to Chinese philosophy and religion, every human had three ethereal souls (hun / 魂) which would leave the body after death, and seven corporeal souls (po / 魄) that remained with the corpse. Each soul governed different aspects of a person's being, ranging from consciousness and memory, to physical function and sensation.

SPIRITUAL CORE: A spiritual core (灵核 / linghe) is the foundation of a cultivator's power. It is typically formed only after ten years of hard work and study. If broken or damaged, the cultivator's abilities are compromised or even destroyed.

SUONA: A traditional Chinese double-reeded wind instrument with a distinct and high-pitched sound, most often used for celebrations of the living and the dead (such as weddings and funerals). Said to herald either great joy or devastating grief.

SWORD GLARE: Jianguang (剑光 / "sword light"), an energy attack released from a sword's edge, often seen in xianxia stories.

A TALE OF NANKE: An opera by Tang Xianzu that details a dream had by disillusioned official Chunyu Fen, highlighting the ephemerality of the mortal world and the illusory nature of wealth and grandeur.

TALISMANS: Strips of paper with written incantations, often in cinnabar ink or blood. They can serve as seals or be used as one-time spells.

THREE DISCIPLINES AND THREE POISONS: Also known as the threefold training in Buddhist traditions, the three disciplines are virtue, mind, and wisdom. Conversely, the three poisons (also known as the three defilements) refer to the three Buddhist roots of suffering: greed, wrath, ignorance.

WANGSHU: In Chinese mythology, Wangshu (望舒) is a lunar goddess often used in literary reference to the moon.

XIHE: In Chinese mythology, Xihe (羲和) is a solar goddess often used in literary reference to the sun.

XUN: A traditional Chinese vessel flute similar to the ocarina, often made of clay.

YIN ENERGY AND YANG ENERGY: Yin and yang is a concept in Chinese philosophy which describes the complementary interdependence of opposite/contrary forces. It can be applied to all forms of change and differences. Yang represents the sun, masculinity, and the living, while yin represents the shadows, femininity, and the dead, including spirits and ghosts. In fiction, imbalances between yin and yang energy may do serious harm to the body or act as the driving force for malevolent spirits seeking to replenish themselves of whichever energy they lack.

ZIWEI STAR: A star known to Western astronomers as the North Star or Polaris. As the other stars seemed to revolve around it, the Ziwei Star is considered the celestial equivalent of the emperor. Its stationary position in the sky makes it key to Zi Wei Dou Shu, the form of astrology that the ancient Chinese used to divine mortal destinies.

ABOUT THE AUTHOR

Rou Bao Bu Chi Rou ("Meatbun Doesn't Eat Meat") was a low-level soldier who served in Gu Mang's army as a cook. Meatbun's cooking was so good that, after Gu Mang turned traitor, the spirit beast Cai Bao ("Veggiebun") swooped in to rescue Meatbun as it passed by. Thus, Meatbun escaped interrogation in Chonghua and became a lucky survivor. In order to repay the big orange cat Veggiebun, Meatbun not only cooked three square meals a day but also told the tale of Mo Xi and Gu Mang as a nightly bedtime story to coax the spirit beast Veggiebun to sleep. Once the saga came to an end, it was compiled into *Remnants of Filth*.